THE
COMFORT
of LIES

ALSO BY RANDY SUSAN MEYERS

The Murderer's Daughters

THE
COMFORT
of LIES

A NOVEL

RANDY SUSAN MEYERS

ATRIA BOOKS

New York   London   Toronto   Sydney   New Delhi

ATRIA BOOKS
A Division of Simon & Schuster, Inc.
1230 Avenue of the Americas
New York, NY 10020

First Atria Books hardcover edition February 2013

ATRIA B O O K S and colophon are trademarks of Simon & Schuster, Inc.

For information about special discounts for bulk purchases,
please contact Simon & Schuster Special Sales at 1-866-506-1949
or business@simonandschuster.com.

The Simon & Schuster Speakers Bureau can bring authors to your live event.
For more information or to book an event, contact the Simon & Schuster
Speakers Bureau at 1-866-248-3049 or visit our website at www.simonspeakers.com.

Designed by Kyoko Watanabe

Manufactured in the United States of America

10   9   8   7   6   5   4   3   2   1

Library of Congress Cataloging-in-Publication Data

Meyers, Randy Susan.
    The comfort of lies : a novel / Randy Susan Meyers.—1st Atria Books hardcover ed.
        p. cm.
    1. Adopted children—Fiction. 2. Unmarried mothers—Fiction. 3. Motherhood—Fiction.
    4. Man-woman relationships—Fiction. 5. Family secrets—Fiction. 6. Domestic fiction.
    I. Title.
    PS3613.E9853C66 2012
    813'.6—dc22

                                                                          2012007682

ISBN 978-1-4516-7301-2
ISBN 978-1-4516-7303-6 (ebook)

For Jeff, always

It is better to be told a hurtful truth
than to be told a comforting lie.
In the end, the truth will make its way out and
will hurt much more than it ever had to.

—*Anonymous*

Part 1

———

BEFORE

CHAPTER 1

Tia

Happiness at someone else's expense came at a price. Tia had imagined judgment from the first kiss that she and Nathan shared. All year, she'd waited to be punished for being in love, and in truth, she believed that whatever consequences came her way would be deserved.

She felt vaguely queasy from the late Sunday lunch she and Nathan had just shared. They'd ordered far too many courses; buttery appetizers, overdressed salad, and marbled meat roiled in her stomach. Black Forest cake had left her mouth pasty with sugar and chocolate. Each time Nathan patted his thickening middle with chagrin, she worried that she'd become Nathan's accomplice in more than one sin.

Since childhood, she'd hated heavy food. Instead of sharing this lunch, she wished they could have waited until tomorrow to see each other, when they could sit on a blanket watching fireworks explode on the Esplanade and listening to the Boston Pops. The Fourth of July was a holiday without the burden of expectations; a perfect celebration for them.

Nathan squeezed her hand as they walked toward her apartment. His obvious pride delighted her. She was twenty-four, he was thirty-seven, and this was the first time she'd been loved by a man of substance. Each time they met, she discovered new love-struck traits—details she'd never admit to anyone, like the way his hands seemed more like a cowboy's than a professor's. Qualities that might seem ordinary to someone who'd grown up with a father, Tia added to her list of Nathan lore.

Last week, he'd seemed like Superman when he came over carrying a toolbox, planning to install a showerhead that sprayed more than a weak stream. Attached to the handle was a card where he'd written, "This is for you to keep here."

The words made Tia feel as though he'd use it again.

No present could have pleased her more.

Mostly, she found Nathan perfect. Muscled arms. A wide back. His sardonic New York edge, delivered with a crooked smile— worlds away from the street humor of the South Boston boys of her youth—cracked her up, while his innate competence wrapped her in a thick blanket of security. Nathan's too-rare presence oxygenated her blood. When she ran her thumb up and down each of his fingers, the universe existed in that physical connection. Her life had shrunk to being with him.

She'd spent many hours crying during this year of Nathan. A man with a family couldn't spare a whole lot of attention.

When they reached the two-family house where she lived, Nathan circled her from behind. She leaned back and caught his kiss on the side of her neck. He ran his hands down the length of her body. "I never tire of touching you," he said.

"I hope that never changes."

"People always change." A look of discomfort crossed his face as he disengaged from her. "You deserve so much."

Did he think she deserved having him with her always? Tia put the key in the door. She comforted herself with the thought that he believed her worthy.

The moment they entered her apartment, Tia raced to the bathroom; lately she always needed the bathroom. Afterward, she spent a long time drying her hands and straightening an out-of-place antique perfume bottle he'd bought her. She was constantly rearranging things, trying to make the pink crystal fit in with her Ikea-ware and her mother's castoffs. Tia's apartment became a stage set when Nathan visited. She spent hours before he arrived seeing every book, decoration, and poster through his eyes.

Nathan offered her a glass of wine when she joined him in the living room. "Listen to this one," he said. "I used an old Groucho line today—'I refuse to join any club that would have me as a member'—to illustrate a point, and a student asked me who Groucho Marx was."

Tia put out a refusing palm for the wine. "No thanks. I'm not in the mood."

"It made me feel about a hundred years old. Now, tell me the absolute truth: you know who Groucho Marx was, right?" He pushed the glass toward her. "At least taste it. It's probably the smoothest Merlot you'll ever have."

When she didn't have wine at lunch, he hadn't commented. "I'm in the mood for a Pepsi," she'd said. Maybe he thought she was acting like a teenager and he found it cute. Sometimes it bothered her, the things he found cute.

"*You Bet Your Life,*" she said. "*Duck Soup. A Night at the Opera.*"

"Thank you. My faith in young people is restored."

"There aren't that many years between us." She hated when he dwelled on their age difference. "God knows I'm older than your students."

"And sharper," he said.

"That's right—don't forget."

The moment she shared her news, their romance would change forever, not that it had ever had been sustainable as it was. From the first time they slept together and he'd blurted out "I'm crazy about you," she'd wanted more. First she'd wanted him in her bed all the time, and then she wanted the ring on his finger to be from her. When her need for him hit full throttle, she wanted the crease in his pants to be put there by a dry cleaner she'd chosen, his shirt to smell of detergent she'd chosen.

Tia looked straight at him. "I'm pregnant."

He stood with his hand still extended, the wine sloshing against the edge of the glass like a riptide.

Tia reached for the glass. "You're going to drop it." She put it next to his on the coffee table.

"So that's why you didn't drink with lunch," he said.

He delivered the words slowly; so slowly it terrified Tia. Despite knowing how unlikely it was, she wanted to see a shy smile—a TV smile followed by a movie-style kiss. She put a hand over her still-flat belly, nausea welling again. She pushed away thoughts of Nathan's wife. Much as she tried, Tia couldn't stop thinking of Juliette— where she was, where she believed her husband had gone—but early on, he'd made it clear that topic was off-limits.

"How long have you known?" he asked.

"A few days. I wanted to tell you in person."

He nodded, finished his wine, and then sat. He laced his fingers and leaned over until his arms rested on his legs. He glanced up at her, looking stern, like the professor he was. "You're going to take care of it, right?"

Tia sank into the armchair across from the couch. "Take care of it?"

"Of course, take care of it." He closed his eyes for one moment. When he opened them, he sat up straighter. "What else can we do? What else makes sense?"

"I can have it." She wouldn't cry. If nothing else good in this damned world happened tonight, she'd keep from crying.

"Alone? Like your mother?" Nathan ran his hand over his chin. "You of all people know what a hard road that is, right, sweetheart?"

"Where are you going to be? Are you planning to die? Disappear?" Behind her brave front, Tia shrank to walnut size. She knew where Nathan would be. He'd be in his beautiful house with Juliette. The wife. The wife she'd once spied on. The wife who looked like sun and sky, whose blonde shine had blinded Tia.

"I'll pay for whatever you need to take care of . . ."

"'Take care of, take care of,'" Tia mimicked. "Take care of what?" She wanted to force him to say the word *abortion*.

"My sons are so young."

Tia clutched the arm of the chair. She craved the forbidden wine.

"I can't stretch between two families. Please. Look at what this means," he begged.

Dry skin peeled from her cracked thumb as she wrung her hands. Already this pregnancy had changed her, somehow drying her out while also making her pee twice an hour.

Nathan came and put his arms around her. "Pregnancy makes women romanticize things. You think after seeing the baby, fatherly love will overwhelm me and I'll change my mind. But I can't. I'm not leaving my family. Wasn't I always straight about that?"

Oh God. He was crying.

His family.

She'd thought *she* was having his family.

Stupid, stupid, stupid.

Finally she spoke. "I can't do it, Nathan. What you're asking—I can't."

Nathan drew away. "I'm sorry, but there's no possible way we can be together, Tia. Please. Take care of this. It's the best thing for both of us. Honestly."

By her sixth month of pregnancy, discomfort had become Tia's new normal. Once upon a time so skinny that people pressed milkshakes on her, now she lumbered. She stuck a cushion behind her as she sat on the couch, surrounded by begging letters, photos, and essays from couples hungry for her baby.

Tia had refused to "take care of this," as Nathan wanted. St. Peter's nuns and Tia's mother had done too good a job. She couldn't rid herself of the pregnancy for fear of being haunted into the afterlife, and she couldn't find the courage to hold her child in this life, so here she was, six months pregnant, choosing a mother and father for her baby.

Picking adoptive parents, she was faced with impossible choices. She sorted through hundreds of letters from men and women desperate for the baby growing inside her. Potential mothers and fathers swam before her until she could barely remember who was the librarian from Fall River and which was the couple reminiscent of her scariest Sunday school teachers. They all promised nurturing love, backyards the size of Minnesota, and Ivy League schools.

After three cups of sugary mint tea, missing coffee more with each sip, Tia narrowed the choices to the three most likely couples. She sifted through their pictures and letters, and then laid them out like tarot cards. Then, with the fear of continuing to face this task hastening her decision, she picked the man and woman she deemed most likely to be good parents. She balanced their photos on her big belly and then moved them around like paper dolls, acting out everything they'd said during the phone conversation she'd had with them, both of them sounding so sure of themselves, so smart and together.

"Hello, Tia," she imagined Paper Caroline's voice squeaking. "I want your baby. I'm a pathologist researching children's cancer. My husband has a very large family, and he's always been drawn to children."

"Tell her about being a counselor at Paul Newman's camp. What's the name? You know. The one for kids with cancer?" Paper Peter laid a gentle hand on saintly Paper Caroline's arm.

"The Hole in the Wall Gang." Paper Caroline bowed her head so as not to appear boastful.

A month later, when Caroline and Peter learned it was a girl, they told Tia they were naming the baby Savannah. An idiotic name. Tia called the baby inside her Honor, her mother's middle name—also an idiotic name, but it wasn't meant to be used out of utero, and besides, idiotic or not, it certainly beat Savannah. Why not simply call her Britney and be done with it? If she wasn't so busy caring for her ailing mother, she'd choose new parents for her daughter.

Tia stumbled as she fumed over the choice, bumping into a food cart in the hall of the hospice that had become her mother's home. Clumsiness was Tia's companion. Clumsiness, the constant need to pee, and a life of seclusion. She'd gone from existing for Nathan's visits to carrying a relentless reminder of him. Each time she stroked her stomach, she felt as though she were caressing him. Hard as she tried, she couldn't replace sadness with hate.

Her mother was the only person with whom she spent time. Every other friend from her past—except for Robin, in California, too far away to visit—thought she'd gone to Arizona for a year to work on a masters in gerontology, based on her work with the elderly. In reality, she moved to Jamaica Plain, an entirely different sort of neighborhood from Southie.

Unlike her old neighborhood, where she'd see people she knew on every street, Jamaica Plain was always in flux—a mix not just of ethnicity and race, but class, culture, and age. Her only acquaintance was the librarian, with whom she had a nodding *hi, how are you,* relationship. JP was an easy place to remain anonymous.

She'd wanted to be where nobody knew her name. Being the object of gossip or pity wasn't in her plans. Her mother's savings supported both of them—Tia rarely left the house. Life became mainlining novels, watching TV, and caring for her mother, who'd moved in with Tia until her pain overcame Tia's nursing ability.

She crept into her mother's room on angel feet. That's what her mother had called it when Tia the child tried to sneak into the kitchen for extra cookies. "Sweet one, mothers can hear their children, even when they use their angel feet."

Though Tia tried to pretend otherwise, her mother lay dying as Tia's baby grew.

"Mom?" she whispered.

The room remained silent. Tia dug her nails into her palms and bent over the bed, watching until she saw the slight rise and fall of her mother's chest. Her mother was only forty-nine. Liver cancer had overtaken her in a matter of months, although Tia suspected her mother had hidden the truth for some time.

Her mother had been in hospice for twenty-three days. Maybe

the younger you were when you became sick, the longer you held on, or maybe twenty-three days was average, normal—whatever you'd call the amount of time from entering a hospice until you died. She couldn't bring herself to find out. Perhaps if she had a sister or brother who'd team up with her, she'd have the courage to ask such a vulgar question, but it had always been just the two of them, Tia and her mother.

Dying could be such a long process, which surprised Tia. You'd think that working with the elderly would have taught her more about death and dying, but she'd provided senior recreation, not counseling. Word games were her specialty. In her work world, a client didn't show up for Scrabble, and the next thing you knew, he or she was dead.

You didn't see the person die.

Losing her mother seemed impossible, as though someone planned to cut the string that held Tia to earth. She'd be floating without ballast. Tia had none of the usual family: no aunts, no uncles, no cousins—her mother filled all those roles.

Tia settled into the chair next to her mother's bed. She wondered why, when they so stressed comfort, the hospice didn't provide chairs where a pregnant woman could sit pain free. She slipped a paperback from her tote: a mystery so simple that even if she retained only a quarter of what she read, she could still track the plot. Her mother's copy of *Jane Eyre*, complete with the magical happy ending, was in her bag, but she saved that to read aloud to her mother after supper.

Her mother opened her eyes. "Been here long, sweetheart?" She reached for Tia's hand. "Tired?"

Tia ran a hand over her large belly. "Always."

"You don't have to come here every night, you know."

Her mother repeated this daily. It was her version of "I'm worried about you."

"Tired isn't life threatening."

"When you're pregnant—"

"When you're pregnant, it's what you are. Remember?" Tia asked.

"Was it like that for you? Did I drive you crazy even before I was born?"

Her mother struggled to sit up. Tia offered a hand for leverage and then tucked pillows behind her mother's back. Her mother's skin, once such a pretty, pink-tinged white—pale Irish skin that burned with one wink from the sun; that was how her mother described herself—now looked mean yellow against the sheets.

"I remember everything about being pregnant," her mother said. "Are you going to be able to forget?"

"Mom, please don't," Tia said.

"I have to, honey." Her mother retrieved her glasses from the metal tray attached to the bed. Once the wire rims were firmly in place, she looked healthier. Glasses, jewelry, and other accoutrements seemed like totems against death. Tia constantly bought bright trinkets to cheer her mother. Electric blue beads threaded onto silver cord clanked around her mother's wrist. "They match your eyes," Tia had said, after buying them the previous week.

"Why don't I get you some ice water?" Tia said.

"Don't run away. Listen to me. You need to face how sorry you'll be if you go through with this."

This was the word her mother used to describe Tia's plan to give up her baby for adoption.

"I'd be a horrible mother," Tia said.

"You think that now. Wait until you hold your baby."

Each skirmish in her mother's battle to stop the adoption made Tia feel worse. Every reason Tia laid out sounded lamer than the last.

"I'll be a bad mother."

"I don't have enough money."

"I'm too ashamed of not knowing who the father is."

Rather than telling her mother the truth, Tia pretended to be a woman who'd slept with too many men and, thus, didn't know the identity of her baby's father. The horror of that lie was still better than the truth. She couldn't bear telling her mother she'd been sleeping with a married man—and had tried to steal him.

Everything she said sounded ridiculous. Maybe she'd be a bad mother, God knows she had no money, and immature should be her middle name, but if that were all it took to give up a baby, the world would be filled with orphans.

Tia caressed her belly. *Sweet little baby, I'm sorry.*

Tia had grown up in the wake of her father's vanishing. In a vacuum of knowledge, her mother assumed he'd chosen a life with another woman—living a life with more fun and liquor than Tia's puritanical mother would accept. In her mother's estimation, sleeping with a married man was a sin only exceeded by abortion.

Without the truth, Tia could offer no reasoning that would make sense. How could she admit that she was giving up a child whose existence would remind her of a man she loved but could never have? How could Tia say this to her mother when Tia had no idea if she was being the most selfish she'd ever been, or the most selfless?

"The baby will have a better life than I'll ever be able to give her," Tia said. "Really, Mom. You saw their letter, the pictures. The baby will have good parents."

Her mother's eyes watered. Tia's mother never cried. Not when Tia broke her leg so badly that the bone stuck out. Not when she found out about the cancer. And not when Tia's father left—at least, not in front of Tia.

"I'm sorry." Her mother blinked, and the tears disappeared.

"Sorry? God, you've done nothing wrong."

Her mother folded her arms and clutched her elbows. "I must have done something awful to have you believe your baby will do better without you. Do you think your life at this moment is as well as you'll ever do? Don't you see that your future lies in front of you?"

Tia shrugged as though she were a child shutting down against shame, aching at the thought that she might let her mother die thinking she'd failed in raising her.

"Mom, it's not that."

"Then what?"

"I just don't think it's my path." Tia covered her belly with both hands. Every lie she told felt as though she were pushing her mother further away, now when they needed closeness more than ever. "I don't think she's meant to be mine."

"Please don't make your decision yet. Something's tormenting you, and I know it's not what you're telling me. That's okay. But believe me, if you pick giving in to your pain over choosing your baby, you'll never recover from either."

CHAPTER 2

Juliette

Juliette usually listened to music while she worked, but not today. She was stealing from Sunday family time—and a sunny Sunday at that—while the boys watched a video downstairs. Silence ensured she could hear her sons.

Guilt kept her company, even though she and Nathan had devoted every second of the morning and early afternoon to the boys. They'd taken a short hike at Beaver Brook Reservation, and then eaten a picnic lunch prepared by Juliette, complete with the Rice Krispies Treats she'd stirred up at six that morning, and then played an hour of goofy softball. Afterward, Nathan left for an afternoon of correcting papers, and she snuck up to get in a few hours of paperwork.

It wasn't as though they weren't having togetherness; tomorrow night they'd drive into Boston and watch the fireworks. Still, she worried. Bright light poured in the windows, and her boys were in the living room staring at the television.

Terrific. Juliette hoped her kids appreciated all the unlined women on the street, knowing that their mother had traded their brains, health, and security for furrow serums.

Furrow serums.

Wrinkle serums.
Furrow.
Wrinkle.
Furrow.
Wrinkle.

Furrow had tested better as a problem to be solved than *wrinkle.* Maybe *furrow* sounded like a woman crinkling from thoughts rather than age.

Perhaps they should call it crinkle serum. *Crinkle* sounded kind of happy, right?

Sure. She pictured her business partner Gwynne hooting when Juliette shared that the next time they had one of their creative meetings. Juliette and Gwynne had met in Mommy and Me swim classes, drawn to each other through a shared mutual head-exploding boredom with the minutiae of motherhood, coupled with tendencies to overworship their children. They'd fallen in love with one sardonic glance, the way that best friends sometimes do, recognizing a kinship of lonely childhoods.

Juliette listened for disaster. When she worked, she worried about Max and Lucas. When she devoted herself to them, she worried about business. Nathan tried to solve the problem by telling her to r-e-l-a-x. "Concentrate on where you are," he'd say, as though she could will herself out of worrying. Perhaps a male genetic pattern similar to male pattern baldness allowed Nathan to go to work and be at work. He couldn't imagine life any other way.

She knew Nathan wanted to help. He tried to solve every problem that came his way; he always had. Taking care of people pleased him, so much so that she sensed it disappointed him that she asked for so little when it came to her work, but how could he help with a business built on balm for women's skin? Nathan taught sociology at Brandeis University and researched the plight of the elderly, which, in his mind, she was certain, did not include their crinkles or furrows.

This was the year that her balancing act would pay off. She just knew it. Years of investing every free moment in work—even as she pretended her preoccupation with cosmetics and skin care barely broke from being a hobby; concocting potions until three in the morning and then making breakfast for everyone at seven—would be worth it.

The kids came first. Nathan's schedule, second. Then came cooking, cleaning, birthdays, Halloween, Passover, Chanukah, and Christmas—anchoring her family. That's how she thought of it. Juliette loved her work to an unholy degree, but she worked equally hard to hide her obsession, always a bit ashamed of how much passion she felt about her business.

Creating organic skincare and makeup couldn't be compared with saving lives. juliette&gwynne was even potentially an unkind business, building on women's fear, though she and Gwynne kept it clean and honest. No promises of unborn-sperm-cell-laden cream guaranteed to eliminate wrinkles or furrows were offered, just assurances that their products would make the best of what nature had given. They didn't tout faces frozen in time, but faces and bodies smoothed gracefully. Nothing depressed Juliette more than seeing older women with wind-tunneled faces wearing the Juicy Couture label emblazoned on their behinds.

juliette&gwynne had a place in the world, she and Gwynne assured each other, even writing lists of the ways they helped women:

- *Bought shea butter (only grade-A) from women's collective in Ghana.*
- *Packaging made by a women's collective in Appalachia.*
- *Donated products to a battered women's shelter.*

Gwynne took an extra long pull from her beer last week, when they'd added that last one, and then said, "Are we really comforting ourselves with this? Providing moisturizer and lipstick to battered women? Jesus, Jules, wouldn't they rather have a check?"

"I know, I know." Juliette had leaned back in the cracked leather chair donated from Gwynne's husband's law office. Two rooms in Juliette's falling-apart Waltham house served as the offices for juliette&gwynne//flush de la beauté. "When we make a ton of money, we'll give a ton away."

Maybe someday they'd be rich. She never told anyone, not even Nathan, how she hungered for money. It made her seem like her mother. God save her, Juliette loved things. Well-cut clothes. Thin china. Fat comforters.

All this and healthy, happy children.

First, always first, please, healthy, happy children.

In reaction against her own childhood, Juliette guarded against showing pride. Her mother's devotion to the sheen of one's skin and the drape of one's clothes had resulted in Juliette's impersonating a woman without narcissism. In truth, it was the opposite. Juliette lacked her mother's self confidence, and a shameful amount of her mind was preoccupied with her appearance.

At least, in the case of juliette&gwynne, her secret vice had value. The business was borne of Juliette's vanity. After giving up her Looks column at *Boston* magazine to stay home with Lucas, and then Max, her addiction to high-end products became impossible to sustain. Nathan's professor's salary covered only the basics. She experimented at home, mixing moisturizers from ingredients ranging from frankincense to chamomile, and inventing body scrubs made from sugar, oats, and even coffee grounds.

"Mommy!" Five-year-old Max flew in and leapt on the battered sofa, dislodging papers and product samples. "I'm hungry!" He nestled close to Juliette.

Lucas appeared at the door. "I told you to stay in the playroom." He grabbed his brother by the shirt collar. "Come on. I'll get you a granola bar."

Babysitting money fueled her older son's enthusiasm, but his attention to the job impressed Juliette, even as she feared that in his zeal he might detach Max's head from his body. She uncurled Lucas's fingers from Max's shirt and smiled. "It's okay. Let's all go downstairs. Daddy will be home soon. You guys can draw in the dining room while I make supper."

Juliette took out the chopped onions, sliced mushrooms, and

diced carrots and cauliflower she'd prepared at seven that morning while Nathan and the kids slept, in anticipation of making mushroom barley soup for dinner. With chicken. Now she took out the plastic containers and lined them up in the order in which she'd sauté them before she added chicken stock.

She cut up chicken breasts, leaving on just enough skin to add depth to the soup without overwhelming Nathan's heart.

He'd had her heart from the first moment they'd met, when Nathan moved from Brooklyn to the Hudson Valley in upstate New York, where Juliette grew up. He'd come for his first teaching job, working in the sociology department at Bard College. Her father headed the political science department.

They'd met at her parents' annual holiday party at their house in Rhinebeck, a Hudson Valley town that attracted former New Yorkers. Musky men's cologne vied with the heavy scents of Chanel and Joy. The women either sparkled or were romantic in dusty velvet. Their men wore suits or reindeer sweaters. Juliette stood out in her midthigh-length sapphire dress.

Nathan walked up to her as she stood drinking eggnog and watching her mother work the room. His tie, which from afar looked like blended tones of blue, had Stars of David woven into the cloth.

She reached out and traced one. "Pronouncement?"

"Chanukah gift from my parents."

"Are they marking you?"

"I'm too far from Brooklyn: they're warding off *shiksas* bearing tiny gold crucifixes."

Juliette touched the empty hollow of her throat in some odd reflex. "Lucky me. I'm only half. *Shiksa*, that is."

He swept his arm toward her parents' light-crusted tree, so tall that it brushed the ceiling. Garlands laced with red ribbons and crystal snowflakes were intertwined with evergreen on the staircase, visible from where they stood. He touched a soft blonde wave framing her face. "Where in God's name does your family hide the other half?"

Juliette took his hand. "Come. I'll show you."

She took his hand and led him to the quiet library, mercifully free of glitter.

"See?" She pointed to the library mantle where a cobalt glass menorah sat between matching dreidels.

"I don't imagine you ever played with those."

Juliette placed a careful finger on the glass. "No."

She'd rarely played with anything outside her room as a child. Her parents' home, cared for as though it were a sacred object, was her rival for her parents' affection, and to Juliette is usually seemed as though the house won. Juliette's parents seemed to think the house represented them more than their daughter. Why else would she get only benign neglect, while every corner of the house received unremitting attention?

"Do you live here with your parents?" he asked.

"Not since I came home on college vacations."

"You don't like Rhinebeck?" he asked.

"There's not much here, unless you're involved with Bard." His hair was thick and straight. Hollywood black.

She slept with him that night.

"You're besotted," her mother said the next day when Juliette returned from Nathan's apartment.

Besotted. Her mother had found the perfect word. The night with Nathan had been explosive before slowing to billowing softness. She'd been struck and so had he, the two of them barely able to separate that afternoon. The moment Nathan dropped her off, she'd wanted to be back with him.

Juliette smoothed her rumpled party dress. "You're right."

Her mother removed lint from Juliette's hem. "Don't let him see that—not now. It gives them too much power when they see how much you care."

Juliette thought how sad those words were as she poured olive oil in the pan. How could you hide your love? Did her mother still do that, even as she closed in on forty years married? Her parents were knotted to a degree Juliette envied and hated, but she refused to believe it was built on tricks. Her father and mother loved each other so completely and unreservedly—except for Dad loving a bit more, just as Mom wanted—that Juliette never had a chance. Growing up, their marriage had seemed a two plus one to her, with Juliette the plus to their tight couple. All her life, she'd danced on the outskirts of her parents' love.

Oil sizzled. She threw in the onions. Nathan walked in. Juliette grinned wide, as she did each time he appeared. She still loved him to distraction. Maybe even more. Having children together struck her as the sexiest possible thing you could do with another person.

They kissed. He touched her back with a light hand. His fingers rested on her shoulders in a way that years of marriage told her bore no good. Something troubled him.

"Where are the boys?" he asked.

"Arts and crafts in the dining room." She threw in the garlic and mushrooms when the onions reached peak translucency. "I think I heard Lucas sneak on the TV, but I'm being a bad mother and not noticing until I finish making supper. Now that you're home, feel free to go in and chastise him."

After wiping her hands on the towel tucked in her waistband, she turned and hugged him. The rigidity of his muscles under her hands frightened her.

"What's wrong?" She pushed him away, so she could look at his face. His eyes held emotions she couldn't read, except for the fear. "Your parents? Is your father okay?" Had his father suffered another heart attack? Worse?

Nathan shook his head.

"Work? Did something happen?"

"No." Nathan took a deep breath.

"What then? You look awful. Are you sick?"

He went to the cabinet and pulled out a bottle of brandy. Nathan, never the type to drink when he got home, poured a double shot.

Juliette put down her long wooden spoon. Her parents? Her father? Had her mother called Nathan so that he could break some awful news to Juliette? Bubbles of dread flipped around her stomach. He dropped into a kitchen chair. She sat facing him, so close their knees touched.

When she took his hands, they were cold. She lifted one to her cheek and ran it over her warm skin. "Honey, what's wrong?"

He lowered his face, his hands covering hers. His shoulders shook as he began to cry. Everything inside Juliette froze.

"Tell me."

"I had an affair, Jules. Oh my God, I'm so sorry."

CHAPTER 3

Caroline

After five years of marriage, Peter still made love to Caroline as though realizing his life's dream. Being the object of his lust never failed to rouse her own. Exercising on the treadmill, Caroline labored through work problems, scratching ideas in tiny journals she kept in her pockets. Riding the train to work, she caught up with medical journals; driving to visit her parents, she listened to audiobooks. Only with her husband did she remember her corporeal being. There was no other time she left her mind and lived inside her body.

Peter thought her beautiful, he thought her sexy, and he made her believe it, if only for the moments she lay with him. She didn't live under illusions. Much of her belief system boiled down to "What it is, is." Caroline knew she was more wholesome than bombshell. Before Peter, she'd limited her relationships to men who marched to the same beat as she did: quiet songs, gentle dances. Peter unlocked her fervor.

"Come on, you're incredible," Peter declared when she scoffed at his compliments. Where her honest doctor eyes saw wheat-colored hair not dramatic enough to call blonde, an easy-to-forget face, and a slat-like build, Peter declared her graceful and pure, and then de-lineated how those qualities turned him on. She knew it was her difference from every woman he'd grown up with that excited him: she was his upper-class unattainable woman—just as his unrestrained fervor, so different from the boys she grew up with, provided the same thrill for her.

After, they lingered in the bedroom, as they did every Sunday. Coffee cups, plates covered with crumbs, and orange rinds littered their bedside tables.

"Listen to this, Caro." Peter cleared his throat and, using his public voice—the one he used at investor meetings—read aloud from his laptop:

"Forecasters believe the strongest economic growth in two decades is in front of us. Businesses are investing in new plants and equipment and rehiring laid-off workers. Most economists predict 2004 should be an excellent year, and that this should be a predictor for years to come."

"Mmm," Caroline responded, the words not really registering. Peter grasped financial concepts instantly, while she found economic analysis so dry that it crumbled before it traveled from her ears to her brain. "Online news?" She pulled up the covers a bit.

"Yes, but it's a well-regarded site. Do you know what this means?"

"Not a clue, actually, beyond the facts as presented. But I'm sure you do." Caroline smiled, waiting for Peter to spill his theories. He shared his thoughts as they occurred to him. Peter tended to think out loud, while Caroline let ideas percolate for days, weeks, or longer before opening them to question.

"It means folks will be investing like crazy," Peter said. "They'll think they're hopping on the money train. Do you know what *that* means?"

She leaned her head on his shoulder. They were close to a match in height. "No." He did their accounting; she kept their space in perfect order. Having disparate interests freed each of the boring and baffling portions of life. "Do you want to watch the fireworks tomorrow night?"

"Yes, and don't change the subject. Listen, we're in a perfect-storm place. The naïve of the world—meaning most—will believe,

once again, that uptrends in stocks and real estate will continue forever—exactly the mythology which leads to insanity in the market."

"Ah. Interesting. The masses moving in lockstep." She picked up
Pediatric Blood & Cancer.

Peter pushed down the journal. "Caro, I'm not just commenting.
This could be important to us."

Like the obedient student she'd always been, Caroline let the
magazine drop in her lap and turned to her husband. "Okay. I'm
listening."

"If we time this right, we'll have an opportunity."

She nodded as though she'd have some part in *this*, when in reality, *we* meant Peter, who meshed with money. Building a pile of cash
excited him beyond the security and buying power it represented.

"When the business goes public next year, I'm betting our company stock prices will soar. Everyone wants . . ."

Her attention wandered a little, knowing what she was going to
hear: Sound & Sight Software, Peter's company, would provide a
platform for X and integrate Y, etc., etc.

She nodded and picked up her coffee cup, trying to read the journal lying in her lap.

"That's why we should start looking for a baby now," Peter said.
"Do you see what I'm saying?"

Now Caroline looked up. She clutched the handle of her mug.
"What?"

Peter put a firm hand on her knee. "Were you listening?"

She shook her head. "Not closely enough," she said. "Say it again.
The part about the baby, not the money."

"But they're very related, hon. Look: soon I'll need to focus on
business in a different way. I feel it. Now's the time to concentrate on
getting our baby. Before work explodes, before everything crashes,
when I can be the one to pick up all the work left from guys who got
lost in the wreckage."

Peter shared her love of work: both of them were busy puritans
turning the wheels of life. However, to Peter, life included a family—
preferably a large one. He would be a spectacular father. Caroline

couldn't imagine a better man for the job, but she didn't long for motherhood. That twenty-four-hour-a-day enthusiasm for the activity of children wasn't in her.

Her own mother's passion for Caroline and her sisters had always been evident. Caroline didn't want to offer her own children anything less, but she lacked the instinct for self-sacrifice. Once home, she didn't want anyone forcing her to put down her journals or interrupting her studies.

Becoming a mother terrified her so much that Caroline could barely hide her relief when she couldn't get pregnant, and Peter's sperm had turned out to be the problem.

But then Peter, in his usual style of *Okay, how do I solve this problem, and how quickly can I make it go away?* began investigating adoption. She'd left all the research and decision making to him, a stance he'd always accepted. Peter liked being in charge. That's why he'd chosen identified adoption, deeming it safer. He wanted to see the mother for himself, not leave their life decisions to anonymous social workers. "Better the devil you know," he'd declared.

Peter researched while Caroline did something totally out of character: she went into denial. Now, once again, the truth of every matter faced her: *what was, was.*

"Now?" she asked. "Really now?"

He sat up straighter and crossed his legs, pushing away the blanket. "It's not that I'm saying now or never, but now is the best time."

"I'm not sure. It's so busy at work, and—"

"Honey, we'll always have a reason to say 'Not now.' We'll always be busy. But we can make time, and we'll make room." He scanned their cramped bedroom. "Though we'll need more space. We might as well do it all up at once, eh? Look for the right neighborhood, right schools. Find the right house. My guess? Real estate will also drop soon."

Caroline—calm, always-good-in-an-emergency, hard-to-ruffle Caroline—felt as though she'd have an anxiety attack if he said one more word. "No," she said.

"No?"

"I love our apartment," she said. "I love our neighborhood."

"We need to find a place with great schools."

"We can find private schools," Caroline insisted. "Like you said, we'll have the money. I won't do well in the suburbs."

"That's just fear talking. I know how much you hate transition, but really, you're going to be a wonderful mother wherever we are."

No she wouldn't.

"You're perfect. Calm and loving. Smart. You're always grounded. I adore that about you." He stroked her arm.

"Grounded? How romantic."

"And funny. Did I mention funny?"

She managed a smile. "No one ever described me as funny."

"Oops, I meant that *I* was funny. And that you were smart to marry me."

She *had* been smart to marry him. He lightened her, he cosseted her, he made her into a better person—more aware of the world beyond her boundaries. But she didn't want to change anything. Their life: she loved the way their life was now. A baby would ruin everything.

Part 2

———

AFTER

CHAPTER 4

Tia

"If you give away your child, you might as well give away your legs, because you're going to end up a cripple."

Tia remembered her mother's words as she studied her daughter's face, captured in the photographs spread over the kitchen table. In the moment, her mother had seemed cruel, but now Tia recognized her mother's desperate attempt to cram in last bits of wisdom before dying.

Tia ignored Sunday's *Boston Globe* as she scrutinized the pictures. Each year, around her daughter's March birthday, a blandly pleasant note and five photos arrived from Caroline Fitzgerald. She studied five-year-old Honor: cross-legged on a pink duvet, dressed up in a red velvet dress, sturdy legs pumping a swing, holding a doll, digging an ambitious hole on a sandy beach. The pictures had remained on the table since they arrived in yesterday's mail, Tia returning repeatedly to memorize the images. Hunger to see her daughter peaked every March, when Honor's birthday, the arrival of Honor photos, and the anniversary of Tia's mother's death collided.

Tia's fantasies of motherhood weren't grand visions. She yearned for the comforts of simple physical and mundane mothering; daily maternal tasks such as pouring milk and braiding her daughter's hair had become her daydreams. It seemed impossible that her daughter couldn't feel her love on some cellular level. Tia imagined that when she had sweet thoughts of her girl, love emanated from her and entered Honor.

She chewed on her lower lip as she lifted a close-up of Honor clutching a doll, searching for evidence of her and Nathan in the image. Honor's dense, shiny hair reminded Tia of Nathan. Like him, Honor was heavy boned in an appealing way, like thick, rich soup. Only the child's intense stare revealed any resemblance to Tia. She brought the picture closer, but couldn't read Honor's expression.

Sometimes she prayed to be free of her yearning for Honor, but more often, Tia held that ache close. Longing was her connection to her daughter, and she couldn't bring herself to wish it away.

Tia splashed the tiniest drop of whiskey in her morning coffee, and then, as homage to her bad and Nathan, she spread rich salmon cream cheese on a bagel. Nathan had introduced Irish-Italian Tia to lox. He swore that Boston bagels were a farce compared to those in New York, but Tia had never known any other kind.

Nathan also introduced her to unrequited love. Some men bruised your heart, but when they left, the damage healed. Nathan had bitten chunks clean off, and Tia feared she'd search forever for the missing pieces. She'd never be safe from him. If there were an inoculation, she'd shoot the vaccine straight up.

Holding the bagel away from the table so no crumbs fell on the photos, Tia studied the top image. Her daughter looked a lifetime older at five than she had at four, but how could Tia judge? She possessed only a vague knowledge of children.

Everything her mother had predicted about losing Honor had come true.

The thought made whiskey a perfect companion for her bagel.

Her mother had died just days before Honor was born. Tia last saw Nathan the day she'd shared the news of her—their—pregnancy. The losses braided tighter each year, until today when Tia couldn't think of anything except how stupid she'd been to ignore her mother's wisdom and how much she wished she could somehow tell her how sorry she was for not telling the whole truth.

The moment Tia arrived at her office Monday morning, she opened the windows, knowing that when Katie arrived, her coworker would wrap her cardigan tight and stare at Tia as if they worked in Antarctica, when, in fact, whispers of spring blew over the chipped windowsill.

Good scents were rare at the Jamaica Plain Senior Advocate Center, where Tia worked. Hope was not in bountiful supply. Each day, Tia fought a battle against caving in to her clients' sadness. The greatest gift she offered them was the strength and invincibility of her youth—she knew that—but she feared that if she wasn't careful, instead of inspiring her clients, she'd become a geriatric twenty-nine-year-old, groaning when she rose from a chair and moaning from self-pity. Perhaps this was Katie's problem also: only thirty-six, and already she shivered when the temperature went lower than seventy degrees.

Katie entered, shuddering. "Brr."

"Should I put the heat on?" Tia dreaded Katie's disapproving clucks.

"I'll be okay." Katie shook as if coming in from a blizzard. "What did you do this weekend?"

"Not much." Tia closed the window.

"We took the kids to the Cape." Katie exhaled as though she usually spent her weekends building homes with Habitat for Humanity.

Tia knew how to make Katie happy. "You deserved a break," she said as she sat at her battered metal desk.

"Thanks for taking the messages." Katie gave a delicate shiver and reached for the pink paper Tia offered. They were equals at the agency, both counselors for the elderly clients, but Katie made it clear that with her master's degree in social work, she considered herself superior to Tia and her bachelor's in psychology. Katie's palatial Beacon Hill home dwarfed Tia's one-bedroom apartment in

Jamaica Plain. Katie thanked Tia for assistance as though Tia were her receptionist.

"Whose picture?" Katie plucked at the shiny photo sticking out from Tia's worn address book.

"That's my cousin's baby." Tia grabbed at the photo, but Katie held it out of reach.

Katie peered at the picture. "Cute. Pretty eyes. A little pudgy, though."

Tia snatched Honor from Katie's hand. "What's wrong with you? She's just a little kid."

"Obesity's a huge issue. You've never worried about weight, I bet. You're thin. Like me." Katie ran her hands down her sides. "I watch my kids like crazy. Jerry's family runs chunky."

Tia tightened her lips and tossed the picture in the trash, anxious to remove Honor from sight and out of conversation.

"What are you doing?" Katie stepped forward as though ready to rescue the photograph.

"I have too much clutter." Tia's stomach clutched as the picture fell.

Her daughter was only twenty miles away in the suburb of Dover, but it might as well be millions. Millions of dollars and millions of opportunities Tia shouldn't take from Honor, who'd get privileges Tia never knew. Bars, not parklands, had dotted South Boston, a mainly Irish neighborhood where she got to be exotic simply because her father's Italian side colored her mother's Irish genes, giving Tia pale skin and near-black hair. Her mother used to make the sign of the cross as they walked by taverns Tia's father patronized before he disappeared, whispering advice as she crossed herself.

"Forget these men," her mother would say, lifting her chin toward a gang of boys hanging on the corner. "Find a Jewish man. They make the best husbands." Her mother's low murmur conveyed the shame she felt—shame that her husband, Tia's father, had left them, and maybe shame that her words betrayed Southie. Her mother had felt disloyal when she strayed from South Boston's casual anti-Semitism. Her mother grew up in Southie, and she raised her daughter there, but she worked at Brandeis University—"Jew U.," as many in Southie called the school. Tia's mother didn't side with any of what she called "that ridiculousness," but she loved her loyal neighbors too much to take them to task.

Perhaps Jewish Nathan made a good Jewish husband for his half-Jewish wife, one of the few details he'd shared about the sainted-wife-who-will-never-be-mentioned. God knows that if one measured goodness by his panicked reaction when Tia hinted at marriage, then Nathan measured up as a prince of husbands.

Katie leaned down to take Tia's trash basket.

Tia put her hand on the rim and held it in place. "What are you doing?"

"Straightening. Devin won't be in for three days."

Jamaica Plain Senior Advocate Center could afford a janitor only once a week. Tia kept hold of the pail as Katie pulled at it. "I'll empty my own basket," Tia said.

"Fine," Katie said. "Just don't forget that today is Dumpster day."

Imagining banana peels and apple cores falling on Honor's face panicked Tia. She reached into the pail and pulled out the photo, drying unseen moisture by pressing it to her shirt.

"What are you doing?" Katie drew back as though Tia were swinging bits of bacteria her way.

"It's bad juju, tossing away a child's picture. Didn't you know that?"

Eight hours later, Tia climbed the bus steps. Darkness draped her mood, though nothing had gone wrong. In fact, it had been a day of reaping benefits from the previous month, when she'd walked door to door asking local business owners to donate small treats and trips for her clients. Lately, she'd put "happiness" on her client's goal sheets—just plain-vanilla happiness, even if it were only for an afternoon. At noon that day, she'd taken clients to Bella Luna for lunch: four women, plus Tia, sharing two pizzas and six desserts as they sat under the three-dimensional stars decorating the restaurant.

Tia jerked backward as the bus lurched forward. She faced a row of construction workers, their roughened hands clutching lunch bags, thermoses, and work gloves. She ran her hand over the latest mystery she was reading. She'd put Honor's picture in the middle of the library book in a vain attempt to press out the crumples she'd caused by stupidly tossing it in the trash. As she stroked the book, a proper repentant action took form. Tia would finally put all the pictures in an album. Now, tonight, she'd start preparing for the visit she expected on Honor's eighteenth birthday.

Before giving up her baby, Tia had taken legal steps to guarantee that Honor could contact her in the future. She hoped that ensuring access for her daughter might mitigate, even if only in the smallest way, the pain of having lost her child. The adoption, though identified, wasn't an open adoption; there would be no contact except the pictures Caroline sent. However, at least with the papers Tia had signed, Honor could easily contact her once she came of age and made her own decisions.

Leaning her head against the cloudy bus window, Tia tried to imagine Honor's life at that moment. Her child's parents—Dr. Caroline and software king Peter—were probably driving from work to their bright white house, which was bordered by stately evergreens. Tia saw the home each year in the photos. She imagined a well-paid nanny, earning far more than she did, reading to Honor, whose glossy, dark hair would spread over the nanny's shirt as she leaned into her. Or maybe Caroline was already home, and Honor sat tight and close against her mother.

Did they talk about Tia? Caroline and Peter seemed the types who'd tell the truth and have a library of the you're-so-special-that-we-chose-you books, which Tia couldn't resist reading in the library.

The bus passed the Harvest Co-op, where she'd shopped since moving from South Boston to Jamaica Plain. The small store soothed Tia, unlike the frozen tundra of a supermarket where she always ended up buying too much produce: vegetables so doomed for the trash that she might as well toss the broccoli in the supermarket garbage can as she left.

Her longtime friend Robin kept reminding Tia that she needed something besides her old people and Fianna's Bar in Southie. Robin nagged Tia to visit her in San Francisco. She said *yes, yes, yes* every time Robin asked, but both knew the real answer would be *no*. One of the many Tia-secrets Robin knew was that she'd never been on a plane. Imagining flying felt like diving in space, and Tia's stomach turned at the idea.

Robin and Tia grew up next door to each other. The commonality of both loving and having escaped South Boston gave their present closeness additional fuel. The difference was that Tia couldn't stay away and Robin, once she'd come out of the closet, couldn't bear to go back.

Southie's overwhelming traits made for the yin and yang of the neighborhood. Growing up, it seemed as though all her friend's parents had seven children, two of whom died tragically—either from drugs or suicide—and yet this same neighborhood that bred secrets and gangsters specialized in loyalty and taking care of one another. Tia would never find anyplace where she could count on her neighbors as she did in Southie. If she'd kept Honor, the girl would already have twenty honorary aunties and uncles. No one in Southie would understand how she could give up her daughter.

In JP they'd sympathize with her choice, but Tia hadn't decided if that were a good or bad thing.

An aged couple crept up the bus stairs one painful step at a time, the woman leaning on a walker. A heavy middle-aged woman spread over the designated handicapped bench closed her eyes against the man and woman.

Tia stood and touched the elderly woman's shoulders. "Please. Sit down, ma'am."

The woman's smile warmed the very air around her. "Thank you, dear."

Her companion, so in sync that Tia couldn't imagine he wasn't her husband, put a hand under her elbow to guide her. Tia cut her eyes at the teenager sitting beside Tia's now empty seat, choosing him, despite his tattoos, ripped jacket, and untied shoes—such a strange mark of toughness—rather than the young woman sitting on the other side. Even at ninety, a man couldn't easily accept chivalry from a woman. The kid ignored her. Tia tapped his shoe with hers. She widened her eyes at him and nodded toward the couple.

"Um, wanna sit down?" he asked the older man, rising with reluctance.

The older woman reached over and patted the teen's scorpion tattoo. "What good manners. Your mother would be proud." He half smiled enough to change from a thug to a boy, and as he helped the man, the woman winked at Tia.

People rose as the bus approached Green Street. Tia glanced at the stores outside. She lined up behind an exiting girl; a Pre-Raphaelite angel with gold hoops the size of dinner platters, and stepped off the bus one stop early. She headed to the gift shop.

Once home, Tia splashed milk on Cheerios. She stood as she ate, watching *Jeopardy!* on the small television on the counter, alternating bites of cereal with clearing the previous day's dishes, and then ended her meal by placing her supper bowl in the loaded dishwasher. After wiping the counter, she reached for the shopping bag she'd brought home.

Tia gathered photos of Honor and straightened them into a neat stack.

Rough tapestry covered the scrapbook she'd bought. Tia searched her desk drawers until she found a silver Cross pen that had belonged to her mother, testing it before writing. "*Birth Name: Honor Adagio Soros,*" she wrote in her best Catholic schoolgirl handwriting, and under those words, "*Adoptive Name: Savannah Hollister Fitzgerald.*" Cobalt ink sank into the thick ivory pages.

Below her daughter's names, Tia wrote "*Father: Nathan Isaac Soros,*" and "*Mother: Tia Genevieve Adagio.*" She pasted in a photo she and Nathan had taken of themselves at a secluded park. They'd balanced Nathan's camera on a rock to take the picture. Nathan smiled at the unmanned Canon with a crooked grin; Tia thought she looked sadly brave wearing the happy face she'd always put on for Nathan.

Under the picture of her and Nathan, she placed her only pregnancy photograph. Taken by her mother just weeks before her death, it was a picture her mother had insisted Tia keep forever. The late afternoon sun lit Tia's large belly and left her face in shadow.

She picked up the image she'd kept from Honor's ultrasound—white swirls in a grey background—and pasted it below the pregnancy shot; beside it, she put the newborn picture from the hospital, Honor's face still pinched from exit and entry. Had Tia been more kindly inclined toward Caroline and Peter, she might have given them the picture five years ago, but giving them Honor had seemed sufficient.

Tia dreaded the day Honor asked why Tia had abandoned her. She couldn't tell her the truth: keeping Honor would have bound her to Nathan forever, giving Tia license to call him, meet him, and lose herself again. Hundreds of times a day, Tia would have looked at Honor and thought about Nathan—Nathan who lived with his wife and two sons. She refused to saddle her daughter with her own longing. She didn't want to watch her daughter pine for a father as Tia still did.

When Tia and Nathan's affair had reached the four month mark, she'd longed to see him as he was before she knew him. "Please," she'd say, "bring me some pictures of you as a boy, as a teenager, in your twenties."

Finally, she realized that she'd reminded him enough times, and that she'd never see him any way other than how he appeared in front of her. He wouldn't give her any more of himself than what showed up in her apartment once a week. She didn't need him to spell it out—apparently there were degrees of cheating, and he wasn't willing to take his past out of his house and show it to her. That belonged only to his wife. Tia didn't want that for her daughter. Carrying that craving ate away at a person. Even now Tia wondered what Nathan had looked like at every age, what he looked like now. Not knowing made her feel as though something was always out of reach; as though she was always undeserving.

She carried a large wooden chair to the hall closet, the weight forcing her to drag it the final few feet. Standing on it, she brought down a softening shoebox from the top shelf and carried it to her desk. Grabbing a handful of old family shots, she wondered where to start. The album she planned to put together would help Honor understand her roots. Tia wanted to be ready for the day Honor came looking for answers.

She measured her own bony shoulders and photo scowl against those of her great-grandmother and ancient aunts. Tia pictured Honor, years forward, judging how much Tia had taken from her.

Tia turned from the family photos and grabbed the pile of annually received Honor pictures. She picked one from each birthday collection, tucked them in a beige folder, and went to find her coat.

Back home again, Tia poured herself a shot of Jameson. She carried the drink and a slim white bag to the living room. She drank half the shot and then arranged the copies of the photos she'd made at CVS, putting them in order from baby Honor, to Honor at age five. On top, she put a copy of the newborn picture stolen from Honor's first moments on earth.

Dear Nathan.

Tia touched her hand to her chest and slowed her breathing. She'd had no contact with Nathan since he walked away. She wrote and rewrote, until she'd composed a version that fit her imagined scene of Nathan reading the letter. Under her name, she added her phone number, her email, and her address. After a moment's thought, she wrote the word "work" and underneath the name and address of the senior center.

She folded the letter in thirds and tucked it in with the pictures of Honor. Tia wrote the address of a house to which she'd never been invited and the return address of an apartment that Nathan had never seen.

She lifted the pen and wondered, *Why now?*

For five years, she'd imagined sharing Honor with Nathan. Fantasies of his seeing the light, his running to her—"I missed you! I want to see our baby!"—had been her presleep soothers for five years. Reaching out to Nathan had tempted Tia since the day she gave birth.

So, *Why now?*

Tia could think of no answer except *Why not now?*

She stamped and sealed the envelope and placed it in her purse. In the morning, she'd mail Nathan their paper baby.

CHAPTER 5

Tia

A week after mailing the pictures, Tia hadn't heard a thing. Nathan remained underground. She dawdled as long as possible before leaving the house that morning, hoping her phone would ring that second, or the next, or right after that.

Tia tried to fool herself that she'd sent Nathan the pictures without expectations, but she could only lie to herself so much. Finally, she left her apartment. Crocus shoots poked through in her front yard. She'd assumed the gardening chores since moving in almost six years ago, throwing in fall bulbs and buying flats of annuals when they went on sale in late June. Flowers bloomed all summer. Tia reminded herself of those masses of daisies and irises when Katie insisted that Tia suffered from a prickly view of life.

The past Friday, Katie suggested that Tia might benefit from making an effort to celebrate one joyful thing about her life each day. Tia didn't suppose her coworker would appreciate Tia writing "I don't have to see Katie on weekends" on Tia's happy list. Still, Katie's advice managed to worm into Tia's brain, and she found herself rummaging for her life's blessings as she headed down Green Street. A blessing: her mother's job at Brandeis had allowed Tia to afford college, a blessing that Tia hadn't truly appreciated until she spent a year after high school working at the Gap. She prayed to never fold a pair of jeans again.

Blessing: she'd matriculated and graduated.

Not such a blessing: two months after graduation, she met Nathan, who had a grant studying those working with the elderly and chose as his research site the agency where she then worked.

Okay, Katie. Good news, bad news. Blessing: I got a college degree. Blessing: I fell in love with a good man, a wonderful husband and father. Curse: He wasn't mine.

Tia's first appointment waited on a wooden bench in the hall. She knew Mrs. Graham lived for their appointments, because her client told her this each week, which made Tia want to weep for Mrs. Graham's loneliness. Tia thought she'd do better by her clients if she took them home instead of writing reports about them. She'd tuck them into her best chair, buy a giant-screen TV so they could watch old movies, tote home the newest best sellers, and tempt their worn-out palates with home-baked treats. Her clients needed so much more than she could offer in sixty-minute sessions.

The agency was housed in a church, where the side lobby served as a client waiting room. The building smelled of years of dinners cooked in the mammoth kitchen and sweat from the men and women of Narcotics and Alcoholics Anonymous who filled the meeting rooms each night.

"Hey, Mrs. G," Tia greeted Mrs. Graham. "You look sharp. New dress?"

"For goodness sake, this dress is probably twenty years old." Mrs. Graham preened, even as she tossed her head at the compliment. "So, when are you going to call me Marjorie?"

"I wish I could." Their exchanges were stale from overuse, but Mrs. Graham, like so many of Tia's clients, thrived on a repetition of affectionate conversation. Weekly, Mrs. Graham reminded Tia how much she disliked the agency policy that forbid calling clients by their first name. Her boss believed that it gave respect to the clients—but Mrs. Graham found it the opposite.

"I miss the sound of my given name." Mrs. Graham pressed her lips until they whitened. She shook her head. "Sam's so far gone he never says it."

"Your friends must call you by name."

"Friends? Either they're dead, or I'm too dead on my feet from ministering to my Sam to see them."

Tia leaned forward and put her hand over Mrs. Graham's. "How about I call you Marjorie when we're alone?"

"I'd like that." Her expression lightened, and years flew away. Tia saw the woman, not the client. Mrs. Graham's strong bone structure and her lovely widow's peak gave testimony to a memorable face. "It gets lonely, you know. Nobody wants to see an old lady. We're invisible."

Tia's clients deserved recognition. They should also serve as warnings. The senior center should distribute tiny medallion likenesses of their clients engraved with the words *Don't Deny Your Future* and affix them to young people's dashboards instead of Saint Christopher medals.

Tia picked up a yellow legal pad and ran down a checklist of urgent and recurring items. Meals. Visiting nurses. Respite services. These referrals for Mrs. Graham and her dementia-cursed husband were the supposed reason for their meeting, but Tia believed the list was far less important than the hour of friendship and connection.

"So, Marjorie, brass tacks," Tia began their session. Mrs. Graham enjoyed Tia's tough talk, as it offered the woman a chance to do the same. "Have you given any more thought to putting Mr. G on the waiting list?"

Mrs. Graham's wrinkles deepened as she frowned and shook her head at Tia's suggestion. "Send him to a home? Must we talk about that again?" She closed her eyes for a moment. "No. No one else would tend Sam like I can. Thank you for worrying about me, but no thank you. If Sam goes away, it's because I'm dead."

At this point, Tia was supposed to give Mrs. Graham the social worker nod, to indicate deference and understanding, and then pull out brochures to encourage her to join Tia in checking out nursing homes for Mr. Graham. Mrs. G's fragility, high blood pressure, and erratic blood sugar demanded it. Tia knew that if she opened the poor woman's pocketbook, she'd find the box of licorice that Mrs. G chipped away at all day, Mrs. G's self-prescribed mood stabilizer. Mr. and Mrs. Graham should be marked as being "At severe risk" when Tia filled out the Grahams' weekly report, but she knew that check mark would lead to a home visit by someone who wielded more influence than Tia; someone who'd bully and push Sam and Marjorie Graham into leaving the home where they'd lived for their entire marriage.

Tia hadn't the heart to take them away from each other. She made a vow to get Mrs. G to come in for extra visits so Tia could keep a closer watch on her.

Tia went straight from work to Southie. She exchanged her button-down oxford shirt for a tight Red Sox T-shirt she kept in her desk. She rimmed her eyes with a thick black line and pulled a tighter notch on the worn red belt holding up her black jeans.

Tia hated Friday nights in Jamaica Plain, where politically active men who made her feel inadequate filled the bars, men whose eyes remained locked on Tia's chest as they lectured about building cooperative housing for immigrants. They made her crave the old neighborhood. A Southie guy might rant about immigrants ruining the world as he stared at your breasts, but he didn't try to pretend that he wasn't looking. Most importantly, if you wrote a Southie guy a letter about his long-lost daughter, you'd hear back from him—even if he only said, "Stay the fuck away!"

She switched trains at Park Street to catch the Red line, getting off a stop early so she could walk the scenic route to Fianna's Bar. She missed the speed of this train. Living in Jamaica Plain she was forced to use the slower Green Line, which ran along trolley tracks for half the routes.

Ocean air sweetened the street. After-work runners crammed

Day Boulevard, taking advantage of the wide street next to the beach. With each step toward her bar, she felt more relaxed. Southie's proximity to the water had driven up real estate prices to the point where her friends couldn't afford to buy houses—she knew that—but still, it made breathing possible for her in a way that JP never would.

Glossy wood and brass railings ran the length of Fianna's, nothing like the old-men bars where Tia's father once drank. Mirrors lining the walls made everything seem shinier and happier than the truth. Dining customers sat in booths reserved for those having a meal; tables ran a pecking order. At the back, farthest from the bar, cliques of newcomers hung out. Most of them lived in the sanded-wood-floor condominiums and ran the Sugar Bowl ocean loop—the mile-long cement ring surrounding Castle Island, the pride of South Boston—dressed in their college T-shirts. In the middle of the room sat the middle-aged local women—genteel women from the Point; the best area of Southie—who found the bar a respite from taverns filled with men like their husbands.

Up front was reserved for Tia's friends, kids who weren't kids anymore, because they owned the place.

Tia had once fantasized showing Nathan off at Fianna's after they'd married, or at least after he'd left his wife. Nathan would fit in, she'd thought, bringing front and center his raised-in-Brooklyn side instead of his college-professor side. The women would admire Nathan's built-to-brawl body, how he looked tough but not too forceful.

Tia and Nathan never went to Fianna's. During the Nathan year, Tia rarely went at all. Since Honor's birth, she visited too often.

"Hey, Ritchie," Tia greeted the bartender. He and Tia went to school together; two of the few in their crowd who'd transferred from Catholic to public school. Ritchie's mom was broke after his father died; Tia's mother didn't want to waste the money she'd hoped would finance uncovered college costs.

"Lookin' good, Tia." Ritchie winked. He poured Kahlúa, milk, and ice into a silver shaker and shook until it frothed to a peak. Her drink would be extra strong.

Tia carried the drink to the table where everybody knew not only her name but also her mother's name, that Tia's father was a drunken deserter, and that Kevin had popped her cherry.

No one knew about Honor.

"Yo." Kevin lifted his chin in greeting.

Bobby Kerrigan pulled out the chair next to him. Bobby's crush on Tia began when they were fourteen and continued right through his marriage, his divorce, and all his relationships after.

Moira Murphy and Deirdre Barsamian—formerly known as the Sweeney sisters—Irish twins, were dressed alike. Loose sweatshirts hid their marriage-and-motherhood fat. Michael Dwyer, the crowd's big shot, had hung his suit jacket over the back of his chair, a reminder to all of his significant city hall job.

"What's up, Tia?'" Michael asked. "Save any old ladies today?"

"You wish your work was even a quarter as important as Tia's," Bobby said.

"Really? City hall doesn't compare to some center for old ladies?" Michael asked. "No offense, Tia. I was just kidding."

"Yeah, being the pope of payback jobs is gonna get you into heaven," Bobby jabbed.

"No offense, taken, Michael." The smooth sweet drink eased through Tia one muscle at a time. "Why don't you come by some time? To the center. Maybe you could find us some funding that I don't have to beg for. Writing grants is killing me."

Tia smiled wide. Michael loved playing important and she wouldn't mind some of that largesse coming to her agency.

"I'll see what I can do." Michael winked at her.

"Hey, how's Robin? Any chance she's coming back?" Kevin quickly covered his question, which rang so obviously of his crush. "Maybe she'll fly in and surprise you with a ring. The two of you can finally get married."

"Really, Kev? You're really going there?" Tia asked.

He put a hand on Tia's arm, suddenly all serious. "Hey, you know I'm just joking, right? I don't care if she's a dyke; she's a good shit. Better looking than anything around here, present company excluded, of course."

Tia fell into the drone of meaningless talk.

Jokes flew.

Old stories were retold.

Moira and Deidre did their wickedly spot-on imitations of any-one missing.

Six? Seven? How many drinks? Southie bartenders poured them twice the size of those downtown or in JP, so she was twice as high as the number of drinks would suggest.

Ritchie shouted last call for the second time.

"I'll drive you home, Tia," Bobby said.

"Better pray she doesn't puke in your car," Kevin said.

"Fuck you, Sullivan." Bobby took Tia's coat off the back of her chair. He placed a gentle hand on Tia's back.

They remained quiet on the ride. Tia feared she would throw up if she tried to make conversation. Bobby hit the disc button, and Eminem came on.

She and Nathan had made love listening to CD's Nathan brought her, from the romance of Sam Cooke, to the pounding beat of The Pussycat Dolls. He layered soft over exciting in and out of bed. One minute he'd bring her to a crashing explosion; an hour later, he'd ask if she got enough intellectual stimulation from her job.

Nathan brought her an array of new music, books, and films. He introduced her to cutting edge ideas in the literature of gerontology, singers like the Nigerian-German Ayo, and encouraged her to watch documentaries like *Waste Land*, which he thought would broaden her world.

He told her she was beautiful, smart, *and* good. "The whole package," he'd say. "That's what you are." She fought her fear that he considered her some sort of Southie idiot savant.

Ayo's "Down on My Knees" was the soundtrack of her pregnancy, breaking her heart, until she finally deleted it and all the other musi-cal and literary traces of Nathan from her life.

They pulled up in front of her house. Bobby turned off the engine. "I'll walk you up."

"Mmm, don't bother." She tried not to slur. "Just get home safe. The roads are such a mess Friday nights."

"You're plastered. Let me make sure you're okay."

"I'm fine," she insisted.

"I want to help you." Bobby's strawberry-blond hair and blue eyes shined in the dark. Too bright.

Tia tried to flip the lock to get out. Bobby leaned over the console of his shiny red Corvette and released it for her. Bobby made the only real money in the crowd, realizing earlier than most how valuable Southie property could be, especially the houses on the waterfront. He knew when to pull back and when to buy property for himself.

Bobby's hand on her shoulder felt good. Warm and comforting, like a big blanket of you're-going to-be-okay. She rested against him. Just for a minute. Bobby's extra pounds made good leaning material. The music played. Bobby went slowly. He put an arm around her and strummed his fingers on her shoulder in time to the song. He reached for her hand. He tucked her fingers in his.

"You get more beautiful every year." Bobby brought her hand to his lips. "Honest. You've spoiled me for anyone else."

"Where'd you learn those lines?" She let him trace the top of her shoulder. "Corny old Bobby."

"Excuse me, college girl." He tipped her face to his and planted sweet kisses on each cheek. Bobby Kerrigan, secret softie. "You know I like that, right? That you went to college? How else do you get any-where in this world? I admire you, Tia."

You drive me crazy, Tia. You make me so damned hot, Tia, Nathan would say.

Bobby's hand went lower. He played with the bottom of her Red Sox shirt. She pulled away, for a moment becoming, while not sober, not as drunk. His palm brushed her waist where pregnancy stretch marks and puckered skin striated her flesh into an unrecognizable terrain. If he touched her, he'd know her secrets.

She hadn't slept with anyone since the day the stick showed that positive pink line.

CHAPTER 6

Juliette

Juliette opened her eyes to the welcome sight of Nathan holding her favorite mug: sturdy, big, and rough textured. She struggled to a sitting position, already wanting her first sip, Pavlovian in her response to the rich smell of dark roast. "You'll never leave me," Nathan used to joke. "You couldn't live without your morning coffee delivery."

Teasing like that was long gone. Much more than trust had been broken when Nathan cheated; a level of ease had disappeared. Kidding about affairs was crossed off the marital banter list six years ago, when the idea of getting her own morning coffee sounded just fine—a terrific bargain to never have to see him again. But, well, life was filled with *buts*, wasn't it?

Max's screech drifted in through the bedroom door, followed by Lucas's louder bellow.

"What are they fighting over?" Juliette asked.

"Some shirt that Max swears you gave him but Lucas says still belongs to him."

"What does it look like?"

"Blue?" Nathan sat on the edge of the bed. "Maybe green?" He ran a hand down her arm.

Nathan was forty-two. She was a year younger. Worry lines,

which on Juliette portended the not-too-distant day when she'd become invisible, added gravitas to his good looks.

"Are they dressed?" Juliette brushed off his hand, though even as she batted away temptation, she considered it. Locking the door and making love, even if it was silent surreptitious sex, offered a moment's sanctuary from Wednesday, the worst day of her week. Deliveries poured in. Customers woke up realizing they had to look perfect by some weekend function, and only juliette&gwynne could perform that miracle. Lucas and Max both had practices to which she had to somehow shuffle them in between her work.

Juliette hated Wednesdays.

Increasingly louder shouts came from the boys.

"I better make sure they're okay," she said.

Nathan held his hands up. "Stay. I'll deal with them." He leaned over and kissed her. "Rain check?"

She squeezed his love handle. "Rain check."

By the time she'd brushed her teeth and pulled on her robe, the sound of fighting had given way to the clicking of computer keys. Both boys, but particularly Lucas, at fourteen, thought their parents' refusal to allow computers in their bedrooms was insane. For Juliette, it meant keeping her boys safe. She'd read too many times about some nut going after a kid he'd met on the Internet. She could easily imagine her sweet Max drifting out to a playground where, instead of a fellow Civilization video game player, he'd find a thirty-five-year-old killer pervert.

Juliette stood at the door of the upstairs study, enjoying the sight of them bent toward the screen—Lucas light-haired like her, Max dark like Nathan—and wished she could let them be. Instead she entered, kicking away clutter and boy debris. In her sons' world, computers, soccer balls, and dirty laundry coexisted quite happily. She was eternally grateful they had moved to a house with enough space to hide the boy's messes.

"Good morning, honeys." Juliette leaned down to kiss Lucas's head. His hair, still damp from a shower, smelled sweetly grassy. She inhaled until he ducked away.

"Morning," he muttered without looking up.

Juliette hugged her younger boy, who smelled far less sweet. "Mmm. Shower time, it's getting late."

"Can we have something special for breakfast?" Max, bounced with enthusiasm in that way only young boys could.

"Could you clean this room before breakfast?" She pointed in turn at a crumpled sweatshirt, a bowl lined with dried flecks of the previous night's chips, and mugs flaky with sugary remnants of something unhealthy.

"Will you make waffles if we do?" Max wiggled his eyebrows and gave a "Don'tcha love me?" grin.

Waffles.

She held back her sigh, dreading the extra time making the batter, dragging out the waffle iron, and, with a working woman's guilt, heating the damned syrup.

"Okay—you clean, I'll make waffles." She pulled her robe tighter as she left and walked downstairs.

No whipped cream, though.

The number on the scale had crept up again that morning. She could hear her mother's lecture on metabolism after forty.

She opened the front door to fine mist and damp newspapers. Four years after moving, Juliette still missed their Waltham paper delivery guy who'd wrap them in plastic at the slightest hint of wetness.

She lifted out yesterday's mail still piled in the oversized bowl on the hall table and replaced it with the newspapers, where they could dry without getting wetness on the wooden top. Last night she and Nathan had both arrived home late, which meant rushing to prepare dinner, helping the boys with homework, and answering too many phone calls and emails. Email had overtaken postal deliveries in importance. Unless there was a package, she expected little but magazines and bills.

Emerson College alumni bulletin for her.

Contexts for Nathan. The magazine claimed it made sociology "interesting and relevant to anyone interested in how society operates," so why did Juliette always pick up *Vogue* instead?

Junk mail for Nathan. Junk mail for her.

American Express bill.

Last in the pile was a hand-addressed letter forwarded from their Waltham address. The return address was Jamaica Plain. It had been sent to Nathan.

She recognized the last name.

Adagio.

Jesus Christ.

Tia Genevieve Adagio. Such a pretty name. She'd forced that name from Nathan. "Tell me her name!" she'd screamed. "Tell me, goddamn it! I'm sure she knows mine."

Juliette almost crushed the envelope. She should give it to Nathan. Didn't she trust him now? They were doing so well. The act of giving it to him would strengthen the confidence they'd regained. He'd open it in front of her. That was the right thing to do.

She hid the envelope in the living room—the company room— kept so clean they barely used it. After closing her eyes and praying she'd find an innocent, forgivable reason for the contact ("I'm dying and must say good-bye!"), Juliette slit open the envelope.

Pictures slid out and then a letter. A somber little girl stared at Juliette.

Dear Nathan,

This is our daughter. Her adoptive parents send photos each year after her birthday (March 6). As you can see, she resembles you.

They named her Savannah (I know, it's an awful name; in my mind she's Honor—the name I gave her at birth), but they're good people. Caroline and Peter Fitzgerald. She is a doctor; he has a software company. They live in Dover. (I know you will wonder. I do know you.) They will always love and care for her.

I expect our daughter will call me someday. At her birth, I arranged things to allow this future contact to happen easily. I expect that if she calls, she will ask *about you. I plan to help her get in touch if that's her wish.*

Tia

Juliette stared at the child, gripping the photos with icy fingers. She placed her other hand on her chest, trying to slow her rapid, shallow breaths.

Did he know he had this child, this daughter? Tia had written "This is our daughter" as though it were a given fact. We. Have. A. Daughter.

Had he seen her, spoken to her? Had they had any contact since Nathan's confession? Please, God, please let the answers be no.

"Mom!" Max called down the stairs. *"Mom!"* he repeated when she didn't respond.

Juliette shoved the letter and pictures back in the envelope and stuck it into her bathrobe pocket. "I'm right here, Max, you don't have to scream." Her words sounded muted, despite the fact that she'd yelled, just as she'd told Max not to scream.

Max's head appeared over the stair railing of the second floor. "Where are my blue sweats? Did you remember that I have practice?"

Juliette twisted her wedding ring and willed the pounding in her chest to subside. "Left side of the closet, hanging beside your denim jacket."

He grunted his version of thanks.

"And shower before you get dressed," Juliette nagged on autopilot. She straightened the mail until it was piled in size order, trying to think about anything other than the envelope pressing against her hip.

She stumbled into the kitchen.

The pictures, the resemblance to Max, to Nathan—for a moment, she thought she'd choke on her rising fury. Memories of her husband's betrayal rushed through her until there seemed to be room only for anger. A daughter? How could her husband have not told her?

Tia's letter didn't say, "You have a child." Or "I never told you I was pregnant, but . . ."

Yet she hadn't known that they'd moved.

What did he know? What did they know together? What else had they hidden from her? Memories of being left out, of Nathan and that woman as a couple while she floundered in the dark, threatened to drown her.

Not many miles away, Nathan's daughter was waking, or having breakfast, or maybe getting ready for preschool. A child of his that wasn't hers.

Surely her eyes would give away her distress. Blinking, squeezing back tears, she stumbled toward the table and sat on the hard kitchen chair. Once sitting, she dug her nails hard into her thighs. She had to calm down somehow, or the children, Nathan, would read her in a minute.

Breathe deep.

What could be more of a betrayal than having a child with another woman?

Dissociate.

Not telling her: didn't that say his loyalty was more to that woman than to her?

Think about this later. Figure this out later.

She needed to find out more of the facts before opening herself to lies from Nathan.

Juliette was well schooled in keeping her own counsel. Growing up with a mother whose version of "Good morning" was "You are not wearing that ugly outfit to school" gifted her with an enduring ability to maintain a calm front. Her mother thrived on knocking self-pity and crying out of Juliette, so early on, she learned techniques for preventing tears.

Soon Lucas, always first, would stomp down the stairs, ready to eat a ridiculously large amount of whatever she offered. He combusted calories impossibly fast. He'd grown taller than his father this year. Nathan pretended not to notice, but Juliette saw how often her husband looked as though he were stretching towards greater height when next to Lucas.

Screw the waffles. She pulled eight eggs from the fridge. Four for

Lucas, two for Nathan—a burst of rage took her breath away—and two for Max.

Focus on food.

Max was built husky like Nathan, with a similarly sluggish engine. *Don't think about the letter.*

Juliette's metabolism had once burned fast. No longer. Now she wrestled her lust for bubbling pans of macaroni and cheese topped with crisped, buttery crumbs.

Had pregnancy broadened Tia? So tiny she'd been, when Juliette found a way to see her, needing to put a face in her nightmares.

Food. Stick to breakfast.

Nathan's lust for food was broader than Juliette's. He hungered for steak and for things soft, sweet, and savory. Juliette could make him weak with her cheddar biscuits. She should poison a batch for him.

Was he still seeing Tia? It didn't seem so from the letter. But who knew? Who really knew one's husband? Once she would have said she did, but no more.

Nathan thirsted for his students' awe. Juliette knew that. They treated her husband like a minor rock star, with his exciting politics and edgy lectures, and he held his face to the attention like a flower to the sun.

Lucas slid into the kitchen moments before the last bit of egg transformed from liquid to solid. Juliette sprinkled in shredded cheddar and then scrambled the last bits.

"Juice is on the table," she said even as Lucas picked up his glass. He grabbed a handful of raspberries from a dish on the table.

"Sit when you eat," Juliette ordered. Motherhood was little more than a series of repetitive commands and tasks these days. She remembered the moments when Max switched from holding her finger, to slipping his hand into hers, and then to rejecting her touch.

"Why are mothers so keen on these things?" Nathan walked in carrying their three newspapers. Oh, he was so important, the sociology professor—of course he must have the *New York Times*, the *Boston Globe*, and the *Wall Street Journal*.

Lucas surprised Juliette by picking up the slack when she didn't answer Nathan, perhaps discomforted by her unusual reticence. "What things?" he asked.

"Things like requiring sons to sit when eating, as though vitamins and minerals can be fully absorbed only when they're in proscribed positions." Nathan grinned at his all-American athletic blond son, at Juliette. He swiveled, seeking the missing Max.

Nathan held out his arms for an embrace. Juliette held the blistering frying pan between them.

"Hot. Watch out," she warned. "This is heavy."

Nathan looked puzzled. He leveled hurt eyes at her. They were close in height. His mournful dark eyes, refugee eyes, velvety full-of-shit eyes, met hers. "Is something wrong?"

She slammed the pan on the wooden block protecting their table, their precious Fairfield Antique Show table. She slid his portion of eggs onto his plate.

"Whole wheat toast," she said. "I protect your heart, Nathan. No seeds; you don't like seeds." She slammed a platter on the table. "And I warm the toast plate each morning? Did you know that, Nathan?"

"Umm, it's great, Mom." Lucas, her poor, confused boy. "Thanks."

Nathan, apparently stunned into silence, reached for the pitcher of juice.

"Put the dishes in the sink when you're done," she said. "Make sure Max eats his eggs. Tell him I didn't have time for waffles."

"Aren't you eating?" Nathan asked. "Where are you going so early?"

"I lost my appetite. Work." She began walking out and then turned. "I love you guys." She couldn't confuse Lucas by making her love sound specific to him and not their father. Besides, she did love them all; she just prayed that love didn't damn her to a life of turning a blind eye.

Juliette climbed the stairs to her bedroom, grabbed clothes, and brought them into the bathroom. After locking the door, she turned on the faucet, fell on the rug, and wrapped her arms around herself tight and rocked. She gripped her upper arms hard enough to leave red marks.

She'd thought it was over: the heartache, the mistrust, watching him for signs of deceit each time he walked in the house. For such a long time, she'd wondered if he was simply riding the comfort of his own lies when he'd promise the bad times were all behind them.

There had been too many threads she hadn't wanted to cut: children, the world they'd built together, and, of course, love. She never stopped loving him. Forgiving him became her best choice.

She'd finally let go and believed him.

Now Juliette spun right back to asking herself why. Why had he slept with another woman? She'd revered him for the judgement and rectitude she'd believed he possessed.

Tia's huge orphan eyes had probably begged her husband for love and protection. She must have been exactly the right ticket when Nathan tired of his über-competent wife, good at so many things. Perfect Juliette: providing gourmet meals and mother-of-the-year nurturing, spicking-and-spanning his house. She even brought in more money than he did these days. The idea that he'd turned to that girl because his ego needed lifting drove Juliette insane. She'd always thought so much more of Nathan.

How dare that woman spread her name, cool as aloe, right across the envelope for the world and Juliette to see, as though Juliette didn't know who she was. As though Juliette hadn't once followed her for five shameful nights.

Tia Genevieve Adagio. Silky girl, sliding over Juliette's husband like Salome. Slippery like a baby seal, all dark and tiny, fragile, needy girl, looking up at Juliette's husband as though Nathan supplied the oxygen she breathed.

And now they had a daughter? More than anything else, this knowledge shut out Juliette. Suddenly Tia and Nathan were the couple, while Juliette pressed herself up to the glass of their secret family.

* * *

Juliette drove up Central Street and parked in the small lot behind the shop. The back as well as the front entrance was marked with their full name: juliette&gwynne//flush de la beauté. They'd wanted to open their shop on a street rife with beauty and flush with money. Gwynne chose the moneyed zip code of Wellesley's suburban main street for their location, and Juliette had come up with the name, confident that women would fling money at anything French. Juliette created products. Gwynne managed the business. They were synchronized as friends and business partners. When Gwynne sneezed, Juliette grabbed a tissue.

That's why she had to stay in the car for a few minutes. Juliette was transparent to Gwynne, and Juliette didn't want her friend reading her mind.

Gwynne would scare the shit out of Juliette if they weren't best friends. Besides having four daughters ages six to thirteen, a solid marriage, and the dancer's body that Juliette's mother wanted for Juliette, Gwynne was smart and funny. Thankfully, she had a wide streak of neurotic self-doubt and anxiety that required a steady diet of predawn runs, Effexor, and an occasional sleeping pill, enabling Juliette to keep her envy in check.

Juliette, privy to the secrets of the privileged, wondered why so many lovely women thought they were garbage. She slipped the envelope from her purse. A light rain fell, pleasing Juliette, offering safety in the confines of her car, hiding her from the world for at least that moment.

She fingered the cheap paper.

The cheap envelope.

Stationery and matching envelopes waited in Juliette's desk, something to suit any mood. Thick paper so rich it caressed the ink. Ivory. Dove grey. Palest blue. None right for the letter she'd send to Tia. For that, Juliette would go to Walgreens and buy ninety-nine-cent crap in blaring white.

Juliette skimmed the letter again, unable to concentrate on words, feeling only Tia's contamination.

"Our daughter," she'd written to Nathan.

"She resembles you."

Juliette took the pictures from her lap, where they'd dropped. Her fingers shook. This child would wreck their life.

The resemblance to Max astonished Juliette. Like this child, her boy had been fat legged and adamant. The photo marked Savannah as Max's sister. Lucas's also, but that wasn't as screamingly obvious. Savannah? An unlikely name for this solemn-looking child.

She flipped through the pictures, one for each year of the child's life and one as a newborn. The child's serious expressions, more intent each year, tapped open Juliette's heart. Warmth toward the girl, so unexpected that Juliette almost cried, trickled in. Nathan's mother showed in the child; Nathan's mother, who still wore the sober face of an immigrant. Nathan's parents were fifty years in New York but still expected the real Americans to send them back to Hungary. They carried a fearful gratitude for having escaped the Communist noose around the neck of the Hungarian Jews. Nathan, their only child, born eleven years later, accepted the dreams his parents fed him, along with rich milk, red meat, and their veneration of education.

Nathan's parents still gasped in joy each time they saw their strong, good-looking American son; Juliette, their *szép*—beautiful— daughter-in-law; and their handsome grandsons.

Shouldn't they know they had a granddaughter?

Juliette examined Savannah's face. She brought the photo closer. Even as she wanted to shred it, she recognized that the child looked like family.

But Nathan's, not hers. Not theirs together.

Gwynne knocked on the car window. Rain dripped in as Juliette rolled it down.

"What are you doing out here?" Gwynne held the *Boston Globe* over her head with one hand and pointed at the pictures with the other. "Who's that?"

Juliette shoved the pictures and letter into her large leather bag. "One of those Sally Struthers kids."

"The Christian Children's Fund?" Gwynne twisted a corner of her mouth up. "Are you sure that's the best place to give?"

No doubt Gwynne had a list of better charities in her purse, ready to be whipped out and given as a guideline for giving. If she didn't love hot showers and air-conditioning so much, Gwynne would be in some jungle saving the planet, bringing her kids with her. She was big on exposing her kids to the right thing to do, often saying she prayed that didn't backfire and lead to raising four nihilistic ladies who lunched.

"It's called the ChildFund International now." Actually, Juliette had sponsored a child and was embarrassed that she'd pulled it out as a cover. Somehow that seemed so wrong.

"When did you start that?" Gwen asked.

"I don't brag," Juliette said. "One is supposed to give quietly."

"Give quietly to Christian funds?" Gwynne and Juliette were both married to Jewish men. Two blondes with dark men; they were quite the clichés. Juliette's father was nominally Jewish, but her parents didn't pay religion or culture much attention past the annual Christmas party.

"Are we going in?" Juliette asked.

Gwynne moved back from the door, arms up. "I wasn't the one out here mooning over little Christian babies."

Who adopted Nathan's daughter? Who were these good people, this doctor-woman and computer-man from Dover, a town so old money, it made the town of Wellesley appear nouveau riche?

Their shop still held the cool basil-lemon scent they sprayed each night before leaving. Minimalist displays were in the same perfect order in which Gwynne and Juliette left them each evening. Outside, engraved into a steel plate in flowing black lines, the shop's name topped the large glass window, the same simple logo used in every brochure, card, and advertisement—all designed to capture the taste of the women of Wellesley and the surrounding circle of the wealthiest towns in Massachusetts.

Since they'd opened five years ago, they'd done everything possible to build a loyal customer base, from hiring top designers for their packaging, to using the highest-grade organic ingredients. Even when euros sped past dollars, they'd continued using expensive oils pressed from flowers grown in the soil of Ireland's Burren. Child care was provided in a big, bright room carpeted in sunshine yellow. Juliette and Gwynne cut no corners in building their premium brand.

Juliette's experience at Emerson doing theatrical makeup, plus the fashion column she'd once written for *Boston* magazine, combined with Gwynne's eye for art and head for business, had come together in such a perfect storm of success that they'd recently moved from selling their products only at their shop to selling the juliette&gwynne makeup and skin care line regionally.

In the last three years, they'd both purchased homes in the town where they'd opened their shop, the town they'd originally chosen because it was so far above their economic stations. Juliette had made their first skin creams in her Waltham kitchen; now a small manufacturing plant produced their products. Recently, every exclusive women's store that Juliette visited displayed the matte black slashed with deep pansy-purple that signified a juliette&gwynne product.

That letter threatened every bit of the happiness Juliette had earned.

Leaving Gwynne to deal with the shop, Juliette slipped into the bathroom and locked the door. She sat on the black restroom chair and again slid out the photos and letter. She studied the child's face and memorized the adoptive mother's name before zipping them into the deepest compartment of her purse. Then she stood before the mirror, applied another coat of lipstick, and readied to give her usual morning greeting to the staff as they arrived.

Helena and Jai were first to show up after Juliette and Gwynne. Not only did they work together, they were roommates who drove in together, left together, and spent the weekends together at bars made for women wrapped in dresses as tight as bandages and the men who wanted them.

The two young women were the juliette&gwynne brow specialists. Brows, the women of Boston's western suburbs knew, could make or break your face, so there were definite Helena and Jai camps.

Helena, the designated sophisticate, arched women into minor-league versions of Catherine Zeta-Jones. She could thin a brow into submission, dye it to resemble mink, or teach a client how to make her anemic brow resemble Brooke Shields wings if she so wished.

Juliette preferred Jai's minimalist approach, making a woman's brows just clean enough to pop her eyes. One time she'd made the mistake of saying this at dinner, which sent Lucas, Max, and Nathan into hysteria. Max, then eight, took to telling gory stories of women's eyes popping out, strings of eyeballs hanging from bloody sockets.

As she went from room to room, Juliette considered her options. The plans she'd begun formulating would sound crazy if she gave them voice—not that she intended to talk about them. But she needed information. Acting in a play where she didn't know the lines would never happen to her again.

Six years ago, after Nathan engraved the words *I had an affair* on her, she hadn't known how to look at him. For too long, she hadn't been able to ask anything except *why.*

"Why, Nathan? Were you unsatisfied?" she'd ask. "Bored? Tired of me? What did you need that I didn't provide?"

Those questions never elicited a satisfying answer. What could he say that would help her understand? "I was restless"? "Being around the kids and you bored me"? "I missed your adoration"?

At some point, she accepted that it was all that and more, and that it didn't matter why he did it, but that he'd done it.

It wasn't his answer that mattered, but hers.

She had to find out not only if she could stay with him but also how to do it without punishing him every day. He implored her to go to couples therapy with him, but she refused. Every time she pictured herself sitting with Nathan and some faceless shrink, she panicked. In these imaginary sessions, she was picked over, criticized, analyzed, and found wanting.

For weeks she'd shut herself away with the computer. One site, complete with audio, screamed *Heal Yourself!* The next began with a warning that their chances of staying together were fifty-fifty, and did she know this was also painful for the cheater and his lover? That they suffered from depression and contemplated suicide? Further into the site, she learned she could affair-proof her marriage, but only by sending $79.99 for the books and tapes. Sent in discreet packaging.

After the panic elicited by that site, she found one promising that many couples emerged from their affairs stronger than ever, but, it warned, they had to assess their relationship: Were they committed to healing? Were they willing to talk to each other? Then she wondered if she should be going to therapy with Nathan.

At times she'd felt as though she did only two things: care for the children and read about infidelity online. During one sleepless three-o'clock-in-the-morning online session, she read that marriages were "far less likely to recover from serial cheating than a single affair." Juliette marched into the bedroom demanding to know if there had been anyone else. If she'd had a flashlight, she would have shined it in Nathan's eyes,

Even after he swore to his fidelity to his one secret lover, intent on his claim that he'd never been with any other woman during their marriage—as though he should get a medal—Juliette studied the characteristics of cheaters, finding an online test that promised to determine how likely a spouse was to cheat. She flipped out when Nathan's score showed moderate risk. She wanted him to test at an impossible zero. Of the seven indicators of likelihood for cheating, Nathan had three risk factors: he was *attractive*, he had *opportunity*— wasn't a college simply fishing grounds for affairs?—and he had a *high sex drive*. Thankfully, she could truthfully mark "No" for his being a *risk taker*, being *entitled*, seeing *love as a game*, and having *relationship problems*.

Except, of course, that he slept with someone for a year.

Juliette took her cold comfort from the fact that they were under the 50 percent mark for "yes" answers.

After searching for solutions in books, online, and couples therapy, and finding no respite from pain in her rush to bludgeon herself into recovering, she finally discovered her own best answers. Three things were true: She loved Nathan and didn't want to leave him. The thought of raising her sons alone terrified her, and it would hurt them. And as with any grief, she needed time to pass before she could find her way back to her marriage.

Juliette held closely to the belief that it wasn't her fault. Nathan assured her repeatedly that it wasn't her fault, apparently doing his own online searches. He printed out a consoling list of why men and women had affairs:

- *For the ego stroking you get when someone pays attention*
- *For the selfish desire of a temporary pleasure*
- *For confirmation of your attractiveness or worth*
- *To get adoration*

Juliette's volcano of righteous anger churned with hurt until the day it miraculously began receding a bit at a time, and then shrank into a small lump sitting on her chest, eventually hardened, and became a tiny but sharp pebble that she could tuck away until a reminder tripped her up.

Now he'd brought that rock right back up to the surface, and once again she could barely breathe without feeling that goddamned so-called buried pain.

Once in her office, a cool-blue-and-white escape from the ubiquitous pansy and black throughout the shop, Juliette turned on her computer, readying to Google "Caroline Hollister Fitzgerald." Like Juliette Silver Soros, Caroline used her maiden name as a middle name. Already Juliette knew something about her.

She needed facts. There was no way Juliette would be left out— the proverbial last one to know—again. If knowledge were power, then she'd get her strength from learning exactly what was going on.

She found Caroline's image on the Web site of Cabot Hospital in Boston, where she was a pathologist specializing in pediatric cancer.

Caroline's hawkish nose told Juliette that looks didn't rule Caroline's world. Many women would have pared down that nose. Caroline Fitzgerald lived in Dover, so surgery costs weren't likely a factor in her decision. Thin lips gave her a tense look, but her eyes overcame all her sharper features. Intense olive eyes framed by long, sandy lashes stood out from everything else. One coat of juliette&gwynne bitter-chocolate mascara, and Juliette could make those eyes striking. They'd pop.

Juliette found the computer folder labeled "Promotions," from their early days, and opened a file labeled "Deep Discount," seeking the flyer that they'd once used to romance customers in the hopes of building a following.

"Please accept our offer of childcare while enjoying our signature day of beauty." Juliette entered Caroline Hollister Fitzgerald's name and printed the invitation on creamy ivory paper topped with a double line of black and pansy stripes.

CHAPTER 7

Juliette

Two days later, Juliette drove to Boston. She needed to be alone, away from the shop, the house, and the boys, if only for a few hours. And Nathan. Jesus, did she need to be away from him. She didn't even want to be in the same town.

Of course, her destination would hardly bring relief.

Juliette hadn't said anything about the letter yet. She refused to show it to Nathan until she knew more. She needed control over her life, and, like a smart lawyer, she didn't want to ask any question to which she didn't know the answer.

Of course, she knew she should talk to Gwynne before her constant thoughts about the child and that woman drove her completely insane, but she didn't. If Gwynne knew what Juliette was about to do, she'd lock her in the linen closet.

The road curved as Juliette followed Route 16 to Route 9. The last time she'd driven to Boston had been for a meeting with her lawyer, when she and Gwynne rewrote their partnership agreement to adjust for the changes in their growing business. That day, she'd headed downtown. Today she headed to Jamaica Plain.

It was late morning. Time would soon slip away. Juliette's freedom ended when Max's soccer game began at four. Nathan would meet her there, because—oh yes—they were a children-first family.

Juliette loathed her growing bitterness. She missed the sweetness that came with loving Nathan. She wished they were back at Cape Cod, the way it had been when the boys were little. Nathan spent hours digging in the sand with Lucas and Max, dribbling wet sand over dry, digging deep moats so the boys could dangle their feet inside.

Nights were lobster, warm butter, and cold wine. Scrabble and lovemaking. Waking brought happiness.

She'd believed Nathan when he told her it was just stupidity. Just greedy, meaningless sex. She'd believed her research. He was an idiot. She's believed that she'd forgiven him.

Now she worried that her anger had simply lain dormant. During their struggle, the worst of it had been the awfulness of hating Nathan. In truth, Juliette thought she loved him too much.

Juliette slowed for the red light ahead, realizing she'd been speeding. Route 9's amalgam of stores interspersed with stretches of tree-lined road became denser with cars and business as she neared the Boston city limits. Already the Atrium Mall loomed on her right. Gwynne and Juliette had considered opening their shop at the upscale Atrium, they realized foot traffic suited them better.

Keeping her eyes on the road, Juliette rummaged in her pocketbook, which she'd plopped on the passenger seat, until her fingers felt the crackle of the bag of M&M's she'd grabbed from her stash. Every Halloween she bought enough miniature bags of M&M's to keep her through the following October. Full-sized bags would add a dress size a year.

Hiding food at forty-one was pathetic, as though she were still a child sneaking candy past her mother and shoving it to the very back of her dresser drawer.

Since receiving the letter two days before, Juliette worked at not being alone with Nathan. She spoke to him as little as possible, alluding to work problems and PMS, both tactics guaranteed to give her lots of space. He didn't find her work very interesting, much as he tried to pretend otherwise, and like any man, he shied away from anything to do with her cycle.

Swallowing back her unspoken words made conversation almost impossible. Keeping quiet required muffling her voice with food: she'd used the brownies she'd baked late last night, and the lasagna from Thursday, so thick with meat and mozzarella that as she watched Nathan devour the food, an instant heart attack from cholesterol overload seemed possible.

That morning at breakfast, Juliette stuffed herself with four pieces of toast and then finished both the kids' and Nathan's crusts. Her waistbands were already getting tight, and she couldn't afford it.

After breakfast, she'd scoured the stove and then scrubbed the counter until the granite screamed.

Pathetic, aiming her anger at appliances.

Cleaning.

A women's rifle range.

Clorox.

A woman's bullets.

The now smeared and creased photos of Savannah called constantly. Repeatedly she took them out, worrying at them like an erupting blemish. Perhaps she was hoping that the image would finally evaporate, and then Max would no longer seem like a middle child.

She glanced in the rearview mirror. A chin hair fit for Methuselah had popped out and heralded the end of her useful beauty years. Once she'd been able to count on being attractive, now it required every product she'd invented. She plucked at the hair with a forefinger and thumb, despite it being fruitless and doing nothing but inviting a car accident.

Juliette pushed her oversized sunglasses higher on her nose and pulled Max's baseball cap lower on her forehead. She wore Lucas's shapeless old jeans jacket and sweatpants.

NPR blared. She snapped it off and pulled off the Arborway. She drove down Morton Street to Tia's workplace, clueless about her motive, except she hoped Tia had gained a hundred pounds and that her skin resembled a leper's. A roughened complexion had been Tia's weakest feature; at least, at the distance from which Juliette had spied on her years before. Perhaps hormones and time had ravaged it into pits and craters.

So thoughtful of Tia to include her work address and the name of the agency where she worked, but Juliette was puzzled when the GPS led her to a church. She didn't want to get too close, but finally she left her car and walked down a weedy slate path. The massive entrance door, guarded by an expanse of overgrown evergreens and untrimmed bushes, was locked. Juliette backed away.

A foot-worn side path ended at a parking lot behind the building. A brick propped open a heavy back door, where a young man in a brimmed cap sucked on a cigarette. A brush broom leaned against the wall.

"Help you?" He stamped out the butt and swept it into the pile of trash to his left.

"I think I'm lost," Juliette pretended. "Is this the Spaulding Nursing and Therapy Center?" She looked around as though bewildered. "This looks like a church."

"You're lost all right, lady. What you want is down the parkway. You're at the Jamaica Plain Senior Advocate Center. This is a church—their offices are here." He peered at her. "Sure that's not what you're looking for?"

Juliette bent her head to the silver clipboard she held, the kind with a slim box for holding papers. "Nope. Says right here: Spaulding Nursing and Therapy. I'm an inspector for the city."

"Okay then. Good luck." He took his broom, removed the brick holding the door open, and walked back into the church.

Maybe she had an untapped aptitude for deceit. Perhaps if she left Nathan, she'd give up beauty and become a private eye.

Now that she knew she was at the right place, Juliette returned to her car and drove around back, parking within sight of the now closed door. Across from the church, masses of trees and vines filled an empty lot.

Full of nervous energy, but without a single task, she sorted through the receipts in her wallet. Then she cleaned out her glove box, wishing that it were Nathan's car she was inspecting, so she could search for evidence of further betrayal.

When she'd discovered a forgotten card from Tia in Nathan's glove box, a year after Nathan's confession—crushed way in the back—Juliette had been hit all over again by his betrayal. Just a ghostly thought of the card brought back that feeling.

That sickening card, dated soon before Nathan's telling her about his affair, showed a simple red heart. Inside, the printed message read,"Meant to Be." Written in perfect script were the words *You own me. Tia.*

Now Tia owned Juliette. If possible, Juliette would have used the card to carve Nathan's heart into the same million pieces into which he'd lacerated hers.

Tia came out.

She hadn't gained weight—if anything, she was smaller, sharper. Her skin seemed no worse, but no better either. Her hair was still short, but she'd cut it into ragged pieces that were more *Oliver Twist* than *Vogue*. How did her lack of style make her seem more vulnerable? She was the type that men lined up to rescue.

Look at her. Miss Delicate, who'd abandoned her baby like so much rubbish and then used the child as an excuse to contact Nathan. Why hadn't she kept her daughter? Too selfish? Had the baby only been a scheme to keep Nathan?

Juliette studied her from a distance. Learn your enemy. She wore cheap, nasty knockoffs that had the look of H&M. No makeup except for a garish line rimming her eyes. Scuffed clogs completed her careless look.

She was still beautiful.

Supper should have tasted like ashes that night, but instead compliments flew as Nathan and her sons forked up buttered noodles, beef chunks, and carrots so tender from wine and time, you'd think they'd been cooked with love.

Now, at eleven thirty, Lucas and Max slept. Juliette mopped the kitchen floor until she feared she might wear away the finish. Nathan spent three hours hidden in his study.

Finally, Juliette put down the sponge and went to the bedroom. She propped herself on pillows and studied juliette&gwynne's financial statement for the previous quarter. This part of the business bored her to the point of wanting to bash her head against the wall. Numbers were Gwynne's responsibility, and Juliette would happily leave every box in every spreadsheet to her. But Nathan's father had lectured Juliette on the importance of keeping watch, and she'd promised him that she would.

"Remember Bernie Madoff," he'd warn her, as though Gwynne spent her nights concocting phony invoices. Juliette wanted to ignore him, but breaking a promise to her ever-vigilant father-in-law seemed sinful. Each time he called her sweetheart, the word inflected from his worry as much as his accent, Juliette felt protected and loved.

Nathan carried in a load of laundry. Juliette lowered her files and pad, and studied him over her reading glasses. Concern showed on his face. Nathan noticed moods, performing domestic tasks when he sensed tension.

"This was next to the stairs." He placed the basket on the bench at the foot of the bed. "Where do you want it?"

Juliette creased the papers she now gripped too hard. "There's fine."

"You okay?" He sat on her side of the bed, forcing her to move over. "What's wrong? You've been weird for days."

"I'm fine."

Nathan ran a hand down her arm. "You don't seem fine."

In his sweatshirt and jeans, he looked like Lucas. Juliette studied the bare thigh revealed by her short nightgown. Spots from old sunburns had morphed into age spots. "Work," she said. "Just work."

He took off Juliette's reading glasses, a move earned by sixteen years of marriage. As though he were a righteous man, he laid a gentle finger between her brows and rubbed where her glasses always pressed in a line.

Words backed up in her throat. Her fingers curled until she ripped the report on sunscreen sales.

"Whoa! You're more than a little tense. Is business okay?" He touched the report as though to look. Juliette pulled it back, clutching it against her chest so the words weren't visible.

"Everything's fine," she said.

"So what's wrong?"

She shook her head. "Nothing. Really. Just in a sad mood, I guess."

"Poor baby." Without saying anymore, he pulled off his clothes, got into bed, and stroked her back.

Even as Juliette meant to move, push him away, and run to the kitchen, where she'd shovel in forkfuls of noodles cold with congealed butter, and wine, and strings of icy beef until she'd eaten away her desires, she remained motionless, feeling him work against her rigid muscles. Without saying yes or no, she let him proceed.

She lay facedown. Broad, warm hands that had once run over Tia's hips, Tia's breasts, Tia's flat stomach and slender thighs pulled up Juliette's nightgown and stroked Juliette's back.

Numbness crept up her body. Nathan's hands might as well be moving over layers of blankets. He traced her shoulder blades.

He urged her to turn over. Juliette faced the ceiling.

She squeezed her eyes shut, praying for the release of orgasm or tears. She prayed for the release of knowledge she didn't want.

Juliette pulled Nathan's hand away, his touch too intimate. He thought her ready and climbed on top. This she could take, his weight, him inside pounding without tenderness.

Years of marriage had given Nathan too much awareness, and he used his familiarity to bring her to climax despite herself, almost as though Juliette's body was cheating on her heart.

He rose above her and came in a rush of murmured love. He collapsed as he melted, pressing his warm lips to the spot above her collarbone.

An image of Savannah swam before Juliette. Mouth full at the bottom and sweetly curved on top. Nose the tiniest bit broad. Eyes so large and dark the blackness seemed blue. Chubby hands cupped the sides of her serious face.

CHAPTER 8

Caroline

Caroline drew the curtains in Savannah's room. Her daughter slept so soundly that Caroline or Peter had to wake her each morning. There seemed something unnatural about a five-year-old child who didn't bound from bed, a child who slumbered, waiting for her parents to bring her to the surface. The clattering of drapery rings didn't disturb the girl, whose face remained grave even in sleep. Sometimes Caroline thought Savannah had inherited, through proximity if not genetics, Caroline's worst characteristics. Caroline hated waking. Like Caroline, Savannah was tense, a perfectionist, and a watcher. Caroline had insisted on naming their daughter Savannah, a romantic gesture to the city where Caroline and Peter had honeymooned, hoping the name might make her witty and romantic—even daring—all the qualities Caroline believed she lacked.

Savannah stirred when Caroline sat on the eyelet quilt covering the bed, arching into Caroline's hand as Caroline drew finger pictures on Savannah's back.

"Ice cream cone," Savannah mumbled.

"Guess again," Caroline said.

Savannah turned her head and opened her eyes. "Do it under, Mommy."

Caroline lifted Savannah's pajama top, still warm from sleep. Using a light touch, she traced an *M* on the child's skin three times.

"*M*. Like in *Mommy*," Savannah said.

"Right," Caroline said.

Savannah rolled over and squinted. "Really?"

"Really. Now go to the bathroom, and then we'll pick out clothes." Caroline worried about Savannah's nervous distrust, wondering where it came from.

Savannah returned from the bathroom with a shining pink face and toothpaste-fresh breath. The child liked to get clean first thing. She had a natural sense of order that Caroline found endearing.

Caroline and Savannah sorted through possible outfits, serious at their task. Savannah would travel no farther than the random destination chosen by Nanny Rose—sometimes the Dover library, sometimes the playground, sometimes only the backyard—but they prepared for each day carefully, united in their attention to the task, as though Savannah reported to some important children's workplace. Caroline worried about not having enrolled Savannah in preschool, but having a nanny was so much easier than rushing back and forth to school. She'd let herself buy a few more years of freedom from school obligations. With Savannah's birthday being in March, she'd still enter kindergarten at five years old.

Okay, time to stop fooling myself.

Ballet classes, swim classes, music classes—all the enrichment provided through Nanny Rose's research and driving—didn't make up for not having sent her to preschool. Caroline knew that, but she pretended that seeing other children once or twice a week was enough, except on the days when she forced herself to read the list in her mind: *things I should be doing for Savannah.*

Caroline didn't mind that Peter left for work early most days, leaving her to ready Savannah for the day. These were their best mother-daughter moments. Time-limited tasks allowed her to stay patient.

Specificity calmed Caroline, and focus was her best friend. She went to work eagerly each day. She was puzzled at how coworkers longed for the weekend, as desperate as if they were escaping indentured servitude.

Ten minutes past the time when Nanny Rose should have arrived, Caroline strained to pretend she was fine, just fine. Calm, in fact. See Savannah, Mommy's fine. Smile. Hug. Turn on television—just this once.

Truly, Caroline knew, she had no reason to be concerned. She always allowed at least an hour of grace when scheduling around her knowledge of Nanny Rose. After five years, Caroline knew Nanny Rose's foibles. When estimating Nanny's arrival time, Caroline took into account Nanny's traffic backups, Nanny's hour of primping, and Nanny's tendency to get caught up watching the *Today* show and then rush in babbling about what Matt had said that morning, as though he and Nanny Rose were pals. Despite being five years younger than Caroline, Nanny Rose seemed to be from an older generation.

Caroline accepted all of Nanny Rose's shortcomings: her lateness, her constant crushes on Caroline's other service providers (the pediatrician, the pediatric dentist, the guy who repaved the driveway, the landscaper); she even swallowed her rage at Nanny Rose's dismissal of Caroline's nutritional standards, feeding Savannah Fritos and Oreos. She accepted it all because Nanny Rose often told Caroline how much she loved her job. Nanny even added, in her usual guileless fashion, how she'd never earn as much money anywhere else.

She opened the heavy living room drapes by pulling a satin cord. Nothing disturbed the perfect picture of a rolling lawn, Japanese maples lining the insanely expensive wood sliced walkway, Adirondack chairs dotting the grass. They had too much house, and it shamed Caroline. The money they spent on Nanny Rose, the housekeeper, the lawn man, and the handyman would probably support three families—perhaps four thrifty ones.

Oh, she'd forgotten the carpet cleaner who serviced the antique rugs thrown over the wooden floors that gleamed in every room.

Everything had been built plumb, linear, modern, and of the finest materials. Granite and rosewood surrounded a stove far more professional than Caroline's cooking skills.

Peter grew up wearing secondhand and thirdhand clothes handed down from cousins and then passed on to his brothers. Now he was eager to buy himself the shiny new things he constantly desired, and Caroline feared the next would be a sibling for Savannah. In contrast, Caroline had grown up with everything she needed—except a role model for how to be a decent absentee mother.

"Mommy, can we play Bitty Twins?" Savannah pushed a miniature stroller holding two dolls tucked under a blanket. American Girl products littered the house. For every secret worry Caroline experienced about feeling too little for her child, she spent more money.

"Who do you want to be, Mommy?" Savannah asked. She stood poised to take on whichever playing-house role her mother rejected.

Caroline forced a smile. "Who do you want me to be?"

"You be the nanny, and I'll be the mommy." Savannah looked self-important and busy as she bent over the carriage. "Now, girls, Mommy has to leave. Be big girls. Mommy does important work fixing sick babies. That's why we have Nanny."

Savannah nodded at Caroline as though feeding her a cue.

"Yes, here I am. Ready to give hugs and kisses," Caroline said. "Nanny Caroline at your service."

"No," Savannah said. "Say 'Nanny loves you, girls.'"

"Nanny loves you, girls," Caroline repeated.

Savannah pulled the carriage deeper into the great room, settling herself on the cushioned window seat. "But *Mommy* loves you better." Savannah wagged a pudgy finger at the Bitty Twins. She pulled at the patchwork blanket fussily, drawing it up so high that only their noses showed.

Tires screeched. Caroline looked out the window and exhaled with gratitude at the sight of Nanny Rose pulling into the driveway. As instructed, Nanny cut a hard right and parked close to the edge of the blacktop, allowing Caroline a quick escape.

* * *

Caroline devoted the morning to finishing a pile of reports. She forced herself to put down her pen and remember to thank her secretary when Ana handed her a container of spinach and orange salad. After giving the lunch to Caroline, Ana held up her own grease-laden McDonald's bag and said, "Maybe you'd smile more if you had some of this."

Caroline offered Ana a weak grin and reminded herself that the young woman was efficient, responsible, and always on time, thus Caroline overlooked Ana's annoying habit of trying to get her to "smile!" Caroline had been exhorted to look happier all her life and was well sick of it.

Her small office resembled a cage. Simplicity in this small space was important to Caroline, especially considering the amount of paper her job produced. She could easily be working amidst teetering heaps of forms in triplicate, like so many of her colleagues, but Caroline had been strict about organization since her first day at Cabot, four years ago.

At a right angle to her desk stood her microscope table, the surface around the instrument kept clear for current slides. She'd placed her computer monitor in the far left corner of her desk, leaving the main section clear for three neat stacks of files, sitting under three wooden paperweights burned with the words *Immediate, This Week,* and *Long-Term.*

Peter had teamed up with his father, whose hobby was woodworking, to make the paperweights for Caroline, and she loved them beyond all reason.

Caroline riffled through reports while waiting for a sample from a rectal biopsy so she could perform an evaluation of what they suspected would be an abnormal colon. She was afraid it was Hirschsprung disease, which untreated could lead to the infant having an intestinal blockage.

There wasn't much about her work that didn't interest her. Being part of a long-term study—analyzing the effects of proton beam therapy on retinoblastoma—never failed to be absorbing. Most important, of course, was the pot-of-gold possibility of finding a way to erase the horror of that particular childhood eye cancer, but along with that hope was the constant draw of the chase.

One of the reasons that Caroline preferred pediatric pathology to pediatric surgery, which she'd once considered, was that she didn't have to deliver heartbreaking news to parents. If the biopsy revealed Hirschsprung—and the baby's symptoms were pointing in that direction—then the surgeon would be the one to break the news that their tiny daughter might need ostomy surgery.

She glanced at the wall clock. At four, she'd give a lecture to medical students; before that she'd work on biopsied tissue from a patient with suspected neuroblastoma. Due dates loomed for grant reports. Caroline took the last bite of her salad while reading an email from someone at the National Institutes of Health.

Details consumed her with a worried anticipation that actually felt pleasurable. If only she could transfer a portion of that delight to caring for her daughter.

"Caroline?" Ana stuck her head in the door. "Your nanny left two messages while you were at the meeting. She wants you to call."

Please don't let there be anything wrong. Caroline had turned off her cell when the meeting started and never turned it back on. Some days even the time it took to swallow felt like an unaffordable luxury. She nodded at Ana. "Thanks," she said as she picked up the office phone and began dialing.

"Peter," she said when he picked up the phone. "Please, please, call home, okay? Rose called twice, and I don't have a minute."

"What is it?" he asked.

"I just know she wants to be called."

"And you can't even make a phone call?" Peter asked.

"I just did." Caroline swallowed the cold dregs of her morning coffee. "I have to get to the lab in less than a minute. Please, call."

"Baby, I have five people in my office. Just call Rose back and then call me if you need me. Okay?"

She didn't want to take the time to argue. Instead she called Nanny

Rose's cell and the house phone. No one picked up, so obviously the problem had been resolved and they'd gone out. Nanny Rose never picked up the phone while driving—Caroline and Peter forbade it.

"Hi, Rose," Caroline said to voice mail. "I'm off to the lab. Hope everything is okay. I'll talk to you later, or you can call Peter if you need anything."

The house looked too dark when Caroline returned home. Nanny Rose's car wasn't in the driveway. Caroline glanced at the dashboard: 8:05.

Damn.

Rose had never called back, so she assumed all was well and didn't think about it again.

Damn. Damn. Damn.

Blue television light flickered from the family room. Caroline pressed the button to lift the garage door, tapping her fingers on the wheel with impatient concern. A pool of yellow light illuminated Peter's empty parking spot. She turned off the ignition and rushed through the connecting door to the house.

An unknown teenage girl sat with Savannah in the dim family room, lit only by the television and a reading lamp on the lowest setting. A bowl spotted with soggy bits of cereal sat in front of Savannah, who beat her spoon in what sounded like "Row, Row, Row Your Boat" rhythm on the bottom of the melamine dish. Pictures of a French-labeled ballerina, puppy, bicycle, and cup decorated the dish, as though Savannah, who'd barely begun reading English, might learn a second language as she spooned up Rice Krispies.

Jeopardy! played on the giant screen hanging over the sleek, low bookcase stuffed with Savannah's fairy tales and princess books. No matter how many girls-can-do-anything stories Caroline bought, Savannah chose *Fancy Nancy*.

Savannah rocked the Bitty Twins and hummed to them softly.

The unfamiliar teenager looked up. "Hi." Her T-shirt was cut lower than Caroline's cocktail dresses.

Savannah drummed faster. Caroline covered the child's hand with hers, tightening her grip until Savannah dropped the spoon.

"Nanny had to go home," Savannah said. "Maybe she was mad?"

"No. She wasn't mad at you, pumpkin." Caroline loosened her hold on her daughter's hand and stroked her soft cheek. Her heart flopped. She swallowed, full of sorrow for this little girl she should treasure far more. She turned to the stranger/babysitter. "And you are . . ."

"Janine." For a moment, it seemed she would offer no more. She lifted a graham cracker from a pile and bit off half. Crumbs sprayed from her mouth as she added, "Rose is my aunt."

"Nanny had to go home," Savannah repeated. She turned to one of the Bitty Twins at her side and laid her hand on the doll's belly. The competence of Savannah's large hand belied her age. "Cause of her head. Can we wash the Bitties?"

"Soon, Savannah."

What had happened to Peter? Apparently, Nanny Rose had one of her excruciating migraines. Peter was usually the parent who came home when needed. His office was closer to the house, and his days were filled with interoffice memos and ticked-off clients, not critical medical decisions. His work was not unimportant, just less important than Caroline believed her own work to be, though he never let her forget that his work paid massively more than hers did. Peter's money bought all their luxuries. Organic cherries! Salmon so wild it might leap from their grill! Bitty Twins! Peter underwrote her work, as he reminded her too often lately. Nevertheless, when emergencies arose, he could get home far more quickly than Caroline.

"Daddy got stuck," Savannah said. "Can I sit in your lap?"

Caroline put down her briefcase and lowered herself onto the couch. After pulling Savannah onto her lap, she looked to Janine for further illumination. Savannah leaned into Caroline's chest. Without Nanny, Savannah had been given no postdinner bath, or a proper dinner, for that matter. The scent of sour child drifted up from Savannah.

"I took the train and then a cab. A long cab ride." Janine held out her hand as though the amount matching her transportation outlay must certainly be waiting in Caroline's pocket. "Mr. Fitzgerald said he'd pay from the time I left my house until you got here. So, that's four hours. So, that's eighty dollars. Plus, you need to get me home and then pay me for that time. So, that will be, like, a hundred dollars or maybe more."

Caroline's head pounded.

"Mommy, can I have something real to eat?"

"Will you drive me or are you going to call a cab? What time does the train leave?"

"Can the Bitty Twins come in the bath now?"

"Mr. Fitzgerald said someone would drive if it got dark. My mother doesn't like me out after dark alone."

"Did you fix anyone today?"

"Could you drive me all the way home? That would be easier."

Caroline's mouth remained closed as though someone had glued it shut. She wanted to be lying in a warm bath, still as a corpse, with a warm washcloth draped over her eyes.

The front door opened. Savannah leapt off her lap and ran into Peter's arms. He knelt and wrapped his arms around her, his face lit with affection. Peter didn't mind if Savannah smelled sour or asked him a million questions.

"I'll drive you," she told Janine.

CHAPTER 9

Caroline

Caroline knew she took too long getting home from dropping off Janine, and she certainly shouldn't have stopped for coffee, but it was that or fall asleep on the ride home from Boston. Now she'd have to take an Ambien to counteract the caffeine.

She sipped the coffee each time she hit a light, and every light was welcome. More than anything, Caroline missed being able to move on her own time. Her research would approach a tantalizing moment, where clues led to roads she was certain could break hypotheses wide open, and still she'd have to leave for home. Before Savannah, there was never a problem in digging in, feeling hours slide by like seconds as her notes piled up.

Peter was never a problem previously. He also found that same active joy in breaking the back of problems at work, but now he also found that joy with Savannah.

She pulled into their driveway.

"Caroline?" Peter stood in the doorway. Not glowering, but nowhere near smiling.

"How was she?" Caroline asked.

"She was scared." He folded his arms, looking remarkably and uncomfortably like his father. Peter's parents had kept their children at the center of their lives, just like Caroline's mother.

Caroline's father left his children—Caroline and her two sisters—
to his wife, but nobody complained. Whatever Dad provided, he'd
provided well. When he taught them to swim, they learned the skill
perfectly, breathing as evenly as Olympic athletes. When he cooked
a Sunday breakfast, the French toast came out flawless: crisp and
buttery, soft in the middle.

Her father's love was never questioned. No one in the family re-
sented that his deepest energies were saved for his work. They didn't
confuse his love and his energy. He earned enough that they lacked
for nothing, and he instilled the morals that ensured they never
asked for too much. They learned by example: work, family, and
community all needed fealty, but the labor could be divided.

Caroline believed herself to be more like her father than her
mother. She wished she could get away with the pattern of adequate
yet simple paternal gestures: make a perfect Sunday breakfast, read a
story each night, and devote the rest of her time to work.

"Any problem getting her to bed?" Caroline asked.

"She was really upset. I think she felt abandoned."

"I didn't abandon her." Acid from the coffee burned in Caroline's
stomach. "I thought you were taking care of it."

"Whoa! I didn't say you abandoned her, I said she felt that way.
And I never said I could come home. You virtually hung up on me!"

"Peter, I was in the middle of—"

"Jesus, Caro. You're always in the middle of something lately."

Peter's frustration baffled her. What was she supposed to do?
Should she not lean on him?

"Sometimes I think you forget our lives have changed," he said.
"Savannah has to take precedence."

Caroline could scream, but wasn't he right? She twisted her
head from side to side, feeling everything inside her upper body
cramp into an iron column. Peter put his hand on the back of her
neck, and Caroline arched in, wanting comfort even as she hated
his words.

"You have to learn to compromise." Peter dug his thumbs into the
spot on the side of her neck that always tensed first.

"Mmm . . . but sometimes I just can't," she said. "Really. Some-times I simply can't."

Peter removed his hands from her neck and stepped into her line of vision. "What if she fell out of a tree, Caro? Honestly? What if a car hit her? Would you come then? Would that make you leave the hospital?"

The phone rang before six o'clock in the morning.

That couldn't be good.

Peter leaned over her and grabbed the phone. Having grown up in a large family meant that he was always on call for disaster. Caroline listened to Peter's side of the conversation, trying to fill in the missing sentences.

"Uh-huh. No, no, we'll be fine."

Nanny Rose.

"No, really, you don't have to send her."

Was Rose offering that twit of a niece?

"When my mother gets migraines, she steams with eucalyptus leaves. You should try it."

Peter was the ultimate fix-it guy, as her mother often reminded her. "You have someone special there, Caroline. Don't take him for granted."

"No, it's okay. No, don't call her." Peter said.

Caroline waved her arms, *No, no,* at Peter. After yesterday's argument, she didn't want him taking the day off. He held up a hand to stop her, turning away and covering his free ear.

"No. It's fine." He held the phone after disconnecting with Nanny Rose. "I better call Ellie and tell her to cancel my appointments."

Caroline sat cross-legged on the bed. "Peter, you just told me how difficult it is to take off so much time."

"What are our options? We're not leaving Savannah with that Janine." He rolled over and swung his legs off the bed.

Caroline put her hand on his shoulder. "I'll do it. I'll take the day off."

He cocked his head to the side. "Really?"

His look of incredulity annoyed her no end. Who did he think got Savannah ready for Nanny every morning? Took her to the doctor? The dentist? Who smiled as Savannah dragged her from store to store until they finally found a Halloween costume that met with their daughter's approval?

"Okay," he said when she deliberately didn't speak. "Terrific."

Caroline gave a faint smile. Even if he meant it to be flattering, his words didn't seem like a compliment. "You don't have to make it sound like I'm running into a blazing building." She twisted the edge of the comforter into a complicated knot. She had to teach a class in two hours. Three surgeons were expecting her in the afternoon. Reports were due. It was close to the end of the month. Moreover, weren't they interviewing a new part-time pathologist to cover weekends?

"Maybe I can take her into work with me," Caroline said. "Ana could watch her when I'm out of the office. I'll bring in the iPad, for movies. Or books—I'll download some new books."

"An iPad can't watch Savannah. Forget it. I already said I'd do it." Peter lay back and put his hands behind his head. He stared up at the ceiling as though he preferred it to looking at Caroline.

She opened her mouth to defend herself, but nothing came out. She fell down on the bed beside Peter. He continued looking at the ceiling, his jaw tight, his mouth pressed to a deep drawn-in line.

"Come on. Look at me." Caroline placed her hand on his bristly cheek, trying to turn him, but he remained a mummy. "Haven't you ever said something in the excitement of a moment? Wanted to do something good and then realized it was impossible?"

He turned and looked at her. "Not when it comes to my family."

It was Saturday, and Caroline wanted to please Peter and Savannah. She hurried downstairs while Peter showered and Savannah slept. Caroline had at least twenty minutes before everyone gathered for breakfast.

She had an appointment for a makeover in a few hours, and if that wasn't unusual enough, she planned to bring along Savannah. When she'd received the baffling offer for a free makeover, she shocked herself by scheduling an appointment, desperate enough to think it might bring her back to life. Somewhere she'd lost her physical desires. Her need for Peter, once so strong, had at first dissipated, then disappeared, and now she dreaded his touch.

Believing that a facial and having cosmetics smeared on her face might help her was ridiculous, but Caroline wanted a miracle, even one from a jar.

Despite being a bit nervous, as this was so wholly outside her ken, Caroline felt unexpected optimism about going to juliette&gwynne, though she hoped their affected use of lower-case letters didn't portend a place so chichi that Caroline would be dressed wrong no matter what she chose—which, considering her closet, was not unlikely.

She wondered what database had lifted her name from obscurity and deemed her worthy of Juliette Soros's personal ministrations. Caroline lacked familiarity with the world of beauty authorities, but when she'd mentioned Juliette's name to a lab assistant, she'd reacted as though Caroline had been granted an audience with the Queen.

Caroline mixed eggs into a bowl of broken bits of bread, her quick version of French toast. As the soggy mess sizzled, Savannah rode into the kitchen on Peter's shoulders, smiling as she always did when near her father. Peter was lit up in that way he did only with Savannah. Had he once produced such high wattage for Caroline?

"Look!" Caroline tipped the pan toward them. "French toast eggs."

"Way to go." Peter swung Savannah down and placed her in a chair in one graceful swoop. His wide shoulders that tapered to a trim waist made him appear taller than five foot eight. He and Caroline could see eye to eye if Peter stretched just a bit. Caroline scraped the bready eggs from the pan onto three waiting plates.

"Syrup, anyone?" Peter poured a stream from a dangerously high starting point.

"Daddy!" Savannah bounced in her chair. "You'll spill it!"

Peter twirled an imaginary moustache while speaking in a vaguely faux-Teutonic accent. "Amazing Daddy spills nothing."

Caroline squeezed Peter's shoulder. "Does Amazing Daddy kiss Amazing Mommy?" She tried to smile brightly, wanting to escape the bleak fog between them.

"What do you think, Savannah? Should we give Amazing Mommy a kiss?"

Savannah giggled. "Oh, yes please! Kiss Mommy."

Peter turned and pressed his warm lips to Caroline's cooler ones.

The shop in Wellesley exuded so much charm and relaxation that Caroline tensed under the expectation. Downy chairs upholstered in white matelasse embraced well-dressed women. Stacks of glossy magazines invited perusing. Purple accents in the room, reminiscent of royal robes, softened the matte black decorating scheme.

Juliette Soros walked in, smiled, and after a brief but warm introduction, turned to Savannah. Juliette was almost Caroline's height, but where Caroline was a straight line, Juliette curved in a true hourglass. Her perfect nose was the one Caroline would choose if she could. Caroline always noticed noses first. Unfamiliar desire stirred at the sight of all the glossy, hopeful packages. An alien and uncomfortable greed overtook her for a moment.

"Aren't you lovely?" Juliette said to Savannah. "I'm Juliette, and I promise to make sure you have fun while you're here, sweetheart. Why don't you come with me?"

Juliette smiled and stretched her arm toward the child. Savannah tucked her hand inside Juliette's as though she'd always known her. Juliette then directed her kindness at Caroline. "You too, Mom. Follow us."

Caroline followed her daughter and Juliette to a private room, where the woman ushered them in as though they were the most important people in the world.

"Make yourself comfortable." Juliette's grin showed straight sparkling teeth. Caroline ran her tongue over the rough spot where she'd chipped a tooth in high school soccer. Her mother's stiff-upper-lip background made her dismissive of imperfections inflicted by childhood accidents. Caroline's youngest sister carried a ragged scar on her chin from when she'd fallen off the porch and been given a Band-Aid when stitches had been needed.

"Please, have a seat." Juliette indicated a sleek leather and chrome chair facing a mirror and a bank of glossy white drawers.

Caroline wondered how much of Juliette's golden beauty was artifice and how much a lucky draw from the genetic lottery. While still holding Savannah's hand, Juliette put a warm, sure hand on Caroline's back and with gentle pressure prompted her to a chair. Once Caroline sat, Juliette leaned over her shoulder and gave an approving nod as she looked at both their reflections.

No amount of cosmetics could make that much of a difference. Even Juliette's honey-colored hair looked natural.

"We're going to have some fun," Juliette said before turning to Savannah. "As for you, cutie, I have a surprise for you."

Juliette winked at Caroline and then reached for a medium-sized box. "This is for you, sweetheart."

Savannah gave a shy smile and glanced at Caroline for permission.

"It's okay, hon. Open it." Caroline glanced at Juliette, trying to gauge her reaction to Caroline's words. Did she think Caroline prudent and caring, or rigid and overstrict? "We've trained her about taking things from strangers."

"Wise. When my boys where her age, I hated any moment they were out of my sight." Juliette laughed. "I still do."

Savannah held the box, seeming excited even as she approached the present as cautiously as she did everything.

"Being a mother is terrifying, isn't it?" Caroline said.

"It is. I haven't been able to ignore a phone call since having children. Of course, you also have the terror of your work. Analyzing a person's chances for life or death. What a difference from this." Juliette swept her arms around the room, with its frosted bottles of creams, the brushes, and the tiers of lipsticks, and rolled her eyes.

"How do you know what I do?" Alarm prickled at Caroline. Had someone at work mentioned how badly she'd aged? What had they said? Ideas rolled through Caroline's mind in rapid succession as she stared at her mirror image in uncomfortable full reveal.

"Oh, that's how I—we—picked you. We find local women who work in professions where they can't indulge themselves. Women like you: locked away in a lab, and working on childhood cancer, no less. We offer special services as thanks to those who do the most difficult work. We hoped you might provide an entrée into the field. It's our way of giving back, since we've had such success."

"Oh." Caroline nodded. "I did wonder. Why didn't you say that in the letter?"

"We didn't want to raise expectations until we've met with you." Juliette put a hand on Savannah's shoulder. "Let's get this little girl settled, so you and I can begin."

Juliette led Savannah to a small leather couch. "Tell me what you think, honey." She indicated the still unopened box. "I'm more used to boys than little girls."

Savannah stroked the chalky black paper and deep purple ribbon. "Can I keep the ribbon? For my dolls?"

"Of course you can." Caroline worried she sounded snappish and that Savannah sounded beaten down, as though Caroline withheld ribbons on a regular basis.

Caroline waited for Juliette to return from the child care room, where she'd taken Savannah to play with her paper dolls, the new kind where clothes stuck by the magic of static cling and required no scissors.

Juliette's skills baffled Caroline, who'd watched with awe as the popular girls in high school stood at the locker room mirror and with a few puffs and sprays transformed themselves into ideal American beauties. In contrast, Caroline's clumsy attempts at using lipstick felt showy and garish. Her instinct was to wipe it off as quickly as possible. At her wedding, Peter's mother and sisters had been determined to wrestle her into a Kabuki mask, but the moment she was alone, she'd rubbed away most of what the makeup artist had smeared on her face. Her first kiss as a married woman was what she wanted: bare lips touching bare lips.

The door opened. Juliette slipped in. A black smock covered her silk shirt and slacks. "Savannah seems happy. Someone from the child care room will get you if there's any problem, so not to worry."

"Oh, she'll be fine. Savannah's quite placid with strangers." Did that sound bizarre, as if she handed Savannah off to strangers regularly? "What I mean is, well, she's an unusually self-assured child."

"I'm sure that's a credit to your good mothering." Juliette held three protective smocks up to Caroline's neck in succession. Pink followed by black and then navy blue. "First I judge which best flatters your complexion, so we can start you off with the right background."

"Won't the color thing throw off the effect? Make it seem better than it really is?"

Juliette laughed. "It's all false here. Makeup's an illusion, right? So we begin with the best canvas. Like you do when choosing your clothes, no?"

Given the choice, a white lab coat would be Caroline's fashion choice. Otherwise Caroline stuck to the safe beige palette in which she'd been raised.

"Navy," Juliette decided. Silken fabric billowed as she settled the blue cloth around Caroline. Juliette studied her in the mirror. "You should wear this color often."

Caroline nodded as though she believed that wearing navy blue would make a difference in her life.

Juliette ran a finger down Caroline's cheek. "You're not wearing any makeup, are you?" Caroline shook her head no. Juliette poured a bit of oil on her fingers and spread it over Caroline's face.

"I'm just giving you a quick cleansing. Later, we can schedule you for a facial if you'd like," Juliette offered. "With Paloma. She's our best. Don't tell anyone I said so, though; I'm not supposed to have a favorite. She'll give you a full skin diagnosis. But I'll give you some instant gratification."

Juliette's sure fingers massaged oil into her face. Oh, Caroline could lie there for years. Then the scientist in her took over. "Oil?" Caroline asked.

"Extra virgin olive oil purified by juliette&gwynne. Nothing is better. It cleans the skin, removes makeup, tones and conditions, and you simply rinse it off with tepid water. I could go on and on—but Paloma will say it all much better than I can."

"Do you use it?" Caroline liked the idea of being purified, but she felt tired just imagining doing so much to her face each day and each night. Juliette pressed the oft-aching area over Caroline's sinuses. That alone was worth the trip.

"There's nothing we sell that I don't use, or wouldn't use, based on my skin type," Juliette added. She wiped a warm washcloth over Caroline's face. The slight scratch of the fabric sweeping away the oil felt brisk and wholesome.

"What do you use to wash your face?" Juliette asked.

Caroline smiled before giving her answer. "Ivory soap."

Juliette chuckled. "99.44% pure, right?" After patting Caroline's face clean, she assessed Caroline's forehead, the sides of her nose, and her cheeks with confident fingers. "That's why your skin is so dry."

Juliette smoothed cream over Caroline's face. "When we make your skin softer, you'll look less lined." Juliette's eyes met Caroline's in the mirror. "Cleaning with a better product, using proper moisturizer—all this will help. Add plumping ingredients to where you want to see plump. Paloma will give you the details."

"Maybe she can fit me in as an emergency case," Caroline joked.

Juliette chuckled and squeezed Caroline's shoulder. "Not to worry. I'll manage everything."

Apparently Caroline's humor was too dry for Juliette—had she thought Caroline serious? God knows, she barely had time for this morning's visit. Did other women do this all the time?

As Juliette applied more layers of colors and creams than Caroline had ever dreamed of using, she startled at seeing herself become almost lovely through the miracle of cosmetic alchemy.

Juliette held up first one jar of color, then another. She striped five different shades of foundation on Caroline's jaw—foundation, something Caroline thought reserved for the aged—until one satisfied her. As she blended, she gently lectured Caroline about the importance of sunblock. Caroline the doctor, who knew the importance of using it, spent her life fighting Caroline the daughter, whose outdoorsy mother believed only sissies used sunblock.

"Look at this! Your eyes are your key feature, Caroline." Juliette stepped away to admire the thin lines she'd just applied to Caroline's lids. "Green eyes. So beautiful! Like Savannah. Her brown eyes are so incredibly dark! They'll be her key feature, also. They're remarkable. Does your husband have those dark eyes? My goodness—they look Italian or Greek."

"Savannah's adopted," Caroline said.

"Oh. Close your eyes." Juliette applied mascara. "Now open. I have a friend who adopted all of her children. Three boys."

"How old are they?" Caroline thought she sounded too hungry for the information.

"They range from ten to about fifteen. Older than Savannah. My friend's pretty active in all sorts of support groups."

Caroline had never joined any adoption groups or participated in any counseling that might help her on the path to being a good adoptive mother. Beyond buying the right we-chose-you books for Savannah, she and Peter had done little to learn about being adoptive parents. Caroline knew they should participate in more structured learning, but he'd resisted, and she'd taken the easy way out by following his disinclination.

Peter swallowed Savannah into their family whole, as though by pretending that everything was peachy keen, he could make it so. Peter wanted Savannah to merge with her cousins and blend in with the family brood.

"Is it all okay? With your friend?" Caroline asked.

Juliette brushed a light coat of pink across Caroline's cheeks. The effect was delicate and opalescent—like the inside of a shell. Dawn, Juliette called it. Then she tipped her head and stepped back as though weighing the choices she'd made in painting Caroline's face.

"Sometimes she has problems," Juliette said. "She gets angry when people say that adoption is as natural a process as giving birth and should be treated the same. She thinks that leaves no room for adoptive moms to talk about their problems."

Caroline nodded, encouraging Juliette to keep talking.

"After her experience, I realized that biological mothers get more of a break than she did. We get to have postpartum blues and all that. You know. You're a doctor."

"A pathologist. I work with tissue samples more than people. I'm not sure I've really thought of it that way." Caroline gripped the arms of the chair. "But you're right." Peter's sisters complained about their children incessantly, but Caroline never dared join the discussion.

"Exactly. We act as though adoptive parents should be so grateful they have children at all, that they don't deserve to complain."

CHAPTER 10

Tia

Tia had less than ten minutes before Bobby arrived for their . . . Jesus, it was a date, wasn't it, this Saturday night dinner Bobby had asked for, almost bribing her with promises of getting out to somewhere other than Southie or JP? She didn't know why she'd agreed, or how his driving her home had allowed her to open the dreaded relationship door she'd considered shut and crosshatched with steel, but here she was.

It had been a long time since anyone had touched Tia. That was one reason she remembered pregnancy with warmth; despite her isolation, she'd never been alone.

The June night that Tia conceived Honor—and she knew it was that night—she'd worn a white linen dress made of fabric so soft and fine that the slightest breeze lifted the belled skirt. A wide red belt hugged her small waist. High-heeled sandals showed off her first-ever pedicure.

They'd walked down three steps to enter the hidden bar, stopping a moment to let their eyes adjust from the June dusk to the dim bar light. The location, a side street off Mass Ave in Cambridge, surprised Tia each time they arrived. Who expected a postage-stamp dance floor and middle-aged waitresses wearing black rayon skirts and white blouses in a part of town usually known for poetry readings? Most of the drinkers were born-in-Cambridge townies. Tia recognized them; they carried the same working-class DNA as she and her Southie friends.

Patrons listened to long-forgotten songs and danced to the lush music that replicated the soundtrack of Tia's childhood. On Sunday mornings, instead of going to church, Tia's mother had played Herb Alpert. Al Green. Etta James. Frank Sinatra. Music that made Tia nostalgic for a past she'd never known; times that seemed more glamorous than her life would ever be.

Nathan had worn a pressed shirt. When she leaned against him, Tia tried not to think about who'd ironed it so stiff, and who'd made it smell of bleach and wholesome living.

After ordering drinks, Nathan stood and held out a hand. "Dance with me?" he'd asked, as though worried that she'd say no; as though he didn't own her dances, her thoughts, and her future.

Nathan pressed her close as they danced. She smelled shampoo and aftershave, scents Tia loved because they were Nathan's, and hated because Juliette undeniably chose both.

She'd let her friendships and hobbies fall away in pursuit of her Nathan obsession. To the world, Tia seemed devoted to her work, as though she were solely dedicated to the needy men and women in the nursing home where she'd then worked, as though crafts programs for the elderly were her only reason for existing.

Tia turned her head so that her cheek lay on the solid muscle of Nathan's arm. He engulfed her. "Moon River" played, and then gave way to Sinatra singing "The Way You Look Tonight." Nathan pulled her closer.

"I wish we could always be like this," she whispered into his sleeve.

"I know." Nathan pulled her in closer. "Me too."

He'd lied, of course. If he'd wanted them to be together, he'd be here now. He'd have answered her letter. He'd have looked at Honor's picture and recognized himself.

The downstairs doorbell rang.

Tia pushed the buzzer to give Bobby entry. As she waited for him to climb the winding stairs, she finished the glass of wine she'd poured, and then stuck the glass in the cabinet, unwashed, so he wouldn't see either the dirty glass or a freshly washed one. After she swished mouthwash straight from the bottle.

The tentative sound of Bobby knocking bothered Tia. She'd said yes to him, so why did he tap at her door as though maybe she'd forgotten he was coming? If Nathan had brought out Tia's softer side, she feared that Bobby might bring out the opposite.

Bobby wore a suit, Tia, jeans and a simple silk shirt. Their clothes announced how much more this meant to him than it did to her. Tia hated the inequity, an elephant hulking in the room.

"Sorry." Tia gestured at her outfit. "I thought we were going local."

"No, no—it's my fault. I didn't tell you." His cheeks blazed. Poor strawberry-blond Bobby and his telltale skin.

"Give me a minute. I'll change."

"No, no," Bobby said. "You're fine. I'll take off my jacket." He moved as though to shrug off his suit coat and tug off his tie.

Tia swore she saw the gears clicking in his head: Changing the night's itinerary? Perhaps trying to think of a less fancy restaurant. She stilled him with a hand on his shoulder. "Stop. Give me five minutes."

Tia ran to her bedroom and flipped through her wardrobe. She fingered the white conception dress buried deep in the back of her closet for a moment—still so beautiful, but unwearable, reeking of unrequited love. She chose a black shift and dressed it up with her mother's only good pieces of jewelry, now Tia's only treasures: the lover's knot gold earrings that her father had bought her mother and a filigreed locket holding faded photos of her grandparents.

They sat in leather chairs studded with brass buttons. The Oak Room at Copley Plaza was a place for celebrations of high order: engagements, movie deals, dream job offers. Bobby made his intentions all too clear.

This room was as dim as the bar where she'd danced with Nathan, but Nathan's bar held a yellowed darkness; here luminous rosiness warmed every corner. Chandeliers reflected ornate carved paneling and a tapestry of red-toned fabrics.

"I sold a condo today," Bobby said. "Totally redone, a loft for an artist. Good light. Sold it for big money, especially for today's market."

"I thought the market was down," Tia said.

"Southie's still strong as fuck." Bobby turned tomato again. "Excuse me."

"Bobby. You don't have to apologize for saying 'fuck.'" She rolled her eyes in exaggerated impatience. "So why's Southie still—"

"For one thing, the waterfront. It's a limited resource."

It was difficult for Tia to connect the real-estate-rich area Bobby described with the place where she'd come of age. "I suppose you're right," she said.

"There are incredible opportunities." He started to put out his hand, as though to take hers, and then drew back. "You won't believe this huge building deal—way upscale—that I'm putting together."

"It just seems like they're taking over everything," she said.

"'They?'" Bobby smiled. "Why are the ones who move away always the most nostalgic?"

"Nobody who grew up there can afford to buy a house."

"What? The neighborhood's supposed to cater to the laziest?"

"Not being able to afford half a million dollars for two bedrooms makes you lazy?"

The waiter interrupted with the drinks they'd ordered. Tia practically drained the glass with her first taste. She felt far too sober.

Bobby raised his glass. "To our first fight."

Tia cringed at his words. She raised her glass. "To your first million."

Tia slunk past Katie's desk, ignoring her glare and theatrical glance at her watch. Katie considered tardiness a major character flaw.

Katie didn't ask how Tia's weekend had been, and Tia didn't ask how the new wallpaper in Katie's bathroom had turned out. Despite the fact that their desks were at right angles, forcing them to work hard to avoid staring at each other all day, they performed a well-rehearsed dance of pretending they possessed a modicum of privacy.

After a morning of client meetings and endless phone calls up and down the ranks of city and state bureaucracies, Tia shuffled through papers on her desk until she found her growing to-do list on a lined yellow pad. She refused to commit the list to her computer, because once it went electronic, she couldn't crumple, rip, shred, or otherwise remove it from the earth like she could paper. Didn't they show that on *Law & Order* all the time? Deleted folders apparently lived in tiny wrinkles and crevices of computers that nontech mortals never found.

March To-Do:

Apt inspection for Mrs. Jankowicz
Possible homes for Grahams?
Roundtable meeting-host in April
Remind Katie of inter-agency Senior Fair
Walker Foundation Grant
AA for Jerry Conlin-find JP meetings
Mr. O'Hara eating?

Tia stared at the list. She updated it by crossing out "March" and writing "April" on top of the page.

Tia wished she could spend her days taking her clients to fun places. *Here you go, Mrs. G, we're having lunch on Newbury Street! Look Mr. O'Malley, time to check out the new Grisham from the library! Hey, Mrs. Kuffel, a new Adam Sandler film!*

Mrs. Kuffel was eighty-nine, lived alone, and Adam Sandler was her celebrity pretend grandson.

Tia loved her clients but hated too much of her job. She hated the constant paperwork, the reports, the interagency bullshit, and the grant applications her boss Richard passed down the line to her and Katie.

Richard's laziness strained Katie's and Tia's workload. He tested their patience daily. Tia was convinced that Richard had worked exactly hard enough to reach his position only so that he could then put his feet up on the desk and do next to nothing. Tia believed those "morning meetings" that kept him out of the office until noon or later were appointments with his computer, caving in to his fantasy football addiction.

Katie rustled around, and Tia ignored her.

"I'm leaving," Katie said.

Her clipped words drove a nail into Tia's growing headache. She looked up to see Katie wrapped in her trench coat, sunglasses in hand, ready to ward off both rain and wrinkle-inducing rays.

"You have a meeting?" Tia asked.

"I have to see Natasha's teacher."

Tia simply stared, saying nothing, leading Katie into a rush of defensive words.

"She's had issues with unexplained fears. I don't know what's going on. She's had night terrors. Been stuffing herself with food. In secret. I found an entire sleeve of Chips Ahoy! under her bed."

Tia ached at the thought of the little girl, but her jealousy at Katie's being able to worry out loud about her daughter overwhelmed the ache and brought out Tia's lesser self. "When will you be back?"

"Come back?" Katie stuck her sunglasses on top of her head, pushing back her perfectly Newbury Street styled hair. "By the time I got back, it would be time to leave."

"Why'd you make the appointment so early?" Tia wanted to stop the flow of bitchy words, but she couldn't help herself. Her mother kept telling her to watch her temper. But she never learned, did she? "One day," her mother had said. "One day it will be too late."

"For goodness sake, you waltzed in here at, like, ten o'clock." Katie pulled her coat tight.

"It was nine thirty, and I fully intend to work until five thirty. Plus, I have a late meeting with a client. A home visit," Tia lied.

"What's wrong with you?" Katie asked. "This is important, my appointment."

Tia completely agreed with Katie. What *was* wrong with her? Why couldn't she stop doing this?

"Anyway, isn't Richard coming in?" Katie asked.

Tia screwed her face into an expression indicating the pointlessness of thinking that might be a possibility. "You know how hard it is to handle the phones alone *and* try to get work done." She shook her to-do list at Katie. "Look at this list."

"Tia, you don't understand the strain I'm under. Why are you doing this?"

Tia shut herself off from Katie's accusatory eyes. Tia had gone too far. Another thing her mother had tried to teach her: "Tia, don't try to make other people look bad so you look better. Just be a better girl, honey."

Tia's mother had a natural kindness even when she was too exhausted to do anything particularly nice. Tia worried that her own personality had come from her father's side. Her mother called his family a bitter-edged bunch. She didn't want to be bitter-edged. "Sorry, Katie. I . . . I'm sorry."

"Motherhood isn't a side job. Maybe someday you'll understand." Katie lifted her pocketbook higher on her shoulder and turned away.

"Oh, forget about it," Tia muttered.

"What did you say?"

"Just go, okay?" In truth, Tia was thrilled to see Katie leave. She wanted to be alone.

"This is an office, not a bar. You need to remember that. If I have to, I'll talk to Richard about this. I can't have you take out your nasty moods on me."

"Come, on, Katie. We all get in moods around here."

"Not like you do. I mean it, Tia. I don't know what's gotten into you lately, but you better watch your step."

* * *

Two hours later, Tia heard a knock on the wall outside her open office door. Before she could answer, Richard peeked in, showing first his shaggy head of hair, then his thick glasses and scruffy beard. Richard still lived sometime around 1979—even staying true to aged leather sandals that drew one's eyes right to the disgusting sight of his hairy toes.

"I hear you gave Katie a hard time." Richard crossed his arms over his paunch. "She called me almost in tears."

"Did you hear that she left at lunchtime and stuck me with everything?"

"She told me she had a thing with the kids." Richard looked at her over his smudged glasses.

"She made an appointment with her daughter's teacher. Why couldn't she schedule it later?"

Tia's whining embarrassed her. She sounded like a fifth grader telling on someone. Besides, Richard was the king of leaving early. As far as Richard was concerned, if they met with their clients and didn't set fires in the trash cans, everything was A-OK.

Richard took a deep breath. "I think you know I try to run this agency in a caring way. I extend to you the same understanding and flexibility as I do to Katie."

Tia slammed her pen down. "I'm sick of kids being an excuse for anything and everything. The holy mantle of motherhood comes up, and it's 'Take over Tia. Katie has to change a diaper!'"

Richard looked puzzled and wary. "Parenthood requires certain sacrifices."

"Why do I always have to be the one to sacrifice?"

Richard looked at the silent phone, at Katie's immaculate desk, and Tia's pile of papers. "Are you overloaded?"

"That's not the point." Tia thought she might cry from not knowing what the point was.

Richard closed his eyes and stood very still for a moment, as though he were going into some yogi trance. With his eyes still closed, he said, "Why don't you go home? Take the rest of the day off. I'll handle the phones."

CHAPTER 11

Tia

The scene with Katie and Richard replayed in a loop as Tia hunched against the wind. Once again she'd gotten caught up in the drama of her own anger. Nathan hated when she got in this mood. It was a stylized fight: She'd lash out at him for not being able to commit to her, and then he'd put up his hands, palms out, stagy as hell, as though to ward her off.

They'd been together two months when she first started asking about his so-called intentions. She was still asking when he left her a year after they met. Maybe she'd pushed too early, too much.

"Let it go for the moment," he'd repeat. "Just let us be. It will work out."

Looking back, she wondered how she could have been so naïve. Love had blinded her to the obvious meaning of his words: "Please shut up and join me in denial."

She'd been convinced that he loved her. Had it been her imagination?

"I never meant to fall in love with you," he'd once said.

"What did you mean to do?" Was he saying that, in fact, he didn't love her, and never meant to? Her smile had been stiff with worry. She'd loved him right from the beginning. Smart. Protective. Passionate about his work; about the world. Nathan was a style of man she'd never known. By conversation and car, he took her to exotic places she'd never known existed so close to Southie.

How did he get the time to take her to places like the Fruitlands Museum in Lincoln? Had he been so drawn to her that he'd overcome his guilt at leaving his wife and sons for an entire day, or simply wanted an escape from them?

Shouldn't he have been at the beach with them, rather than spending time with her at Fruitlands, the short-lived once-communal home of Louisa May Alcott's family?

Tia had worked hard to push away those thoughts on that hot July afternoon. She'd spread out the blanket Nathan told her to pack. He laid out his offerings of fruit, cheese, and crackers as he explained transcendentalism. Like the ideas he offered, the food he brought was new to her parochial tastes. Sensuous slices of papaya replaced the crunch of apples. Gorgonzola spread on crostini seemed unrelated to the Swiss cheese on Ritz crackers she'd eaten since childhood.

"These days, people hold weddings here," he said. "Back then, when it was formed, this place was incredibly radical. A commune. A place where they'd plan to separate themselves from the economics of the country, grow their own food, make all their goods—and practice what they preached."

Tia knew Nathan wanted her to ask questions. He loved showing off his knowledge, which was fine with her. It excited her to see how much he knew. "And what did they preach?"

"It's one of the harder movements to define, but in a nutshell, it was a move toward the spiritual." Nathan crossed his legs and became even more intent. "It was meant as a break from what they viewed as the materialism of society at the time, with a core belief in intuition versus dogma."

"And this is where she grew up, Louisa May Alcott?"

"Actually, her family only stayed for about seven months, but those seven months really marked them."

She wiped her hands clean of papaya juice and lay back on the soft Tartan wool. Only one pure white cloud broke the clean blue sky. Nathan lay beside her and took her hand. She traced the calloused ridge along his right index finger. "From marking papers," he'd joke when she called his hands masculine.

Rolling on her side, she offered the small swell of her hip. He traced the line of her thigh with his fingers.

She'd cried the first time they'd made love.

"What's wrong?" he'd asked while wiping the tears from her cheek. "Did I hurt you? Did I make you sad?"

"It's because you made me happy." She didn't know how to explain her fear that she'd never be able to hold on to the happiness she'd just found. "I don't know where this can go."

And for the first time of many times, he'd said, "Let it go"— kindly, but still the words hurt. He'd asked the impossible, as though she had any control over the monkeys who started to chatter in her head from the first time he left her apartment.

Monkey number one said the same thing any random Southie woman would say if Tia stopped her on the street:

He'll never leave her.

He's feeding you a line of bull.

Monkey number two was Tia's mother.

Honey, what you're doing is a sin.

Why don't you find a good man, one who doesn't lie and cheat? Do you think your face will last forever? Claim your prize while you still have bait.

Monkey number three had been Nathan's wife.

Why can't you leave us alone?

He loves me. You're simply a diversion.

The monkeys made Tia a dirty girl; they'd flung their monkey crap all over her until she reeked.

Now, years later, new monkeys had appeared. Nuns who judged her from the corners of their eyes. Righteous mothers pushing strollers. Ogling men who knew she deserved no better than being their personal eye candy.

Hey, baby, give Daddy some sugar.

You know who gives away a child? Whores and bitches. Indulgent selfish women.

I think Honor's crying for you, Tia. Hear her?

Tia took out her cell phone and dialed Robin.

"Geez, I just opened the door to the shop a second ago," her friend answered. "What's up?"

"I need you," Tia said. "Can't you come home for a visit?"

"I keep telling you, Tee, I am home. Why don't you come here?"

That Tia had never flown made her seem so insular and townie, she could tell nobody except Robin. Tia was certain flying would be like the one and only time she'd been on a roller coaster, when she might as well have been hurtled through space, but Robin pushed her, believing that Tia should grit her teeth and move through her fear.

"I need you," Tia repeated.

"I'm here." When Tia didn't answer, Robin gave a soft sigh right into Tia's ear. "What's wrong?"

"I can't get anywhere," Tia said. "No matter what I do, I'm standing in the same place."

"You're being a little existential. Can you break the problem down?"

Tia could weep from hearing a loving voice. From being honest. Sometimes she forgot the weight of constant pretence. "I don't think anyone at work likes me."

"Do you like them?"

"Not really."

"Have you considered that you're in the wrong place? Maybe you think you're standing still because you are. You're the only one who can move yourself."

"Where can I go?"

"Lots of places. There are many more spaces in this world to work than that agency of last hope."

"It's a good place for me."

"No, Tia. It's an easy place for you. Staying in Boston is your default choice."

"Living here is no bowl of ice cream."

"True. It's a plate of white bread and mayo. You know exactly what you're getting."

"There are reasons I can't leave, and you know what they are."

"You keep your address on file with that adoption place. Nathan can find you as easily in California as Jamaica Plain. It's a big small world. Does the word *Google* mean anything to you?"

Tia didn't answer.

"Oh, Tee, he's not looking for you anyway."

"You know there's more."

"Actually, there's not. The postal service works in California, you know. We get letters. And pictures."

"Forget it. We'll talk later."

"Call me back," Robin insisted. "Tonight. No matter how late."

Tia pressed End and then rubbed her thumb along the phone as though it were Robin's shoulder.

When she was ten years old, Tia and her mother moved from the D Street projects to a tiny house smack up against the sidewalk. The place had been renovated from an undersized one-family into two microscopic illegal apartments. Tia's mother didn't care about the size, because they'd finally moved to the Point, Southie's good side, and Tia didn't care because the move brought next-door Robin into her life.

Robin's parents spent most of their time screaming; she practically lived at Tia's. The door to Tia's bedroom opened onto the kitchen, one so small there was barely enough room for two people to eat. Tia ate all her meals in front of the television. Her mother let the girls take over most of the house, grateful that someone was around to keep Tia company, since her new job at Brandeis, as she always told Tia, took the starch right out of her, and all that was left were the wrinkles.

Tia rushed down Washington Street until she hit Doyle's, a bar frequented by political types who pretended they went there for the company and not the whiskey; by granola guys who still liked a hamburger and beer; by JP natives; and by people like her, who just wanted to blend in with the mix.

Tia opened the side door and entered the welcome murkiness. If you wanted a drink despite it only being two in the afternoon, the gloom was perfect. She looked around, afraid that some agency acquaintance might have come here for an afternoon meeting.

High wooden booths crowded the worn-down room. Tia sat at the short bar scarred by years of beer mugs being banged on the counter. She faced a mirror clouded from decades of cigarette smoke. Tia was grateful the antismoking laws had passed. No way could she have stayed cigarette free if bumming were still possible.

She'd stopped smoking when she learned she was pregnant. There weren't many gifts she could offer her baby; at least she'd give her clear, clean oxygen in the womb.

Few people sat at the bar. An old man the color of cigarette ash—both hair and skin—slumped on the stool to her right. Only his glass of ruby wine provided some relief of color. A middle-aged man drooped over a beer. Three green-splattered painters worked on platters of fries as they downed drinks.

Closest to her, on the stool to the left, a boyish-looking man read a wrinkled newspaper as he sipped from a large ice-filled glass. The liquid was clear. Vodka? Gin? Water?

"What can I get you?" The bartender wiped the wood in front of Tia and then put down a worn cardboard coaster meant to blot up a drinker's sloppiness.

"Coffee." For a moment, Tia hoped she'd stop there, but she couldn't dredge up the will. "With a shot of Jameson."

"On the side or in?" The woman's youth and clear skin made Tia want to show off her best side, but she'd lost her chance. Ordering the Jameson put her in a league with her neighbors Ashy and Droopy.

"Is the coffee fresh?" Right, as though Tia were some coffee connoisseur whose decision whether to put her two o'clock whiskey in or out depended on the coffee's pedigree, not on Tia's wanting her caffeine hit spun with whiskey.

"Fresh and hot." The bartender's red hair was long and curly. She looked like an art student who'd be sketching unflattering portraits of her customers later that night. Tia was probably destined to be in an obscure Jamaica Plain art show that Christmas. *Woman Under the Influence* selling for sixty dollars.

"In the coffee, then." Tia forced a grin. She worried about falling further and further away from her dreams of success. Her mother had pushed to get Tia out of the working class. She'd dreamed of seeing her daughter in a life where people bought new cars instead of old clunkers. She'd wanted Tia to own a home. Tia wanted to own a place in the world where she used her mind and heart together.

At least Tia had pushed Honor over the class line.

The boyish newspaper reader came home with Tia.

His hair was fair, his eyes were blue, and he looked like spring. That's how Tia tried to see him as they sat in the high-backed booth they shared in Doyle's back room.

However, his flaxen hair needed washing, his glasses were smudged, and he smelled like Tia's punishment. The clear liquid that suggested purity at the bar turned out to be vodka. She continued with Jameson's, dropping the charade of the coffee, and picked at a hamburger. He wolfed down a veggie burger and fries, eyeing her meat the whole time.

They discussed whiskey-fueled things that seemed vital in a haze of attraction and alcohol. His backpack trip through Greece. His plan to teach literature to immigrants. Her plan to return to school for her master's degree, so she could implement legislative cures for elder hatred, a dream she'd been unaware of until her fourth whiskey. She finished with a soapbox lecture on how poorly the world treated old folks.

Then they went to her house.

He pulled her close the moment the door shut.

She couldn't remember his name.

He slobbered all over her mouth.

Patrick?

Paul?

Jeremy.

"Hey, baby," she said. "Take it easy."

"Mmm?"

"Slow down, buddy." Tia hated how numb her lips were, making it difficult to form words.

In answer to Tia's request, he clutched her so tight that she felt every inch of his hard-on through both their jeans. Then he grabbed her hand and brought it between them. He pushed it down, urging her to press on him. She did nothing. He pressed her hand harder.

Tia pulled away and then shoved him off her. "I said, slow down."

"Can't help it," he said. "You drive me nuts. You're fucking gorgeous."

Tia had stared at herself in the restaurant's bathroom mirror. During the afternoon and evening, she'd unwittingly spiked her hair up and out with her nervous fingers. She'd rubbed her eyes so often that now she resembled a raccoon. The makeup she'd applied that morning had gone from enhancing to slovenly.

"Listen, baby." She tried not to slur. "I hope I didn't lead you on."

Bullshit. Of course she'd led him on. They'd sat side by side in the restaurant. She'd enjoyed it when he ran his hand so far up her thigh that it took everything she had not to press against him. Now the whiskey was wearing off, and his hands felt like an invasion.

He backed away. He ran a thumb across the top of each of her cheekbones. Tia was a sucker for a new move. Hell, they were all new moves now. It had been so long since she'd made love that she didn't even remember where or when it had last happened, only that it had been with Nathan.

He tucked a curled finger under her chin and tipped it up. "You look like some sort of actress, you know."

Tia hungered for admiration, approbation from someone safely anonymous, someone who wouldn't ask her for jack the next day, the next minute. No one who'd wonder if she had a baby hidden away.

He backed her into the corner of the kitchen, against the

washing machine. Pressing-pressing-pressing. He put a too-warm hand—Nathan's hands were always cool and dry—under her shirt and went straight to the breast. Where had the finesse of thumbs to cheekbones gone? He palmed her breast. He pumped against her.

Unexpected wanting shot straight down from her stomach.

He leaned down and covered her mouth with his lips. He tasted of vodka and coffee and the peppery black beans from his veggie burger. His beard grated her skin.

When they'd finished, she wanted to shower.

This was why she'd stayed on the pill since giving birth, because she'd known something exactly like this would happen. Tia couldn't trust herself, and she couldn't trust anyone else.

He sprawled out in her bed, eyes closed, flaccid and damp. The sight made her ill, and yet she didn't know him well enough to cover it. She slipped out of bed and grabbed the chenille robe that had once been her mother's.

She poked his arm with a tentative finger. Then she tapped harder. She used two fingers.

"Hey, hey . . . what?" He turned his head toward her, blinking bloodshot eyes.

"Jeremy, you've got to go." Her voice sounded flat.

He squeezed his eyes shut and then shook his head. "Too tired."

"Sorry. It's time."

"I don't even have my car."

"The bus stops right on the corner, or you can walk down to the Orange line."

"Nah, I can walk home from here."

Idiot. Then why'd you bring up the car?

"But it's far," he said. "And no bus goes from here to there."

"Then what's the difference? You'll have the same problem in the morning." Tia itched with wanting him out.

He tapped her nose. "You'll drive me in the morning, right?"

"I don't have a car."

He screwed up his face with cute. "Hmm, problem. Lucky for you I do have a car. I guess I can walk home in the morning and bring my car back here. Then I can drive you to breakfast."

"I have to go to work," Tia said.

"So, I'll drive you to work."

Tia pulled the robe tight up to her neck. "Jeremy, you got to go."

He looked hurt. "My name isn't Jeremy. It's David."

CHAPTER 12

Juliette

Juliette felt invisible in New York City. Too many people, too many cars, too little space between buildings. Boston was big enough for someone who grew up in Rhinebeck.

Nathan drove toward his parents' home with the expertise of the native he was. The boys were in the backseat. Brooklyn unfolded around them. Coney Island Avenue stretched out in its crazy-quilt spectrum. Gas stations, ethnic grocery stores, and real estate agencies bordered synagogues, mosques, and Pakistani restaurants.

Juliette glanced in the mirror to check on the boys. Max had fallen asleep. Napping, his head lolling back, he seemed younger; his plump little boy face came back into focus.

Savannah's face. A little girl version of Max. Someone who'd enjoy stirring brownie batter, without feeling the need to deliberately make drips that resembled lumps of poop.

Juliette clamped down on her thoughts, knowing that if she didn't, she'd be in trouble. What if Nathan could read her mind? What would he think of her idea that if Savannah knew them, then they could be family? Juliette wouldn't be the outsider. How could she tell anyone that she fantasized about including the girl in their lives?

Juliette had to stop obsessing. Getting through this visit to Nathan's parents required entering a dissociative state. She turned to look at the boys, hoping for distraction, but though Max had woken, he was as buried in electronics as his brother.

Lucas concentrated on his iPhone as though studying the Torah. Juliette supposed that Lucas and Max, so expert at tapping and scrolling on miniature screens, would always have an advantage over her and Nathan. Neither of them managed to adopt new technology fast enough to catch up with their sons, although Nathan tried. Unless she needed it for work, Juliette resisted new gadgets. Smart phones made her feel stupid.

Avraham and Gizi's block seemed the same, although the colorful flags whipping in the wind announcing Easter looked new. She wondered if any sharp entrepreneur had yet designed a Passover banner. Perhaps next year silk-screened streamers heralding pastel matzos and bright silver Elijah cups would swing in the breeze.

As they turned on Albemarle Road, Max stretched and then leaned forward, poking Juliette's right shoulder for attention. "We're here, right?"

"We're here," she answered.

"Why's everyone so quiet?"

"How did you know it was quiet if you were sleeping, dumbo?" Lucas asked.

"I wasn't really sleeping; I was only car sleeping, fecal breath," Max said.

"Language," Juliette warned.

"Hey, guys. We're supposed to be in a meditative mood," Nathan said. "It's Passover."

"I thought Yom Kippur was the reflecting holiday, and Passover was the celebration of freedom," Lucas said.

"How would we know anything? We didn't even have bar mitzvahs." Max sounded accusatory. "Lucas and I aren't even really Jewish anyway, right? Even though we're three-quarters? Since Mamie Sondra isn't Jewish. Benjamin Kaplan said it has to come through the mother."

Mamie Sondra indeed. Juliette's mother insisted the boys call her Mamie instead of Grandma, in recognition of her French heritage about ten generations ago, but Juliette knew her mother chose the word because it sounded younger than *Grandma*. Had she chosen *Grand-mère*, a recognizable word in America? No. She chose a word that made her sound younger and exotic.

"People only pay attention to those obscure rules in the most orthodox communities," Nathan said.

"Then how come Lucas and I didn't have bar mitzvahs?"

"Jesus, who cares?" Lucas said.

"Is Hebrew school what you wanted, Max? More work every day after school?" Nathan made the sharp right into his parents' driveway. "I remember having to schlep two different bags of books to school. Not fun, my son, not fun."

"You never even gave us the choice," Max said.

"What's up with this?" Nathan looked to Juliette for support. She stared back with a deliberate blank face. *You're the full-fledged one, the real one; you answer them.*

"When Josh Simons had his bar mitzvah, he made three thousand dollars!" Max opened his arms, hands up, as though weighing the money. "Three thousand!"

"Oh, so it's about money." Again, Nathan tried connecting to Juliette with his eyes. Again, she blank-eyed him. Now he sent another message, this time with his eyebrows and a small tilt of his head, which in husbandspeak translated to "What? What's wrong?"

His eyes were full of questions. Juliette turned away.

Juliette's in-laws' house smelled of thick Hungarian Jewish food. Smothered red peppers. Gizi's Passover version of stuffed cabbage. Chocolate-walnut torte—a miracle of silky dark chocolate and matzo meal.

Gizi took Max's and Lucas's faces between her hands in turn, studying each boy for a moment before kissing him, first on the right cheek and then the left. Then she turned her attention to Juliette.

"Sweetheart." Gizi smiled as though the sight of Juliette warmed her through and through. "Look at you. *Szép.* Gorgeous. My son is the luckiest man in the world."

Juliette bent down and kissed her mother-in-law's downy cheek. Gizi's skin was barely lined, despite using only Vaseline and a few concoctions, as Gizi called them, on her face. Juliette showered her with bottles of juliette&gwynne products, but Gizi simply lined them on the glass shelves in her bathroom as though they were sculptures.

"Darling," she'd say, "I love them. Look how beautiful!" Meanwhile, Gizi stuck to the wisdom passed down from her mother: Wear a hat outside in every season. Spread Vaseline on your skin when it's damp. Gizi had been the inspiration for Juliette's business: when money was tight for her and Nathan, Gizi counseled Juliette to use honey and avocado mixed with a little olive oil on her face.

"Mama." Nathan gave his mother a tight hug. He loved his parents without reservation. When he let go of Gizi, he stood behind Juliette and squeezed her shoulders. "Does or does not my wife get lovelier every year?"

Nathan's hands weighed on her like iron bars.

"You okay, darling?" Gizi wrinkled her face and peered at Juliette in concern.

"Who's not okay?" Avraham walked in, drying his hands on a towel. "Ah, my boys!" He grabbed Lucas in a bear hug and then gave Max a smacking kiss.

"Everyone is fine." Gizi put a hand behind each boy's back. "Go. We set up the living room."

Set up meant that Avraham had placed snack tables next to each comfortable club chair and loaded them with sodas Juliette never allowed the boys to have, and chocolate and nuts she'd never give them before a meal.

"What can I do?" Juliette asked.

"Keep me company while I finish." Gizi grabbed the towel from Avraham. "You. Take your son for a walk before dinner."

Juliette knew this meant that Gizi worried about how much Avraham would eat and how high his blood sugar would be after the meal, so she wanted him to get exercise.

"Come on, Dad." Nathan put his arm around his father. "Let's leave while they'll let us."

Dirty pots, scraped-out bowls, and wooden spoons caked with batter covered every surface in Gizi's kitchen. Juliette's in-laws hadn't changed a thing since they bought the house when Nathan was ten. Gizi hated change. Each time Avraham suggested remodeling, she'd flick a hand and say, "Next you'll be remodeling me!"

"Okay, what is wrong?" Gizi handed Juliette a sponge. "Get the wineglasses, please. I must wash the dust which has built up since last Passover."

Gizi's overly formal speech, as unchanged as her house, reflected the English for Immigrants course she'd taken so many years before at Brooklyn College. Juliette dragged the old metal step stool to the pantry. She handed down the precious Ajka Crystal glasses. Her in-laws had collected the Hungarian crystal one piece at a time. Juliette found it incongruous; first people ran from their homelands to escape persecution, then their homes became shrines to those countries. Nathan called it the power of cognitive dissonance.

Perhaps cognitive dissonance described Juliette's marriage. Her love for Nathan collided with the painful knowledge of Tia. She'd papered over the dark side of their marriage.

Gizi placed one glass at a time in a warm vinegar and water bath, using a small rubber tub she'd placed in the sink.

"So, no answer to my question?" Gizi prodded.

Juliette didn't bother pretending ignorance. Her mother-in-law sensed the undertones of life with uncanny accuracy. Even when she didn't know what was wrong, she sniffed to the heart of troubles like a bloodhound.

Juliette rummaged for a suitable answer. Certainly she wouldn't say the words pressing at her lips: *You have a granddaughter. Her hair and eyes are the color of dark walnuts. Just like you.*

"I'm feeling blue, but it's nothing serious," she said. "Premenstrual."

Her mother-in-law took measure of Juliette. "I thought you seemed a little bloated."

Wonderful. Juliette's period had ended the previous week. So she was getting fat along with everything else. "Thanks."

Gizi tipped her head. "Oh, Juliette, you are already so beautiful and blessed. I think you can afford a few days of extra salt in your system."

Juliette gave her mother-in-law a hard hug. "I'm going to change. Then I'll help you some more."

The guest bedroom reserved for them was barely large enough for a dresser and a bed—the only furniture in the room. Juliette ran a hand over the carved headboard. It banged against the wall with the slightest movement, as Juliette learned the one and only time that she and Nathan made love in this room. There was the time he'd suggested they use the floor, but Juliette didn't think there was enough space for them to lie down, even one on top of the other, and she was terrified of getting stuck in some awful position.

How could she stay in this room with him? Everyone went to their bedrooms early, leaving Avraham to watch television at an audio level unbearable by anyone but him. The kids had a small TV in Nathan's old room, where they slept, Gizi fell asleep by nine thirty, and she and Nathan read, entwined side by side, in the barely full-sized bed.

Not for the first time, Juliette wished she found solace in alcohol. It was a shame that chocolate and sugar didn't induce sleep.

Ajka Crystal shimmered on the Passover table; the already crimson glasses even deeper-colored, filled with blood-red wine. Emerald bowls held cooked peppers. Browned farfel kugel rested on cobalt platters. Candles flickered. Avraham read from a tattered Manischewitz Haggadah. Max asked the four questions in his breaking voice. Avraham hid the *afikomen* for the boys to find after the meal. Traditionally, only the finder of the hidden matzo got an award, but Avraham never gave anything to just one grandson.

Juliette felt as though her heart might crack in half. She loved her in-laws, but she thought she might explode from not wanting to be in their apartment. The walls of the already small dining room seemed as though they were getting closer to the table. Nathan's knee repeatedly hit hers under the table. Each time she drew away, he made contact again.

Nathan became expansive around his mother and father. She could feel his want in advance, imagine him pressing against her in the tiny bed, still trying to change her mind about lovemaking in Brooklyn. He'd be wrapped around her all night, and there would be no place for her to go.

"A wonderful meal, Mom." Nathan turned to his father. "We're lucky men."

Avraham nodded. "I know. Make sure that you know."

Did Avraham and Gizi know about the difficult time she and Nathan had gone through? Had he told them anything? Their love for Nathan wasn't without awareness.

Gizi reached over and patted Nathan's hand. "He knows, he knows. We have a family from heaven."

Soon after they ate the last macaroon, Juliette grabbed Nathan and dragged him into the tiny guest room. Their still-packed overnight bags sat on the lumpy bed. Tea-colored lace curtains drifted with the air blown up from the radiator. Heat and the smell of lemon Pledge mixed to a noxious thickness.

"I want to go home," Juliette said.

Nathan looked at her as though she spoke in tongues. "What?" He cocked his head to the side as if he might understand better.

"I. Want. To. Go," Juliette said. "Tonight. Now."

"Are you crazy? We wouldn't get home until after one in the morning. What's wrong?"

How could she say that she couldn't bear to sleep in that cramped bed with him? That she didn't want to breathe his air or be awake all night with no place to go. If she got out of bed, no matter how quietly she tried to creep, within minutes Gizi would appear, offering a world of comfort she didn't want.

Would you like some tea? Hot water bottle? A piece of cake? How about some oatmeal? I could make you eggs, darling.

"I'll drive," Juliette said.

"Forget the driving. Give me one reason for this insane idea."

Juliette rummaged for something, anything, to say that would get her out of there. Her head was cracking open. Anything could fall out. At least driving at night, the boys would sleep. Nathan would sleep.

"I said I'd drive." She'd drink ten coffees if necessary. "I just have too much work waiting. I need to go. I need to wake up and get right to work."

"It's Passover, for Christ's sake. What am I supposed to tell my parents? The kids?"

Juliette walked over and looked straight into Nathan's eyes. "I don't care what you say. Just get me the hell out of here. Now. I mean it. Now."

Whatever he saw in Juliette's eyes made him walk out of the room and announce their new plans.

She dodged her in-laws' questions and confusion, almost changing her mind when faced with their hurt. Juliette might have stayed if she could stick the boys in the guest room while Nathan and she slept in the twin beds in Nathan's old room, but there was no way that the boys would share a bed, and it wouldn't fly with Gizi and Avraham, anyway.

The expressions they'd worn as Nathan packed the car haunted Juliette during the silent ride home. Leaving had given Gizi confirmation that her intuition was on target, but if they'd stayed, Juliette would have let out the scream she'd been holding too long.

Nathan drove.

They arrived home at two in the morning.

The boys stumbled into the house as Nathan and Juliette carried in the luggage.

"G'night," Max mumbled as he sleepwalked up the stairs.

"Good night, sweetheart," Juliette said. "Good night, Lucas."

Lucas grunted. He'd not spoken a word since leaving his grandparents. His silence and rigid shoulders let her know that she'd wrecked his plan to visit the Museum of Natural History with his grandfather. Even at fourteen, Lucas still loved wandering through the marble halls filled with dinosaurs, plus they'd planned to see *Cosmic Collisions*, a space show at the planetarium.

After they brought the last load into the house, Nathan turned to Juliette. They were alone for the first time since leaving his parents' house.

"What's going on with you?" Frustration turned Nathan's eyes into slits. Impossibly, he seemed to tower over her. Anger made him seem bigger.

When Juliette didn't answer, he stepped forward and bent his head to her. "What, I ask you, *what* was so important that insulting my parents seemed like a good idea? I kept quiet back there because I didn't want to upset them more than we already had. And in the car, I held back for the kids. Now—now it's just us."

Juliette stepped back. "It had nothing to do with your parents."

"That barely matters, does it, since it's their house we walked out of?" He slammed Max's backpack to the floor and then threw his keys on the entrance table.

"Stop," she whispered, "you'll upset the boys." She moved Nathan's keys from the table to the bowl meant to protect the wood from scratches.

"Now you're worried? After your little stunt, nothing will bother or wake the boys. What time is it? Four in the morning?"

"It's only two." Juliette walked out of the entry and headed to the kitchen.

Nathan followed her down the hall. "Where the hell are you going?"

She stopped short and turned. "Watch your mouth. I'm not one of those googly-eyed girls who worship you."

"Jesus, what's going on, Jules?"

They stared at each other. Nathan's eyes searched for what Juliette wasn't saying. Rushes of words came to her, but they all stopped at her throat. Once she told him the truth, everything would change. Until then, no matter how awful she felt, they were still the four of them: her, Nathan, Lucas, and Max. After she brought Savannah into the conversation, the girl became family, and they'd never be the same again.

"Why are you so angry?" he asked. "You're not making any sense."

She said the only thing that could make any sense at all. Maybe if she leaked a hint, she'd get a clue as to whether or not Nathan had seen Tia, if he knew about Savannah. "It's her," she said.

"Her? Who is her?"

She was relieved that his question seemed genuine. "That woman. The one you slept with."

"Who are you talking about?"

"Was there more than one?"

"You're talking about Tia? Seriously? That's why we left Brooklyn? What the fuck, Juliette?" He dug his hands into the side of his head and shook it back and forth. "Are you having some sort of traumatic flashback?"

A great loneliness overcame her. Being alone with knowledge of such great proportions threatened to sink her.

"Maybe I am," she whispered. She walked over to her husband and wrapped her arms around his waist. "Perhaps that's my problem."

She knew this couldn't continue, but she didn't know how to move forward. All she wanted at the moment was to be the only mother of Nathan's only children.

CHAPTER 13

Juliette

The week after Passover became a temporary détente. Juliette anesthetized herself with Vogue and Elle. Nathan spent most nights behind his desk.

And then came Easter, a holiday that never failed to depress her. Girls in Rhinebeck wore frills and taffeta. Satin ribbons hung from overflowing baskets filled with yellow marshmallow baby chicks, jelly beans, and pink barrettes. At dinner, they sat on stacks of phone books, and ate ham and candied yams. People took pictures because they were so cute.

She hated Easter.

Juliette's parents ignored all the traditions. Was it because her father was Jewish? They'd never celebrated Passover either. Was it because her father and mother taught at Bard, such a bastion of humanism? Her mother taught creative dance; her father, political science—did that make them too sophisticated for chickadee marshmallows and too liberal for petticoats? Easter Sunday, her parents did nothing different from any Sunday, except that after Juliette fell asleep on Easter eve, her mother left a chocolate rabbit on Juliette's dresser. Easter morning, Juliette ate the entire bunny while her parents slept late.

When Lucas was two, Juliette built him an Easter basket worthy of a prince. Nathan had come in as she curled the last ribbons—multitudes of blue and yellow ribbons twirled around the yellow straw.

"What do you think?" She'd held up her masterpiece.

Nathan had laid a tentative finger on the soft white fur of a plush bunny. He held the whiskers, letting them open and spring back. "An Easter basket?"

"Do you have a problem with that?" Juliette had asked.

"Don't get defensive, Jules," he said.

"I won't get defensive, if you don't use that voice."

"What voice?" Nathan crossed his arms across his chest.

"The you're-shocking-me-with-your-level-of-stupidity voice." Juliette placed a protective hand on the blue basket and worked at not crying.

"We'd agreed to raise Lucas Jewish."

"For your parents. I don't think giving him a stuffed animal will make him into a Christian or a Communist. Your parents are safe."

"There's no reason to be sarcastic. I thought we had a deal."

But what was her side of the deal? What did she get? Not having to listen to Nathan sermonizing about how important Jewish traditions were to his family? She longed to create their own traditions.

She felt as though their life had become a series of compromises that always tipped to the Nathan Soros side of the moral scale.

When she tried to change his mind, he'd remind Juliette that since her father was Jewish, the children were actually more Jewish than anything else—as though Max and Lucas were genetic measuring cups.

Easter Sundays now were just like they'd been when Juliette was a child. Her family tradition was being carried on. Another generation of nothing special. Not even a chocolate bunny, though she always baked something out of the ordinary for dessert. Something Nathan considered a bit goyish, like a white cake with boiled icing. She'd paint green grass, a yellow sun, and blue sky by adding food coloring to the frosting. Nothing he could truly object to, but still, it tickled her to serve it.

What a pathetic rebellion. Baking a Christian-style cake to make up for his screwing around and forbidding Easter baskets?

Juliette tugged at the *Times* Style section from where Nathan's legs had trapped the paper.

"Lift," she said.

He lifted without a word.

"Again," she said, going for the magazine section.

"I was going to read that next," he said.

"You can't *call* sections." Juliette pulled at the paper. "If it's not in your hands, it's up for grabs."

Nathan laughed, not turning from the business section. "Who made you the queen of newspaper etiquette?"

Juliette grabbed the paper and pulled until a page ripped away and she held nothing but a scrap of newsprint. "For God's sake, Nathan, just give me the damned paper."

Now he looked at her. "What's wrong with you, Jules?" He lifted the torn Style section and handed it to her.

"You don't need to hoard sections," she said. "Nobody gets more than one at a time."

"Then why are you holding the magazine *and* the Style section?" He smiled, trying to lighten the mood.

"You don't read the damned Style section. You call it crap. You think everything I do is crap and everything you do is some sort of high holy brilliant top-of-the-line gift to God." Juliette threw down the paper and pushed it over to him. "Here. Take it. Take it all. You get whatever you want anyway, right?"

Juliette stomped out of the room and slammed into the bathroom. She turned on the faucets and shower full blast, so he couldn't hear her crying. Jerk. Next he'd probably tell her she was ruining the environment by running the water.

She turned off the water, thinking of Lucas and Max and future grandchildren.

After blowing her nose, she buried her face in a towel, muffling her sadness and anger.

"Go away, Nathan," she whispered when he knocked.

"Are you okay, Mom?"

Lucas.

She curled her toes. She tightened every muscle. "I'm okay, hon."

"Are you crying?" he asked.

"No," she said.

"You sound like you're crying."

Oh, shit. Max. Both of them were out there, sentinel sons guarding their crazy mother.

She ground her palms into her forehead.

"What's wrong, Mom?" Lucas asked.

Your father cheated. You have a sister. I still love your father.

"Leave Mom alone, guys." Nathan's voice was full and soothing. "She had a sad morning. Everyone has one now and then."

"Why did she have a sad morning?" Max asked. "What was she sad about?"

What are you going to say, Nathan?

"When Mom was little, Easter was hard for her. Now I think I've made it just as bad." It sounded like Nathan was patting the door, as though it were her back. "Come on, give her some privacy."

They walked away, and Juliette hated Nathan more than ever. If he knew her so well, why didn't he come through for her more? Why couldn't he always be like that?

Why had he ever gone to that woman?

Juliette removed a load of hot towels from the dryer, wishing she could make a nest of the warm cotton and lie down. Tuesdays were quiet at the shop. She'd come in early that morning, eager to get away from Nathan and her pounding questions.

A key turned in the front door. Gwynne's light footsteps came toward Juliette.

"What are you doing?" Gwynne asked.

"Folding towels?"

"Isn't Helen coming in?"

Helen was their cleaner, towel folder, and official moaner. They tried to placate her with gifts. (Look, Helen, freesia perfume to mask the smell of disappointment! Poppy-red lipstick to smear on your wrinkled lips!) She made everyone miserable, but neither Gwynne nor Juliette had the guts to fire her.

"She's cleaning the bathrooms." Juliette raised her eyebrows at Gwynne.

"Which means you have to fold?"

"I had to go somewhere I wouldn't hear her muttering 'Pigs, pigs, they're all pigs.'"

Gwynne looked at her with skeptical eyes.

"Okay, I needed to do something mindless," Juliette admitted.

"What's wrong? You've been in a funk for weeks."

"I'm fine."

"You are so obviously not fine that I feel as though I should be pouring you tea laced with brandy."

"Really. It's nothing," Juliette insisted.

All that "nothing" burned at her throat as she worked to keep it from bubbling out and scalding everything in the beautiful shop. If she didn't, she might unleash a torrent of "Life sucks!" all over Helen's clean floors.

"You know what they say. Crying gets the sad out of you." Gwynne's light words didn't hide her concern.

"And what gets the Nathan blues out of you?" Juliette asked.

"What's he done now?" Gwynne knew about the affair with Tia. If Juliette hadn't shared it, she'd have exploded like the blueberry girl in *Charlie and the Chocolate Factory*, except instead of bursting from eating too much candy, bullshit would have blown Juliette apart.

She buried her face in a towel. Too late. It had already cooled off, and now it had to be washed again for no good reason. Here she was, adding to Helen's reasons to hate Americans.

Gwynne took the towel from Juliette's hand and dumped it in the laundry bin. "Stop. It looks as though you're veiling yourself, covering your mouth like that."

Juliette flapped her eyelashes, but tears still leaked out.

"Is he seeing someone again?" Gwynne asked.

"I don't think so." She retrieved the towel Gwynne had thrown in the basket and wiped her eyes.

Gwynne fell on the cushy couch and patted the seat next to her. It wasn't elegant, this back room where they had the washer-dryer, old magazines, employee lockers, and tables piled with the cosmetic samples that flew into the store. Old chairs and frayed pillows ended their lives in this room where no one bothered sucking in her stomach.

"He has a daughter."

"He has a daughter," Gwynne repeated.

"Nathan has a little girl. She's five." Juliette leaned back, pushing her hair off her face. She'd released the secret. Made it real. Savannah, Honor, Tia's baby, Caroline's child, Nathan's daughter, no longer lived only in her mind, and now she had to deal with her.

Juliette tried to be friendly at dinner, for Lucas, for Max, and for her plan. She'd worked with Gwynne to craft a strategy for talking to Nathan. She'd be calm. Easygoing. Give him room to have his feelings and reactions before she had her say.

Otherwise, she'd screech. He'd retreat. That would be useless.

What was more frightening in a marriage than the moments you caught your husband looking at you with dispassionate eyes, when he revealed that he didn't like you very much in that moment? So Juliette didn't slam the Swedish meatballs on the table. She slid them.

"Meatballs?" Max hummed in anticipation, imagining the rare treat of real beef.

"Don't be a dope. They're turkey balls, right, Mom?" Lucas stabbed one on his fork.

"Wait until everything's served." Parmesan cheese formed a perfect fat *S* for Soros on the platter of spaghetti she'd placed on a copper trivet. "And the meatballs aren't turkey."

"Real meat? Hey, thanks for the miracle." Lucas spread the cheesy *S* over the pasta. Juliette wondered if a daughter would at least comment on Juliette's food art before smearing it like that.

"Do you really think you can taste the difference?" Juliette asked.

Lucas paused before biting his meatball. "So it isn't meat?"

Max chomped down on his. "Whatever it is, it's good."

"You'd think crap balls were good if Mom put cheese and bread-crumbs in them."

"Lucas, language," Nathan said.

"Maybe they're soybean balls," Juliette suggested.

Lucas took a suspicious sniff. "You're kidding, right?"

"Taste it," Juliette said. "See if you like it. Then I'll tell you."

Nathan swirled a forkful of spaghetti and then tipped it with a quarter meatball. "It's beef," he said after chewing. "Coleman beef."

"Come on, Dad. How could you tell what kind of beef it is?" As usual, Lucas sprinkled salt over his plate before tasting anything.

"Because your mother wouldn't serve any other kind. She loves me too much not to give me natural free-range beef," Nathan said.

"Don't you mean she loves *us* too much?" Max asked. "All of us."

"Sure, she loves us all." Nathan gave Juliette a lazy smile and winked. "But she loved me first."

Juliette poured herself a generous glass of Cabernet.

Surely Nathan noticed. Juliette rarely drank.

Why not forget about it?

She watched Nathan remove his shirt. Crinkly hair covered his chest, some sprouted on his back. Ugly, except not to her. Nathan's back endeared him to Juliette. It was the part of him that he couldn't see, so she felt as though it were hers.

Before Juliette could fall further into her sentimental admiration of Nathan's body, jealousy rushed in to replace her pleasure. Tia had seen his back.

Why did men cheat? That song kept playing. The thought of listening to it forever terrified her.

Gwynne theorized that Nathan's mother and father doted on him too much. "You know," she'd said, "the precious only child of immigrants. First they raise him to do well in the world—constantly assuring him that he's brilliant! So handsome! One of a kind! Then he makes it, and they're all: 'Oh, Nathan! A professor! So brilliant! Your children! So handsome! Your wife! One of a kind!'"

Who could live up to that? Was Juliette supposed to constantly assure a husband who belched and scratched and trailed dirty coffee cups that he was God's particular gift to the world and to her?

Still, Juliette worried that the affair was her fault. She'd become boring: talking about moisturizers and makeovers instead of the Palestinian-Israeli conflict. Maybe she'd become a sexual robot, always following the tracks she and Nathan had laid down early on: *touch this, stroke that, rub this.*

Nathan pulled on his robe.

"What reason did I give you?" Her words sprayed out without care, lacking the coolness she'd planned. She fell back on the bed, picked up a pillow, and held it first over her face and then across her stomach.

He turned to face her, his expression a mix of worry and puzzlement.

"Reason for what?" he asked in a deliberate tone.

"You know." She threw down the pillow and brought her legs to her chest, circling them with her arms. "Her," she said to her knees.

Give Nathan credit. He didn't pretend ignorance. He sat next to Juliette. "Her again? Her doesn't exist anymore," he said. "I've kept my word. I've never even been tempted."

She lifted her face just enough to look at the corners of his mouth where the lies showed first.

Not lying.

Big deal.

Though, really, it was.

But they had business to face. She didn't want to. He touched her leg and she wanted to pull him down and make love in ways that weren't routine, or were, but who cared, because the act would scrub everything out of her brain. She wanted to become stupid with sex.

Well, la-di-fucking-da, Juliette. Tough luck that the past is toddling around somewhere on Max's legs and wearing Nathan's hair.

"You have a daughter, Nathan." His hand froze.

"She's five."

He drew his hand away.

"Maybe you already knew, huh?" she asked. "Did you know about her?"

"Did I know?"

He was buying time. She saw the wheels turning.

"Do you know about Honor?" Juliette asked.

"Honor?" Now he sounded genuinely puzzled.

Okay, so he didn't know her stupid Tia name.

"Savannah?" Juliette asked. "Do you know about Savannah?"

"Savannah? Honor? Honestly, I don't know what you're talking about."

"You don't know the names, or the topic?"

"Neither," he said.

Now he was lying. His lips quivered that millimeter she knew.

"Liar," Juliette said. "I know."

"You know what?"

She knew he wanted to jump out the window. "I know you knew that Tia was pregnant. I know that."

Of course, that woman used the baby as leverage to pressure him to leave Juliette. An obsessive stalker who sent Hallmark heart cards would do anything.

Nathan moved away from her and slumped at the edge of the bed, holding his head in his hands.

"What are you going to do?" Juliette asked.

"Do? Do about what? I barely have a clue what you're talking about. How do you even . . . ?"

Juliette crossed her arms. "I opened the letter she sent you."

"What letter?" A bit of anger tinged his words. "A letter to me?"

Screw you, Nathan. What, you have a privacy issue going on here?

Juliette reached into the top drawer of her nightstand. The envelope looked as though she'd carried it through ten storms. "Here. Read it."

He slipped the letter and the photos from the envelope. He

looked at the photos first. Was Nathan more curious about the child than he was about Tia, and if so, was that good or bad?

He stared at the girl for long minutes. His daughter. Juliette knew he was trying to keep his face impassive; she could see his emotions, she just wasn't sure what they added up to.

He unfolded the letter. Juliette kneaded the bedspread, and then went to lean over his shoulder.

When he'd had enough time to read it five hundred times, Juliette burst out, "What are you going to do?"

"About what?"

"*About what?*" Juliette jumped off the bed. "What do you feel? What do you feel about this child? About her?"

"Juliette, I didn't know about the child until I opened this. I haven't spoken to . . . to her, since—"

"Since when? Since you swore it was over? Since she told you she was pregnant?"

Nathan remained silent.

"Which is it? Which? Answer me!"

He sank his head back into his hands.

"Don't play hangdog."

"Jules, give me a minute at least."

"It takes no time to tell the truth. You don't need a minute. Talk."

He shook his head. "I can't. Not yet. I need to absorb this."

"We have to plan everything together: how you'll respond to Tia, to the news of Savannah, or it will drive us apart. Please, Nathan."

"Enough. You're right, you're right. But you've been thinking about this, obsessing about it—I just found out. Surely you can understand that?"

She paced around the room, picking up a necklace lying on her dresser, putting it in her jewelry box, and then folding a towel from a basket of laundry in stiff, jerky movements. "Damn it, talk to me. Tell me what you're thinking."

"Not yet." He shook his head as though she barely registered. "I need to sort it out."

After squeezing the white towel until her hand ached, she threw it at him. "What are you *feeling*?" she shouted. "Do you feel like you have a daughter? Does this make you feel connected to Tia? What about Max and Lucas? Do we tell them?"

He stood up and grabbed her shoulders. "Give me some time," he said through gritted teeth. "I mean it. I can't handle you like this. Not right now."

CHAPTER 14

Caroline

The San Diego Marriott lobby was nearly empty. Caroline glanced around, guilty as a kid cutting class. She'd tried to give off the air of a doctor called out to tend to a life-or-death situation as she'd slipped out the back of the lecture hall, but she just wanted to breathe fresh air and shake off her jet lag.

"A New Paradigm for Considering the Ramifications of Treatments of Retinoblastoma" had given her a new paradigm for sleeping with her eyes open. The lecturers at the Future of Pediatrics conference obviously meant well—more than well—they were dedicated people willing to share their expertise. If they gave out caffeine tablets when you entered, then she could truly appreciate their paradigms.

The hotel lobby opened to a wide concrete plaza. FedEx was to her right. Across the way was a row of small shops. Caroline turned left and was grateful for the sight of a Starbucks. Good. After spending an hour yawning, she craved caffeine.

"Large coffee," she said when she reached the front of the line.

The barista looked at Caroline without hiding her boredom. "So you want a *Venti?*" Why did this girl crayon her eyes so heavily? The thick green semicircles looked like a grotesque signpost announcing her foul attitude.

Caroline looked up to the wall for help. *Grande* sounded larger, but what was *venti*? *Tall* sounded large also, but it was the name for small, right? Starbucks made her feel stupid. How was she supposed to keep their drink sizes straight? Was she supposed to learn Italian to drink coffee?

She took a chance. "I think I meant *Grande.*"

Green-circle smirked. "That's a medium. Is that what you want?"

The man next in line tapped Caroline's shoulder. "You want a large, right?"

She nodded.

"A *Venti* for the lady and a tall iced latte for me. Skim milk, light ice , please."

"Thanks," Caroline said. "I get lost here." He appeared familiar, a weedy type with wire-rim glasses and an eager-puppy look.

"My claim to fame," he said. "I speak fluent Starbucks." He put out his hand. "I snuck out of the lecture right after you."

As Caroline shook his hand, she realized she'd missed Green-circle's demand for money. She held out a twenty.

"Let me," her new friend offered, his money already in the girl's hand.

"Thank you." Caroline tucked the twenty back in her purse, knowing she'd just given him rights to something. Nothing big. But something.

They sat inside—both Easterners afraid of the sun, as it turned out. Jonah—Dr. Jonah Weber—ran a private practice in Vermont. The Northeast Kingdom.

"It sounds grand, doesn't it?" he said. "The Northeast Kingdom."

"Is it?" Caroline sank deeper into the velvety club chair, awash in good feeling. She'd escaped the lecture and was three thousand miles from the gilded cage to which she returned each night.

"It's beautiful in the extreme. And also horrific."

"How?" she asked.

"How is it beautiful? Or how is it horrific?"

"Both," she said. "Tell me about both."

"The landscape is almost mythical. Craggy, and then suddenly rolling hills. My house has a three-hundred-sixty-degree view. On the other hand, the town is filled with people poor in ways you can't imagine."

"Is your practice small?"

"Actually, too big. I cover a vast amount of territory. I could use help. Not many doctors want to live in a place where mud season outlasts summer. I'm not a pediatrician; I'm a family doctor. Where I live, that means being everything to everybody."

"Did you grow up in Vermont?"

"I did. I escaped for a bit." He looked happy, remembering. "I interned right here in San Diego. Stayed for a bit afterward. I loved being in a place where I didn't need ten pairs of flannel-lined jeans or five pairs of boots."

"So why'd you leave?"

"Not completely sure." He opened his hands as though offering her something. "Crazy?"

"You don't seem the crazy type."

"I think maybe some of us who grow up so specifically one way—like a hothouse flower, or in my case, a mud weed—need that environment to function. Even if we don't like it."

Caroline thought about the solitude she'd treasured as a girl. Lying for hours on her neatly made bed, reading, sketching angled houses during the period when architecture interested her, listening to Jascha Heifetz during the years she played violin. She'd felt complete.

"So you need mud and snow to function?" she asked.

"I guess I do. I haven't thought about it for a long time. I suppose I'm content being where I am."

Caroline snuck a look. The reassuring wedding band circling Jonah's finger took away her tickle of concern. This was safe; hardly even flirtation. Just colleagues playing hooky. Strangers offering each other revelations.

Jonah folded napkins into perfect squares and then triangles. "How about you? What do you need to function?"

All Caroline could think about were things that *didn't* help her function, like Savannah's constant thirst for her and Peter's need for the perfect family.

"Peace. I long for peace," she said.

"Just that?"

"That's plenty. Without it, everything else overwhelms me."

"How is work for that?"

Caroline laced her long fingers. "Work is never a problem. Even when things get hectic, I can provide my own inner peace. I love my work. As long as I also get my quota of quiet."

"And when you don't?" Jonah asked.

She didn't want to answer, so she didn't. She simply gave a self-deprecating smile that he could take any way he wanted. That was the beauty of talking to a stranger. Low stakes.

"How about your husband? Have children?"

He'd noticed her ring.

"My husband is dead."

What?

"Oh, I'm sorry. Recently?"

"Three years ago," she said. "My husband and daughter. In a car accident."

Horror passed over his face. Her stomach cramped. Had she gone insane? How could she take the words back without making him run away?

"I don't like talking about it," she rushed to say. "At all."

"Of course, of course." He covered her hand with his. She pushed away the awfulness of her words. His skin carried the chafing of a winter spent shoveling snow and chipping ice. It felt scratchy and yet good. Not like it came from a hothouse at all.

Caroline arrived home. She paid the cab driver. She opened the car door quietly, still greedy for solitude despite her four-day absence.

It was seven at night. Perhaps Peter had taken Savannah out for dinner. Just the two of them living the high life at McDonald's, acting as though they were free, free, free, until Mommy came home and laid down the law. Peter liked to play these games, putting Caroline in the role of the stern but loving mommy, while he played fun dad, making Savannah his companion in their domestic rebellion game.

Except it was just that. A game.

Where had this Peter come from, this man who wanted to poke and mold Caroline into someone different? He fell in love with her as a quiet researcher-doctor, claiming to love her safe aura of calm, so why was he trying to make her into a fun-loving, mess-enduring cookie baker?

As for the role Peter picked out for Savannah, the girl was as rebellious as an accountant. Savannah watched every move Caroline made as though measuring her against a secret measuring stick to which only Savannah had access.

The garage door was, of course, neatly closed. Peter hated it open, while Caroline disliked the grinding of opening and closing it. She had a crazy fear of it crashing down on her.

She hated their garage. Just as their house was a foolish mini-mansion for the three of them, the garage was a ridiculously massive home for their cars. It embarrassed Caroline, this conspicuous consumption in which Peter reveled—especially now, with so many suffering from the bad turns of the economy. Peter loved reminding Caroline how smart he'd been taking their money out of risky stocks and parking it in bonds at just the right time.

Her parents had managed to provide comfort without the sound and fury Peter required. She feared Peter might bury her in things before he overcame his upbringing. His background seemed perfectly acceptable to Caroline; whenever she said this, he'd bark his seal laugh and say, "Only the rich appreciate the beauty of poverty."

Peter hadn't grown up in poverty, just the bustle of keeping up. His father had hauled groceries long-distance, but he owned his own truck, and, later, three trucks. "Almost a mogul, my father," Peter would say with a pained smile. Peter's mother took in sewing, but it wasn't as though she hunched over an underlit project in a freezing room, wrapped in rags. She'd been the first choice of anyone who wanted a better fit, a copy of a designer dress, the perfect wedding ensemble.

Peter's family enchanted her when she met them. They were a noisy, teasing bunch, so different from Caroline's parents and sisters, who'd been muted except when playing team sports on their lawn—something that she never participated in anyway.

Caroline slipped her key in the door and inched it open. The smell of chocolate greeted her. In Peter's family, food represented everything fun in life, and they shoveled in prodigious amounts. Caroline's family portioned it out as though the supply was finite: here's your half cup of peas and your chicken breast. Two quarters of roasted potato. Sauce was for restaurants, butter available only in pats, cake in the house meant a birthday or wedding.

She followed the sound of Savannah singing, finding her daughter and husband in the kitchen smearing frosting on a platter of brownies. Gilding the proverbial lily. Didn't the brownies taste sweet and rich enough already?

Caroline didn't want to be the bad cop in the house—the "*No, no, no*" parent, instituting the designated fun-free zone. Peter's enthusiasm tamped her down, as though some mechanism forced couples to balance each other until they reached equilibrium.

"Mommy!" Savannah yelled when she saw Caroline. "Daddy, get me down."

"Here you go, sweets." Peter swung Savannah off the high stool on which she knelt at the kitchen island. Dark chocolate smeared the white counter tiles, the red apron tied around Savannah's waist, and her cheeks.

"We're putting gumdrops on top of the brownies," Savannah said. She threw her arms around Caroline, who tried not to flinch at the vision of chocolate staining her beige trench coat.

"Wow. Sugary." Caroline said.

Savannah stiffened and removed her arms from Caroline's hips, where they'd been tightly circling her mother. Caroline saw her face fall.

"Sounds delicious." She tried to imply that *sugary* had been meant as a compliment and not indicative of Caroline's true reaction: that it sounded disgusting, crunching into tooth-achingly-sweet candies on top of an already overrich brownie.

"You mean it?" Savannah asked. She knit her brows together, making frowning lines in her once-again grave face. Not in the house a minute, and Caroline had managed to flatline her daughter's smile.

"Of course Mommy means it," Peter said. He kissed Caroline's mouth lightly. "Didn't you, Mommy." He gave a surreptitious tweak to the top of Caroline's arm, warning in Peter pinch language, *Don't be a party pooper.*

Caroline tucked the blanket around Savannah just the way the child liked. *Flatten the comforter across the top, tuck it around her feet—stopping to give each set of toes a squeeze—and then tuck, tuck, tuck up one side and down the next.* Much like Caroline, Savannah required routine and repetition.

"I love you, Mommy," Savannah said.

"I love you, honey."

Savannah pressed her lips together. She stared at Caroline with those intense eyes that sometimes spooked Caroline, often made her squirm, and always made her want to keep her from getting hurt.

"Do you love me as much as you love Daddy?" Savannah asked.

"Of course I do." Caroline prayed each day and night to love them better than she did.

"Do you love me more than you love Daddy?"

Caroline worried that she was giving subliminal messages to Savannah. Perhaps Savannah, in the way of children, had a seventh sense that measured true love.

Caroline supposed that adults, if they were willing to let in the truth, could also have that seventh sense.

But did anyone want that sort of knowledge?

Caroline started formulating "I love you differently" answers, but overtiredness made her take the easy route. "I love you and Daddy exactly the same."

"Do you love me as much as you love Grandma?"

Grandma was Caroline's mother. Peter's mother was Nana. Caroline worked to keep her impatience in check. "Yes, I do."

Savannah squinted, looking like the teenager she would be, the one who'd measure Caroline for a suit of disgrace. "Okay," she said finally.

Okay. A strange little word from her strange little visitor from some other planet. Caroline's heart splintered in convoluted love. She leaned in close and planted three kisses on her daughter: one on the forehead, one on the right cheek, and then one on the left, just as Savannah liked.

Caroline vowed again to wrench herself off the hamster wheel of worrying about her thoughts and leave behind her wishes for impossible and awful things.

She entered the bedroom.

Peter lay in bed wearing his sex smile.

She calculated how long it had been, wondering if she could claim headache or jet lag or plane backache.

Two weeks.

She'd always been fast at math.

"I missed you, honey," he said. "Really missed you."

He emphasized his words, so she couldn't miss his meaning. Caroline controlled her inner groan. When they'd been in the earliest stages, when their love glittered and twittered around their heads like Disney bluebirds, she'd adored their shorthand. Their secret Peter-Caroline language had been romantic. Code words for "Let's make love" had given Caroline shivers of anticipation.

Now, most times, she felt a shudder of dread.

"Just let me shower," she said. Maybe he'd be asleep when she came out.

"You don't need to shower," he said.

"Trust me, after all those hours traveling, I do."

He made pleading eyes.

Her stomach turned.

"I'll be right out." She didn't look back as she went into the bathroom, afraid the sight of his hot desire would make her even less excited.

She opened the medicine cabinet for aspirin—she really did have a headache—and saw the bottles and tubes promising beauty. All that pristine purple and black packaging, unopened.

Peter sometimes asked what happened with the trip to prettyland. He'd found her irresistible the afternoon she'd come back from juliette&gwynne—even called Nanny Rose to come out, offering triple overtime, so he could take Caroline to a fancy dinner.

Where she'd had nothing to say, because nothing running through her brain could be spoken.

First Peter had filled the empty air by droning about work. Then he engaged Caroline in conversation about Savannah. What did Caroline think about the school where their daughter would attend kindergarten in September? Had Caroline thought about it? Should they enroll Savannah in private school? Had they made a mistake not putting her in preschool? They should probably send her to summer camp, right? What kind did Caroline think would be best?

Caroline pushed the top of the childproof cap on the aspirin bottle.

Sometimes when Caroline couldn't fall asleep, unbidden fantasies—nightmares, she reminded herself—floated up from her subconscious.

Train wrecks.

Car accidents.

Plane crashes.

Peter and Savannah were passengers.

Of course, it was never painful, and there were never flames, just an instant snuffing out of the body and then a quick ascension to heaven.

And Caroline would be alone.

After those thoughts, she couldn't stand herself.

Those horrible things she said to Jonah Weber hadn't come from nowhere.

She swallowed two aspirin tablets, grateful for the bitter taste. She needed punishment.

On the top shelf, far out of Savannah's reach, were her emergency bottles. Ambien. Xanax. She took them down and counted the number of pills left in each.

Five Ambien.

Three Xanax.

As she'd counted the days since she and Peter last had sex, she counted how long since she'd taken a pill.

A week. Okay, she could have one. Which one?

If she took the Ambien, she'd barely make it through lovemaking.

Her indifference—bordering on distaste—for lovemaking was worsening. In the beginning, when they'd first adopted Savannah, she'd attributed it to exhaustion. But now Savannah was five. Caroline no longer woke up in the middle of the night for her daughter, so she couldn't blame her feelings on exhaustion, but her desire to push Peter off her when he touched her had become greater—at times so bad that she resorted to using a blanket of drugs to muffle her aversion during sex.

She nibbled off half a Xanax as carefully as possible. It was difficult with the tiny pills, but she had to make them last.

CHAPTER 15

Caroline

The Xanax kicked in as Peter worked his way from Caroline's lips to her neck. Making love could now move ahead, with her body participating while her mind drifted.

Caroline made soft sounds of pleasure, trying to convey excitement that would hurry him over the edge.

"Now," she murmured.

She wondered if whispering dirty words would hasten the act. Thinking about it, her throat closed up as though she'd been inhaling dust.

Caroline had never been the dirty words sort.

Peter tightened his grip on her.

She'd once found him electrifying.

His breath warmed her neck.

Back then, she'd barely been able to survive two days without making love.

He tensed.

She squeezed her eyes against tears.

The following Sunday, Caroline and Savannah studied three dresses laid out on Savannah's bed, the top fashion choices for Easter dinner at Peter's parents. Savannah deliberated over the dresses with the air of a discriminating style expert. She fingered the taffeta hem of one, placed her pink patent-leather shoes next to another, and then held the last one up to her shoulders and examined her image in the mirror.

"Do you like this one, Mommy?"

Caroline examined it with a serious expression. "Red looks good on you." It did, heightening the drama of Savannah's dark hair and eyes.

"Do I look fat?" Savannah asked.

Dear Lord, the child was five. Where in the world had that come from?

"Savannah, honey, of course not. How could you look fat? You're perfect." Caroline thought of the anorexic preteens and teens whose case histories she read, some as young as eight.

Savannah stroked the red satin sash of her favorite dress. "Janine said I was the kind who blows right up." She sent a laser beam look at Caroline. "That means fat, right?"

Who in the world was Janine?

"Right, Mommy? Didn't she mean I'm fat?"

Ah, it came to her: Nanny Rose's niece. "Sweetie, you don't need to worry about that." Caroline jotted a mental note to ban Janine from the house.

"Am I?" Savannah demanded to know.

Pat answers never satisfied Savannah. When something confused her, she chipped away until Caroline provided a complete explanation.

Caroline took Savannah's hand and led her to the bed. She gathered the sturdy child into her lap and hugged her tight. "You're perfect. Strong." Caroline squeezed Savannah's upper arm. "Feel that muscle!"

"Nanny Rose says I'm meaty. Is that good?" Savannah scrunched her face. "It sounds like soup. Like I'm fat soup."

Inconveniently smart fat soup. It was time for a long talk with Nanny.

"Strong is wonderful."

"Is meaty wonderful?"

"Sure, it's like a muscle, which is always good." Trying to prove her point, Caroline made the biggest muscle she could, flexing her arm until her tendons popped. "See. This is something I'm proud of."

Savannah seemed unconvinced by the demonstration. The child took Caroline's hand and brought it to Caroline's wrist. "Make a circle," she said.

Caroline hesitated.

"Please, Mommy."

Caroline made a bracelet with her fingers.

Savannah circled her own wrist with her own fingers. "Mine don't meet. Nanny said they have to meet to be pretty."

"I doubt she said that, Savannah." Caroline shouldn't have let Nanny nag her into ordering all those fashion magazines. Nanny and Savannah spent hours poring over them. Caroline had thought it cute how they made paper dolls from the magazines, combining arts and crafts with make-believe. Even teaching Savannah a form of recycling. How very politically correct of Caroline and Nanny Rose.

Apparently, what they'd been doing was quietly destroying her daughter's confidence.

"You are beautiful." Perhaps what she should be saying was how little beauty mattered. Right. Except it was a lie in this world, and Savannah was too smart to buy it. Even at five, she'd immediately think that Caroline was declaring her not-beautiful.

Caroline knelt before Savannah. She put her hands on the girl's sturdy shoulders. "You're a great, smart, and beautiful kid, and I love you."

Three blocks from Peter's parents' house, Caroline began wishing they were going anyplace else. A movie. The park. Even the zoo, and Caroline despised zoos.

Savannah slept in the backseat with her favorite stuffed dog, Pudding, clutched in her arms. Peter concentrated on the Red Sox game playing on the radio. He loved the Red Sox. Yet another zealous pastime pouring from Peter in torrential storms. Go Red Sox go! Must have Big Mac now! Let's go to Europe next week!

What was this paradigm of love, where what first attracts later repels?

Perhaps Caroline was too young when they got together, still recovering from life as the hidden middle sister; the afterthought whose absence people noticed only when they saw her empty chair. She'd be curled up in bed reading, having missed the gentle tinkle of the bell her mother rang for meals.

Peter pulled their car next to the others parked on the edge of the front lawn, which sloped right down to the street. This part of Chelmsford had no sidewalks, despite the houses' proximity to each other. Cars overfilled the Fitzgerald driveway. Peter sat still for a moment, hand paused on the radio dial, as he caught the last play of something. She leaned back and gulped her last shot of peace.

Treasures of the past filled the Fitzgerald home. Pictures of the Fitzgerald children in every possible costume—graduation robes, Little League jerseys, navy uniforms—lined the walls. Smaller pictures of grandchildren crowded next to oversized wedding photos.

Peter's sisters bustled in the kitchen with Mrs. Fitzgerald. Her mother-in-law spotted them the moment that Caroline walked in, as the kitchen was a straight shot down from the front door.

"Caroline! Send in Savannah," called Faith, Peter's youngest sibling. "We're coloring eggs. Mom bought Disney thingies."

The baby of the family, ten years younger than Peter, Faith displayed the confidence of knowing there was always someone around to carry you.

Savannah sidled next to Caroline. "Come with me."

"Sure, honey. Let's take off your coat."

Savannah tugged her blue wool coat tighter around her. "No. I want to wear it."

"Savannah, you can't dye eggs in your coat."

"Why not?"

"What's wrong?" Irene Fitzgerald came out wiping her hands on her bright holiday-themed apron. Yellow chicks circled the green grass printed on a bright blue background. Caroline had no idea where her mother-in-law found the fabric to make these things. Was there some special store? A website called bestmomsintheworld.com?

"Everything's fine, Irene." The name stuck in her throat. Peter reminded her time after time how much his mother would love Caroline to call her Mom, and why did she have to make such a big deal of it? "Because she's not my mother," Caroline would answer each time, embarrassed by her immaturity, even intractability, yet unwilling to move one step closer to absorption by the Fitzgerald clan.

"I want to wear my coat." Savannah, usually the most obedient child in the world, when thwarted on something she deemed life or death, planted herself like a redwood.

"What's the problem?" Irene asked. "Let her wear it. She'll take it off when she gets warm enough."

"I don't think it's a good idea to be dyeing eggs in her new coat." Caroline forced out a smile that would never reach her eyes.

"Don't be such a worrywart, Caro." Irene was the only one who presumed to use Peter's pet name for Caroline. "She can wear an apron."

"I want to wear an apron, Mommy."

"How about one with hearts?" Irene asked. "I've been saving it for someone special."

Caroline couldn't explain to Peter's mother why she wanted Savannah to take off her coat. She didn't want Irene commenting to the crowd about it—Savannah stood out enough already. The Fitzgerald nieces and nephews ranged from skeletal to skinny. Among the fourteen of them, with their fourteen shades of blond and red hair, most, Caroline guessed, landed smack in the 90th percentile for height and the 10th percentile for weight.

Caroline had to deal with Nanny and rid Savannah of the idea of normal and of beauty engendered by women's magazines. She'd call her tonight, though she dreaded the conversation. Every time she took Nanny to task for something, the woman would act out somewhere else. Caroline would have found another nanny long ago, but as Peter pointed out, Nanny Rose genuinely cared for Savannah, and that quality meant more than almost anything else.

On the other hand, forcing poor Savannah out of her coat would hardly encourage good self-image. What a stupid idea, and yet Caroline wanted to tear the blue garment off her.

She longed to see the girl running around like her cousins, with her hair spinning out behind her and her shoes scuffed and dirty.

Savannah was such an anxious child.

No, Savannah was a well-behaved and accepting child.

Except occasionally she dug in her heels.

That was a good quality. Did Caroline want a yes-girl?

"Okay, honey." Caroline kissed Savannah on the top of her head. "You can keep your coat on."

Irene put out her hand as though to stop Savannah. "Remember, though, you might get it dirty."

"But you're giving me an apron, Grandma? Right?"

"Nothing stays perfect, Savannah." Irene leaned down and kissed her cheek. "Don't worry, dear. Dirt comes out, right?"

Caroline wondered if they had anything other than beer to drink. She'd thought of bringing a bottle of wine, offering it as a gift, but Caroline's greatest fear when visiting Joe and Irene was of sticking out.

Caroline wandered into the empty living room. Irene's most favored possessions, her crystal and figurines, were locked behind glass in a shelved wall unit that stretched across the entire wall. Joe's mystery books and Irene's volumes of craft magazines tucked in leather binders lined the open shelves.

Caroline knew she should either join Peter playing football outside or join his sisters helping Irene in the kitchen. The grandchildren were scattered throughout the house—at least, those old enough to be out of a parent's arms or eyeshot. But instead she sat on the deep-cushioned couch.

Seasonal Hummels sat on the glossy, dark Colonial coffee table. Irene changed them monthly. Caroline ran her fingers over the little boy painting Easter eggs, the two girls with scarves tied under their chins patting a bunny. Trees and flowers in the unmoving grass held hidden Easter eggs. Grandchildren fought for the privilege of touching the miniature statues, none of them daring to go near them without permission. Even the tiniest child knew not to touch. How did Irene do it? How did she keep all the children—young, middle-aged, babies—in her steady sway?

Caroline picked up a hidden pink egg and rolled it in her palm.

"Better not lose that." Peter's older sister, Sissy walked in. "Unless you want my mother to drum you out of the family."

Caroline opened her hand, so that the egg lay still in her palm. Sissy picked it up with two fingers and returned it to its hiding place.

"Why all alone? Too good for us?" Sissy delivered her dig with a big smile, lifting her freckled cheeks toward her bright blue eyes. She pulled her hair back into a ponytail and then released it back to its natural curly state.

"Just tired," Caroline said.

"So you thought you'd come play with the Hummels?"

"I'm admiring them." Caroline patted the egg-painting boy's miniature head with her index finger.

"Right." Sissy snorted. She couldn't stand Caroline. Peter denied it, but Caroline knew it was true. On the other hand, Faith was Caroline's champion. Faith admired Caroline for being a doctor, for speaking three languages, and for what she thought of as Caroline's elegant lifestyle, all of which drove Sissy crazy.

"Your mother has quite a collection," Caroline said.

"Who do you think you're kidding? Look at your house. Mom's house is probably a joke to you. Bad taste, circa 1985."

"I don't think that. I think your mother's house is lovely."

Caroline spoke the truth. In 1985 Irene went on a Laura Ashley kick, and things had stayed in flowered-English-cottage mode since that time. It might not be exactly her taste, but she found the place warm, preferring it to the cold white McMansion in which she and Peter lived.

Sissy looked around, as though trying to see her mother's house through Caroline's eyes. "Come on, compared to your house?" She took the springtime display statue from Caroline's hands. "You're such a liar."

CHAPTER 16

Tia

"Wake up, David." Tia pushed at his arm, and then poked him when he didn't respond. Her hangover was minor, thankfully, but it still made her want to shove him out of her bed so she could be alone with her headache and queasy stomach. She was three weeks into a relationship with a man she didn't even think she liked.

Tia hadn't ever slept around. After losing her virginity to Kevin, she'd closed up shop for so long the boys taunted her by calling her the Ice Queen. What was this?

"Go 'way," David said into the pillow.

"Gotta go to work," she said.

"No. Going in late," he mumbled from under the covers.

"Not you, me."

"Bye." He snaked a hand from under the covers and gave a limp wave.

Tia wished she could blink her eyes and make him disappear. Or wiggle her nose. Or dive out the window.

"I have a cup of coffee for you," she said. "Come on, I have to leave in five minutes. You have to go."

"Leave me a key." He sounded awake now, and trying to sleaze a key. "I'll lock up," he said. "Don't want you to be late."

Tia stared at the empty glasses on the nightstand. One stained brown with whiskey, one red from the cranberry juice in a Cape Codder. His spring drink, he'd said. Perhaps the mark of an alcoholic was having seasonal drinks. Maybe her father switched to eggnog laced with rum every Christmas.

She'd never have brought David home if she hadn't gone to Doyle's.

Way to be easy on herself. Perhaps she'd never have gone to Doyle's if she hadn't been seeking a David.

Dear God, why did she ever let him in her bed? Becoming imprinted on a man was too easy. Sleep with one damned man in five years, boom, you're marked. Being wanted, even by the worst of them, opened the door to that awful gratitude brought on merely by the knowledge of that desire. Couple that with the simple pleasure of a warm body and having someone who'd know if you died in the night, and *zap*, you could end up married to anyone.

Tia poked him with her big toe. Then she did it again, and then she did it harder.

"Jesus, what's wrong with you?" He whipped off the sheet and sprang out of bed.

"Good. You're up." Tia handed him the coffee, now lukewarm. "Drink up."

Tia's desk at work mirrored what her life had become: messy, unkempt, and requiring more energy than she could muster. She used to pride herself on her orderly work spaces, her lovely apartment, the treasures she uncovered at flea markets and yard sales. Tiny glass stars. Copper candlesticks. Hand-quilted pillows.

"What's wrong?" Katie asked. "You look tired."

"I got to sleep late last night." Tia made a kind of plan. She'd sort all the crap into two piles—files and loose papers—and organize them after her meeting with Mrs. Graham.

Katie raised her eyebrows. "Anything good?"

"Nothing even remotely exciting. Just insomnia."

"What's happening with David?"

Tia regretted ever letting him drive her to work. Katie had sauntered down the street just as David dropped her off, leaving Tia no choice but to make introductions.

"He's just a friend."

"Friend with benefits?"

"Just a friend." Tia gathered her notebook and Mrs. Graham's file.

Tia slipped a piece of candied ginger from her purse, attempting to quell her nausea for the third time that morning.

She had to get rid of David. Now. Find someone normal.

Sometimes it seemed that Nathan had slurped up her entire life, and she couldn't refill the cup. After lovemaking, they'd talked for hours. Nathan's stories of his parents' escape from Hungary opened up a world that made history books pop into three dimensions, making her think about possibilities she'd never known she could have. Childhood dreams flooded back.

"This will sound insane," she'd once told him, "but as a kid, I wanted to—don't laugh—grow up to be someone like Elizabeth Blackwell. I mean, not that I could be the first female doctor, but something meaningful. Someone who could change people's lives."

Nathan hadn't made a joke out of it, he'd said, "It's hardly too late."

"Actually, I think it's kinda late to be the first anything," she said.

"It's not about the *when*, it's the *if*." He'd lain beside her with his hands behind his head, staring at the map of Paris hanging opposite them." Why Paris?" he asked.

She swung a leg over his. "I think it's pretty."

He shook his head in gentle disagreement. "That's not true. People choose maps for a reason. Do you want to go there?"

She'd never told him flying terrified her. There were already too many ways in which she was the weak one in the relationship. Waving Paris away with her hand, she tried to make her dreams seem unimportant. "There are many places I'd like to visit. But I don't know how I'll ever get to them."

He rolled over and pulled her until they were face-to-face. "You can do anything. You're a capable, smart woman. But, and this is a big but, you have to start rooting for yourself."

That hadn't been the advice she'd wanted. What she'd wanted was a great big hand lifting her out of herself.

Tia grabbed her tote bag and stuffed in Mrs. Graham's folder. She shuffled the paper and files on her desk into neater stacks, even digging out her to-do list and placing it on top. After Mrs. Graham, she'd really dig in. "Don't worry," she said to Katie, "I'll let you know when to look for a wedding outfit."

Katie grinned as though already planning what she'd wear to Tia's wedding.

Tia sometimes wondered if she had even the slightest grasp on the realities of her relationships. Was it possible that Katie really liked her?

Smiling wider than usual, Tia turned back and waved as she walked out the door.

Mrs. Graham waited patiently on the bench. Tia gave up trying to beat her to their appointments long ago, after she'd realized that Mrs. Graham had no place to go but medical appointments and Lost Hope. Arriving early allowed Mrs. Graham extra time to feel a part of the world.

"Morning, Mrs. G." Tia slung her bag over her shoulder and gave Mrs. Graham a pat on the arm before inserting a key into the client-office lock. "Marjorie," she whispered.

"Another one died yesterday." Mrs. Graham followed Tia in and plunked down her purse.

"Oh, I'm sorry. Who?" Like all her clients, Mrs. G started the day by reading the obituaries, though it wasn't as fruitful a search these days. She had more dead friends than living ones. Poor Mrs. G hardly had anyone to search for anymore.

"Alma Kelleher." Mrs. G sighed out her sadness. "We went to Saint Clare's High School together. Alma was the prettiest thing you ever saw."

"I'm sorry. That's so sad." Tia paused as Mrs. Graham settled herself in the easy chair across from Tia's aging wingback, "So, how are you today?"

"Not so good."

"What's wrong?" Tia wondered if she could disengage from David without drama, without even talking. Were they already too involved for an email breakup? Or, even better, could she simply ignore his calls and emails and text messages, and all the other ways he'd thrust himself into her life?

"Sam. I can barely get him to move around so I can . . . wash him properly."

Tia refocused on Mrs. G and scratched "Help w/Sam—nurse" on her pad. "We need to talk about help for your husband. It's important."

"If you people really wanted to help, you'd get me a cleaning woman. How's a person supposed to keep up with all this?"

"All what? Tell me." Tia peered at Mrs. Graham. Clients in crisis looked disheveled, often unbathed. Mrs. G wore the same blue-red lipstick as always, her hair was combed into the usual stiff grey helmet of curls, and her lavender cardigan looked clean and wrinkle free.

"The dishes, the washing, the floors—oh, trust me, my dear, old age is no cure for housework." Mrs. Graham pulled her purse closer to her, stroking the brown leather like a pet.

"I'm sorry, Mrs. G." Tia leaned forward and again patted Mrs. Graham's veined hand. She wished she could hug her, whisk her off on a cruise staffed with men and women willing to treat her like a queen. "We can't get cleaning people for you, but that would be the point of assisted living. You wouldn't have to do everything *and* take care of Sam. He'd be bathed and . . ."

Tia searched for ways to reference Sam's accidents—his growing dependence on Mrs. Graham for his toileting needs—without offending her client.

". . . and made comfortable in every way."

"Why does everyone jump to the conclusion that Sam and I should be put away? Why not shoot us? Push us out on an ice floe?"

Tia moved her chair closer, hating how agitated she'd made the poor woman. It wasn't like Mrs. G to get so testy. Her mother had been right. Tia should watch her mouth. She shot off too quick.

"Believe me, I didn't mean to imply that you're incapable." Mrs. Graham needed admiration, not manhandling; complaining was her right. "In fact, you're doing a spectacular job. You put most of the people I work with to shame."

She praised Mrs. G for a few more moments, eager to finish their hour with positive reinforcement, and her client did seem mollified when Tia gently squeezed her shoulder in place of a good-bye handshake.

At four in the afternoon, after three more appointments, a meeting with the Department of Children and Families, a visit to a client in a rehab, and a home visit, Tia was ready to steal an hour and leave early. She jammed the last of her folders and papers into her bottom drawer, shoving a bit to get it closed so Katie wouldn't comment about Tia's sloppy desk again.

"Oh, Tia, do you need some help? Your desk is just a mess." That's what Katie said the other day.

"Then don't look!" Tia had wanted to say when Katie complained, but she was too embarrassed—her desk did look awful. Tia couldn't defend the indefensible jumble.

Tia marched down Washington Street to Doyle's. "Coffee with," she told the bartender, the flat-faced one who barely acknowledged her existence. She didn't care. He knew what she drank, and he poured with a heavy hand.

The initial swallow hit fine. First it warmed her throat, then her heart, and then her stomach.

After the second one, the picture in her mind of sad Mrs. Graham and all the rest of her clients receded just enough that Tia could breathe freely.

David slipped onto the stool next to her.

"How about some company?" he asked.

Tia examined David. His face held no hint of worry. Soon he'd drink, and then he'd hold forth on the evils of sales tax, or the long-range considerations of the euro, to which apparently only he was privy.

He leaned in to kiss her, which she accepted.

"Take me home?" she asked.

He touched her glass. "Mind if I finish this before we go?"

Tia smiled, ready to accept David as her due. She waved her arm, as though bestowing her favors on him. "Be my guest."

He drained her glass and then ran his hand down her back. "Exactly what I have planned."

In her numbed state, Tia could barely feel his hand, and at the moment, she found that level of sensitivity pretty near perfect.

CHAPTER 17

Tia

"Tia, we have a situation."

Not today, please. How she hated the mornings when Richard popped his head in to complain about something or other before she'd even taken off her jacket. She hadn't even drunk her coffee yet. Her head pounded from drinking with David last night.

"Are you listening?" Richard asked.

"I heard you. I heard you. We have a situation." Did he think they worked at NASA? She pulled the lid off her coffee and took a desperate, hot gulp.

"We have a real problem."

"Okay." She shrugged an arm out of her jacket. "Got it. We have a real problem."

"Leave your coat on. We have to go."

"Go? Go where?" Tia tried to put the cover back on her coffee as she followed Richard out the door to the small hallway and then down the stairs.

"To your client's house."

Coffee splashed on her shirt. She tried to wipe it away while holding her cup and at the same time raised her right shoulder to keep her bag from slipping down.

"Who?" she asked Richard's back. Dog hair covered his tweed sports coat.

"A Mrs. Graham."

A gust of warm wind hit them when Richard opened the door to the parking lot. Tia stopped. "We're going to Mrs. Graham's house?"

"Let's go, let's go. The police are waiting."

"The police are waiting?"

Richard turned to face her, his impatient expression emphasized by the deep red he turned whenever he became anxious or angry. "Could you please stop repeating everything I say and get in the damned car?"

Mrs. Graham tugged her sweater closer. Tia wanted to touch her, give her comfort, but two police officers stood by sternly.

She'd never seen Mrs. Graham without lipstick or when she wasn't wearing clothes that were pressed and perfect. The pilled brown cardigan enveloping her looked as though she'd taken it from Sam's side of the dresser.

"Oh, Mrs. G, are you all right?" Tia asked. "Do you need anything?"

Mrs. Graham looked up with an angry frown. She pressed her lips together and shook her head. The boulder in Tia's chest became heavier. Debris covered the rug: baskets of laundry, newspapers, cloths with stains of indeterminate origin, unopened mail, and in the midst of it all, an ironing board with an iron set up like a soldier at the ready.

"A glass of water?" Tia needed to offer something.

"That's not possible, ma'am." The young policewoman's words were without inflection. "Evidence isn't finished in there."

Stacks of dirty plates teetered on the coffee table. Smears of what looked to be spinach—creamed spinach, perhaps—covered the top one.

Mrs. Graham had been accused of attempted murder. That's what Richard told Tia on the ride over. She supposedly fed her husband food laced with pills, and then panicked and called 911.

Tia fumbled at the catch on her bag and rummaged until she found a roll of Life Savers. "Want one?" she asked in Mrs. G's direction, not sure whether to include the policewoman in the offer.

"Why didn't you answer when I called?" Mrs. G's face crumpled with despair.

"I . . ." Tia's voice faded. Oh, Jesus, she must have called after Tia left. Would things have been okay if she'd stayed till five? If she'd returned the call, could she have prevented Mrs. Graham from crushing those pills?

"There was no one else, Tia." Mrs. G held out her hands, palms up, imploring Tia to help. "I needed you."

"Mrs. G, I'm—" Tia stopped when Richard dug his fingers into her shoulder. She slipped the candy back in her handbag.

"There are legal issues here," he muttered into her ear.

"Why are we here if I can't speak?" Tia asked.

"She asked for you. Said she had no other living relative. The police called. I thought we better check it out."

"I'm not her relative."

"She probably meant no other connection. I'll explain to them."

"If you'd called, everything would have been okay." Mrs. Graham fussed at a hole in her sweater.

Tia remained mute, grateful that Richard had forbidden her to talk, choking on waves of Mrs. Graham's grief and blame.

"Can I wash my hands?" Mrs. Graham asked the policewoman on her right.

"Sorry, ma'am, no."

"But they're dirty, so dirty," Mrs. Graham told the officer on her left.

"It won't be long," he said.

"Tia, don't you have a wet nap or something you can give me?"

Tia opened her bag again, frantic for some way to offer comfort. The policewoman held up a broad hand. "Ma'am, please don't."

"Why are we here, Richard?" Tia whispered.

"They need information," he said.

"Sam, he had an accident. I needed to clean him. Please," Mrs.

Graham said, "please, let me clean my hands." Soft sobs replaced her pleas.

Tia dug her fingers into her forearms. "I need to use the bathroom." She stood, waiting to be stopped.

"You'll have to go down the street. There's a coffee shop." The policewoman pointed as though the living room wall were invisible.

Tia ran out before Richard could stop her, before Mrs. Graham could speak again, but her words followed Tia down the hall.

"It wasn't my fault, right?" Mrs. Graham's thin voice pierced Tia. "What could I do? Let a stranger clean him? Sam wouldn't like that. Sam is proud, just about the proudest man in America."

Tia squeezed her eyes shut for a moment, then turned and walked back, stopping at the doorway so she could bear witness as Mrs. Graham spoke.

Seeing Tia return, Mrs. Graham sat straighter. Her watery blue eyes locked on Tia's. "He managed fifty people at John Hancock. Fifty. Everyone looked up to Sam. I don't care what any of you say. He always knew what was happening; he knew it was me feeding him, cleaning him."

"You did a good job." Tia said.

Richard glared at her.

"He knew when people came into the house," Mrs. Graham said. "I couldn't shame him, letting people see him like that."

"You showed him love every day. He knew that." Tears ran down Tia's face. "I'm sorry I didn't call."

Tia walked away. She stopped at the kitchen entrance, seeing where Sam had lain before they took him out. An empty bottle of pills was next to the half-eaten bowl of applesauce into which Mrs. Graham had supposedly crushed tablet after tablet of Ativan tranquilizers.

The medication Tia had persuaded Mrs. G to request from her doctor.

Richard exploded the moment he slammed the car door shut. "What the hell, Tia? When was the last time you made a home visit?"

"Maybe he'll live," Tia said. "How much could she have gotten him to swallow?"

"Live, die, either way we're fucked. When did you last go into that home?"

"Home visits weren't mandated in her case." Tia threw her head against the headrest and then immediately changed her position. Everything smelled like Richard's dog. "She liked coming to the office. It got her out of the house. She'd come when Sam napped."

"Yeah, I can imagine how she got him to take those naps."

"She loved him."

"She tried to kill him."

"She did it for him."

"She did it on our watch." Richard started the engine. "Your watch."

"She didn't want me to come to the house."

"Wasn't that a fucking clue?" He pounded the dashboard. "Do you know how this will read in the *Globe?*"

"There was absolutely no hint of abuse in the home. None," Tia insisted.

"Really?" He pulled out into traffic. "Did you see that house? How could you let her live like that?"

"It's not your fault." Bobby slid closer to Tia on the stone wall lining Day Boulevard. The ocean appeared calm under the inky night sky. He put an arm around her shoulders and hugged her close.

"Of course it's my fault." Tia reached for Bobby's hand. "I should have seen it."

"You said it yourself, she always looked perfect. And home visits weren't mandated."

"Mandated and the right thing aren't the same."

Tia wished she had one of the six-packs they used to bring here when they were kids. She'd asked Bobby to bring her here because she couldn't face the crowd at Fianna's. She couldn't take any jokes tonight. He'd taken her to eat in a faceless diner in Dorchester, and then they'd driven here.

"I should have gone to her house," she said.

"You couldn't know. She worked hard to hide it."

She leaned against him. "I should have seen through her denial." His shoulder felt durable enough to be unbreakable. She slid her hand into his. She needed a friend.

Tia walked to work every day following the incident at Mrs. Graham's house. No more Doyle's. No more drinking. No more sleeping with David. She'd ended that with a sober face-to-face.

Tia had seen Bobby three times that week, each encounter chaste and pure. Twice they went out for dinner, once they went to the movies, and each time Bobby reassured her. Nothing was grey in Bobby's world. You were right or wrong. Memories of awful choices didn't complicate his moral compass.

She longed to walk around with that sort of righteousness. Sam would live, but confusion as to whether that was good or bad complicated Tia's reaction. Certainly, for her, for the agency, it was good. Somehow, the newspapers hadn't written about the tragedy that almost occurred.

Who was she kidding? The tragedy had damn well happened, and she hadn't helped. What would happen to Mrs. G now? To Sam?

Bobby kept telling her to go easy on herself. She'd been Mrs. G's friend, right? Hadn't Tia been the one Mrs. G asked for? How could Tia save people when the entire system was so awful? He kept reminding her that Mrs. G had declined her help. Tia couldn't do it alone, right?

His talk soothed her, but she knew better. She'd messed up. Maybe she'd obeyed the letter of the law, but she'd been lax in not probing deeper with her client.

Tia pulled out her iPod and tried to follow Bobby's advice by walking faster and faster. *Fresh air! Exercise! Endorphins! Don't blame yourself!*

She sped up again, walking so quickly that she reached the coffee shop by work in half her usual time. The line at Fazenda Cafe didn't seem as daunting as usual. Without headaches and hangovers, things almost flowed.

Now if she could only find a way to find Bobby as exciting as she did comforting. She wanted the grain of his skin, the tone of his voice, and the texture of his hair between her fingers to electrify her like Nathan's had.

She pushed away her obsessive Nathan thoughts, using a visualization technique Bobby had shared, though he hadn't known she'd use it for this purpose. Nathan became a massive rock that she pushed off a cliff.

Adios, Nathan.

"Two blueberry scones," Tia said to the kid behind the counter when her turn came. "And a corn muffin." Richard liked muffins; she and Katie were scone addicts. Tia would bring treats for all of them.

Act positive, you'll be positive.

And she'd find a way to visit Mrs. Graham at Suffolk County Jail. Richard kept saying no—he wanted to consult with their agency counsel first, but everything moved so slowly, she feared both Grahams would be dead before she could visit.

Richard and Katie were waiting for her when she walked into the office. Too bad. She'd wanted to surprise them by leaving the pastries on their desks.

She wasn't even late. Why where they posed like that? They looked like cops, standing in front of her desk with their arms crossed.

"What's up?" Tia held her purse tight to her chest. "Did Sam die?"

Shamefully, she prayed the old man would live, so she could escape with her hands a little cleaner, when in truth, death was his better option.

"Good morning." Richard gave Tia a look that felt like a slap. "Question: anything slip your mind lately?"

Katie looked at her like she had mud smeared on her face. Had they found out about some reports she hadn't filed?

"What are you talking about?" She inched toward her desk. Katie blocked her. Richard held a file folder.

"What's going on?" Tia asked.

"We found out." Katie jutted out her chin. "There's no more hiding it."

"Found out what?"

"Do you realize what this will cost us?" Richard smacked his folder against her desk.

Her desk looked wrong. Everything on top was messed up differently than it usually was. Odd piles lined up across the edge.

"How could you?" Katie shook her head, as though mourning Tia. "Our clients, they're the ones who'll suffer, you know."

"I haven't got a clue what you're talking about."

If only that were true. The anxiety that Tia had been pushing away for weeks bloomed full in her belly. *Pop.* In an instant, she had a stomach full of acid.

The Walker grant.

Richard peered at her. "Ah, you remember. The fact that you may have put us out of business finally dawns."

How late was she? Tia had been pushing the Walker grant out of her mind for so many weeks that the deadline had become too fuzzy to recall.

"How could you, Tia?" Katie's eyes were red and swollen. "Do you know what you've done to us?"

The coffee began leaking; she felt wet heat in her hand, but with Katie and Richard blocking her desk, she couldn't put it down. With the bag threatening to fall apart in her hands, she held it out to them. "I brought us coffee. Scones. A muffin for you, Richard."

"This isn't the time to joke around." He massaged his forehead with the palm of his hand. "It's serious."

"I just thought you'd like a muffin." Tia's hands shook.

"We'll be lucky if we have desks to eat at when this is through. The Walker money is sixty percent of our budget!" Richard's voice rose. "*Sixty percent!*"

Tia bit her lip against asking him when he'd last supervised anything in the agency. "I'm sure it will be okay. People are late with grants all the time, right?"

"Not two months late!" Katie said. "They called yesterday, before you got here, because they wanted to know if we were still in business. They're reallocating our money and want to earmark it for another agency in JP."

Daphne Morrow probably called. Daphne should have known better than to talk to someone other than Tia. Maybe Tia should call Daphne's supervisor and spill her guts about what a pain it was to work with Daphne.

"You're not getting it," Richard said. "We may not be able to get those funds back."

"The Walker Foundation is enraged." Katie said. "You made us seem very disrespectful of them."

"They said they repeatedly tried to get in touch. That you ignored their emails." Richard leaned too close. "Did you think you deleted them? Don't you know they're still on your computer?"

They'd rummaged through her computer. Jesus. They'd been looking for a way to get rid of her. Richard couldn't do it based on Mrs. Graham, not when he'd barely supervised her since he'd hired Tia.

The coffee bag was going to break. Finally, not knowing what else to do, feeling foolish, she grabbed a newspaper from the wastepaper basket, placed it on a file cabinet by the door, and rested the bag on the improvised mat.

"Just tell me what to do. I'm sorry, okay? This was a mistake. I mixed up the dates."

"No you didn't," Katie said. "I saw it written in your desk calendar. You knew."

"You looked through my stuff?"

"I told her to," Richard said.

"You told her to snoop around my things?"

"They aren't your things. They belong to the agency. I asked Katie. I needed the truth," he said.

"You could have asked me."

"Like I said." He waited a beat. "I wanted the truth."

"I found it all," Katie said. "The reports you never did. The home visits. You didn't fill out any forms. No wonder Mrs. Graham—"

Richard put out a hand to stop Katie. "This is all in the formal letter from the board." He took an envelope from his breast pocket and handed it to Tia. "Sorry, Tia. You gave me no choice. You're fired."

CHAPTER 18

Juliette

Juliette thought she couldn't imagine a life without Nathan, but these past two weeks had given her a taste of what it would be like. She and Nathan fell asleep as far apart as two people could while sleeping in the same bed. Then in their sleep they'd become one again. She'd wake to find herself leaning against him, the two of them making a pool of warmth, his back, his rump, comforting her. She'd rise up from the depth, and they'd turn as one, and he'd curve to her, and for a moment, they danced their usual night ballet. Then she'd remember, and she'd throw off his arm and move to the outer tundra of the mattress.

He swore he hadn't known about the child, but he knew something. What? Judging in a vacuum of silence was impossible. He wouldn't talk; she didn't push. She retreated into a fog of pretence, giving him time and air, grasping for ways to hold on to the brittle illusion that things wouldn't change.

Juliette was happy to be going to work this Saturday, a day she usually hated leaving the house. She flew through her last-minute chores. Loaded the dishwasher. Sorted the teetering pile of mail on her desk. Brushed on one more coat of lip stain.

She welcomed the chance to leave the house. To leave Nathan's brooding; his promises that he'd talk soon. Footsteps banged down the stairs as she hung up the pile of raincoats and sweatshirts that had been flung over the banister.

"Where are we going this summer?" Max carried a rolled-up comic book. Lucas came up behind his brother. Lately they followed her like nervous toddlers.

Before answering, Juliette stuffed one last thing into her already overloaded bag: the latest issue of *Allure*, which touted juliette&gwynne's all-natural mascara as an editor's choice. Of course, the issue would have been delivered to the shop, actually three of them, but they usually lost at least two to overentitled customers who ripped out pages or even stole entire issues. Juliette's copy was pristine and suitable for framing.

The mention in *Allure* would bring an avalanche of orders. Juliette should be flying high.

"April is barely over, and you're worrying about summer?" Juliette tugged at the bag's zipper. Each season, she bought a bigger bag, and then it became too small.

"Look at it another way," Lucas said. "Summer is only two months from now. Dad would call it an example of the theory of relativity."

"So are we going to Rhinebeck?" Max's pajamas were too short in the arms. Juliette put buying new ones on her mental list.

"Guys, can we talk about this later? Are we having some sort of summer planning emergency? We always go to Rhinebeck."

She and Gwynne alternated Saturdays in the shop, except during bridal and holiday season, when they both went in. Maybe she'd take the next few Saturdays for Gwynne.

"Is Dad coming?" Lucas tried to sound casual, but she could hear the strain. Fear, even. Why not? Nathan and Juliette passed each other in the hall like frosty college roommates putting up with each other until school let out. How could the boys not notice the tension?

"Look, I promise that we'll talk about summer tonight, about when we'll go to Rhinebeck, summer jobs, camp, the whole thing, okay? But later. I have to open the shop before women line the street."

"Sure," Lucas said. "Better go, Mom. Wrinkle emergency!"

"Dry skin alert!" Max jumped up and waved his hands as if alerting rescue personnel. Lucas picked up the theme. "Pimple crisis in Wellesley—news at eleven."

Their jokes sounded forced, as though her sons needed to prove that everything was okay: see, we can make fun of mom, just like usual! Juliette's throat thickened.

"I love you both. Make Dad take you for haircuts."

Max wrapped her in an unexpected bear hug. "I love you, Mom."

"Love you." Lucas leaned in and gave her an awkward pat on the back.

Juliette hugged Max back too tight and then kissed Lucas on the cheek. "Haircuts."

Juliette opened the shop, locked the door behind her until the rest of the staff arrived, and carried her coffee back to her office. Coming in early meant she could . . . she could what? She didn't know what she needed to do. What did you do when your life unraveled?

She took everything off her desk and piled it on the long, low cabinet to the side. The furniture polish she sprayed on the now empty desk filled the air with orange-scented chemicals. She compounded her ecoterrorism by grabbing paper towels instead of a cloth and wiped the hell out of the desk. One towel for spreading the polish. *Fuck it.* Another for wiping down the desk. *Fuck Nathan.* And then another to dry it. *Fuck her.*

Juliette wiped down her phone and placed it on the desk, using yet another paper towel. She lined up her stapler, her tape dispenser, and her in-and-out box, fiddling with everything until she'd achieved perfect order. Last she took the silver picture frame she'd received as a gift from Nathan's mother the day they opened the shop.

"Family first," Gizi had warned Juliette. "Never let your work be obscuring that."

Be obscuring that. Nathan's mother used sophisticated words in vaguely ungrammatical ways, but her English as a second language became a form of poetry.

Family first
Never let
Your work
Be
Obscuring
That.

The family picture was way out of date. Nathan held an infant Max as though he'd just won an Oscar. Nathan had been a wonderful father right from the start. In the beginning, when Juliette fretted about cutting Lucas's infant fingernails, convinced she'd snip off a tip of his minute finger, Nathan did it without a word and continued quietly doing it until Juliette felt comfortable.

She scrolled through the list of good things about Nathan.

He was warm and kind. Most of the time.

He was smart.

He was interesting.

The physical side of their relationship had always been incredible, although that thought opened the door for unbearable questions.

He understood why her parents drove her crazy.

He knew how much she loved his parents.

He was Max's and Lucas's father.

She loved him.

She didn't want to be without him.

Juliette replaced the frame and picked up her now sterilized phone. She looked over her orderly desk, calmed by the precision. The cleaner her workspace, the sharper her decisions—not always right, but fast. Bullet-paced decisions.

Juliette woke up her computer. She clicked into her address book and scrolled down the list until hitting *F* for Fitzgerald.

Juliette arrived first the following Saturday for her date with Caroline. The shabby appearance of the small Newton coffee shop calmed her. Stuffed chairs and old wood tables matched the dim lighting.

Despite the lunchtime hour, Juliette was too nervous to eat. On the phone, she'd told Caroline only that she had something important to discuss about Savannah. Reassuring Caroline that she had good intentions, while holding off on the truth, had been a tightrope of conversation. Juliette danced on the head of a lie as she intimated that she had information from her friend who'd adopted children.

Now Juliette realized that while she'd succeeded in convincing Caroline to show up, she'd not done a good job of thinking out her plan for this meeting.

Caroline walked in, looking around with a blank expression. When Juliette signaled her over, Caroline raised her hand in a tentative wave.

"Hi. Nice to see you again." Caroline put a newspaper on the table and then pointed to Juliette's coffee cup. "I'm going to get myself a coffee. Would you like another?"

"I'm fine."

Juliette watched as Caroline walked away. Caroline wore no makeup. Not even the brown mascara that Juliette had promised Caroline would make her sparkle all by itself.

Is this what was wrong with her? That she thought about mascara at a time when her life was falling apart? Had Nathan found Tia because he needed a woman who wasn't so shallow?

Caroline returned with a barely lightened coffee. "I must admit I'm quite anxious to hear why you wanted to talk—you sound nervous."

Juliette tried to order her thoughts. How did you tell a story like this? Finally, she simply dove in and began talking. Caroline listened, taut and still, without comment, as Juliette related the history of how they all fit together. When Juliette finished, Caroline remained silent for a long, agonizing time. When she finally spoke, her voice sounded thin and reedy.

"This is insane."

"I know it must sound that way."

"So that's why you sent me that invitation." Caroline clenched the twisted napkin she held. "I suppose I was quite gullible. You must have thought me quite a fool."

Caroline went back to silence. Juliette tried to read the undertones of her words. At this moment, Juliette didn't know if Caroline wanted to kill her, quench her curiosity, or simply walk away in disgust. In her shoes, Juliette could never remain calm.

"Get the hell away from my family, and me!" Juliette would yell. "What do you want? If you have anything to say, say it to my lawyer."

"Did you mean anything you said?" Caroline asked. "When I was at your shop, were you telling the truth about having a friend who'd adopted her children?"

"That was true. I do have a friend whose kids are adopted, and she had a difficult time admitting to any moment of not loving motherhood."

Caroline's nod at Juliette's answer seemed doubtful.

"What are you looking for?" Caroline asked. "Did your husband send you?"

Juliette tried to imagine Nathan sending her on a mission like this. "No. When you came to my shop, he didn't even know about your daughter."

"But he knows now?"

"Yes. Now he knows."

"And he knew nothing about Savannah?"

"He knew about the pregnancy, but nothing after. At least, that's what he told me."

"Told you when?"

Juliette found it a bizarre relief to talk to Caroline; too many secrets knocked around Juliette's head. One day Max would say he wanted toast, and Juliette would spill out, "You have a half sister, Max, so please, would you stop whining about toast!"

She told almost everything, censoring only the parts that made her sound crazy. Like stalking Tia and carrying Savannah's picture everywhere she went.

"You haven't spoken with your husband about this since you confronted him?" Caroline asked when Juliette's torrent of words finally stopped.

"No."

"Why are you here? What do you want from me?"

"This will sound false, disingenuous, but honestly, I'm not sure."

"I've always thought when someone said 'honestly' in a sentence, they were lying, or at the very least, suspect. Are you?"

"Lying or suspect?" Juliette asked.

"Either."

"I'm not lying. I don't know what I want. But maybe I am suspect, because there are things running through my head which you may not like."

"Such as what?"

"Such as thinking Savannah should somehow know my family. She has wonderful grandparents who'd give an arm and a leg to hold her. Nathan is their only child, and they've done everything possible for our sons since they were born. I think of that each time I look at her picture."

Caroline sat so straight that there might have been rods inserted in her back. "Savannah already has wonderful grandparents who love her."

"Of course." Juliette realized she'd revealed too much. "Please, please don't think I'm suggesting that I expect anything from you or your family."

Caroline laced her fingers and brought her knotted fists to her chest. "Something drove you here. Like something drove you to have to meet Savannah and me. Either you aren't sure what it is or you aren't telling me the truth. Which is it?"

Juliette was sorry she'd come.

"Are you trying to get Savannah?" Caroline leaned forward like a hawk studying a hummingbird. "You and your husband?"

"God, no! Nathan would go insane if he even knew I was here."

"Then what is it you want?"

"I . . ." Juliette wondered what to say, what was her truth? "I love my husband," she said.

"Love brings you here?" Caroline crossed her arms over her chest.

"No. Of course not. That sounds crazy."

Caroline tipped her head to the side. "You want to tie yourself to her." She spoke slowly, analyzing Juliette in a manner that made her want to run away. "What are you looking for?"

Exhaustion overcame Juliette. She had to go home. Climb into bed. "Honestly? I simply don't know."

CHAPTER 19

Juliette

Juliette's heels clicked as she paced outside the restaurant, watching for Nathan's car, each tap another impatient demand to see him arrive.

After leaving Caroline, she'd driven back to the shop and almost hidden away to keep from confessing to Gwynne that she'd met with Caroline. Disaster watcher Gwynne would be alert to all the possible problems Juliette might have wrought with her visit. Lawsuits! Restraining orders! End of marriage! Gwynne lived each day waiting for something awful to happen. Juliette swore that her friend kept a pressed black dress ready for funerals at all times.

Caroline had asked her what she wanted. Juliette hadn't lied when she said she didn't know. She knew it was wrong that Nathan's daughter was out there and they didn't know her, and yet it also drove her crazy that Nathan might get to know her.

What if Nathan had come to her when he'd found out that Tia was pregnant? Would she have opened her heart to the baby?

Juliette had picked this restaurant for its stuffy atmosphere, hoping the mahogany-lined walls and deep carpet might muffle Nathan's expected outburst. He arrived noticeably nervous, looking hopeful and dressed for an occasion. Like perhaps this was to be their fresh start—the one for which he kept asking.

* * *

"*Have you gone completely nuts?*" Nathan dropped his fork on his plate, the *clink* enough of a disturbance to attract the attention of the diners at the next table. "You went to see the child's mother?"

"Nathan, we can't close our eyes to the situation."

"There is no situation. The child has a mother and a father—and from what you've said, damned good ones."

"No. Something is wrong, I can feel it."

"A doctor and a businessman living in Dover? Money? Education? What's their sin? Are they secret child molesters?"

"Don't even joke about that."

The busboy came over to clear their salad plates. The three of them played the game of civilized folk as the young man brushed crumbs from the white tablecloth.

The overly hair-gelled waiter placed a steak before Nathan and gave Juliette her salmon. She'd refused the potatoes, hoping the sacrifice would bring her luck.

If she took just one of Nathan's steak fries, would the spell break? Would the luck fairy give a damn about one fry?

The waiter left. Juliette dug into her green beans.

"I'm sorry," Nathan said. "You're right. I shouldn't joke about this."

She would never eat potatoes again.

"It's just that I'm confused. Hell, confused doesn't even begin to encompass what I'm feeling." Nathan opened his hands in a gesture that implored her to listen. "I love you. I love the boys. I love our family."

"I know. Even as I wonder how you could, how you could do what you did, I know you love us." Juliette cut off a piece of salmon with her fork. "I simply don't know if I can trust you. Not if you could keep such a major thing like . . . like a child from me." How did one even describe a relationship such as the one he'd never shared? A pregnancy? A daughter?

"I want to rebuild your trust."

"You can start by talking about Savannah."

"How will that help?" Nathan dipped a steak fry in a pool of ketchup. "This is about us."

"And she is connected to us."

"I just don't see how."

Again, he made his pleading hands, only this time a fry swung from one. Juliette snatched it from his hand and shoved it into her mouth.

This man was unhinging her.

"Take whatever you want." Nathan pushed his plate toward her.

"See, see, that's what I mean."

"What? You wanted it, right?"

"You're always offering the wrong thing."

Nathan looked confused. Hurt.

Jerk.

"How did we get here?" Juliette asked.

"I brought us here."

"Did I push you? Did I push you away?"

"Thanks for the out, but I can't put any of this on you."

"Then why?" Juliette shoved her plate away.

"Maybe I was just greedy."

Juliette thought of how Nathan tore through books, and meat, and even television episodes. They'd get a DVD of some cable TV series he'd never seen, like *Curb Your Enthusiasm*, and then he'd make her watch two, three, four—the entire series—until it was two in the morning. Was that what he did with women? Was Tia an episode that Nathan had gobbled?

"How can I know you won't get greedy again?"

"I'm asking for faith. I've never lied to you since the affair. Can you believe me when I say I know how much I hurt you?"

He knew her. He knew she wanted to believe.

"I want to be first in your heart," Juliette said.

"Don't you know you always are, have always been?"

"First and only. No understudy."

"Of course."

Juliette smiled without mirth. "Don't look at me as though you've just won the war."

"Really? We're in battle?" he asked.

"We're battling for our marriage. Or not. We can't pretend the child doesn't exist." Juliette saw his eyes open up, appearing to have let Savannah in for a moment. "Your parents. What if they ever knew that we'd kept this from them?"

Nathan pulled the wine from the bucket next to the table and re-filled his glass, the waiter rushing over as he did. Nathan held a hand out to keep him from the table.

"How can you allow a child to think her birth father didn't want her?" Juliette held out her glass. "How can you not want her?"

"I just don't have answers yet. This is all new to me."

"She told you, right? That she was pregnant. So it's not really all new."

"Yes. But I was more worried about us than anything else."

Juliette shook her head. "Forget then, talk about now."

"What is it you want me to do?"

Juliette opened her purse and pulled out Savannah's picture. She slid it across the table. "Look at her. Really look."

Nathan took the photograph that Juliette had sealed in a pliable plastic frame. Nathan's hand shook. He bit his lower lip.

"She looks like you. She looks like Max." Juliette saw it on his face, a longing. Nathan had grown up with the veneration of family that Juliette inherited through marriage.

What if they could take Savannah into their home to visit and have some sort of open family? It happened all the time. They wouldn't wrench her from her home, they'd expand it—give her more warmth, more love. Children could always expand to accept more people who loved them. Max, Lucas, they'd be shocked at first, but then it would work out.

And Juliette would not be ashamed. She'd be proud they'd worked this all out for the best interest of the child. Juliette imagined the feel of the girl's silky hair under her hand.

Juliette and Caroline would become friends.

"She does," Nathan said. "She reminds me a little of Max. But, my God, there is so much of her mother in her."

* * *

Juliette slammed the car door shut. She should have taken her own car. "You didn't see your face, Nathan. That's why you think it's no big deal," Juliette said as he started the engine.

Nathan leaned his elbows on the wheel and pressed his thumbs between his eyes. "All I said was the girl looks like her mother. Is that so surprising? So horrible?"

"You didn't see your face," Juliette repeated. "It was like you saw a ghost. A ghost you love."

Nathan tried to take her hand. She snatched it from him. She'd seen that gentleness come over him when he talked about Tia.

"What you saw was me looking at the child," he said. "For God's sake, I'm looking at a five-year-old daughter I've never seen."

Juliette panted, gulping air to catch her breath. "She's your daughter with *her*; that's what makes it special, right?"

"I thought that's what you wanted, for me to see the child, to become involved, to get emotionally invested."

"With the child, Nathan. Not her," Juliette whispered.

CHAPTER 20

Caroline

The sky darkened as Caroline listened to Savannah complain on the phone. She switched on her office lamp and watched the light pool on her desk pad.

"Mommy," Savannah asked, her voice made tinny by the cell phone. "When are you coming home?"

Caroline held the phone so tightly that her fingers cramped. A headache thudded over her left eye. When she removed her reading glasses, "Some Clinical Findings at Presentation Can Predict High-Risk Pathology Features in Unilateral Retinoblastoma" became an abstract of tiny, blurred letters. She was supposed to lead a discussion about the article at tomorrow morning's staff meeting and she'd hardly cracked its twenty-six dense pages.

"Guess what Nanny Rose is making you tonight, pumpkin." Caroline said. "SpaghettiOs!"

In their home of hundred-dollar takeout dinners, junk food was the way to Savannah's heart.

"But when are you coming home?" Savannah asked.

Caroline looked at the array of work in front of her. "I'll kiss you when I get home. Even if you're sleeping."

"You're not coming until I'm asleep." Savannah's tone was more flat than accusing. Caroline wished Savannah sounded angrier, more surprised. Not so accepting.

"I told her to sprinkle on extra cheese." Caroline switched hands and sorted through memos on her desk.

"Okay."

"How are the Bitty Twins?" Caroline chirped with excessive enthusiasm. "Why don't you and Nanny Rose make a Bitty Twins beach outside?" Although it was only late April, temperatures had soared into the eighties. Caroline had been searching at midnight the previous night for the summer clothes she'd put away.

"Mommy! It's nighttime."

"Oh, you have a silly mommy. I love you, bunny nose."

She did love her.

"And I love you, Mommy."

She simply didn't want to be with her all the time.

"You promise you'll kiss me when you come home?" Savannah asked.

Caroline closed her eyes. "Of course."

Caroline opened the door connecting the garage.

Waiting on the other side, in the extra study they barely used, Peter sat in their sleek cherry rocker. The chair matched a burnished red leather couch, part of the furniture they'd bought with a vision of the room as Savannah's future homework site. Peter's feet, planted on the glossy wood floor, seemed positioned for a quick rise. Nothing in the room was out of place except Peter's rumpled pajama pants.

"Do you know what time it is?" he asked.

"Sorry." Caroline ran her fingers through her hair and caught a whiff of stale hospital and lab. She clutched a bag from Cabot's gift shop. The hospital's small store stayed open late enough for her to have popped in during a coffee run.

She held out the bag as though offering appeasement. "I got a present for Savannah."

Peter turned off the television and tossed the remote on the coffee table. "For God's sake, Caro. Savannah has about three million toys. What she doesn't have enough of, it seems, is you."

"That's not fair. Do you know what I was doing tonight?"

"I'm sure it was important. That's the problem. Everything about your work is important. When do we get to be at the top of the list?"

Please shut up, Peter.

Caroline longed to look at the miniature Johnny Town-Mouse in the bag, just the right size for tucking in a pocket. Savannah loved tiny toys. Caroline planned to put the stuffed animal next to her daughter's slippers for a morning surprise. Driving home, she'd anticipated waking Savannah the next morning and watching her delight when she saw the mouse, wearing a tiny blue blazer, just as he did in Savannah's Beatrix Potter books. Maybe if she wasn't too tired, Caroline could fashion a little mouse bed . . .

"Are you going to answer me?"

"Sorry. I thought it was a rhetorical question."

"Sarcasm doesn't help, you know."

"I didn't know I needed help," Caroline said. "That we needed help."

"See. There you go." Peter sighed.

"There I go *where*? What? What?"

"We're drowning here. I feel like our family is sinking under the weight of your work."

She dropped the small bag on the table and fell on the couch, too tired to stand, too exhausted to keep the argument going. "Perhaps I should look at my work schedule and figure out a better way to handle all this." Caroline waved her hands as though "all this" hung on the walls.

Peter dropped down next to her. He put a hand on her knee. "Have you ever thought that maybe you could stop working," he said. "Just for a little while?"

She shook off his hand and turned to face him. Did her husband know her at all?

"I think it might be better for Savannah," Peter continued. "I'm not sure about this whole nanny thing. Savannah seems—"

This nanny thing? Nanny Rose had been with them since Savannah was three weeks old.

"I think of how I grew up, with my mother always there, always available. It was a good way to grow up. I'd like that for Savannah. I think she should have it." Peter cleared his throat. "Your mother was always home. Didn't that mean a lot to you?"

"I didn't know anything else." Caroline could barely squeeze out the words.

"You had security. You never knew worry."

This was how you murdered a marriage. A husband brought up something so awful to the wife that it could end their world, and he presented it as a serious option.

"Maybe *you* should stop working." Caroline spoke in a dead voice. He'd become such a stranger at that moment that she didn't much care about his answer.

"I know you love your work." He squeezed her knee. She tried to control her reflex to slap away his hand. "But so do I, and we have to be honest about this. I make—what?—ten times the money you do?"

"I could take a different job," she answered, as though anything about this ridiculous discussion deserved serious consideration. That's what he'd done: put garbage on the table and made her pretend it could be dinner.

"Even if you could find work paying anywhere in my ballpark— not even mentioning for the moment that I own the company—can you imagine me home all day?"

"No, Peter. I can't." Caroline rose. "What scares me is that you can imagine it for me."

Caroline crept into Savannah's room with the tiny toy clutched in her hand. Savannah slept wrapped in her quilt, her thumb resting near her lips.

After patting the blankets tighter around Savannah, Caroline sunk to the floor. As she sat cross-legged beside the bed, watching her child's chest rise and fall, she considered Peter's idea. Perhaps she shouldn't have jumped down his throat. Maybe she should at least consider the possibility.

Maybe everything would come together for them, for the entire family, if she stayed home. She'd fall back in love with Peter and stop holding her breath each time he touched her. She'd fall into sparkly parent-child love with Savannah, like Peter had with her, instead of trudging through motherhood.

"Mommy?" Sleepy surprise infused Savannah's words. "What are you doing?"

"I told you I'd kiss you when I came home, right?" Caroline pressed her lips to Savannah's satiny cheek.

"Cuddle me?"

Caroline dropped the mouse on the rug and climbed in with Savannah. The little girl inched as close as possible, all warm flannel and sturdy little girl. "You feel good, Mommy."

"So do you, sweetness."

A welcome torpor overtook Caroline. She closed her eyes.

"Are you going to stay with me?"

"I am, pumpkin."

"All night?"

"All night." Caroline could barely form words.

"You are my good mother." Savannah patted Caroline's arm. "Just like the fairy godmother. In *Cinderella*."

CHAPTER 21

Caroline

An internal alarm rang in Caroline's head at four forty-five the next morning, reminding her of the eight o'clock consult she had for a suspected case of necrotizing enterocolitis. If it were that severe intestinal inflammation, they needed fast diagnosis to get treatment started.

She carefully untangled herself from Savannah, grateful for the child's sodden sleep. She snuck out before six, leaving a note where Peter couldn't miss it, showering in the guest bath and dressing quietly.

The Mass Pike was blissfully quiet compared with the usual time she commuted. Within forty-five minutes of leaving home, she'd grabbed a coffee and yogurt at the cafeteria, slipped behind her desk, and powered up her computer.

She combed through her mail, separating it into Attention, Trash, and File.

Her cell phone blinked. Caroline had turned off the ringer. The text message alert came soon after. She tried to ignore it, but she became frightened of a crisis; something horrible that she'd forgotten. "Whre are u?" Peter had texted.

"Emrgcy," Caroline responded. She'd already written that in her note: "emergency at the lab."

"We mst tlk. Tnite," he texted back.

Email pinged on her computer.

Mixed in with notes from colleagues, lab notes, and requests from schools and hospitals, an email from Jonah stood out.

They'd written numerous times since the conference in San Diego: innocent communications about mud season in Vermont, the Red Sox opener in Boston, but mostly about their work. They had an online collegial coffee break relationship. In the weeks since she'd met him, she'd learned that a young woman in his practice suffered from denied anorexia. That made Jonah concerned for her life, which led Caroline to write him about a case she'd seen recently—unfortunately, at the autopsy stage.

She told Jonah that she lived her quiet widowed life surrounded by books, which led to Jonah confessing that he spent most of his nonpatient hours reading by the fire. Detective mysteries and thrillers were his favorites, he'd written with an abashed air. In response, she'd admitted to her soft spot for celebrity biographies when she needed total escape.

Caroline clicked on Jonah's email with more anticipation than she thought appropriate. She scanned it quickly and then reread it for the details. He was in Boston, and he wanted to see her. Excitement and fear rushed in a lethal emotional mix.

There was no question that Jonah wanted more than conversation and that Caroline should back away. Still, she lingered over the email. The idea of spending simple time with someone who didn't see her as a mother, a wife, and a failure enticed her, although the thought of another person wanting attention held zero temptation. What she craved was hours lost with her slides and her journals, slowly uncovering answers until everything crystallized into near immutability. In her work, even the worst truths had clarity. Home life held murkiness that threatened to suck her down permanently. Each morning, she woke to living an ill-fitting role until she reached the hospital.

Nanny Rose called during an online conference to say she'd need a day off in three weeks, and, by the way, did Caroline think it was normal for a woman her age to still be breaking out? Should she go on that birth control pill they said helped?

Peter called to repeat that they needed to talk and to point out that Caroline should at least give his idea some consideration. "Just rent the idea," he said.

Caroline's mother left a message reminding her about the fitting for Caroline's sister's wedding. The dressmaker expected them all on Saturday morning at eight sharp.

Her sister-in-law Faith wrote for Caroline's help in preparing her grad school application.

Caroline's secretary whispered that her time reports were late. Two days had gone by with nobody knowing how many hours Caroline had put into which project. Caroline shocked herself by barely caring.

Worst of all, Caroline had to duck into the ladies' room after lunch because she'd looked at her feet and started crying. Her shoes were scuffed and ugly. The hem of her slacks looked worn. Her knees felt bony and old. She'd never cared about how she looked before, knowing she wasn't beautiful, but she was fine. Perfectly okay. It never mattered much because she'd always had a more-than-fine mind. Now her psyche felt like a blanket with holes, allowing facts and ideas to slip through.

By the time she arrived home—on time—she was ready to take a shower and climb into bed with a book. The day hadn't been difficult, filled with the usual, but the usual had become a constant snafu: situation normal, all fucked up.

She didn't take the shower or go to bed. She threw together Annie's Whole Wheat Shells and Cheddar, tossed in peas, and called it a balanced meal.

She bathed Savannah for an extra long time—allowing the Bitty Twins to join in, and even blow-drying their hair, to Savannah's delight.

Instead of talking to Peter about his idea, she kissed him with a pretence of passion, poured them each a glass of wine, and then initiated lovemaking, putting him to sleep as efficiently as she had Savannah.

* * *

Surfing porn would feel less threatening than the sites Caroline visited behind the closed door of her home office. At three in the morning, loneliness turned into total isolation, the sort that allowed her to visit Web sites such as Insight: Open Adoption. Juliette's visit, coupled with Peter's insane ideas, kept her awake in a way that begged for attention. Another Ambien terrified her; she was weary of meeting life by shutting down. It was time to research her life.

After Googling repeated iterations of "adoption," Caroline returned to Insight. She opened a file, labeling it "Adoption Psych," and began taking notes and highlighting information to which she felt connected. Entire passages begged to be cut and pasted into a Word document.

"No matter where your child is adopted from, you will, as adoptive parents, need to 'deal with' your child's birth family whether you know the birth family or not. This birth family is a part of who your child is."

She thought of Juliette talking about the grandparents Savannah would never know.

"Many adoptive professionals encourage prospective birthparents and adoptive parents in the preplacement process to choose the level of contact 'they are most comfortable with having.' The philosophy of comfort does not take into consideration several very important factors, one being that open adoption should not be based on making the adults involved comfortable; rather it should be about providing for the needs of the child."

Caroline considered this for quite a while. Wasn't it weird, even unfair, that she and Peter, Tia, Juliette and her husband, that all of them knew more about one another than Savannah knew about any of them? Was limiting her daughter's knowledge to fairy tales and children's stories of "we chose you" for Savannah, or was it comfort for her and Peter?

"Much of the open adoption experience is uncomfortable and awkward, especially in the beginning . . . Patricia Martinez Dorner, author of *Children of Open Adoption* and *Talking to Your Child About Adoption*, encourages us to see open adoption as just another form of blended family . . . The adopted child is also able to know his birthparents as they are, rather than creating a fantasy birthparent. Instead of spending countless hours conjuring up an image of a person they do not know, they can use that energy for other things. Two, it gives the child a sense of wholeness."

Caroline copied these words into a document and then ordered the book. It was old—maybe out of date—but it was a beginning.

CHAPTER 22

Tia

The phone might as well have rung from the roof for how muted it sounded, competing with a too-loud episode about skin cancer on *The Doctors*. Tia, stretched out on the couch with the remote in her hand, didn't move except to pull the pilled blanket tighter over her legs. The fleece throw had hung over her mother's couch for years before Tia inherited it. Not that it was some family heirloom: her mother probably got it for five bucks at Old Navy after Christmas. But that it had once warmed her mother offered Tia a bit of peace.

Tia's days consisted of watching television and checking on her unemployment case. Katie—who would have imagined?—had convinced Richard not to fight Tia's claim. She'd even called Tia to let her know that it looked like Sam would definitely survive. Mrs. G wouldn't be going to jail, just to an assisted living home, with a guarantee of psychiatric care. Of course, that might as well be jail for Mrs. G.

Tia glanced at the clock, wishing it would spin forward to three, when she'd let herself think about adding Kahlúa to her coffee. After that, she'd shower in readiness for Bobby's nightly arrival.

Tia let the call go to voice mail. Bobby was the only one she wanted to speak to, and he'd call back. Or she could call him. Bobby's store of patience seemed infinite, even in bed, and what man had patience there? Sometimes she couldn't bear his touch; other times she'd cling to him as though he were her only source of sustenance on the planet.

In a matter of weeks, days—Tia could barely remember—after she'd been fired, Bobby had become her ever-patient steady boyfriend. If she had his old football jacket, she'd wrap herself in it. Tia wanted to be back in high school, except this time it would be Bobby whom she'd make out with at the Sugar Bowl. She'd sleep with him, marry him, and have his babies. When the babies became children, she'd send them off to school with carefully packed nutritious lunches. Then Tia would have returned to school and become a professor, or a doctor, or a lawyer.

Five rings went by, and then Nathan's voice filled the room like a shot to her central nervous system.

"Tia. It's Nathan."

As though there were any chance that she wouldn't recognize his voice.

"We need to talk."

Now? She'd sent the letter so long ago.

"It's about . . . the child."

Tia clutched the blanket.

"I . . . my wife. For God's sake, Tia, how could you have just sent that to my house like that? Did you even think of the possibilities?"

Tia shrank from his accusation. Guilt shamed her. Then anger followed.

Did you even consider what happened to me after having your baby? Did you think about that baby even once?

What was it like going through the world not even knowing if you'd had a boy or a girl?

"Call me. On my cell. I have a new number," his disembodied voice announced.

Tia already knew that. His old one didn't work. She'd wondered if he'd changed it so she couldn't call. Nathan said his number twice, and Tia scribbled it down. Then she saved the message in case she'd written the number wrong.

In case she wanted to hear his message again.

Stupid! She reminded herself that he'd called to berate her, not love her.

Still, he'd called. The last time Tia had heard Nathan's voice, she'd been five months pregnant, when she'd made her final attempt to convince Nathan to include her in his life, pleading, "But you love me! I know you do."

It had been like that with Nathan too many times. She'd plan long, rational speeches and end up pleading, "I know that you love me. I know it. I know it. I know it."

Eventually Tia forced herself to face the probability that she'd projected onto Nathan her own obsessed madness. For too long, she'd assumed his love for her was genuine, like the words he used to describe his feelings: "Oh, Tia, you are so unlike anyone else—so real, so authentic. I love you."

Perhaps Nathan's "I love you" was really "Love ya, babe!" Or perhaps it was "Hot for ya, baby, but I'm too civilized to say that."

Could he love her and also love his wife?

Could he love her and turn his back on all knowledge about their child?

Tia prayed that a ghostly film of her presence hovered over him, as his did over her. She wanted to haunt him.

Each time something awful happened, the silver lining had been the same: Didn't her desperate need for comfort provide dispensation? Wasn't she now allowed to call Nathan? Hadn't their closeness during their year together earned her that right? After her mother died: *I could call Nathan!* When she fell and broke three ribs: *Nathan will help me!* Even after she'd been fired, her first thought had been to call Nathan.

But she never did. Honest moments made her recognize that she was an infrequent presence in Nathan's mind, while he was just moments from her thoughts at any given moment. Robin was the one she called for help, allowing herself to fantasize about having Nathan's comfort only while waiting for sleep.

Tia splashed cold water on her face. She considered a shower, wanting to be alert and ready for whatever Nathan might offer, but she feared that even a few minutes' delay could take him away forever. Just taking the time to fill a coffee cup could be dangerous. What if, in those moments, he changed his mind about talking to her? What if, at the very moment Tia watched hot coffee splash into a mug, his wife used her purity and beauty to beckon him away from the phone?

First she read the number she'd written down, then she scribbled it larger. Only then did she dial Nathan.

"Tia?"

"Caller ID ruins the surprise, doesn't it?" she said.

His voice, oh damn, his voice ran through her.

"Hardly a surprise, considering I called you a few minutes ago," he said.

She squeezed herself in concentration, trying to establish his mood. Reading Nathan had once been her talent. The pitch of his voice told Tia how playful she could be. At the time their affair hit the final notes, Tia found herself adjusting every word to Nathan's frame of mind. Today he sounded cautious.

Still, she detected a note—a small note, but still a note—of curiosity. Tia the Nathan scholar could detect interest in his voice, no matter how minute.

"I was surprised to hear from you," Tia said.

"That hardly makes sense, considering what you sent."

"I mailed those pictures almost two months ago."

"I didn't get them until quite recently." Nathan used his sincerity voice. "Juliette intercepted them."

"What do you mean, intercepted?"

"I moved, you know," he said.

Nathan excelled at changing subjects. "No," she said. "I didn't. How would I?"

A sticky silence hung for a moment.

"Good question," he answered. "How would you? Anyway, it's not important. Listen. Truly, I only recently found out about the pictures. Juliette opened the envelope, but she didn't tell me until now."

His words unfolded a million questions. Tia froze, unsure what part of his statement to address first.

"She looks like us," he said into the quiet. "The child."

Tia clutched the phone. Us. They were still an "us." She opened her top drawer and took out the picture of Honor. Yes, Nathan was right. They'd finally merged. In their daughter.

"She's striking," Nathan said.

"What does *striking* mean?"

"Unusual. Her looks sort of—"

"I know what the word means." Nathan, the eternal professor. "What do *you* mean by that? Are you saying she's not pretty? Not cute?"

Had his princess-pretty blonde wife said that? "Oh, she's not very pretty, but she's striking, Nathan."

"No, I meant *striking* as in she struck me. Floored me, in fact."

"How?"

"She looks so much like Max, my younger son," Nathan said. "Juliette couldn't stop talking about it."

Coffee curdled in Tia's stomach, imagining Juliette studying Honor's picture. Thinking about her. Commenting on her. "What else did Juliette have to say?" Tia worked at not putting verbal quotation marks around the word *Juliette*.

"Tia, this is difficult for everyone."

"It's only difficult for you because I opened your eyes. If I'd never sent those pictures, you'd have gone your entire life without knowing whether or not your daughter was striking."

Now he was quiet.

"Did you care at all? Did you wonder if you had a son or a daughter? Were you ever going to call?"

"Are you asking if I ever cared about the child or about you?"

"It doesn't matter." Tia held on to thoughts of Bobby. He'd held her after she'd been fired, even when she'd been so drunk that she'd puked on her own shoes. She wouldn't let Nathan confuse her with his I'm-the-real-person-here-with-my-wife-and-family bullshit. "Because you never did call, did you?"

"Juliette thinks I should see her."

Tia and Nathan met the next morning in an anonymous coffee shop in Quincy, a city close enough by miles but far removed from either Jamaica Plain or Wellesley. Chosen by Nathan, of course, who offered to pay for a cab.

Tia took the Red line train.

He waited in a leather booth. Tia tried to hide the intensity of her reaction, how she caught her breath, how the blood rushed to her head. He looked good. Older, but still as desirable. Maybe a bit heavier. Solid. She itched to run her thumb over the top of his hand.

"Does your wife know we're meeting?" Her voice shook.

"Not really." Nathan took her hand and squeezed. She recognized the feel of his skin too well. "I got you coffee and a scone."

"Not really" meant no. Reluctantly, she pulled her hand from his. She shifted her weight on the leather banquette. The booths were built too high. Tia hated having her legs dangle; hated being unable to feel the ground beneath her feet. She wore heels and a sundress with a cardigan thrown over her shoulders. "Nathan clothes": the sort of girly stuff he liked.

Nathan pushed the scone toward her. "Try it. My muffin is actually pretty good."

"Why so surprised? Decent things exist of Starbucks and Whole Foods," Tia said.

Nathan put down his muffin and smiled. "Don't you love to pigeonhole me? Nothing changes, eh? Still my girl from the 'hood, aren't you?"

"Who's pigeonholing now? And I'm not your girl from anywhere anymore, am I?" Tia broke her scone into a pieces. She wondered how to seem more intelligent, less "girl from the 'hood." It bothered her then and still did today: she played his bad girl, and he represented her good man. "I'll assume the answer is no, she doesn't know you're here."

"I need to know what you want, Tia. Why you sent those pictures. Juliette, well, you can only imagine how this affected her. It was terrifying when she found out."

Juliette. Juliette. Tia whispered it in her mind using soft French-sounding *J*s.

She hated hearing "Juliette" from Nathan's lips: so sweet, so pure and elegant. Soon she'd hate all words that began with the letter *J*.

Jonquil.

Je t'aime.

Joy.

Tia sounded too hard, starting with *T. Truck. Trouble. Tether.*

"Juliette wants to know about these people—the adoptive family," Nathan said. "And so do I. Now that you broke the silence, we want to know the entire picture."

Nathan wore a crisp blue shirt so perfectly ironed that Tia wondered how it was done. Tia never could get those paper-sharp creases or crisp, smooth fronts. Did other people have better irons than she could find? Perhaps women like Juliette had access to tools that only upper-class women could get: beauty weapons sold on secret Web sites and irons you needed a password to buy.

"Why would *J-Juliette*," Tia stumbled on the name. "*Juliette,*" she repeated, "want to know anything, much less everything?"

"She feels connected. The girl is my daughter, after all."

"Your daughter?" Tia gripped the edge of the table. "She may be your biological material, but she's not your daughter. And—how can I emphasize this enough—she is nothing, *nothing*, to your wife."

"You say *wife* as though you're describing something awful," Nathan said. This was the most directly he'd ever spoken about Juliette; Tia's words were the most straightforward he'd ever heard from her. "Why are you angry at her? Shouldn't it be me who gets your fury?"

Tia had no adequate answer. He was right.

"Juliette sounds the same way when she speaks of you."

"Maybe that's our problem," Tia said. "We haven't yet figured out how to truly hate you, so we turn it on each other."

Nathan rose and walked around the table. They'd been facing each other. Now he took the seat next to her, so they were hip to hip in the booth. Tia felt his heat. Their thighs touched, and she wondered if it was an accident.

He put an arm around her shoulders and pulled her closer. He gave her the kiss hello that hadn't come before. It was brief, their lips barely brushed. But it was a kiss.

She blinked at the rush of feeling his arm, a weight she thought she'd never feel again. Why on God's earth would she feel comfortable and safe with him? She tried to squeeze the foolishness away.

"We'll figure this out," he said. "I promise."

Before this morning, Tia hadn't known they had something to figure out, or that she and Nathan constituted a "they." Now, suddenly, they were parents together.

"Juliette wants to go with me to see her."

Tia took calming breaths. She traced the swirl of white marbleizing the black counter. "We're the ones who should see her. We should be the ones to judge how she's doing."

Nathan took her hand. "Perhaps you're right."

Nathan's sincerity couldn't be trusted.

"Yes. Perhaps you're right," he repeated. "I'll be in touch."

CHAPTER 23

Tia

Tia crackled with energy when she returned home from Quincy. Even before entering her apartment, she began cleaning, clearing the umbrellas, shoes, and junk mail cluttering the table and shelves in the hall. Orphaned gloves, cloth supermarket bags, and a chewed-up ice scraper were immediately consigned to a throwaway pile.

She supposed the scraper was a ghost of a tenant past, some lost item she forgot to throw out when she moved in. Perhaps she'd been hopeful then and had thought that she'd soon buy a car.

After grabbing trash bags and the vacuum, Tia returned to the hall. She shoved everything into the bags without looking, ran the Hoover quickly over the worn oriental runner, and then brought the bulging bags to the garbage cans outside.

Mess, she'd made a humiliating mess. Despite having nothing but time since being fired, she'd barely spent a moment with a broom or dust cloth. Before, she'd straighten up each morning before leaving for work. She'd deep cleaned each weekend, even if only for herself. "There's no excuse for dirty," her mother said every time she'd put a dust cloth in Tia's hands. These words first surfaced when they'd lived in the projects. Tia's mother had nothing but contempt for those who chose beer over Pine-Sol.

Tia could hear exactly what her mother would say if she saw her daughter's apartment at the moment.

"No excuse, Tia. There's no excuse for living like this."

And why was she coming to Jesus now? She tried to pretend the rush of energy racing through her wasn't inspired by thoughts of Nathan visiting.

Okay, she wouldn't lie to herself, but this place needed a deep cleaning whatever the impetus. How could Bobby come in here without wanting to throw up? His tolerance and compassion made her feel like screaming. Why would he sit in the midst of her dust and dirty dishes and not even say something, like, "Hey, ever think of running the vacuum?"

Nathan, what would he say? "What's wrong, Tia? Do you think your home is reflecting your state of mind?"

She could hear Nathan saying something like that, and she wanted to show him just how okay her state of mind was.

Not that she was expecting him to come to her apartment.

Right.

But he might.

"Wow." Bobby took a deep breath. She'd opened every window to let spring air wash the apartment.

"Wow, what?" Tia asked.

"Wow, everything looks terrific. Is that a terrible thing to say? Don't get prickly on me." He pulled her close. "And you look great. As always."

In fact, although she'd scrubbed the apartment and carefully arranged her best ornaments—placing her collection of cobalt glass in the exact spot where afternoon sunlight refracted from it, and placing her most artistic paperweights on top of loose papers, while hiding the milk glass vases that might seem tacky to Nathan—she'd done little to make herself look good besides showering. Instead of spending time smearing herself with eyeliner and blush, she'd gone through her books, looking for the ones that would make her seem more intelligent and thoughtful. She hid her cheap mystery paperbacks in a box under the bed, leaving out only the ones Nathan would think interesting, such as novels written by Norwegians and Africans.

"The apartment looks great, not me."

"Baby, you don't need makeup to look good. You look energized, and that makes you look even cuter than you usually do. Look: I have something for you." Bobby stepped into the hall and came back holding out a pot of pink and white hyacinths. "I saw these and thought of how much you like them."

Tia took the pot and dipped her nose into the sweet fragrance. Hyacinth and freesia were her favorite flowers. The deep purple pot set off the bloom's paler color.

"You like hyacinths, right?" Bobby shut the door and locked it. Careful Bobby.

"People steal these, you know," Tia said.

"People steal them?"

"Right out of the ground," she said. "Because they're so popular. And expensive."

Tia placed the pot on the kitchen table, moving it to the right and then the left until she was satisfied. She pressed her thumb into the dirt, checking to see if the flowers needed water. She looked at Bobby. "I love hyacinths. And I love that you remember."

Tia admired her shiny white sink as she washed the flowerpot dirt off her hands. She'd scrubbed the porcelain until almost all the black marks were gone—she'd even looked up and tried out best practices, even making the concoction suggested by the Porcelain Enamel Institute:

". . . mix household scouring powder with water to make a slurry, and mop it over the area. Let the solution stand for approximately five minutes."

She shouldn't feel so prideful. Slurry, that's all it was.

"Make love to me." Tia circled her arms around Bobby's waist.

* * *

Tia climbed on top. She was ready before Bobby began. Her synapses fired at a million miles per minute.

Nathan. Nathan. Nathan.

She rode Bobby to the sound of Nathan's name in her head; the chant sent her over the top. "Oh God," she murmured.

"Oh Jesus," Bobby answered as he arched into her.

Afterward, Tia curled up in Bobby's arms and stroked the reddish chest hair that wasn't Nathan's. Everything about Nathan was dense and dark.

Her fingers itched to touch Nathan. She settled for resting her head on Bobby's shoulder, which, like Nathan's, was thick and muscled.

"Damn." He kissed the top of her head. "From now on, I'm bringing hyacinths every time I come over."

"Are you hungry?" she asked.

"You cooked *and* cleaned?" His voice teased, but hope showed on his face. He knew Tia didn't cook—hated it, in fact. If she cooked for Bobby, he'd think it meant true love.

"There are some eggs in the fridge," she said. "I don't remember how old they are, though."

Bobby sat up. "I'll make us an omelette. Going out is too much work." His kiss was gentle. "Did you send out any resumes today?"

"I cleaned today."

He took both her hands in his. "I'm not trying to pressure you. I just want to be part of your life; I want to make your life better."

Tia's chest tightened. "You're too good to me." She laughed so as not to cry. "Am I good to you?"

He stroked her hair as though petting a kitten. "Of course you are, baby."

Nathan was never coming. She'd acted like a love-struck girl, cleaning for him. God himself must have looked down on her scrubbing and laughed until He and Jesus cried.

Nathan called because his wife ordered him to check up on Tia, that's all. They had a hidden agenda, something to do with Honor, and Tia had better face that truth.

* * *

The clean living room brought Tia a feeling of purification. Her life offered possibilities. She could let go of Nathan. Seeing him had led to nothing worse than cleaning the house and making Bobby feel like the hero into whose arms she wanted to be swept. Nothing awful had happened.

Tomorrow she'd work on her resume.

Bobby placed the tray on a clean, uncluttered coffee table, took off the two plates, and set them down with a flourish. "Dinner is served."

Cheese bubbled from perfect omelettes surrounded by slices of apple. Mealy apples, but apples nonetheless, and English muffins, although he'd rescued them from the depths of the freezer and probably had to scrape frost off them. The English muffins looked miraculously good, perfectly toasted with butter melting into each nook and cranny.

"I opened that bottle of Charles Lafitte I put in the fridge last week," he said. He handed her a wineglass filled with fizzy gold champagne.

No one but Bobby had ever brought her champagne just because she liked it.

"A toast," he said.

"To what?"

"To being here. I've thought about it for a long time."

"And has it turned out like you'd hoped for?" Tia bit into her English muffin.

"You make me happy. Maybe it's like they say: every pot has a cover. I've always felt like you were my cover." He kissed her buttery, crumb-flecked lips. "I want to make you happy."

"I don't want to make you unhappy."

He drew back a bit. "What are you worried about?"

With Nathan back in her life, no matter how tenuous the connection, one misstep portended disappearing into him again. She might as well live her life dancing on the edge of a knife.

"I had a baby." Her words came out twisted and tight.

He stared at her, looking baffled. "When?" he finally said.

"Five years ago this March."

He sat beside her and took her hand. "What happened?"

"I loved a man who didn't love me," Tia told Bobby. "Or he didn't love me enough."

She dug shaky fingers into her knees.

"He was married.

"I sinned with him.

"I couldn't sin again, so I didn't get rid of her.

"But I gave her away."

She told him everything she could.

They sat for a while.

Quietly.

He handed her a tissue but didn't touch her.

"Do you still love him?"

Tia pressed her lips against repeating his question back.

Did she still love him? Did it count that her blood pumped faster since seeing Nathan? That his name was the only one she wanted to say, and that she could still feel the skin of his hand under her thumb?

"No. Of course not," she said.

"How about the baby?"

"What about her?"

"Do you love her?"

"How does that matter?"

"It just seems like such a sad thing to give up a baby." He took her hand. "I hate thinking of you going through it. That's all. I'm not judging. He's the one who should be judged. He's the one who was married. He's the one who deserted you."

All she could think to do was throw out an easy axiom: words that would keep them at a distance from discussing Nathan and Honor. "Water under the bridge, I suppose."

"I don't believe you," Bobby said. "You look too unhappy. God, this explains so much about you. Maybe about us."

"Us?"

"You had to keep everyone at a distance, right? Including me. I think knowing the truth will make all the difference."

"I suppose." Maybe Bobby was right. He'd be the one—the one who knew. She could trust him. He'd provide a safe haven.

"It sounds like you were under pressure to give her up."

"From who?"

"From him. He pushed you away; he pushed the baby away. You weren't thinking straight. And your mother was dying. Jesus, Tee. You couldn't possibly think straight."

Honesty could never go all the way, not between a man and a woman. How could she tell him that Honor would have reminded her too much of Nathan? That she'd been the worst sort of coward. That she'd been that stupid with love—or thought she'd been. In the end, was there even a difference?

"It's all his fault. This is so wrong." Bobby's face reddened with anger. "Damn it, she's your daughter. She belongs with you."

"It's too late for that. She's five years old. I signed her away. Jesus, I still remember the words: *final and cannot be revoked.*"

"We can at least talk to a lawyer, right? It can't hurt. There are always loopholes."

Loopholes. Spoken like a true son of Southie. More than anything, she knew she should say no. More than anything, he tempted her to say yes.

CHAPTER 24

Juliette

The shop was cold. Or maybe Juliette was cold. Either way, she shivered as she sat in her desk chair. Perhaps someone had walked over her grave. That's what Nathan's mother said when anyone shivered.

Jews could be so awesomely dark. Would Juliette's father have been gloomy if her mother hadn't been around to lighten him? Her mother's soul was made of helium. Juliette worried that she too had a buoyant soul. If she were more melancholy, then Nathan wouldn't have lost interest in her and strayed to more troubled women.

At that moment, Juliette felt dark enough to depress an entire circus. She'd hoped that finally sharing everything with Nathan would make her feel better, but instead it seemed as though she'd given him the keys to the candy store. Now he had a reason to see Tia. In the weeks since she'd confronted him about the child, he'd given her only the most cursory of answers about what he'd done or was planning to do.

"Nathan," she'd begged repeatedly, "don't leave me out. Not anymore."

He'd given her a tortured look. "I'm kind of lost right now, Jules. Give me some time, okay?"

Juliette lost her fire after confronting Nathan. When he sealed

himself away, he'd taken her anger with him. Perhaps her love also—
without fire, she feared they'd die.

"Juliette?" Gwynne stuck her head through the doorway, her expression creased with concern. "Someone's here to see you."

Juliette threw her head into her hands. It was too early to face a
client popping in for an emergency eyebrow consultation or pleading for her to choose a lipstick guaranteed to produce a three-carat
engagement ring, or a company rep who hadn't done her homework
and didn't know that juliette&gwynne sold only its own products.

"Can you make them go away?" Juliette put her fingers to her
temples. "Please. I'm not up to anyone right now."

"Don't think I can make this one disappear." Gwynne placed her
hands on the edge of Juliette's desk and bent until her face loomed
so close that Juliette was forced to look up.

"Who is it?" Juliette became anxious, hoping this wasn't the day
she'd always dreaded, the day an angry client appeared covered in
rashes, disfigured by a juliette&gwynne product. Juliette trusted
their ingredients, their merchandise, but who knew what toxin a
woman might mix in and then blame them.

"It's not a client." Gwynne covered Juliette's hand. "It's Tia."

Juliette tried to control her shaking as she walked to the front of the
shop. Madge, their sixty-three-year-old receptionist, whom they'd
chosen as an advertisement for the beauty of age, pushed papers as
she stared at the unfolding drama.

Sparks were in the air.

Juliette faced Tia as though preparing for a duel. They'd never
been this close. Juliette gripped her own upper arms so tightly it hurt.
Tia looked so young, younger than twenty-nine. She was twelve
years younger than Juliette. Prying that information from Nathan
had been like pulling rusty nails from petrified wood.

"What does it matter?" he'd asked.

"It matters," Juliette had answered.

It seemed like a generation of difference.

Tia's clothes looked cheap. Her thin black T-shirt was cut too low, almost showing the top of her bra. Her jeans were worn past fashion.

And she looked good despite her awful outfit. All I-don't-care pixie-pretty. Her enormous brown eyes, the color of damp soil, were ten fathoms deep. Those were the eyes in which Nathan had been lost.

Such a tiny waist. A baby had grown in there?

Tia stared back at Juliette. Judging from the intense stares of the handful of clients who'd drifted into the waiting area, their tension must have been apparent. Madge continued to pretend not to look, even as she memorized every move to report back to the rest of the staff. She might not know exactly what was going on, but enough tension crackled to alert Madge to put on her gossip-columnist hat.

Finally, Gwynne stepped in. "Juliette. Maybe you should take your . . . your appointment to your office." She gave Juliette's elbow a gently purposeful squeeze. "I'll bring in coffee."

Gwynne was letting Juliette know she'd check in. Did Gwynne think they'd end up on the floor pulling hair and slapping?

Juliette nodded. "Why don't you follow me?" She turned her back as she bit off the words.

They walked silently down the hall to Juliette's office. She gestured for Tia to enter and then followed. She indicated the chair across from her desk. Juliette had no plans to share the couch or sit kitty-corner-intimate in the two cushioned chairs angled by the window. No, she'd give Tia the glossy oak chair reserved for problem employees.

"What can I do for you?" Juliette set her face in a corpse-like mask.

"I think there's a different question," Tia said. "What is it you think I can do for you?"

"I don't know what you mean." Juliette's father-in-law drummed this into her: in business, make the opponent name the price first. This was the business of her marriage.

"Oh, come on." Tia's nervous laugh made Juliette want to throw her bowl of paper clips right at the young woman's head. "I'm certain you know what I mean."

Heat steamed from Juliette's brain straight to her twitching fingers. She picked up her coffee cup and pretended to take a sip from the empty mug. "Actually, I don't."

"Honor," Tia said. "My daughter. What's your interest in her? Why did you send Nathan to talk to me?"

"Send Nathan?"

"You know he came to see me, right?"

Juliette prayed the mug handle wouldn't crack in her grip. "Of course," she lied. "But what made you think I sent him?"

"'Juliette wants to see her.' That's what Nathan said, that you wanted to see my daughter. Why?"

That bastard. He hadn't even told her he'd spoken to Tia, much less that he'd gone to see her. Why keep it secret?

Juliette could only imagine.

"Actually, I don't owe you an explanation for anything," Juliette said. "I have no idea why you came here or what you expected."

"I want you to stay away from my daughter." Tia folded her hands in her lap as though she were in school.

"I want you to stay away from my husband."

"I'm not planning anything with Nathan." Tia grasped the arms of the chair, looking like she was about to leap out. "I came here to tell you that there are no rights for you with my daughter. None of this is your business. Neither of you. *Leave her alone.*"

"You gave her away."

"I found good parents for her," Tia said. "Great parents. I think about her every day. Nathan never did one thing for her. He didn't even acknowledge her."

Juliette closed her eyes, praying Tia would disappear.

"Did you think you could just go around meeting my daughter without even telling me? Leave her alone."

Juliette opened her eyes. "Your daughter? Do you know her favorite food, what her bedtime book is? Do you know what color she likes?"

Tia bit her lip, looking like she was about to cry. "You think you know me, don't you?"

Juliette didn't want to feel Tia's sadness creeping toward her. "She's Nathan's daughter. That connects me to her."

"Please, leave her alone."

Tia looked so frightened. Juliette worked to remain invulnerable to her. This was the woman who'd ruined her life. "I can't promise you that."

Tia stood to leave. She walked away, but when she got to the door, her hand on the knob, she turned back to Juliette. "He kissed me, you know. Nathan kissed me. Why do you think he did that?"

Juliette called Nathan the moment Tia left. Seconds later, their fight began, mainly a one-sided battle. While Juliette ranted, Nathan muttered "Uh-huh" into the phone, supposedly because he was walking on campus and afraid someone would hear him. Juliette believed that excuse as much as she believed anything else he'd said.

"Honest to God, Jules, I was doing this for us. For our protection."

"We can't have secrets. Don't you think I know that? But I needed to find out the facts."

"I planned to tell you. I honestly did."

When Juliette got home, Nathan was there, but, of course, so were the boys.

They had dinner. Afterward, Nathan opened the mail and paid bills. Juliette answered emails and cleaned the kitchen. Then the two of them kissed the boys good night. Finally, they were alone in the family room, Nathan in the club chair, Juliette on the couch. Juliette put down the magazine she held as a prop and turned to Nathan. He held the remote in his hand, ready to switch on the television.

"You kissed her." The TV remained off. "I can't believe you kissed her."

"Kiss? It was a chaste peck on the cheek, Jules." He leaned over and touched her hand. "It meant nothing. It was just a hello."

Juliette pulled away. "How could you not tell me you visited?"

"I didn't go to her house; we met at a coffee shop."

"Where?"

"What difference does that make?"

"What difference does it make to tell me? Why can't you just answer me instead of repeating my questions?"

"Quincy, we met in Quincy."

"Because you didn't want to be seen?"

"Honey. Keep your voice down—do you want the boys to hear us?"

Juliette grabbed a pillow and held it over her stomach, squeezing it so hard she felt the stems of the feathers that filled the downy cushion.

"You're an idiot," she whispered. "Quincy? It's the opposite of convenient."

Nathan remained silent. He looked sick.

"Was Quincy one of your old stomping grounds?"

He put down the remote. "Sweetheart, you told me we should see Honor."

"Savannah. That's her name." Juliette worked on not screaming, not crying. "I said we should see the child, not that woman."

"Was I supposed to march over to Dover and demand to see the girl? I've never had any contact with them."

"You didn't give the child up, *she* did."

"Actually, I did." Nathan looked miserable in a way that twisted Juliette's heart into frayed rope. "By walking away from Tia without a word, I walked away from the baby."

Juliette clenched her eyes shut against hearing him say the name. She kept her head bowed so Nathan couldn't see her face.

"I asked her to get rid of it," Nathan said.

Savannah's face—so like Max's—rose like an apparition.

"I asked her to have an abortion," Nathan added, as though his words hadn't been clear enough.

It didn't seem possible to keep two such disparate thoughts in her head: horror at the idea of that little girl having been snuffed away, and a hopeless, retroactive wish that the abortion had happened.

"I couldn't go to see the child, however you thought it might happen, without telling Tia. It wouldn't have been fair. You can understand that, can't you?"

"You can't even hear yourself, can you? Who do you think I am?" She stood and walked in circles. "I'm not your mother, filled with bottomless love and sympathy."

"You're a good woman. I know that. Why else would you have even brought up the idea of seeing Honor?"

"Savannah," Juliette murmured. "Savannah, Savannah, Savannah."

"Savannah," he repeated. "I love you, Jules."

"Promise me you'll never see her again. *Never.*"

"How can I do that and also do what you want: see Hon—Savannah?"

"She. Gave. Her. Up." Juliette said the words one deliberate syllable at a time. "She has no legal rights. The only ones we have to speak with are Savannah's parents. Her legal and only parents."

"Wishing something doesn't make it true. Like it or not, Tia gave birth to her."

"And then she gave her away. Don't you get it?"

"Don't you?" Nathan's patient tone gave way. "She gave her away because of me, because I abandoned her."

"Is that what you think? That your fragile girlfriend was forced like Little Nell out into the cold? You tore the child from her arms, did you?"

Juliette went to Nathan, leaned over, and grabbed the arms of his chair. "What do you think I'd have done, if I were pregnant and you said, 'Give it up?' If you told me, 'I'll have nothing to do with you?' Would I have aborted Max? Given Lucas away?"

"That's so different—you're comparing totally different circumstances."

"No, Nathan. There are bottom lines, and this is mine. Nothing—*nothing*—would have made me give up my child."

Nathan looked up. He shook his head. "It's different with her."

"I cannot believe that you're taking her side."

"There are no sides. It's simply a situation," he said. Nathan the rational. "A horribly sad situation."

"Apparently it's a situation in which you can go anywhere, while I'm only allowed access to you. Oh, except when your girlfriend charges into my office."

"She's scared. She thinks we're ganging up on her."

"Why shouldn't we?" Juliette clenched her fists. "She slept with a married man. She gave up a baby. I owe her nothing."

"I'm sorry. I don't think it's the same for me," Nathan said. "It just doesn't seem fair. I know I was awful. I did a terrible thing to you. But, Jules, I also did a terrible thing to her."

Nathan stood in front of her, and she saw regret and yearning in his eyes—a wistful sadness for someone who wasn't Juliette.

CHAPTER 25

Nathan

Nathan stared at his wife, waiting for her, willing her to soften, aware that he was asking for a miracle: a second round of absolution.

"Get out." Juliette spoke so low Nathan almost missed her words. "I want you out of here. Go."

"Go?" Nathan pretended not to understand. Jesus, it was all happening too fast for him to figure it out; to take care of everyone's needs. He felt as though he were a cardboard clown head, popping up and down at a carnival booth, with everyone trying to knock him down.

Juliette bent her head to the side and studied him, her eyes hot with hurt anger. He wished for the millionth time that he could erase everything he'd done wrong.

"Nathan, it's too goddamned late to play games."

"I love you, Jules. You know that."

She stared into his eyes. "You love me, you love me. I know you love me. But that's not the issue. I don't know what to think about you. You're defending her to me, asking my understanding. Do you understand at all what is tearing me apart? Even after all of this, you did it again. You . . . your sin of omission is leaving me out. Once again, I'm the outsider."

He watched his wife trembling in front of him. Without a word, she walked to the bedroom, Nathan followed right behind. Still silent, she looked around as though an answer lay somewhere in their bedroom, and then she walked over to the door and shut it with a quiet deliberation that told Nathan she'd wanted to slam it so that the roof shook.

"I don't want the kids to hear."

He rose and caught up with her as she released the doorknob. "Jules, listen. You're not the outsider. Oh, Jesus, never. But I need to make things as right as I can with her before we sort this all out."

Nathan reached for her; he touched her shoulder.

She shook him off. "Don't."

"I thought we were in this together."

"If we were in this together, you wouldn't have gone there without telling me. You have a relationship with her whether you screw her or not, and you just proved it." Juliette grabbed a nightgown and opened the door to their bathroom.

"Please, don't." He wondered about the intent of his own words. Don't what? Did he mean "Don't leave me"? "Don't walk away"? There seemed to be a million things that Nathan didn't want her to do. Juliette never changed in the bathroom, always allowing him the quiet sexual simmer of watching her undress—an unspoken pleasure of their marriage.

She didn't pretend to misunderstand. "I can't give you any more."

"Please, Jules. Let's not get overdramatic. A kiss? God, it wasn't a real kiss. We're talking friendship, past connection. She simply gave you her point of view."

"Don't tell me about overdramatic. Her? She? Why not name your beloved?" Juliette brought the nightgown closer to her chest. "Tia Adagio. Ms. Mother Teresa of mistresses."

"Jesus, she's not my mistress, Juliette."

"Listen to yourself! So indignant."

"It was a million years ago."

"Six. Six years ago." Juliette balled the nightgown between her hands. "If you were done . . . if you and that girl—that woman—if you were truly done, you wouldn't have lied to me about seeing her."

"I didn't lie."

"But you didn't tell, Nathan." She began weeping. *"You didn't tell."*

He didn't know what to say. Her rare tears silenced him. She was right. He hadn't told.

Juliette threw herself on the bed. Tears leaked from her eyes to the bedspread. Nathan lay beside her. He touched her hip, and this time she did not smack him away, so he leaned over her and kissed away her tears.

Nathan loved Juliette. He hated that he'd hurt her.

Her skin was, as always, soft, warm, and welcome under his fingertips. There was never a time he didn't want his wife. That's what she didn't understand. He needed to make Juliette understand that they were two sides of the same coin—connected by their children, their love, and their years together.

He'd seen this woman give birth to their sons.

He kissed her salty lips.

His wife.

He unbuttoned her shirt.

Heat rose, love rose, this woman, he loved her. In the best way. The right way.

He kissed her throat.

She pushed him away. "Don't touch me. Go sleep in the guest room. Your study. The fucking lawn. I don't care where, as long as it's not here." She drew her knees up close and cradled them in her arms. "I want you out of here tomorrow."

Nathan cleared his throat as he prepared to wreck his son's lives. His boys sat across from him in the pink and orange Dunkin' Donuts booth. He'd pled with Juliette to reconsider.

"How can we do this to the boys?" he'd asked Juliette.

"I didn't do this to the boys," she'd answered. *"You did."*

"Max, Lucas—I have to go away for a bit." Nathan had rehearsed this conversation, trying to find the best words, but in the end, he could do no more than simply get it out and over.

Max's eyes widened. Lucas tightened his grip on his muffin until it crumbled between his fingers.

"You're leaving?" Max's voice cracked. "Leaving us? Leaving Mom? Are you getting a divorce?"

Why had Nathan chosen this stupid place? Could he have picked a worse place? People pressed close on all sides, and even if he didn't know any of them, they might recognize him or the boys. Soccer. Little League. Town meetings. Word got around. What if Max cried?

Shit, shit, shit.

Nathan still couldn't believe Juliette really meant it; that she'd thrown him out.

"You should be the one to tell them," she'd said. "You made this particular bed."

Nathan looked at the array of crap in front of them. Huge, frothy drinks filled with cream, chocolate, and caffeine competed for table space with sugary donuts and oversized muffins greasy with butter. Or lard. Without Juliette watching him, he'd probably drop dead of heart disease within a year.

"No, no, we're not getting divorced. It's a break," Nathan said. "Just a break."

"Bullshit. Since when do families take breaks?" Lucas asked.

"Why do you need a break? How long of a break?" Max chewed at a ragged fingernail. "Where are you going? Why, Daddy?"

Nathan's chest contracted at hearing Max call him *Daddy*, a word he hadn't used in years.

"Mom's making you leave, right?" Lucas asked. "She's been acting crazy lately."

"Don't you dare blame this on me, either," Juliette had warned. "You want to lie, then lie—you're good at that."

"It's not about Mom. Sometimes adults just need some space."
Yes, Lucas. It's bullshit. I have nothing else to offer.

"Space?" Lucas snorted. "That's what this is about? Space? You're an asshole."

Nathan debated taking on Lucas about cursing; neither of his boys had ever sworn at him.

"I know you're angry, Lucas, but that doesn't give you license to curse."

"Asshole," Lucas repeated.

"I don't understand," Max said.

"So if Max and I say we want some space, do we get to walk out?" Lucas banged the fleshy part of his palm hard against the table. The elderly couple next to them looked up. Nathan sent them an apologetic smile. *You know how boys are,* his grin said.

"Your mother and I have been married a long time. Sometimes, in these situations, people need a breather."

"You need a 'breather' from Mom?" Lucas made finger quotes in the air. "This just gets better and better."

"Not a breather from Mom."

"Then who? Us?" Lucas swept his hair from his eyes. Nathan saw how muscled he'd become; how close Lucas was to being a man. Nathan didn't want to leave his sons.

"No, no, never from you," he said.

"What's left? The house? You want to get away from the house? The yard? The car? The driveway? What the fuck is it, Dad?" Lucas was crying. He'd worried about Max breaking down, but not Lucas. Jesus, how had he done this to his boy?

"Come on, guys. Let's go." Nathan stood. He leaned over Lucas, placing an arm around his shoulders. Lucas got up, pulling away from Nathan with a dismissive shrug. Max stood close to his brother.

Nathan guided his sons outside. Once in the warm air, he had no idea where to go, what to say. *Yeah, boys, I need to get away from that old driveway. The yard and I need some time apart.*

Lucas was right. He was an asshole.

A week later, Nathan was living at a hotel. He hated it. He felt as though the staff judged him each time he came and went, as if they knew he was staying at the Royal Sonesta because he'd failed his wife.

Feeling his mother's eyes on him, he cleaned his room for the maid, so she wouldn't think him an awful slob. He didn't want to make her job any harder by leaving toothpaste in the sink. Now, even though it was evening, and there would be no maid coming, Nathan rushed around putting his dirty laundry in a bag. Chores made for one less empty minute.

It was already well past seven. Tia expected him at seven thirty, and the Cambridge hotel was at least a half-hour drive from her apartment. He grabbed his car keys from the hotel water glass on the bureau.

The last time he'd been at a hotel without Juliette, he'd been with Tia, the first time they slept together. Nathan and Tia drove the hour from Waltham, to be as far as possible from prying eyes, to an anonymous box built for businessmen and tourists.

They had fallen on each other the moment the door shut behind them. Whoever said the first time wasn't good had discounted the was-great parts. Maybe he'd been too fast, and maybe they were clumsy, their bodies crashing against each other, but frantic hunger outshone the awkward moments.

Tia's body had amazed him, all tight muscle. Having all that and then going home to Juliette's lushness had been an embarrassment of riches.

There was nothing justifiable about his time with Tia, except that it had felt good, great, and he'd chosen not to deny himself. When he met Tia, six years ago, Lucas had been nine and Max was four. Life had become a round of chores piling upon chores, at home, at work—even visits to his parents were filled with carrying enough baggage to care for a tiny country comprised of two small pashas, with his parents offering their worship in the form of adoration, pushing yet more stuff—toys, books, clothes—on Juliette and him to cram in the car for the ride home.

Not that he slept with Tia because his parents doted on the kids. God, the thought made him sound appalling. But he'd gone from feeling as though he were on the edge of conquering the world—marriage to his stunning Juliette, a prestigious professorship, publishing his studies—to spending weekends doing laundry and following Max and Lucas around the playground while Juliette caught up with work she'd put to the side all week.

Not that he blamed her for a moment. But his father had remained the center of his mother's world, even as she made room on that pedestal for Nathan, and he'd thought it would be the same in his marriage.

With Tia, he'd gone from being the daddy who was secretly sick of reading Caldecott Medal–winning illustrated children's books to Max, and Harry Potter to Lucas, and from the husband tired of washing dishes after the dinners Juliette cooked, to appearing handsome, smart, and exciting. Even as it frightened him, what a god Tia seemed to think him. The young woman's adoration became addictive. He felt in love with her loving him.

It sickened him, but if Nathan took up some retrospective truthfulness, they both fell in love with him.

Now, after working as long as possible, he burned time in the mall across from the hotel. He'd roamed from one chain to another: Sears, Yankee Candle, Swarovski—who knew there were so many ways to throw away money—looking for the store selling something that could make Juliette happy. Make her speak to him. If he bought her a crystal flask, would a genie emerge and grant him forgiveness?

Then he'd come back to his hotel room and call Juliette, begging to come home. Every night she threw another ultimatum his way:

"Make it right with Tia, so we never hear from her again."

"Find out if you love her."

"Convince me, Nathan. Convince me it's truly over."

But she didn't provide a single clue as to how he was supposed to make any of these things happen.

Finally, he'd called Tia.

"You're here." Tia's two-word greeting sounded wary. She stood in front of the apartment door with her arms crossed over her small chest.

"Are you going to let me in?" Nathan asked.

She gave a crooked half smile and stepped aside just enough to let him squeeze past. Waves of fresh shower scent washed over him, but her fragrance was unfamiliar. A different soap, something sharp and lemony, not the flowery scent in which he'd once become lost.

Her hair stuck up in angry points, shorter than it had ever been. When they'd been together, her almost-black hair covered her head like thick mink, a cap revealing her vulnerable neck. She'd worn poppy-red lipstick and nothing else. Now, black and blue outlined her eyes. Her tight body, formerly draped in gauze and silk, looked scrawny under a black tank top and jeans.

"Why are you here?" she asked.

"Can we sit down?"

"I'm not sure. Are you here because she sent you?"

"No."

She stepped aside. He walked into the living room and sat in a battered-looking chair. Tia followed, her anxiety apparent in the forward thrust of her shoulders.

"Can we just talk?" he asked. "No bull?"

She fell on the couch and crossed her legs.

"I'm expecting somebody," Tia said. "We don't have a long time."

"Who?" Nathan immediately regretted the jealous-sounding word.

"Who?" Her sudden sweet smile reminded him how it felt to care for her; vulnerability he could hardly afford.

"None of my business," he said. "Sorry."

Tia should hate him. It would make all this easier for both of them. He could do nothing worse than open her up to caring.

"I admit that I was a coward." Nathan chose his words with effort, working to avoid mentioning Juliette and still include everything his wife had demanded as the price for his return. "I deserve nothing and should get even less. That said, we need to talk about . . . everything."

He scrambled his questions into an order least likely to anger Tia. He took a deep breath and tried to speak like a normal person. "What's going on with you?"

"I've met someone." Now she leaned forward. "I think it's serious. I told him about Honor."

"Did you tell him about us?"

"I told him about you. There is no 'us.'"

"What did you say about me?"

She fell back against the couch cushion. "For God's sake, what do you care? Anyway, he wanted to know about Honor, not about you."

"What's he like?"

"He's a good man."

"Good. I'm happy." He was. "What does he think about you having a daughter?"

"He's great about it."

Tia's clear subtext was *unlike you.* "I want to see her," he said.

"I'm not sure if I care what you want anymore," she said. She chewed her lip too hard for him to believe her.

"Is my name on the birth certificate?" he asked.

She didn't say anything.

"Is it?" he asked again.

"'Take care of this for me, Tia.' That's all you offered me. Now you need me? I have nothing to give."

"Why did you let me come, then?"

"I'm not sure." She stared at him with that searching look he'd hated when they were together, a look that meant *What about us? Do you love me enough? Want me enough? Will you care for me?*

He didn't look away. Wasn't he supposed to find this out? "Do you love her?" Juliette had asked. "Does she love you?"

Had he ever loved her? She'd popped into his life, twenty-four years old and from a different world, exotic to him, sexy, and thrilled to work on his research study. He'd never expected to sleep with her. When he did, his only excuse was desire. She drove him crazy. When Tia fell in love with him, he tried to convince himself that he was in love with her, not just crazy in lust. It made him feel less disgusted about his choices.

"How do I find my daughter?" Nathan asked. "Please. How can I see the parents?"

"*Go see her,*" Juliette had said.

"*How?*" he'd asked.

"*You figured out how to conceive her without me. Now figure out how to see her.*" Juliette had insisted that he meet his daughter but refused to give her the information to complete the mission.

Nathan couldn't imagine where to start. Was he supposed to find their number, call them out of the blue, walk in, and demand to meet his daughter?

"Ask your wife," Tia said.

Nathan couldn't read her true intent. She looked heartbroken. He walked over to the couch, sat beside her, and took her hand. "Please. Let's not play any more games."

She shook her hand from his. "I think you should leave." She turned her head, but he heard the tears clogging her words.

"Tia, I'm sorry." Nathan moved closer. "I'm so sorry for everything."

CHAPTER 26

Caroline

Caroline closed the lid of her briefcase, pushing down to make it latch. She had about ten journals to read when she got home, plus a file bulging with memos, and, most important, she needed to go over notes for a presentation she'd be making, "The Effects of Chemotherapy in Combination with Focal Therapy on Intraocular Retinoblastoma to Avoid Enucleation and Radiotherapy." Just reading the title exhausted her. She could easily sink into her desk chair and close her eyes, but she'd promised Savannah she'd be home on time, and she was going to do it.

Her phone rang just as she'd finished arranging neat piles of papers for the next day. Jonah's name appeared on caller ID, an unwelcome sight. After a moment of hesitation, she reached for the phone. She'd never answered his email. She didn't even remember giving him her phone number, but she supposed that finding her at the hospital wasn't difficult.

"Jonah." Caroline greeted him with his name.

"Surprised?" Jonah paused. Caroline heard him swallow.

"I am."

"I'd really like to see you."

"Are you drinking?" Caroline asked.

"A little. Just enough."

"Just enough for what?"

"Just enough to call you and tell you how much I'm thinking about you."

He slurred his words. Caroline wanted him off the phone. Now. "Jonah? It's never going to happen."

"I sense that you're unhappy. Like me. Maybe we can help each other."

"Jonah, go see your wife."

Caroline arrived home in a positive frame of mind, her exhaustion lifted, determined that she and Peter could work things out. Stress gave him those crazy ideas, like her leaving her job. Maybe they'd take a family vacation.

The house smelled of lemon polish and whatever treats Nanny Rose and Savannah had spent the afternoon baking. Oatmeal cookies?

The quiet house gave no clue to her daughter's whereabouts. She peeked into the playroom, the kitchen—already cleaned, and she was correct about the oatmeal cookies—Savannah's room. All were empty. Crunching a cookie she'd picked up from a flowered plate on the counter, Caroline wandered into the backyard.

"Mommy!" Savannah ran over from the sandbox. "You found the cookies! We made them."

Caroline pulled away from Savannah's dirt-streaked hands, kissing her sweaty hair, which was falling out of a loosening ponytail. "They're delicious. Good job."

"What are we having for supper?" Savannah asked.

"Cookies and milk?"

"Really?" Savannah's eyes gleamed at the idea.

Caroline tweaked the girl's nose. "No. I'm going inside to change. Rose," she asked, "did Peter call?"

Nanny Rose looked up with those annoying knowing eyes she'd been using lately, sniffing out the problems between Caroline and

Peter. "He'll be home soon," she said. Maybe she'd somehow sensed Jonah's presence.

Caroline glared at her. *Stop smirking. Nothing happened.* But something happened, right? Hadn't she almost considered meeting Jonah? How much guilt should one carry from almost meeting someone? She imagined Peter talking to another woman. Emailing. Sharing pieces of himself. Getting that far and then stopping.

Would she laud him for stopping or damn him for taking even the smallest step?

She'd damn him.

"Savannah, why don't we make something silly for supper?" Caroline said.

"Yes, Mommy!" Savannah hugged her tight. Caroline took her daughter's small face in her hands, turned it up, and planted fairy kisses all over her face. Savannah loved those soft, teeny pecks.

An hour later, Caroline deeply regretted her decision to make a fun supper. Cooking was never fun. Perhaps she just wasn't a particularly fun person, period.

As she rolled yet another little meatball, Caroline remembered her mother taking turns teaching Caroline and her sisters how to prepare dinners. Until Caroline took herself out of the lineup, she'd been forced to participate in an agonizing cooking lesson once a week.

"Can we make a smiley meatball face? Like Daddy does?" Savannah's hands were slick with fat from the raw meat, just as hers were. Caroline tamped down her desire to scrub the girl's skin, throw the whole mess in the garbage, and eat a simple salad. That's all she wanted tonight: greens with perhaps some grapes on top, pecans sprinkled in, and apples slices circling the lettuce.

Caroline laid down the last meatball she could bear rolling and rushed to the sink. She squirted lemon soap on her hands and then placed them under hot—too hot—water. "Come here, Savannah. Let's wash your hands."

"Not yet, Mommy. I want to make meatball snakes."

"No. It's time to put everything in the oven. Daddy will be home soon. We need to bake the meatballs before we put them on the spaghetti casserole."

"No. I want to put snakes on the casserole." Savannah stuck out her lower lip in her stubborn pout. "The spaghetti will be the worms, and the meatballs will be the snakes. Except the round ones, they'll be the maggots."

"Sweetie, why would we want maggots on our food?"

Savannah shrank back. "You said we could do a silly supper, Mommy."

"I didn't say disgusting, though. Maggots are nasty things."

"But they're funny. They were in a book."

"No they're not. They're gross," Caroline said. "And we're not making them. Put down the meat, come here, and let me wash your hands. Now."

"No. I'm making maggots. You promised."

Caroline slammed a pot on the side of the sink. "Jesus, Savannah. I didn't promise you could make maggots."

"You promised to be fun!"

"Get over here. *Now*."

"*No*."

"I said now!"

Savannah lifted the greasy plate covered with meatballs and held it protectively to her chest as though Caroline were about to take it from her.

"That's disgusting, Savannah. Put it down."

"*No*. It's not disgusting." Savannah clutched it closer to her chest, backing up on the chair she stood on until it tipped over. Savannah fell, still holding the bowl, the meatballs scattered over the wooden floor. "I want the silly supper," she sobbed.

"What the heck?" Peter walked in, put down his briefcase, and hurried over to where Savannah lay. "Honey, what happened?"

"Mommy didn't want me to make meatball maggots."

Peter looked like he was trying not to laugh. Caroline wanted to kill him.

"Come here, Cookie." He gathered Savannah into his arms, mindless of his suit, his white shirt, and his silk tie, and kissed her grimy cheeks. "How about we clean you up, and then I'll order pizza?"

Peter walked into the study, smiling, and looking content. "She's asleep. It took three books, but she's finally down for the night."

"I'm a terrible mother," Caroline said.

"What are you talking about?" Peter sat beside her on the couch, removing a journal from her hands. "Baby, every mother fights with her kids now and then. I'm surprised the Department of Social Services never came to our house when I was a kid. You should have heard poor Dad trying to referee when my mom went bonkers."

"No. This is different. It's not about losing my temper; I'm not a good mother." Caroline emphasized every word. "As in always, not as in tonight."

Peter put his hands on her shoulders and squeezed. "What are you talking about? You're a great mother."

"Listen to me. This is who I am. This is the woman you asked to stay home and be with your daughter full-time." Caroline drew away. "Look at me. I can't stand getting dirty. I get so bored playing with her that I could bash a Bitty doll against the wall. I don't want to bake cookies. I don't want to have playdates, and I can't stand reading *Adoption Is for Always* one more time."

"Caro, if you spent some time with other mothers, you'd know that's all normal. You should hear my sisters."

Caroline tried to suck back the words already sliding down her tongue, ready to jump off and strangle her and Peter, but she couldn't. She didn't. "Peter, I feel as though I'm losing my mind when I'm with her. She bores me. Do you hear what I'm saying? Being a mother drives me crazy. There's no way around it. I am failing her. She deserves better."

"All you need is to calm down. This is a tough age, right? 'Play with me, play with me.' She just needs more friends. We'll get her into a kid's program this summer Now, let me get you a glass of wine."

"You're not listening." Caroline pressed her fingers to her temples.

She rocked back and forth and then covered her mouth with her hands. "I don't know if I can do this."

"Do what? What are you talking about?"

The last brick holding back her wall of denial tumbled to the ground. Caroline threw her head against the back of the couch, closed her eyes, and then spoke. "I had coffee with the wife of Savannah's father."

"Savannah's father? His wife? What are you talking about? Tia didn't know who the father was." Peter seemed to inflate in front of her. "Who is this woman? Why were you talking to her? What the hell is this about?"

"She called me." Caroline gripped her elbows and took a deep breath. "Apparently Tia lied. She had an affair with this woman's husband. They live right over in Wellesley."

Peter stood. He paced around the study, taking deep breaths. "You're talking to some crazy lady who claims her husband is Savannah's father? What's it about? Do you hear yourself? You sound nuts."

"I'm not nuts, and she's not crazy—"

"Some woman calls you and says her husband had an affair with Tia and the child is his, and you don't wonder if she's just the slightest bit off? You don't tell me? What's going on?"

Caroline thought of telling him about juliette&gwynne, where and how they met, and then realized Juliette would sound even crazier if she told him that particular story. Maybe he was right. Perhaps Juliette was crazy. Aching fatigue washed over her.

"Forget it," she said.

"Forget it? You're kidding, right?" Peter raked his fingers through his hair. "We can't forget this."

Caroline couldn't imagine how she'd agreed to Peter's insistence that she meet with Tia. She needed to do more research, more reading. She clutched the steering wheel, snapped on NPR, and then snapped it off when the voices bored into her brain. No, Peter wasn't the wait-and-read type.

He'd rushed right into protection mode: "What does this mean? What do they want? Where is Tia in this?" Then, being Peter, he needed action.

"First things first," Peter had said. "You spoke to the wife of the supposed biological father. What does that tell us, besides the fact that they have problems in their marriage? They haven't a bit of legal standing."

So here Caroline was, on a reconnaissance mission, something for which she was spectacularly unsuited, but Peter was convinced that if he went, it would scare Tia, and God knows what she'd do if they frightened her. Tia might not have legal rights, but she could make their lives unbearably messy.

Traffic barely moved on Centre Street in Jamaica Plain as she looked for the landmark restaurants and stores Tia had mentioned when giving Caroline directions: Fire & Opal Gifts. Purple Cactus. Boing.

Peter suggested simply showing up at Tia's door, but Caroline didn't have those rights. Appearing at someone's door uninvited was the height of rudeness. Caroline's mother had drummed good manners into all her children, and unsolicited guests topped her bad behavior list.

Their conversation had been brief. Caroline asked to see her, Tia asked why, and Caroline said she'd rather talk in person. How could she explain that she wanted to check out Tia and see if she knew about Juliette?

"See if something is up, Caro," Peter had ordered. "Who knows, maybe Tia and this asshole are seeing each other. Maybe they have some fucked-up idea of coming after Savannah." Peter had smacked one hand into the other as though it were the asshole's head. "Over my dead body they'll get near my family."

Caroline offered to go to Tia's apartment, making it easy for her, but the suggestion was answered with silence. Finally, Tia had said, "Let's meet at City Feed. It's just down the street. We can get coffee there."

Caroline pulled into a one-hour parking space. She didn't imagine they'd talk longer than that.

City Feed and Supply, part granola-looking sandwich shop, part upscale market, appeared new, all shiny glass windows and polished floors, and yet the store also seemed to declare "Of course we're here. What else could be on this corner?"

A few wood tables were to her right, where Tia waited, staring, both hands wrapped around a classic thick white diner mug. Caroline placed her handbag on the empty chair, smiled, and put out her hand.

"Thanks for coming."

"No problem." Tia's hand was cold. She looked almost the same. Of course, she wasn't pregnant, but even pregnant, Tia had seemed delicate, so different from Savannah. However, look at those eyes: her daughter's eyes stared back at Caroline. Savannah's full, pink lips that kissed her good night were Tia's lips.

"Do you mind if I get coffee?" Caroline asked. "Can I get you anything?"

Tia shook her head and then pointed with her sharp chin toward the counter, showing Caroline where to go.

The prospect of lying already had her off base. Peter's concocted cover story, about needing information regarding Savannah's family health history, sounded thin and obvious.

Her one mission was to judge Tia, and Caroline felt awful about it. If Caroline and Peter even considered Juliette's idea that Savannah should know her father, Caroline felt bound to let Tia know, but Peter would explode if she did more than take Tia's measure.

Caroline tried not to let the coffee slosh over when she placed it on the table. She'd poured in too much milk in hopes of calming her stomach.

She sat.

She took a sip.

"How is she?" Tia asked.

Now Caroline saw the trembling hands, the bitten nails, and felt a surge of protectiveness toward Tia, over a decade younger than she was.

"She's good," Caroline said.

Tia gave a dry smile. "Can you give me a bit more?"

"Sorry." Caroline wrapped her own shaky, cold hands around the warm mug. "It's just . . . seeing you. It's disturbing. Not that you're disturbing me—it's just unsettling."

Tia circled her fingers in a figure eight pattern, making slight marks on the table. "Does she look like me?"

"Yes. Somewhat. You must know that from the pictures, though," Caroline said.

"I guess."

Tia's starving eyes belied her diffident words. She looked so greedy for news of Savannah that Caroline felt even more ashamed of hiding her real reason for coming.

"What does she like to do?"

"She loves her dolls. Despite all our attempts to get her interested in blocks and trucks, dolls and stuffed animals are her favorites." Caroline brought the coffee to her lips, buying time, and then sipped. "Savannah loves to sing. And bake. She's a very smart little girl. She's reading. She'll be in kindergarten next year, you know."

"Does she like nursery school?" Tia asked.

Caroline realized how stingy she'd been in her once-a-year letters. Along with the photographs, she'd stick in a note; oh God, she'd used the heavy monogrammed note cards her mother placed in her Christmas stocking each year, scribbling a few miserly words. "Savannah loves planting flowers!" "Savannah's favorite author is Rosemary Wells."

"She hasn't gone to preschool." Guilt rushed through Caroline as she realized how wrong she'd been about not sending Savannah to preschool. Keeping her with Nanny Rose had been easy. Convincing Peter and herself that the playdates that Nanny arranged were enough had been her out.

"When does she get to see other children?" Tia asked.

"She goes to a play group twice a week. At the library." Caroline didn't mention that it was Nanny Rose who brought the girl. "We'll probably look into something more regular now that it's almost summer. But, like I said, she has the library play group. And we have kids from the group come over the house."

Play group, indeed. Listen to her fancying up story hour. And it was Nanny who invited the other little girls over, not Caroline. In just a few moments, Tia had demonstrated how much better a mother she'd have been. Caroline had been content with too little for Savannah. She'd made Savannah into a lonely little girl with no one but Nanny Rose and the Bitty Twins for company. She promised herself she'd find a summer program for Savannah.

"She has playdates, right?" Tia asked. "When I was growing up, the mothers were always dumping their kids on each other."

"Well, our neighborhood isn't that conducive to . . . running in and out of each other's homes."

"Right." Tia laughed. "Not unless five-year-olds have started driving."

"What else do you want to know?" Where had Caroline's head been all these years? She hadn't even wondered about Tia. Had she truly convinced herself that it was a big relief for Tia to give away Savannah?

"Is she happy?" Tia studied Caroline. "What kind of temperament does she have?"

"She's sort of studious. No, that's the wrong word. She's solemn."

"You mean she's sad?"

Caroline saw heartbreak on Tia's face and hastened to correct this impression. "No, no, not sad. She's thoughtful. I don't think she's a carefree sort—not genetically. What was her father like?"

Tia drew back. "I told you. I don't know who her father is."

Caroline gripped the edge of the table. She hated lying. Peter should have come. She got as close as possible so she wouldn't have to speak loud. "I'm sorry, Tia, but I know that you do."

"What's this about, Caroline? Why are you really here?"

"The wife of the man . . ." What words were there for this? "Savannah's father, his wife contacted me."

"Nathan's wife sent you?" Tia looked horrified. "Juliette? Juliette sent you?"

CHAPTER 27

Tia

"History proves that adoption laws favor the biological parents," the lawyer said.

Bobby had given her this lawyer's phone number—someone he'd sold an apartment to last year. See, that was the beauty of Southie. Everyone helped everyone. They weren't too busy earning buckets of money to support one another.

Who the hell did Caroline think she was? Keeping her daughter locked up all day with some damned nanny; she couldn't even get it together to send Honor to nursery school. In Southie, even the dumbest mothers knew enough to let their kids see other kids.

"On the other hand," the lawyer said, "It's been a long time. The chance of a court reversing an adoption after five years is practically zero. It would be considered only if there were extraordinary circumstances. If someone lied, or consent wasn't given."

Tia ran a hand over the scrapbook of Honor she held on her lap. "What if the father hadn't known; hadn't given his permission?" She gripped the phone tighter. "Would that count?"

"It would still be a hell of a long shot, a million to one—but if that's true, I'd at least consider your case. The father would have to be on board, of course. On top of that, there'd have to be compelling evidence as to how and why it would be in the best interest of the child to take her from the parents she's known since birth."

The thought of talking to Nathan about this made Tia queasy. The thought of disappointing Bobby made her want to cry. Anger that Nathan's wife had been in contact with Caroline made her brave.

"Let me get back to you," she said.

"Come over," she'd said. "Tonight."

She refused to tell Nathan more than that. When questioned, she simply repeated her words, hung up, and then, with a fast email, canceled her plans with Bobby.

"I have to take care of old work business tonight," she wrote. "Nothing bad, don't worry. Will call tmw."

She paced her apartment as she waited for the hours to pass until Nathan arrived, switching the television on and off, hopping from site to site on the computer, even doing jumping jacks at one point, but none of the frenetic activity calmed her.

The last time she'd seen Nathan, she'd put on makeup and fussed over her clothes. This time she didn't bother. Screw him. She'd spent enough time putting on pretty dresses and smoothing magic powders on her skin. Now she wanted to cover herself with war paint, smear jagged lines of red down her face. Greet him with a whoop of hate.

Nevertheless, impulse drove her to shower, open the windows, and let in fresh air. Run a vacuum over the rug. Tia told herself it was for her own self-esteem, as though dusting would improve her mood.

Soon, but not soon enough, the doorbell rang.

She took a deep breath and looked in the mirror hanging by the side of the door. Anger brightened her eyes in place of eyeliner.

Tia opened the door. Nathan stood still and quiet.

More than anything, she hated that she still wanted him.

"Guess who I saw last week?" Tia asked.

"Did I miss the beginning of this conversation?" Nathan came toward her. "Can I come in?"

Tia wanted to say "No. We can talk just fine right here in the doorway."

She moved back, and he entered.

"How about I come all the way in, okay?" Nathan pointed toward the living room.

"Let's sit in the kitchen." Tia turned, and Nathan followed.

He sat at the table.

"Do you want anything to drink?" She forced these words out, determined not to come across as foolish.

"What do you have?" he asked.

"What I have is a feeling of being played by everyone, including you and your wife. She wants to see Honor. You want to see Honor. And somehow I'm expected to help the two of you?"

Nathan held up his hands as though blocking her from coming closer. "Whoa! Can I have that drink? Or at least a glass of water?"

Tia threw open the refrigerator, grabbed a beer and slammed it on the table, then splashed some Jameson into a glass.

"What's this about?" Nathan looked nervous.

Tia gulped half her whiskey. "Caroline, the woman who adopted Honor, came to see me. Because guess who went to see her?"

"Jesus," Nathan said.

"Exactly. Apparently, your wife has a deep interest in my child. Now, why would that be?"

"What did this Caroline say?"

"'This Caroline,' Nathan? That's what you call her? This Caroline is the woman mothering your child."

Nathan looked down. He pressed his lips together as he traced the circular design in the linoleum with his foot.

"What?" Tia asked. "What are you trying to not say?"

"'My child.' Juliette says it, and you say it, but I can't make it feel real. My sons, they're my children. I don't know this little girl, so is she my daughter?" Nathan held up a hand at her. "Don't jump down my throat. It's true."

"No. It's not true. Feelings don't make or not make her your child. She *is* your child. That's your problem, how quickly the conversation is about you."

He pressed his fingers to his forehead until the skin looked bruised. "What now?"

"I need to know why Juliette went to Caroline." She walked to the counter, shuffling mail to keep from shaking him, touching him. "Please. The truth, Nathan."

Nathan ran his fingers up and down the neck of the green beer bottle. "She told me that she'd looked up some stuff about these people: Caroline and her husband. Honestly, I don't know why she actually met with her or what she said. Anything I say is only a guess."

"Then guess. I need to know."

"Probably something to do with throwing me out. I didn't tell you before. I'm sorry." He gestured toward the chair next to him. "Sit. Let's talk like people who have a child in common, no matter how badly we've done for her or each other."

Tia returned to the table, her legs suddenly wobbling. "You left your house?"

Tia's world contracted to Nathan once again. He nodded, affirming her words, a gesture too small for such a momentous announcement. He didn't speak for a few moments. "I have no idea what she said to her. To Caroline."

"Why does she care?" she asked again. "Be honest."

"Juliette thinks the child is part of our family," Nathan said. "The pictures tore her apart in more than one way."

"*Our* family? You and her?"

"And our sons."

Tia could barely get words out. "Your sons." Her vocal cords didn't want to respond. Her words were barely audible. "She thinks Honor is connected to your sons?"

"And my parents."

Tia was stunned at the thought of Nathan's wife wanting to connect to Honor, folding her into Juliette's family, folding her over and over, making Honor the filling in the Soros omelette, until Tia's parts disappeared forever.

"Opening your letter and seeing Savannah was a shock for her. Can you understand that?"

Tia gripped her arms. Calling that lawyer had been the smartest thing she could have done. Not telling Nathan about it would be the second smartest. Jesus, how hatefully vulnerable she still was to him.

Nathan placed a hand on her knee. "It's okay. Really. It's going to be okay."

She rocked herself in the hard wooden kitchen chair. Nothing coordinated in her apartment. Everything was an unstable as her life. Wobbly unmatched chairs ringed an oak table that bore gouges left by the previous owners.

She bent, trapping Nathan's hand between her chest and her thighs, and let tears spill on his skin. She felt the wiry hairs on his hands, the protrusion of his knuckles. She smelled and felt his familiar skin.

He pulled her from the chair and led her to the couch. His firm touch on her back felt like yesterday, and like coming home. Wrapping her arms around his waist offered the hard leather of his belt and the feel of rough denim. His stomach was a bit softer, but still Nathan's.

Wanting Nathan hit her hard and fast. All the years of hope and need bubbled up and just about knocked her over. All blood and sensation rushed to her core. She loved and wanted this man like no other.

She tugged at his belt.

He put his hand over hers, pressed, and then pulled away, pushing her gently until she stood. Legs shaking, she walked back to the kitchen, to the chair she'd left.

"We can't," he said.

Cold enough to shiver, humiliation stole her words. Everything in her became bound up in not crying. The horror of being pushed away, unwanted, left her without a tether, until only mortification existed.

"I'm sorry," he said. "For everything. I don't know if you can believe this, really, I want nothing but happiness for you. But I can't be the one to provide it."

"What if?" she asked. "What if we'd met another time, a time when you weren't married, would you have wanted me then? *Would you?*"

He met her eyes. She watched him struggle.

"I don't know," he said. "I just don't know."

The ringing phone jarred Tia from a sodden sleep.

"Did I wake you?" Robin asked when she heard Tia's hello.

Tia turned to look at the clock, a dull whiskey headache turning with her. "It's three in the morning. Yes, you woke me." She smelled a faint aftermath of Nathan on her arm. He'd left as quickly as he could, not meeting her eyes after hugging her good-bye.

"Sorry. It's only midnight here." Robin's voice sounded pleasantly toasted. Not too much. They could instantly measure each other's alcohol intake.

"Midnight is already too late," Tia said. "What's up?"

"I'm in love."

"How do you know?"

"Because I can't think of anything else but her."

"Sometimes I feel that way about Oreos. Should I marry them?"

"See, you're in Massachusetts—you can marry anything. Me, I can't even marry the love of my life."

"So move back."

"Are you kidding? I adore California. Just have to change the laws."

"I almost slept with Nathan," Tia confessed.

"Oh God, no. Why?"

"Because he was here. Can't even say I was drunk."

"Why was he there?"

"She threw him out."

"Why?"

"I'm not positive, but I think it had to do with those pictures I sent. She found out about Honor."

"You should be looking for a job, Tee, not sleeping with that dickwad."

"I didn't sleep with him. Almost; I said almost."

"Well then, I am very proud of you."

"Screw that. It's him you have to be proud of. He pulled away from me. He was the saint, not me."

"Stop that," Robin said. "Don't you dare blame yourself for anything. He pulled away? That means he got close enough to try. Screw him. Who cares if he had some latent crisis of conscience?"

"He doesn't care anymore. He probably never did. Now he's not even attracted to me." Tia pulled the covers closer around her, winding the sheet between her thighs. "What's wrong with me?"

"You believed in him. You thought he was some sort of savior saint, but, sorry, he thought of you as an exciting lay. Nothing's changed, Tee."

"Actually, something very big changed. Before he left, I got him to agree to go with me to see Honor."

"Are you kidding? Is that a good idea? Did they—the adopters, whatever you call them—did they agree?"

"They will. I know they will." A stray desire for a cigarette shot through Tia. "Tell me about your love."

"Come meet her." Robin said. "Tee, I don't think this is such a good idea. Seeing Honor. What good can come from it?"

"Isn't meeting my daughter good enough? I'm her mother. No one can take that away from me."

Silence rang loud from across the country.

"What?" Tia asked. "What are you thinking?"

"I'm just not sure if that's a good enough reason," Robin said.

"Don't you think it's right that I check up on the people I gave her to? They wrote a letter and that's that: here you go, take my daughter? Was that right?"

"That's the decision you made, Tee. You have to stop torturing yourself about it."

"Well, if you don't like that I'm going to see her, you're really going to love this one. I called a lawyer." Tia pulled the covers tighter around her shoulders. "To find out about the adoption."

"To find out what about the adoption?"

"Maybe I made a mistake. Maybe she should be with me."

"This is a big, big mistake."

"You think everything I'm doing is a mistake. I think my mother would be proud of me." Tia wished she could see her friend's face. "I'm sure of it."

CHAPTER 28

Juliette

Loneliness so overwhelmed Juliette as the weekend approached she'd decided to take the boys to Rhinebeck, despite knowing they'd be there for their annual Memorial Day trip in just a matter of weeks. The idea of the three of them being alone in the house one more day made her determined to run away from home. Either the boys watched her as though she were some fragile chemical mix about to boil into oblivion, staring and motionless while she placed breakfast on the Nathan-free table, or they acted out every angry thought that entered their adolescent brains.

Last week Max melted down when they were late to Little League practice. "Dad would have gotten me here on time!" he'd shouted before marching away. Three days later, she overheard Lucas tell Max he was an asshole for siding with Nathan.

Siding? Worse yet, Juliette had been so weary that she pretended she didn't hear.

She exited the Mass Pike, gripping the wheel as she drove onto the Taconic State Parkway, a road where deer often darted from the woods. She wasn't used to being both driver and watcher any more than being both mother and father.

Nathan saw the boys often, which was good for them, but every visit in the weeks since he'd left brought her pain. Having him ring the doorbell instead of using his key just about killed her. Max shuffled out to the car wearing careful comb marks in his hair, while Lucas dressed sloppier every week.

Each time Juliette saw Nathan, she watched for signs that would tell her what to do.

Had he gone to her?

Did he love her?

If he and that woman got together, would they take Savannah back and become their own little family?

Not that Juliette thought it worked that way. Adopting a child wasn't like borrowing a snow blower. "Oh, we'd prefer you give that back now, please."

"Mom, are we there yet?" Max asked.

"If we were there, would we still be on the Taconic?" she answered.

"You don't have to snap at him," Lucas said.

After Nathan left, Lucas appointed himself Juliette's judge and conscience as he tried to fill the father role. She glanced in the rearview mirror. Lucas had a new crop of blemishes. Max's hair was so short that he looked like a war victim. His last haircut had been a disaster.

She shook her head at seeing her sons through her own mother's hypercritical eyes. Juliette never felt worse than when she found herself adopting her mother's harsh views.

"How about we go to the fair tonight?" Juliette wanted to make it up to them for being sad and short tempered. "We'll be in Rhinebeck by three."

"You're kidding, right? You think I want to pet sheep?" Lucas asked.

"I want to go," Max said.

"Then go, fat burger."

"Don't say that," Juliette said. "We'll all go, or none of us go."

"All of us? All *three* of us?" Lucas's sneering tone would drive her crazy or drive her off the road in a fit of guilt-laced rage.

"Grandpa and Mamie may want to go." Juliette held the steering wheel with one hand and reached behind with the other hand cupped. "M&M's, please."

"Yeah, right. Mamie will love that idea." Lucas pressed his feet so hard on the back of her seat that Juliette swore she felt the tips of his sneakers.

"Max?" Juliette shook her hand impatiently and again took a quick look in the rearview mirror. Max held up a giant bag of M&M's and poured the candy into her hand. They'd bought it at CVS before getting on the Mass Pike, adding it to the chips in a can, spray cheese, and three kinds of soda she'd already put in the basket. Nothing she'd brought on the trip was organic, nutritious, or homemade, making it seem like their car belonged to an entirely different family.

Juliette shoved the candy in her mouth. Shells cracked, grainy chocolate coated her tongue, and she felt a moment's relief.

She pulled into the driveway beside her parents' perfect blue-grey Queen Anne–style house.

Juliette still felt as though she competed with this house for her parents' consideration. Each time the house's stately white balusters got a glossy new coat of paint, she had the urge to carve her initials into the gleaming wood.

It irked Juliette how her parents had trusted every one of her actions and choices since she was a child. There were only a few things her parents checked on. Her father made sure that first her bikes, and then her cars, were in good order, and her mother kept watch over Juliette's beauty—making it clear that she considered Juliette an extension of her own loveliness.

Displaying some rebellious spirit, at least enough to worry her parents, might have brought relief, but she seemed destined to be the vigilant one in the family. Her parents were the ones who stumbled after too many drinks. They were the ones performing not-furtive-enough experiments with marijuana when Juliette was seventeen and should have been the one getting stoned. Watching them giggle their way to the bedroom had turned her stomach.

"Lucas, get the large bag from the back," Juliette ordered.

Lucas struggled to pull her overstuffed suitcase from the trunk. "Jeez, Mom, what the hell do you have in here?"

Juliette started to scold him for swearing and then stopped. If she was going to ask him to do Nathan's jobs—carry the heavy bags, check the tires before they got on the road—then she might as well let him complain like Nathan.

Sliding down the slope of bad parenting took no time at all.

"Max, you take your and Lucas's backpacks." Juliette knelt on the backseat, reaching for the few snacks they hadn't stuffed in their mouths and cramming the remains in wrinkled plastic bags. These she pushed deep into her parents' outside trash bins.

Juliette recognized the depth of her parents' concern over Nathan's absence when they offered to take her and the boys to the county fair. Her mother and father took her to the antiques show at the fairgrounds when she was a child, but never the county fair. "Why would I want to see cows?" That had been her mother's point of view. "Your school takes you, right?" That had been her father's way of alleviating his guilt.

"Grandpa," Max said, pulling at her father's arm, "can we get fried dough?"

"Darling! Why in the world would you want that? Grandpa and I are planning to take us all to Gigi's tonight." Juliette's mother turned to Juliette and gave her a familiar once-over. "The food is wonderful, but it's casual. No need to dress up or fuss."

Juliette's mother wore the same style of clothes as during Juliette's childhood. Perhaps they were the same clothes; her mother remained the same size. If a shirt or skirt wanted to make it into Sondra's closet, it had best complement her dancer's body and bring to mind Audrey Hepburn.

"A little fried dough once in a while won't hurt the boys," Juliette's father said.

"But it might hurt you." Her mother gave a significant glance to his midsection and then kissed him full on the lips. "I need you around more than you need the cholesterol." She patted him on the butt with a flirtatious grin, and Juliette thought she might throw up from having to once again witness—with her boys, no less—her parents' constant displays of affection.

"Eww," Max said.

Lucas walked away, pretending to be fascinated by a bulky white horse lumbering toward them.

Her father laughed and then stage-whispered, "Tell you what, Maxie. What happens between grandfather and grandson stays between grandfather and grandson. Right, boys?"

"Does that mean yes?" Max asked.

"That means it's time to take our leave." He flung an arm around Max's neck. "Come on, Lucas."

Lucas looked at Juliette and then shrugged, walking away as though choosing the lesser of two versions of hell. She watched with mixed feelings as they left. Alone with her father, the boys would get more attention. Unfortunately, so would she.

"Fried dough. My God, what is he thinking? You'll see how your father suffers later. And, of course, how I suffer with him." She tucked her arm in Juliette's. "Come. Let's see if we can find anything that doesn't smell or offend."

Juliette hated her mother's casual dismissal of an entire cultural happening. She hated it more that she, Juliette, also loathed the damned fair.

"So, no Nathan." Sondra led them away from the animal corrals, which were divided into horrifying lines of pigs, cows, bunnies, and goats. The place was an animal prison.

"You look great, Mom," Juliette said. "So does Dad." This was true. At seventy and sixty-eight, either of them could pass for ten years younger.

"Don't change the subject. However, thank you. We try to stay in shape, though I have to watch him every second." Her mother gave the fond smile she reserved for Juliette's father.

"I use your picture as a model of good skin care for all my clients," Juliette said. That was a total lie. The last thing she needed was her mother's picture staring down at her all day, but Juliette was well schooled in the art of deflecting her mother from topics Juliette wanted to avoid. Talking about her mother's youthfulness might keep away the subject of Nathan.

"That's flattering, sweetheart. You look nice also. Although, truthfully, you've put on some weight. You're at that age, you know."

When Juliette didn't respond, Juliette's mother sighed. "Sweetheart, I know that it's because of Nathan. Women go in one direction or the other when their husbands leave. Most of my friends got thin as rails, but some just started stuffing themselves and didn't stop. Honey, is that the road you've taken?"

The road she'd taken. As though Juliette had casually deliberated between staying slim or putting on weight. *Fat or skinny, fat or skinny? Oh, why don't I just get plump as a pigeon? That will be fun!*

The sweet smell of cotton candy drifted over.

"He didn't leave," Juliette said. "I threw him out."

Her mother looked shocked, as though Nathan were such a catch that only the most foolish woman would let him go.

"Why in the world—"

"I'm hungry." Juliette unlocked her arm from her mother's. "I'm getting a hamburger. Over there." She pointed to a shack where teenagers flipped burgers and shook baskets of fries. Juliette hungered for the grease, the salty meat, and the blood-soaked bun.

"Oh, no. Not that, Juliette. Perhaps there's a salad around here somewhere." She put her hands on her hips—her lean boyish hips; nothing like the monsters jutting out from either side of Juliette.

"I don't want a salad. I want something substantial."

"Let's save ourselves for tonight, at Gigi's, where at least they'll be worth the calories, okay?" Her mother gave a girlish smile, crinkling her Midwestern blue eyes and swinging her long fringe of blond bangs out of her eyes.

"Mom, don't be such a cliché. It's not like you." This intense scrutiny was curious for her mother. Usually after a few pointed remarks, her mother just went on about herself and Juliette's father. "Gordon said this." "We went here."

Her mother's chittery-chattery expression dropped away. "Cliché? Fine, perhaps I'm a cliché, but you need direction. You need to take care of yourself. Sorry to be blunt, but honey, looking good is your business. What have you done, eaten nothing but chips and cookies since he left?"

"Did you not hear me say I threw him out?"

"It's not always about who did the throwing. The question is why you made him go." Her mother stopped walking and took Juliette's hands between hers, forcing Juliette to look straight at her. "Maybe I wasn't mother of the year, but I do care about you."

"I don't doubt that." She did doubt that.

"Take my advice under serious consideration. It's no picnic out there without a man."

"It was no picnic in there either, Mother."

"Why? Did he sleep with someone else?"

"Mom!"

"Don't act so surprised. What? You think it never happened to my friends? But not to me. Do you want to know why?"

"No," Juliette said.

"Because I've kept your father front and center. He's my life, and he knows it."

"We all knew it."

"Don't be such a child."

"Once I *was* a child, Mom."

"But you're not anymore. This isn't about poor, ignored baby Juliette. Grow up. You want to take care of your children better than I did? Get their father back."

"You don't know the whole story."

"So tell me. But try listening to me like a woman, not my daughter."

"Is that even possible?"

"It is if you can rise to the occasion." Her mother pulled her under one of the food tents. People sat at long wooden tables eating every manner of forbidden food. Children nibbled at corn dripping with butter. Men bent over plates full of barbequed meat red with sauce and brown with grill marks. Women clutched burritos the size of small puppies.

Next to Juliette, a sunburned woman ran her tongue up a mountain of ice cream heaped into a cone. Juliette noticed the thick slab of fat hanging over the woman's jeans and felt superior and then ashamed. She was just her mom with a veneer.

Her mother dug into her straw bag and took out two bottles of water, offering one to Juliette.

The sunburned woman was about Juliette's age. She sat with a companion who had thirty pounds on Ms. Sunburn, and whose complexion spoke of sugar and whiskey.

Juliette took the water with gratitude. "He cheated on me."

"I figured. That's what I said to your father, though he tried to defend Nathan."

"Dad defended him?"

Her mother touched Juliette's arm. "Oh, Juliette, don't worry about that. Your father is simply worried about you being alone, so he blusters a bit."

"Dad didn't believe Nathan would cheat?"

"Dad doesn't like to think ill of people. Come on, let's walk—I can't stand the smell here."

Her mother brushed a drop of water from her yellow linen slacks. Mom showed her age in odd ways, like her refusal to wear white before Memorial Day. Still, even as Mom closed in on seventy, and Juliette ran a business where women paid large sums for her beauty secrets, she felt homely and oafish next to her mother.

Her mother flicked Juliette's hair from her face. "You remind me of your father. He's always thinking the best, always trying to convince me how marvelous the world is. Maybe that's why Nathan got away with cheating for however long you let him. You thought too well of him. It didn't even occur to you that he could be doing that."

When Juliette didn't respond, her mother added iron to her

words. "Look at you, weepy and getting chunky, waiting for Nathan to come to his senses. To make his decision."

"I'm not doing that!" Was her mother right? Hadn't she told him to find out if he loved that woman? To go see the child? "Fine. You're right, Mom. You're right about everything. But there's a small detail you don't know. He had a child."

That stopped her mother. "The woman has his baby?"

"She gave it up for adoption."

"My Lord. Well, you certainly are becoming more interesting, Juliette."

Juliette didn't know whether to laugh or cry, so she laughed, and then her mother joined in. They laughed hard enough that their mascara ran, and they had to find the ladies' room. After they'd dried their hands and reapplied lipstick, her mother offered a summation.

"Have you thought that maybe the answer isn't 'Love me or love her'? We live in an imperfect world, Juliette. You may have to decide whether you want a flawed marriage or no marriage at all. Is it too broken to live with?"

Juliette wondered if she could live with Nathan knowing that he still cared for Tia, even if he just cared for her because she was the mother of his child.

He wanted to come home. He told her so each time he visited the boys. Juliette hated the empty space next to her in bed. She despised coming home to a house without Nathan. At dinner, with just the three of them, she felt as though they sat on a wobbly stool. But she didn't know if she'd feel any better with him lying next to her.

It might be a whole new kind of loneliness.

CHAPTER 29

Nathan

"I'm waiting in front of your house." Nathan pushed *End* button on his cell phone and disconnected with Tia. He'd spent the morning making sure that his clothes were perfectly pressed, his shave close—dressing to see his daughter as though getting ready for a date.

He still yearned to impress her, he wanted to show Caroline and Peter Fitzgerald that he wasn't a loser, and he needed to demand courage of himself.

"We have to do it," Tia had said. "We have the opportunity. Juliette can't get mad at you anymore, right? She's the one who threw you out."

He wouldn't tell Tia that he'd told Juliette they were going to see Savannah. Tia had already sounded halfway to hysterical when she'd called, saying, "Caroline came to me for a reason, and we need to find out what it is. We need to see if Honor is safe."

There is no Honor.

She is Savannah.

It's Lucas and Max that I'm worried about. How can they be safe without me?

"We have to step up to the plate. Please. Come with me," Tia had entreated him. "Who knows what's going on? We need to see where Honor is, and what she's like, and who she is—"

Last night he and Juliette spoke briefly, their conversation revolving around the kids: soccer practice, summer camp schedules, and which nights he'd take them out to dinner. Then Nathan threw in the question: "Can I come home?" Perhaps it was his imagination, but he thought there was a chink in her armor when she hesitated before answering. Then, when after saying "No," she added, "not yet, we'll see," he knew she was wavering.

While half listening about the cost of Max's soccer camp, he considered telling Juliette about this visit to meet Savannah, and then, just as quickly, he reconsidered it. Then, he flipped again, realizing he had to tell the truth.

When he finished speaking, Juliette had been silent. Then he heard her muffled sobs. Why was she crying? Wasn't this what she'd wanted? Hadn't she told him to make it right with Tia? To go see his daughter? To see Tia, and then convince her it was finally over? That's what he was trying to do, damn it. She'd made him feel as though he were torturing her. It was as though that previous conversation had never happened.

"I just can't talk to you." She'd spoken so slowly, it was as though she could barely release those depressing final words.

What had that meant? Can't talk to you now? Ever? This fucking week?

He missed his wife and sons so badly that he felt like the loss hung from his chest like a lousy badge. Patches of his old nemesis—eczema—broke out behind his knees. His stomach pitched in circles. Sleep seemed an impossible dream, and the circles under his eyes grew darker each day.

Tia slipped into the car, unusually quiet.

"Do you know where you're going?" she asked.

"I already put the address in the GPS."

"How do you know where they live?" Tia's questions jabbed like challenges. She exhausted him, but he owed her, and he knew it.

He wanted to pretend that the other night had never happened.

Bury it under a pile of being good. Coming that close to Tia had been playing with rocket fuel and matches.

"A little thing called the Internet," Nathan said.

"I forgot how thorough you are."

He turned a bit and smiled. "Once you liked that."

"Once you liked me."

"I never stopped liking you, Tia."

"But you stopped loving me," she said. "If you ever started."

He kept his eyes glued on traffic.

"Did you ever love me?" she asked.

"Of course I did. I'll always love you."

"How will you love me? As though you're my distant uncle? A brother? A kissing cousin?"

He took her hand and squeezed. "Don't you think we'll always care about each other in some way, for what we share?"

She pulled away from him. "I've spent the past six years trying to stop loving you."

He didn't know what to say. That she'd spent years in love with him while he barely thought of her was so damned sad.

"You broke my heart, Nathan," Tia said simply, quietly. "Everything I did, it was about you."

"I don't think I knew that." Nathan said. "I'm sorry."

"I was stupid." Tia shook her head. "Robin says I was never real to you."

The truth stung.

Occasionally Nathan admired women's willingness to examine one another's relationships, but most of the time it drove him crazy. Like Juliette and Gwynne: Nathan was positive that Gwynne knew everything he did, especially the bad things. At times it made him uncomfortable to be with Gwynne, knowing she'd heard about everything, from his affair, to how he compulsively checked his hairline every morning.

He glanced in the rearview mirror, saw a truck barreling down, and switched to the right lane.

"Robin says I was the whore to your wife's virgin." She tapped him on the leg in the familiar manner of old lovers. "You know, the virgin-whore complex."

"I know what a virgin-whore complex is."

"Sorry, I forgot for a moment what a genius you are."

Had she been this sharp tongued when they were together? God knows he could have ignored anything, he'd been in such a sexual headlock with her.

Keeping his marriage vows had come easy after getting over Tia, like a pacifist who'd adopted nonviolence after dodging combat bullets.

Nathan had fooled himself: he'd worked overtime at the task. Except for moments when a stab of sexual memory excited him, he'd just about put Tia out of his mind. Yes, there had been a discomforting curiosity about the baby, but then when he never heard from her, he convinced himself that she'd had an abortion. He'd managed to believe that Tia was out of his life forever, and he and Juliette would live happily ever after. He'd been so grateful for her forgiveness that he forgave himself and then absolved himself of the memory of Tia.

Nathan never tried to find out what happened with the pregnancy. Battling for a pardon from Juliette overtook everything in his life. He walled off thoughts of Tia. He'd convinced himself that his renewed devotion to Juliette and the boys made him a good and faithful husband, and a father above reproach. The past disappeared. Abracadabra: his affair was expunged via good deeds.

Denial, sure, but that's how he moved ahead. His ability to rationalize, figure out things—assure himself that he was a good man—now seemed like the actions of a delusional man.

Juliette never let go of the *why*, which seemed to bother her more than the actuality. She searched for a reason that would put his infidelity into a paradigm she could understand and thus prevent from happening ever again. As though if he revealed the truth, she'd then understand how to prevent him from straying.

Why the hell had he been unfaithful? The real answer made him seem like garbage. Sharing the truth of his hunger, his want to see himself through the eyes of a besotted woman, would make him seem like . . . like exactly the man he'd been.

Juliette had never been less than a satisfying lover. No woman ever felt closer or more right, though, truth be told, some had been more exciting, but only in the way that one occasionally wanted wasabi to electrify the tongue.

Now Tia provided agitation, not electricity. Sleeping with her had been stupid. Had he really believed he could get away unscathed?

He'd learned to live without lightning, but it had come back to knock him on his ass.

Caroline and Peter Fitzgerald stood in the doorway, the child between them, each with a hand on her shoulder. He studied the couple before staring at the girl, afraid of seeing her.

Tia moved closer to him, and he inched away.

The neutral set of Caroline Fitzgerald's mouth, neither smile nor frown, gave away little. She had an unthreatening appeal, willowy and wholesome.

Nothing about Peter Fitzgerald's expression was neutral. His tight lips were locked, maybe against words that might escape. Judging from the man's expression, his first words could be a demand that they leave. He thought Peter unlikely to win if they fought, Nathan being rougher and wider, but Nathan could be very wrong. Despite Peter's average build, he had the air of a street kid who'd know how to fight dirty. Nathan wouldn't bet on himself if they were tangling over the child's safety, not after seeing how the man clasped the child and glared at Nathan.

Nathan looked at the girl.

His daughter.

The words barely computed, but seeing her struck him in the gut.

She was lovely. Rosy cheeks. Hair so dark he'd call her Snow White if she were his daughter. His princess. He smiled. She looked back with mistrustful eyes. She grasped her father's hand. Peter leaned down to her. "It's okay, pumpkin," he said.

"Why don't we go inside," Caroline said.

Tia and Nathan followed the family, Savannah clutching Caroline's and Peter's hands as they walked through the large white-tiled hall to the living room. Unlike Nathan's home, all warm wood, cushions, and jewel tones, this house shone with aluminium and gloss. Sun bounced off the burnished surfaces, showing everyone in an uncomfortable clarity. Tia looked tired, Peter irate, Caroline anxious, and Savannah—the poor child seemed confused and terrified.

"Want to get the cookies we baked?" Peter asked Savannah.

The girl moved her head in an infinitesimal nod. "Okay."

Hearing her voice for the first time knocked Nathan out. She sounded so little—a little, little girl. He'd somehow built her into a large and unwelcome presence; now the sound of her tiny voice washed away his resentment.

Savannah peeked back as she walked away, staring at Tia but also catching Nathan's eyes. He worked to hold her glance without appearing stern. Seeing her in three dimensions confused him, and he whipped between curiosity, fear, and some atavistic pull. He wanted to take out his phone and capture her face in a picture. Show his mother. Look at it later.

"What have you told her?" Tia asked the moment Savannah was out of sight.

"The truth." Caroline didn't embellish. "Why did you want to come?"

"Because she's my daughter," Tia said.

"She's been your biological daughter since she was born."

"But you never came to see me before," Tia said. "I needed to know what changed and what was going on. See if everything was okay for my daughter."

Tension showed in Caroline's shoulders as she rearranged magazines on the coffee table, first straightening them and then fanning them out into a decorator design. Caroline reminded him more of Juliette than she did Tia. Sympathy for Caroline's rigid stance stabbed at Nathan. Caroline and Peter certainly hadn't bargained for a visit like this when they adopted Savannah.

"We haven't been formally introduced," he said. "I'm Nathan Soros."

Caroline scrutinized him. "Yes, I know. Does your wife know that you're here?"

"Fair question. She does." Nathan heard Tia take a sharp breath.

"So what exactly is your intent in seeing Savannah?" Caroline asked. "Do either of you realize the possible ramifications of this? This could work out very well, or very badly. Have you—all of you, including your wife, Nathan—have you even thought about her?"

"Why did you say yes to our visit?" Nathan asked. He really wanted to know—this wasn't a truculent question, and he prayed Caroline would understand that from his tone.

CHAPTER 30

Caroline

Caroline realized she should get off her very high horse. Riding so far above the ground helped no one, least of all Savannah. If Tia's face got any tighter, it might shatter. The poor woman's hands shook even as she folded her arms around herself. Savannah must be terrified by that fear. What did she make of it?

Having Tia and Nathan come here might be the very worst parenting decision they'd ever made.

Dear Lord, she hoped this wasn't going to damage her girl. How had she been so righteous and convincing when urging Peter to allow it: "Better to face the truth," she'd said. "These are her biological parents. She'll try to find out more about them sooner or later. This may be the right time."

Then she'd read to him straight from her research sites: "The philosophy of comfort does not take into consideration several very important factors, one being that open adoption should not be based on making the adults involved comfortable; rather it should be about providing for the needs of the child."

But maybe she'd been wrong. Or they'd been wrong.

Caroline took a calming breath and ordered her face to relax. "We let you come because we thought it might be healthy for Savannah to have a more open adoption. Even in the best of homes, adopted children fantasize about their birth parents. No matter what, she will always wonder about you—she already does. Peter and I agree, better to put that overwhelming curiosity to rest."

Before Tia or Nathan could comment, Peter and Savannah returned. Peter carried a large tray covered with a platter of cookies, glasses, and a pitcher of iced tea. Savannah, who'd recently entered an everything-pink phase, clutched the pink glass sugar bowl she'd picked out for the occasion. Lost for ideas of how to prepare for this meeting, Caroline had taken her to Target to pick out serving pieces for tea.

Peter set the fuchsia lacquered tray on the coffee table, and Savannah placed the sugar bowl beside it. The moment Peter sat, Savannah sidled between his knees, staring openly at Nathan and Tia.

"Do I have to go away with you?" Savannah clutched the fabric of Peter's pant leg, looking at Tia and Nathan with an expression somewhere between fear and awe.

"Oh, honey, of course not," Tia said.

Nathan leaned toward Savannah. "We just wanted to meet you. That's all."

Savannah nodded. "Are you my real daddy?"

Nathan shook his head. "No, honey. Peter is your real daddy. I'm just the man who made you with Tia."

Caroline began to understand why women were drawn to this man. His concentration on Savannah didn't waver as she pondered his answer.

"Is this lady my real mommy?" Savannah asked him.

Tia's eyes went from the child to Nathan, as though not sure who to absorb first, her hunger shaking Caroline. No one should look at Savannah with eyes like that. How could the child breathe under such pressure?

"No, Savannah," Nathan said. "She's the woman who made you with me. Caroline is your real mommy."

Savannah turned to Tia, moving a little closer to her and Nathan, while keeping a pudgy hand on Peter's knee. "But I was the baby in your stomach, right?"

Tia nodded. She stared into Savannah's eyes. "Yes. You grew in my belly. I have a picture with me."

Tia picked up the large leather bag at her feet.

Caroline and Peter's eyes met. She telegraphed, *Is this okay?*

I hope so, his eyes answered. He looked as helpless as Caroline to stop or even slow down the crazy train.

Tia rummaged in her bag and drew out a large brown envelope.

"What is that?" Peter put out his hand as a stop sign.

"Some pictures I thought Hon—Savannah would like. From before she was born."

"Pictures?" Caroline wanted to snatch the envelope from Tia's hand and shuffle through them, edit them, even as Savannah stretched out a hand to see them.

"Just one, okay?" Peter's question was not a question. "Let's not overwhelm anyone."

"Right." Tia opened the envelope on her lap and peeked in until she drew out a tattered photo. "I should have copied this so I could give you one."

Tia held out the photo to Savannah, but Caroline intercepted it. She glanced down and saw a pregnant Tia sitting in shadows. Savannah left Peter and sidled over to Caroline, who was closer to Tia. Caroline felt the weight of Savannah's warm palm on her forearm.

"This is me?" Savannah tapped the image of Tia's swollen belly. "Before I was born?"

"Yes, baby, that's you before you were born." Caroline lifted the girl to her lap. "And then as soon as you were born, you came home with me and Daddy."

"Like in the *Tell Me Again* book?"

"That's right, honey, like in the book."

Savannah asked for the *Tell Me Again About the Night I Was Born* book at least twice a week, always making Caroline repeat her favorite lines, and then once again tell the story of Peter and Caroline bringing Savannah home.

"Tell me again how you carried me like a china doll all the way home and how you glared at anyone who sneezed."

Savannah squinted at Tia. She left Caroline's lap and took a few cautious steps toward Tia. "You don't look too young," she said.

"Too young for what?" Tia asked.

"Too young to take care of me."

"That's in her book," Caroline said. "Where the pregnant woman is too young to be a mother, so she gives the baby to the baby's mommy."

Why *did* Tia give her child away? All those lies Tia told about not knowing the father's identity, her intimations of some sort of abusive episodes with men, her fragile emotional state, all of it had been lies. Peter hadn't allowed his wife to ask Tia a single question. He'd been too thrilled that they'd been chosen to be Savannah's parents to risk irritating her.

"I guess I was too young in ways you can't see," Tia said.

"Like what?" Savannah asked.

Tia blinked rapidly. Nathan put an arm around her shoulder. "Like I wasn't married, and I didn't have a job or a good place to live," she said.

"That's why you gave me away?" Savannah asked.

Oh, Jesus, please, let me take this child's pain. That's what Caroline should research: how to surgically remove a child's pain and transplant it in the mother's body.

"We knew that your Mommy and Daddy would do a better job," Nathan said.

"So you gave me away, right?" Savannah's lip quivered.

Tia's tears spilled, and she reached out and took Savannah in her arms.

Caroline hugged herself as she watched Tia twine her arms around Savannah. "I just couldn't do it right, honey," Tia said. "I just couldn't. I'm sorry."

Savannah leaned into Tia. "It's okay," the child said in a quivery voice. She touched her biological mother's back with a tentative child's pat. Tia responded by leaning her head upon Savannah's, their dark hair mingling.

Who comforted whom was impossible to determine. For a few

moments, they fit in a way that shattered Caroline's heart. Then Savannah broke away and ran back to her father.

Savannah looked at Peter, tears mixing with the panic on her face. "I am staying here, right? Right, Daddy?"

Caroline spent an hour with Savannah before bedtime, reading *Adoption Is for Always* three times and then repeatedly writing words like *Love* and *Special* on her back before her girl finally fell asleep. Savannah, once Caroline calmed her, declared herself lucky, because unlike the girl in the book, she was able to meet her birth mother and birth father. Caroline felt grateful that whatever happened, this one truth felt right. Savannah wouldn't spend her life imagining who Tia and Nathan were. Caroline prayed that somehow, in that way, the almost disastrous afternoon had blessed her daughter.

After Caroline's initial gratitude that she could soothe Savannah, and that her girl seemed to have weathered the drama, the time spent rubbing letters on her back became no less boring than the day before. Still, despite the tediousness of bedtime—the long hour spent reassuring Savannah how much they loved her, that no one would take her away, and that she was their girl forever and ever—once Savannah slept, Caroline remained in her room. She sat on the rose-colored carpet next to her daughter's bed, legs crossed, listening to Savannah's soft breathing.

After all the tears and hugs, Savannah had asked Caroline a final question. "Can I see the other-mother and other-father sometimes? Not for a long time, just for itsy little bits. Just to see."

"Just to see what?" Caroline had asked.

Savannah had shrugged, and unlike the motion of a child avoiding truth, it was the gesture of a girl who truly didn't know. "Just to see what they look like."

Caroline found Peter in the family room kneeling on an old oilcloth his mother had given them after one of her cleaning sprees. Caroline remembered her urging it on them after a Sunday dinner. "You'll be surprised. It will come in handy one day. Take it. I have three of them."

Caroline hadn't asked why Peter's mother had three red oilcloths. She hadn't a clue how Peter's mother imagined they might use it, and yet here Peter was, kneeling on the slick material, his tool box open, a row of tools laid out neatly beside him.

"What are you doing?" she asked.

He looked up, a wrench in one hand and a pair of pink handlebars in the other. "I bought a bike for Savannah."

"You didn't tell me."

"I forgot. It was in my trunk."

Caroline didn't think it was likely he forgot. Buying toys for Savannah was Peter's sedative. She knelt beside him and picked up a piece of the bike. "A two-wheeler. Do you think she's ready?"

"Maybe I'm rushing it." Peter looked drained and tired despite his brave smile. "Maybe I'm the ready one."

The bike pieces were spread out in a deliberate pattern. Caroline was sure he'd laid them out in the order they would be put together. He was always careful. They were alike in that.

"I'm so sorry, Peter."

"We've fought enough. Let's just let it go for now." He held out his hand. "Phillips head, please."

Caroline began crying. "I didn't want to hurt you. I didn't want to hurt Savannah."

Peter ran a chamois cloth over a piece of chrome.

"I don't want to hurt any of us," Caroline repeated when he remained silent. "I wish I could do a better job with her. Really. I wish I could be the wife you want. Be the mother Savannah needs."

Peter leaned over the handlebars as he attached them to the body of the bike.

"You must hate me." Caroline fell on her knees beside him on the oilcloth. "I'd do anything to be able to take all my words back. To feel different."

Finally he looked at her. "I just don't know what to say. I can't believe we put Savannah through this today."

"I should have told you awhile ago how I felt. I'm not cut out for this. I'm not a natural, like your mother or mine. I can't be like them."

Peter threw down the cloth and stood up. "Well then, what the hell are we going to do? Can you answer that? Can you figure that out? We've ignored the obvious too long—Savannah deserves more than we're giving right now. This is making me crazy. Just goddamn crazy."

He picked up the bike he'd been working on, and for a moment, Caroline feared he'd fling it across the room. He lifted it and tensed his arm. Then he slowly lowered it down.

"You're a mother now." He spit each word out as though wanting raise welts.

She didn't answer.

"There are some choices you don't get to make anymore," he added.

Everything locked inside Caroline gave way. An unbearable sadness and feeling of failure washed over her. "What you're saying, it doesn't even make sense to me. Maybe it's just not working. Us. Maybe we're not working."

"You have to jump there? Is that what you think I'm saying? I'm just trying to—"

"I know what you're trying to do. You're telling me I don't get to have things the way I want them to be. But somehow, somehow you do, Peter. You wanted a child, and so we have one. And I love her. I really love her. I love you. But I'm crumbling. I see how much I'm failing Savannah, and it's killing me. I just don't know what to do."

Peter remained silent.

Caroline didn't have the will to fight. "Sometimes I have to take pills to get through," she almost whispered. "That's how I try to manage, Peter. And it's not working. I want to make you happy. I want to make Savannah happy. But maybe I just don't have the right stuff. Maybe you're both better off without me."

She walked out of the room.

"*Where are you going?*" He ran to the garage door. "*Answer me.*"

"Out," she said. "Just out."

* * *

It was past one in the morning when Caroline came home. Peter sat in the family room, an unopened magazine on his lap. The room was cleaned of tools and the oilcloth.

"Where were you?" he asked. "You didn't answer the phone."

"I'm sorry. I couldn't." She stood in front of him.

"Where were you?" he asked again.

"Thinking. I went to my office. I don't have anywhere else. It's not like we're bar types."

"But we're pill types?"

"I became one," Caroline said. "I didn't know how else to stay quiet."

"You thought you had to stay quiet? Are you frightened of me, Caro?"

"I'm frightened of us. Who we're—I'm—becoming. Our life seems to make you happy no matter how awful I feel."

"I hate that also, Caro." He took her hand and tugged her down. "It's true, though. I want you to change. How did we get here?"

"I couldn't admit how awful everything was . . . is for me." she said. "I can't do that anymore. It just backfires."

"And here we are. You're unhappy. Savannah is a wreck. And I charge around like a raging bull, as though I can make everything the way I want it by stubborn will."

"You're only trying to make a family."

He raised his shoulders, as though indicating *big deal.*

"What are we going to do?" Caroline lowered her head to her husband's shoulder. "I don't want to lose us, but I don't know what to do. I honestly can't keep going like this."

"Are you leaving? Are you asking me to leave?" he asked.

She couldn't answer because any way she turned, she didn't see a life she wanted.

"Caro? Answer me!" He put a hand under her chin and forced her to look up. His eyes were wet. "Please don't ask me to choose between a life with you and Savannah and one without, because I can't."

She'd never seen him cry before. It wrung her out, seeing him pucker his lips and press them together. Savannah did the same thing when things got bad; she'd done it when Tia moved to hug her.

Caroline had been ready to pry Savannah away in that moment.

Caroline knew the truth now. She knew she might not love spending time with Savannah, but she loved her as deeply as any mother loved their child. She'd gladly suffer wounds to her own flesh to keep her from harm.

She was Savannah's mother—maybe not a very good one; maybe even a reluctant one—but she'd never have given away her child. It had probably been the right thing for Tia to do, but Caroline couldn't imagine it.

Oh, who the hell knew? Here she was practically running away from her child, judging the woman who'd at least been honest about what she couldn't do. How did you reach for that kind of truth? Juliette was probably the only real mother among them.

Did Peter have a clue who Caroline was? God knows she could never tell him about the temptation of Jonah. Carrying that toxic secret alone would be her punishment. The same Peter who would never have denied his child's existence was the man who'd never cheat or even contemplate doing such a thing.

Caroline probably wasn't going to be a great mom, but what if she was the best one available? Could she walk away from that?

CHAPTER 31

Tia

"Now I've lost both of you."

Dignified homes and flawless gardens flew by as they drove away from Caroline and Peter's house.

"You lost both of us many years ago," Nathan said, not unkindly.

Tia wished she could hate him, but he'd been so good with Savannah, while she'd been so awful. She'd said horrible, stupid things. Everything inside her ached at the memory of holding Savannah.

Tia's mother would have loved Savannah. She seemed like such a special little girl. Did Caroline and Peter know? Did they care enough?

"Don't you think she was special?" Tia asked.

Nathan didn't answer, but Tia realized he was thinking, not avoiding her question. He was probably a good father to his sons, boys who were real to Tia for the first time.

Savannah's robust build pleased Tia. It made her happy that her daughter seemed sturdy and safe. Tia had resembled a strand of wire at that age. Her father had been sinewy and powerful, seeming as though he'd take off like a jet plane any minute. Everything about Tia's mother looked durable and practical except for the screwy curls leaping out in all directions.

Savannah's face blended together her and Nathan in a way that she'd never tire of seeing. Was that motherhood? Did Caroline spend time staring at Savannah until each feature made indelible tracks in her mind?

"Your question answers itself."

"Thank you, Buddha." Tia moved as close to the door as possible and leaned against the cool glass. What would it be like to wake up and see Savannah every morning?

"Actually, I think you mean Roshi. That would be a Zen teacher."

"Actually, I meant Buddha, Professor. Silent Buddha."

He laughed. Give Nathan credit: he was usually willing to laugh at himself. "Yes. Savannah seemed special to me, but the thing about being a parent is that your own child always seems special."

Tia turned to face him. She tucked a leg up and reached out to touch his arm. "Then she does feel like your child?"

"I don't know how to describe it."

"Did she feel like your sons feel to you?"

"Oh, Tia, of course not. I was there when they were born. I've been with them all their lives, and I always will."

"So she's secondhand. Like me."

"You're being reductive. Reducing a complicated problem to a simplistic one-dimensional thing."

"I know what *reductive* means." What the hell did he think of her?

Perhaps the best thing about having Nathan back in her life, however briefly, was seeing how ill suited they were. *Be careful what you wish for.* Robin had sworn that the worst thing that could happen to Tia would be having Nathan leave his wife for her.

Robin had also said that seeing Savannah was a mistake. But Tia didn't think it had been, except maybe how it made her hungry for more.

Tia had spent all of Memorial Day searching Macy's sales rack for a suit. Nothing in her current wardrobe remotely resembled a proper interview outfit. She supposed she must have worn something decent when Richard interviewed her, but whatever that outfit had been, it was long gone.

Now, wobbling a bit in her brand-new high heels, she climbed down the dingy concrete steps of the Merciful Sisters Senior Center, located in yet another church. This one was Catholic and in the basement. The location provoked equal measures of remorse for the years she'd spent avoiding Mass and anger at the guilt always coloring her life.

She'd had Savannah. She'd stayed true to the teachings there, voting with her heart when she got pregnant. Choice for everyone except Tia seemed to be her position on the politics of abortion.

Tia reached a large, open space divided by furniture rather than walls. Three desks were jammed into one corner. A tall lean woman wearing black trousers and a mannish white shirt occupied the first desk. Thick white hair, coiled in a bun on the top of her head, accentuated the clear blue of her eyes. The empty desk beside her held the look of recent activity: an opened file, a pen laid down, a newspaper ready to be read over a lunch of yogurt and almonds.

The third desk was swept clean. Limp cardboard that once could have been called a blotter covered worn oak; perhaps that desk waited for her. Was she supposed to brighten it with knickknacks, anchored by the glass paperweight Bobby had bought her for luck? She'd tried to smile when she'd seen the multicolored globe of the world nestled under white tissue, tucked in a satin-lined box, padded with foam—Jesus, it would survive an attack from Mars—and labeled with the shop's name in gold script, but her smile felt like a grimace. They were moving into the presents-for-no-reason stage of their relationship. Bobby kept moving ahead as though they were predestined.

He talked about custody in a tone so deliberately even that Tia knew he'd love to discuss it constantly. She kept telling herself this was only an exploration, though letting Bobby pay the legal bills added a weight of expectation.

Ultimately, she feared there'd be a price. She teetered between Bobby's optimism and Robin's warnings, and kept staring at the picture of Savannah that had made its way to her wallet.

Any possibility of custody meant having a job. The lawyer said that was an immutable fact. He'd also hinted about her relationship with Bobby in a way that made Tia think that being married would help enormously.

Not that she'd stay with Bobby for that, but couldn't it be a side benefit without becoming an indictment of her intentions?

"You must be Tia." The white-shirted woman rose and came to greet Tia, holding out her hand. "I'm Sister Patrice." Tia felt the woman's strength and saw kindness in her gaze. Elders deserved someone like her at the head of their senior center. Perhaps in working with her, Tia would learn to be satisfied by doing good works. Maybe she'd yearn less, learn to be present through devotion.

Apples and cooked sugar scented the air, as though pies had been baked recently. Arts and crafts supplies filled plastic bins. Piles of old greeting cards sat waiting to be pasted on cardboard boxes. Soon the cards and boxes would be decoupaged together, lined up in neat rows, like the ones she'd seen in the lobby.

Tia could already imagine herself at Fianna's in December, begging friends to save their Christmas cards. They'd bring in bags of them. Year after year, she'd drown in Hallmark, her request tapping into people's desire to be charitable with a minimum of effort.

At the other end of the room, a pale woman tapped at a computer. Tia couldn't tell whether she was staff or a client. Pictures of soldiers lined half a wall.

"These are the soldiers we've adopted." Sister Patrice swept her arm toward the pictures. "One for each of our clients."

"You certainly have a lot of clients."

"We do." Sister Patrice's smile revealed perfect teeth. The nun was at least in her early seventies, so they were probably dentures, but good ones. Only a smattering of wrinkles lined the woman's pink skin, but still Tia felt her age. She'd worked with seniors long enough to have a feel for people's ages. All the Botox in the world couldn't take away the aura of age.

"Come. Sit." The nun put a hand under Tia's elbow and led her to a set of club chairs angled toward each other. "Would you care for a cup of tea? Coffee? Thank you for coming early. I thought it best we meet before the hordes arrive."

"I'm fine, thank you." Tia imagined seniors descending the steps, using their canes to tap their way over to sing around the old piano. Her stomach contracted as she envisioned Mrs. Graham humming and smiling. Tia should have connected her with a group such as this. Mrs. Graham liked music.

Tia's failure with Mrs. Graham was too immense to dwell on for more than a few minutes. Once again, she chased away the memory.

"You seem more than qualified for the job." Sister Patrice looked up from a brown manila file, which probably held Tia's resume and cover letter. "But I see no references. Why is that?"

The need not to lie became stronger than her desire to impress this good woman. "I totally screwed up my last job. Excuse my language, Sister."

Sister Patrice's face creased into another smile. "Intensely truthful words for an interview."

Tia tipped her head. "Is that good or bad? I could use honesty at the moment."

"From me or from yourself?"

"Probably both," Tia said. "But I suppose more from myself."

"Why don't you tell me what happened," Sister said.

"A toast to Tia!" Michael Dwyer lifted his glass. "Once again, a working slave like the rest of us."

Everyone at the table yelled "To Tia!" in unison. Moira, Deidre, and Michael had already been at Fianna's when Tia and Bobby arrived.

"I'd have stayed on unemployment until the very last check came," Moira said. "You impress me."

Moira's sister tipped her beer mug toward Tia. "For real, hon. Good job. By the way, if the place is run by the Sisters of Notre Dame, it's an up-and-up place. The one who hired you, she's got a good reputation. My aunt told me."

Moira and Deidre thought their place in heaven was secured by having an aunt who was a nun. They mentioned her at least once a night, perhaps as a reminder to God. Still, it was nice to hear.

"Not like that jerk who fired you." Bobby put a proprietary arm around Tia. "I'm proud of you. Plus, it's in a great neighborhood."

"I worked in a good neighborhood before," Tia said.

"Yeah, sure. Nothing like having a courthouse, a cemetery, and a T stop as neighbors." Bobby winked at Michael, which made Tia want to walk away and never look back.

He'd deny it until his tongue fell out but she could feel his racial fear leaking out. She knew he hated her living in a neighborhood where cultures and races were so mixed up there wasn't even an apparent majority. Bobby didn't mind a bit of melting pot, as long as the soup was on the pale side.

"That cemetery is a treasure." Tia doubted Bobby had ever been there. Khalil Gibran, e. e. cummings, and Anne Sexton were among the writers buried there. Chimes, sculptures of spectrally dressed trees, and decades-old statues lined the paths, along with crypts so ornate and dignified that dying didn't seem truly awful if you got to spend eternity in one of them.

"You're right. It's a terrific place," Michael agreed. He liked to show everyone how sophisticated he'd become since working for the city. His stamp of approval meant that Tia's opinion could now be accepted.

"Okay, but that T stop is a pit," Bobby insisted.

"What exactly do you mean by pit, Bobby?" Tia asked. "Not enough white people?"

"Don't put words in my mouth." Bobby gave her a sideways hug. "Your prickles are showing."

He was playing to the crowd, that's all. Pressed, he'd always do the right thing. She believed that. Bobby's goodness wasn't the kind that came out in words but in deeds. Unlike Nathan, who could talk your ear off about his beliefs, but had he ever come through for her?

Moira and Deidre smiled fondly at Tia and Bobby. Somehow,

without Tia noticing, they'd become the Chandler and Monica of their crowd—finding each other after years as friends.

"Bobby, get me another drink. Please." Tia forced herself to smile.

"We'll get the next one at dinner," he said. Bobby's *we* sounded irritating and overly loud.

"Why don't we all get a bite?" Michael suggested.

Bobby held up a hand. "It's gonna be just us tonight. No offense."

"None taken, pal. New romances need room, right?"

Even when they were kids, Michael had acted as though he were the godfather of their crowd. Bobby kept telling Tia not to let Michael get under her skin. He means well, he's good people, Bobby would say, always needing to defend him—to defend everyone in the group.

Bobby looked at her as though he'd won the biggest prize at the fair. "How new can it be, huh?" he replied to Michael. "I've known her forever. Now I just have to make sure it stays this way."

They drove to a restaurant on the waterfront. The tables had candles, white linen, and three different kinds of bread in the baskets. Tia tried not to compare it to the places she'd gone with Nathan, even as she remembered Helmand, the Afghan restaurant in Cambridge, decorated like a Fabergé egg, where the food had been served on hand-painted pottery. Nathan had ordered tasting plates, offering her bits of magical pumpkin kibbe and crisp bread dipped in exotic sauces.

"This is nice." Tia sat in the chair Bobby pulled out for her.

"You look good dressed up like that." He bent and kissed the top of her head.

"You think so?" Tia asked. "I thought I looked a bit corporate for a job in a church basement."

"It must have worked; you have the job, right?"

"I guess. She thought I'd be a good match for the place. I don't know why, though."

Bobby nodded as the busboy slid embossed amber water glasses in front of them and placed leather-bound menus beside their bread plates. "You undervalue yourself. That's how you ended up with sleeping with that asshole."

Undervaluing, indeed. As though she were property. Maybe Bobby thought Tia was a bargain on the market. Tia looked around for the waiter. "I guess," she said again.

"Why'd you stay with him?"

Tia wondered what Bobby wanted to hear. How lost she'd been? That it was all sex? She doubted he'd appreciate that answer. That Nathan had drugged her and tied her down? He'd made Nathan into the Machiavellian older man, and her, the naïve innocent.

In truth, Tia thought she'd been the jerk. She'd loved an unavailable man. Now she had to carry another transgression: wanting to sleep with Nathan yet again. She'd cheated on Bobby through intent if not deed.

"I suppose a shrink would say I was chasing an unavailable man. Reenacting scenes from my childhood."

Bobby's eyes showed more kindness than Tia deserved. "My poor girl. Do you know how much I want to take care of you?"

"I guess I'm beginning to."

"And do you believe that I will never leave you?"

"I do."

"Give me your hands," Bobby said.

Tia held them out. He sandwiched them between his, and ran his thumb over her knuckles. His thick hands engulfed hers. "I love you." This was the first time he'd said these words. "We can have a life together. You can redo my place however you like."

Tia imagined living in Bobby's large apartment with that broad ocean view, sliding across that glossy oak floor to make coffee in the morning, and seeing pure blue morning light instead of the ancient man across the side yard coughing and spitting into his handkerchief.

"We can be a family," Bobby said. "I know it's too soon for a ring. But we're getting there, aren't we? We can go all the way. We'll get your girl back. I swear. I will work my damnedest to make sure you see her."

And there it was. The last opportunity for Tia to tell Bobby about seeing Savannah and Nathan.

She took a roll and ripped it in two, and then in half again.

"Would you like wine or champagne?" Bobby asked. "To celebrate?"

"Celebrate?"

"Your job!" He reached over, took a piece of her fluffy white roll, and popped it in his mouth. "Your job. Us. Honor."

Savannah. She needed to tell him. Her name was Savannah.

CHAPTER 32

Juliette

Juliette and Nathan watched the Flag Day Parade from the curb, the equivalent of front row seats, smack at the corner of Rhinebeck's largest intersection: Main Street and East Market. Juliette's parents sat in folding stadium chairs, a container of lemonade on her father's lap, paper cups on her mother's. She assumed that water bottles were hidden in her mother's large straw bag.

Juliette hugged her knees while she watched Nathan grin and pump his fist as Max jumped on and off his skateboard. Having Juliette and Nathan in the same place had lifted Max into a state of giddiness, and he was acting like a kid again. No matter how often Juliette reminded him that his father was just visiting, Max jumped around as though he were Roo and Juliette were his gently scolding mother, Kanga.

Juliette wished she could fly back in time to when she read A. A. Milne's *Winnie the Pooh* to her sons, to when she and Nathan tucked in their boys each night and did that wonderfully cozy mommy-daddy thing where they simply gazed because the sight of their sons satisfied them.

Max was the easy one. Last night, when Juliette tried to talk to Lucas about Nathan's impending visit, he asked Juliette to leave him alone and shut up about the visit already. Who cared if *he* was coming? But once Nathan arrived, Lucas seemed to relax a bit more each minute.

Her mother's words echoed. Perhaps nobody better than Nathan waited for Juliette. Certainly there was no one else who shared Max and Lucas, no one who'd want to die at bad news about the boys. The teenage years terrified her. Car crashes, drugs, pregnant girlfriends. She imagined the worst. Only Nathan could share that emergency room state of mind.

An antique fire truck came down the street, followed by a flag-festooned dump truck carrying a bright red Elmo.

A little girl wearing a Brownies uniform marched by, her mouth set in a grave line. She waved two pinwheels and gave a tiny hop-skip every few feet, reminding Juliette of her own turn in the parade. Years ago, Juliette had been chosen to carry the flag. She'd practiced for weeks, wearing a path up and down the driveway.

On that parade day, after blocks of marching in anticipation, when Juliette finally arrived where her parents sat, instead of searching for her they were talking to friends, her father with his arm hooked around her mother. Squeezing her eyes shut for one moment, she'd sent them thought waves. *Look at me! Look at me! Look at me!*

Finally, her father had looked up, chucked his chin at her, and grinned. Then her mother clapped, her hands held up high, but it hadn't been enough for Juliette; she'd wanted them to be watching for her, not catching sight of her by chance.

Nathan touched her knee with his. "Thanks for letting me come." He looked as though she'd given him the moon and stars.

Her mother had warned her not to love Nathan so obviously. *Don't dote on him so,* she'd said. *Otherwise, he won't dote on you.*

Now, feeling his desperate want—see, *he's* doting, Mom—she wanted nothing more than normal. *Their* normal. Before this mess. When they did things like eat dinner, read the paper, and all the adult versions of side-by-side play.

"The boys missed you," she said. "They're not used to being here without you. They don't like it."

"There's no one to play basketball with them," Nathan said.

"My father took them fishing," Juliette said. Nathan appeared haggard. She wondered if his lack of sleep was from worry or something else. Like late nights.

"Your father fishes?" Nathan's laugh lines crinkled. "Gordon? I didn't think he even knew what sports were."

Juliette shrugged. Nathan loved taking little jabs at her father. Perhaps the similarities between them—professors—forced Nathan to put down her father to bring himself up. An alpha thing.

"My mother says it's good for his heart." Juliette shaded her eyes and looked for the boys. She noticed Lucas pulling himself taller and puffing out his chest as the cheerleading contingent approached. What sort of lessons about women would her sons learn from Nathan? It frightened her that living apart could sour their outlooks on love.

Before Nathan had left, the boys had worshipped their father. Now Lucas tracked him in wary circles, and Max offered the soft underside of his belly like a puppy begging for pats and approval.

"How about I take you out for a fancy dinner tonight?" he asked Juliette. "Just you and I." Nathan tapped his fingers on the curb. Nathan and Max both had thick peasant hands. Lucas had the same long, articulated artist's fingers that Juliette inherited from her father.

"You just arrived," Juliette said. "We shouldn't leave the boys."

They hadn't spoken about where he would sleep. Her parents had spare bedrooms galore, but she wanted him in her bed. What she didn't want, however, was having that longing. Desire for Nathan weakened her.

"Then I'll take everyone to dinner." Nathan's shoulder touched hers for a fleeting moment. "Unless you'd rather it just be us and the boys."

"Let's stay home. You can bring dinner in. That's what I think the boys would like. We'll be together without pressure."

"How about later? After dinner, will we have any time alone?" Nathan started to take her hand, pulling back at the last moment, leaving her with just a brush of his flesh against hers.

"We'll see." She turned back to the parade before she could follow her craving to touch Nathan's cheek. Old men marched by carrying rifles on their shoulders, wearing uniforms that hung over their hollow chests and strained across their stomachs.

It went by fast, a life.

Juliette wondered if they should have gone out, she and Nathan. Palpable expectations from everyone hung too heavy. She thought she'd scream if her father worked any harder to show that he was having fun, and even harder to insure the boys saw it: *Look how heartily I am welcoming back your father!*

Jolliness wasn't part of her mother's character, but she had charm, and tonight she used it to the maximum. She wrapped everyone in dry jokes after manipulating the seating so that Juliette and Nathan sat side by side. The dining room was suffused with the surfeit of candles her mother lit, the roses she'd crammed into too many vases, and the crackling tension of the boys' hope.

Nathan pressed his leg against Juliette's—probably what her mother had hoped for when she'd shoved them together. He didn't remove it, and she didn't pull away.

"This is great food, Dad." Max heaped another portion of crispy orange beef onto his plate. "And I love this spinner, Mamie. We should get one at home." He whirled the lazy Susan in the middle of the table into dizzying circles until Nathan stopped it with his hand.

"Just what we need," he said. "More perpetual motion to drive us crazy."

"This *is* great food," Juliette said. "I wish there had been Chinese food in town when I was little." She didn't give a damn about the food, but she wanted to wash away the coziness of Nathan's "us" reference before Max and Lucas settled into thinking, *Ah, Dad's home.*

Nathan, her father, her mother, the kids—everyone wanted to weave her into a nice, tight fait accompli. Still, it was a relief to see her sons acting normal. Lucas crumpled a straw wrapper and spitballed it at Max, who flicked rice back at him. Max wasn't trying to be the perfect child. Lucas's mouth had loosened.

"Enough, guys," Nathan said. "Mamie doesn't want you decorating her place in your food. If you're finished eating, we can clear the table."

"No!" Max brought his arm protectively around his plate. "I'm still starving."

"Yeah. You look like you're starving," Lucas said.

"Be nice, Lucas. Here, try some of this." Nathan ladled a heaping portion of shrimp in lobster sauce on Lucas's plate.

A dwindling amount of Chinese comfort food covered the lazy Susan. Nathan had bought enough to feed three families, but they'd eaten as though they were ten instead of six. Even her mother nibbled at a piece of General Tso's chicken.

Juliette and Nathan finally climbed the staircase to the second floor well past midnight.

The rest of the family had gone to bed hours before, obvious in their conspiracy to give them privacy. Lucas left the family room especially early, pretending he'd rather read than watch TV, giving a theatrical yawn after saying good night at nine. He'd held up an old copy of *Jaws* he'd found in his grandfather's study, as though his parents required proof of his intent.

Nevertheless, Juliette remained reading on the couch for hours; at least, she appeared to be reading. In truth, she held a book and turned pages, but little registered. Instead she weighed pros and cons until she thought perhaps she'd go mad. She strained toward her husband emotionally, wanting nothing more than the safety of the private island made by a husband and a wife.

She wanted to hold that comforting cup of coffee.

Now they were alone behind the bedroom door. Juliette leaned against it as though keeping something out.

"You okay?" Nathan asked.

"Not really."

"We okay?"

"Haven't a clue," she said. "Can we leave it alone? Just for now."

"I'm not sure if I can." Nathan put a hand on either side of Juliette, resting his palms flat against the door. "I need to talk to you, Jules. There's so much to say."

"Yes. I know." However, if they talked, they'd probably never get to this. She rested her head on his chest. Or this. She touched him. "I'm not sure if I'm ready."

That was the thing about making love with your husband. You could just damned well touch him. You didn't need to wear lipstick or weigh the pros and cons.

He led her to the bed. She held him back for a moment while she threw off the antique patchwork quilt.

They fell down on the soft white cotton sheets. Juliette breathed him in.

"Let's take our clothes off," he whispered.

"No. Wait." Decisions and choices flew through her in too-rapid succession. One second she wanted him more than breath, and then the next moment, she wasn't ready to feel him without a barrier.

His desire was too apparent, and she felt too brutally hyperaware of everything.

"How was seeing her?" she asked.

"Who?"

"Either. Both."

"We already spoke about it." Her shoulder muffled his words.

"Yes. Right. But I don't really know what happened."

He struggled up and rolled off Juliette. "What happened to leaving it alone?" The moment the words were out, he forced a smile. "Sorry."

Juliette remained flat on her back. The ceiling was perfect. Not one crack. Not a single water stain. "I thought I could, but I was wrong."

Nathan looked good to her. She hated that.

He moved to embrace her.

"Don't."

"I don't love her, Jules. I don't know if I even like her anymore."

"Did you sleep with her?"

"Of course not."

"Don't sound offended. You haven't earned that."

"You're right. It's just that I hate that you think so little of me." He lay on his side next to her. He put a hand on her chin, trying to turn her to face him, but she remained in place, staring at the flawless ceiling.

She couldn't tell whether he was lying or telling the truth, but other than giving him a lie detector test, she didn't know how to determine the answer. She'd read that you could tell by the eyes. Something about the person looking up to retrieve information versus looking down to tell a lie, but she couldn't remember; it might have been the other way around.

"What about Savannah?" Juliette wouldn't cry no matter what he said. She promised herself that if she didn't cry, she could eat pancakes dripping with maple syrup for breakfast. She'd get her father to make them. Max would like that. She'd melt butter and heat the syrup. Put them in her mother's tiny flowered pitchers.

"She's quite a kid."

"What does that mean, 'quite a kid'? How?"

He fell back. Now both of them stared at the ceiling. "She's an honest little girl. She was scared. She thought maybe we were coming to take her away. It must have been horrible for her. It was for me."

"Why did you go together?"

"Honestly, Jules? I'm not even sure. First Caroline went to see Tia—don't ask me why, I haven't a clue—then Tia went nutty and called me right after. She said she didn't trust Caroline's motives and that we had to make sure Savannah was safe with her."

Juliette snorted. "Sure. I believe that."

Nathan rolled over on his side. He put a hand on her hip. "What do you think? Why do you think Caroline met with Tia?"

"I think Caroline was checking up on Tia. She had told Caroline that she didn't know who the father was," Juliette said. "And honestly, I'm sure it didn't help that I'd been so devious about meeting her. If I'd been in Caroline's place, I'd want to know what was going on."

Juliette realized how crazy she'd acted. Caroline must think she was insane.

She had been. Whatever her motives, she'd gone a bit mad, though, still, she couldn't imagine how they could shut away the memory, the reality, of Savannah now. Pandora's box couldn't be shut.

"Caroline seems to be a good person. So does Peter. Her husband. Solid people. Good parents."

"How did you feel? Seeing Savannah?"

"I felt protective. I want her to be safe. I felt a connection, for sure, but I didn't feel like she was mine, not like Max and Lucas."

Juliette didn't know if she should feel happy or sad about that. "Hold me, okay?" She supposed she felt a little of each.

"I miss you." He took her into his arms. "I want to come home, Juliette."

Fatigue overwhelmed her.

"Let's just go to sleep, Nathan."

Nathan pulled the antique quilt over her, clothes and all. Water ran as he brushed his teeth. Juliette never could break him of that bad habit. She thought of washing up, but overtiredness kept her splayed on the sheets.

"Here." Nathan held out a Dixie cup filled with water. "Chinese food always makes you thirsty."

He sat on the edge of the bed and brought the cup to her lips. She hadn't realized how thirsty she was until he gave her water.

She wiped her wet lips. "I don't know. I just don't know if you can stay."

"Now?"

"No. You can stay now, but after." Juliette took his hand. "I need to be certain."

"Have you stopped loving me?" Nathan asked.

"I love you. The question is, can I forgive you? If I can't do that, we won't have any sort of life."

"Don't make this decision now. Not like this. It's all too raw."

"You're right. But there are things I'm feeling that might never change."

"I can tell you this with complete confidence. I will never sleep with another woman except you. I won't. I know that. I'm not sure what it was all about, but I know that it had nothing to do with you."

"I can accept that, and I can even choose to believe it. But here's the problem. Even if I can forgive you for Tia, I don't know if I can forgive you for Savannah."

"Savannah?" Nathan's voice rose in confusion. "I had no responsibility for that. I didn't want Tia to be pregnant—Jesus that was the last thing I wanted. Honestly, I think she wanted to use it to get me to come to her. Leave you. And, of course, I wouldn't. "

"You stayed with me. But you didn't trust me."

"What do you mean?"

Juliette struggled to sit upright. She crossed her legs and pressed her fists into her knees, trying not to cry. "You denied your baby, your child. What in the world makes a man deny his child?"

"It was about you, Jules! You and the boys—I couldn't lose you."

"See, that's the second thing. You should have trusted me, Nathan. You should have told me. Maybe if you'd been honest, we would have had a chance."

Nathan remained quiet for a long time. The faint light from the bedside lamp cast shadows that hinted at Nathan at fifty, sixty, and older.

"Don't let go of us," he begged. "I know you're disappointed in me. I feel the same way. Please. Give us a chance."

Juliette rolled away from Nathan, needing not to see him. She knew he wanted to make things right, and she knew Lucas and Max needed their father home.

Her mother, her father, everyone pushed Juliette to take back Nathan.

It was wrong to make decisions because of that pressure, right?

But making her family happy would make her happy. Wasn't that worth it?

Could she forgive him?

Gandhi said that forgiveness was the attribute of the strong. She just didn't know if she had that sort of strength.

CHAPTER 33

Caroline

"Happy Father's Day, Daddy!" Savannah jumped on the bed, managing somehow to land right between Caroline and Peter. Caroline wondered why she'd not noticed until recently that Savannah moved with tremendous grace.

Savannah leaned over Peter and gave him a loud, smacking kiss. "Ick, you're scratchy, Daddy."

"Think so?" Peter asked. He rubbed his cheek along Savannah's arm. "As scratchy as Mommy's nail file?"

"Worse than the sandpaper in *Pat the Bunny*." Savannah turned and stroked Caroline's face. "Mommy's soft."

"How about for Father's Day, I get to go back to sleep?" Peter asked.

Caroline pulled down Savannah, hoping that they might all sleep for another five minutes or so. "Snuggle time?"

Savannah became still, hands at her sides, obviously trying to please her parents despite her impatience to get up. "Aren't we going to bring Daddy breakfast in bed?" she whispered. "Like we did for you on Mother's Day?"

Caroline rolled over to face Savannah. "Maybe we should do something else, pumpkin. Maybe we can take Daddy out for breakfast."

"But it's Father's Day," Savannah spoke without the whine one might expect of a five-year-old asked to put aside tradition. Kids liked things to be conventional. Once again, Caroline feared that Savannah was too good.

"I know," Caroline said. "They have special breakfasts for fathers at restaurants."

"But we're supposed to cook for him."

Where did she get these rigid conventions of family? The Disney Channel?

Peter dug deeper into his pillow.

Cooking a big breakfast sounded horrendous. "Okay, honey. In a second," she said.

Savannah wiggled closer to Caroline, grabbing a corner of the blanket and wrapping it around her fist. "Mommy?"

Caroline heard the tinkle of fear she so disliked. The sound reminded Caroline of her own failing, rarely bold enough to say what she thought or felt. "What is it, honey?"

"What do you think the other daddy is doing today?"

Caroline evaluated all the possible responses and then chose honesty.

"I would guess that he is with his sons, pumpkin." She and Peter had told Savannah about Nathan's family with as much candor as they thought she could bear. It hadn't been easy, but burying things only made it worse in the end.

"His real children." Savannah stated this as an absolute fact, and though Caroline would have liked to contradict her, she couldn't find any words that could be twisted into a palatable truth. Finally, she simply hugged her girl as hard as she could.

"Daddy and I love you so much."

Really, was there anything else to say?

After eating French toast eggs, they showered and dressed for a visit to Peter's parents. During the ride, they kept their magical feeling of *just us three*. Then Peter parked the car, and Caroline tensed.

"I'm not looking forward to this," she said.

"Don't worry," Peter said. "I'll handle them."

"Handle what, Daddy?" Savannah asked from the backseat.

"Grandma and Grandpa. Sometimes they think what Mommy and I do is silly."

"Like what?"

Like what we're about to do. Caroline laced her fingers and squeezed.

"Well, like having pancakes for supper. You know how we do that sometimes? Grandma and Grandpa think pancakes are only for breakfast." Peter opened the car door and then stuck his head back in after he got out. "I think we should all take a day off—from work, from Nanny Rose, from everything—next week and go to the beach. We should buy kites and fly them as high as the clouds. Now, *that* would be silly, huh?"

Savannah's eyes opened wider than Caroline had ever seen. "Oh, Daddy, could we?" she asked in a reverential tone.

"Why not?" Peter said.

"Mommy? Does Daddy mean it?"

"He does, baby. He's pretty flexible, this daddy of ours." Caroline sat back, waiting for Savannah to ask what *flexible* meant. Caroline looked forward to forming an explanation for her daughter. She was pretty good at that.

"Anyway, I know this all seems sudden, but we want to be settled in a new place before school starts."

Peter's words sort of melted away as he watched his mother. If Caroline had thought about it longer, she'd never have let her own enthusiasm get in the way of the obvious fact that her mother-in-law would flip out when she heard about their plans. Talking about their decisions like this, with Savannah and the rest of the family at the table, was a huge error.

"Are you finished?" Her mother-in-law, who'd been listening with her lips set in pruney disapproval, finally let loose. "Are you nuts?

Because this will finish you. Wave good-bye to your company, Peter." Caroline shrank back as Peter's mother slammed a cherry pie on the table. It was her father-in-law's favorite, which Peter's mother made every Father's Day.

"You've both lost your minds," her mother-in-law continued ranting even as she turned back to the sideboard and grabbed a tall stack of dessert plates. The Sunday roast had been devoured by Peter's tribe of sisters, brothers, in-laws, nieces, and nephews. All the leaves had been put in the long mahogany dining table, and then a card table was added to either end. Peter and Caroline sat with Savannah wedged between them.

Irene Fitzgerald smacked a gold-rimmed plate in front of Caroline. "I suppose this is all your doing, right?"

"Irene, calm yourself down," Peter's father said in an ineffectual attempt to quiet his wife.

"Too good to take care of her own child," Peter's mother muttered, ignoring Peter's father.

"Mommy takes care of me, Grandma." Savannah reached for Caroline's hand under the table and squeezed. "Right, Mommy?"

Caroline nodded. "Right, baby."

Savannah looked at Peter. "And Nanny Rose just helps us, right?"

"Nannies!" Peter's mother practically spit out the word. "Normal people would be quite satisfied with a babysitter."

"*Stop*," Peter said to his mother, infusing the word with a deadly force that Caroline recognized well. Then he turned to Savannah. "Nanny Rose has helped us an awful lot since you were a baby. But soon we won't need her as much. You'll be in school, and then I'll pick you up or you'll go to an after-school program. Nanny Rose is going to take care of someone else's little baby, and you and I will hang out together more. Sound good?"

"Oh, I'd love that." She peeked at Caroline. "Right, Mommy?"

"Yes. You will. And maybe this summer, after we find our new house, you'll meet some of the girls who will be in your kindergarten class."

"And where will this be? Jamaica Plain? Dorchester?" Peter's mother named Boston neighborhoods as though Caroline and Peter planned to send their child to school in a war-torn village where she'd be dodging bullets.

"We're looking at fine areas, Mom," Peter said.

"You live in a fine area now. The finest. How can you take this opportunity away from your daughter? You worked so hard." She sniffed in Caroline's direction. "Look at you, giving up everything."

"Caroline and I have the best interests of our family first and foremost." Peter placed a protective hand over Caroline's wrist. With a smile that Caroline knew was meant to calm Savannah, while also telling his mother he meant business, he said, "Now sit down and join us for this great pie, before we force-feed you a blood pressure pill."

His mother probably sensed that Peter really meant "Stop, or we'll march right out of here." Caroline closed her eyes momentarily in gratitude. Standing up to his mother was difficult for Peter. He loved being the big success in the family; the one who gave his mother bragging rights in the neighborhood, at church, in the supermarket. She rarely passed up an opportunity to talk about Peter's business triumphs, and he basked in his mother's pride.

And here was Caroline, taking it all away.

Everything in their lives was about to change. Peter planned to reduce his hours in the business and hire a manager. They'd live on less money until Savannah was older and he could get fully back in the game.

Their gleaming white home? "Sell it," Peter had said. "I want you and Savannah far more than I want acreage."

Their cars? "Trade them in. Corollas get you there just the same."

Peter's mother shook her head in disgust. "Such a waste. You built up a wonderful business, and now you're going to let it disappear? Why are you being such fools?"

"Ma, let it go," Joe Junior, the oldest brother, said. "Who the hell cares if they sell their goddamn house or he wears a damned apron?"

Joe was the quiet one, but when a door needed closing, he'd eventually shut it.

"Joe!" his mother exclaimed.

"Excuse me, Ma," Joe said. "Who the *heck* cares if they sell their house? It's too big for three people anyway. All it's good for is showing off their bank balance."

Joe's teenage daughter Heather yelled from the other end of the table, "I'll take it!"

"Your house is just fine, miss," her grandmother said. "Your father provides every single thing you need."

"I wasn't saying anything, Grandma."

"Just make sure you don't. I won't have any showing off in this house."

"You're not even making sense, Ma," Faith said. "First you get upset because Peter and Caroline are selling their house, and then you tell Heather not to want it."

With shaky fingers, Caroline plopped a scoop of ice cream on top of the slice of pie in front of Savannah. Then she topped her own.

"You're missing the point," Peter's mother said. "They already have it. Why give it away?"

"Christ, Mom. We're not giving it away. We're selling it," Peter said.

"Who does something so crazy?" She slammed her hands on her hips. "Your father and I struggled to give you kids everything we could, so you could end up with more than we had. How can you go backward like this? Why don't you just move to the exact street in Dorchester where I grew up? Would that make you happy? Maybe you can rent that same garbage apartment."

"You have to stop this craziness," Sissy said.

Caroline tensed, wondering what fresh hell Peter's sister would inject in the conversation.

"Exactly," said Mrs. Fitzgerald. "It's all craziness."

"No, Ma," Sissy said. "You're exactly wrong. You're the one who's wrong. Money isn't everything in the world, you know."

"I never said it was." Mrs. Fitzgerald fussed with straightening napkins on the buffet.

"You kind of did, Reenie," Peter's father said.

"I only want the best for my children," she said. "More than I had for myself—that's what I want for you."

"And we appreciate that, Ma." Peter put an arm around Caroline. "But Caroline and I, we also want to give Savannah the best. Ma, you did a great job. I want to do as well. I never want Savannah to starve for anything, including our company. One of us has to work a little less, and I chose to be the one."

Peter's mother put her hands to her face, covering her mouth for a moment. She blinked her eyes. "Fine, fine. You'll do what you want anyway."

Peter's father patted the empty seat to his right. "Let's give it a rest, okay? Everyone at the table is healthy, no one is starving, and everyone has a job. So, there's nothing to be upset about, right? We'll get enough trouble when we're not looking."

Mrs. Fitzgerald threw her arms in the air. "I give up. Let's eat." She sat to the right of her husband and picked up her fork, waving it at Caroline before digging it into her dessert. "You better discover a cure for eye cancer for this sacrifice from Peter."

"Absolutely, Mom," Caroline agreed. "I'm on it."

Caroline smiled at her mother-in-law. She took a large bite of pie, enjoying the sweet and creamy mix in her mouth. She turned to Savannah and hugged her close, closing her eyes and breathing in her smell of baby shampoo mixed with Caroline's vanilla-tinged powder. Her girl was beginning to raid Caroline's things.

Savannah's first five years weren't splendid. Caroline knew that. And she knew she held much of the blame—not all, but much. Now it was on her to figure out how to change things.

CHAPTER 34

Tia

Sister Patrice's patience awed Tia.

Scorching August heat—barely overcome by the church's ancient air conditioner—addled clients pulling at her arm each time she passed, bathrooms needing cleaning ten times in a day, none of it rattled her. Sister managed to find the good in everyone—even Ed Parker, who attempted to pick up the skirt of every woman who passed. "At least he still has a spark," Sister Patrice would say repeatedly, usually after putting a plate of cookies in front of him to keep his hands busy. Ed refused to wear his teeth, so eating took him a good, long time.

The goodness of her new boss soothed Tia through the days of knowing that she was at the wrong job. In her month working at Merciful Sisters, Tia had learned this about herself: working with the elderly suffering from early dementia was a job for the serene or the jolly. Tia fit neither category.

At Merciful Sisters, Tia was available every moment. The staff had fifteen minutes to set up before the clients arrived and fifteen minutes to clean after they left. The other seven and a half hours were devoted to entertaining the elderly men and women for whom this church basement was everything.

Merciful Sisters was a good place. Compared to some senior facilities, it was paradise on earth. Sister Harmony's biscuits were so delicious that Tia swore she was developing the first potbelly of her life.

Father Gerard came in from the rectory with a different leather-bound classic each week. They'd sit in a joyful circle of ideas—that's what he called the reading hour—and listen as he read in his rough brogue. This week it was *Ivanhoe*.

They had painting class, and they adopted soldiers, and sang, and took trips to shows. Last week Tia had a shaky elderly woman on each side, holding tight as she led them down the aisle of the Colonial Theatre to see a revival of *Guys and Dolls*.

Tia hated it all. The day-in, day-out cheerful care wasn't in her. She knew this was a wonderful place, but she could barely make it through her days, and she was frightened of her future. Perhaps she needed to buck up and accept that this was her life.

"Here you go." Sister Harmony handed her a platter of meringues. "A special treat. Pass them out, dear."

Tia took the plate. That morning, Sister Harmony had explained how she'd been waiting for a dry day to make these meringues—angel kisses, she called them. Apparently, humidity made angel kisses weep.

Her clients made Tia weep these days. She wanted to enjoy spending time with them; she hated having to put on a face. They deserved more than cookies, and Tia realized she wanted to find ways to work on that. Maybe going back to school. Maybe teaching.

She gave Ed plenty of distance as she held out the plate to him. "Only two, Ed," she warned. "These are for everyone."

"Make sure he doesn't cheat," Alice Gomez said. "He thinks everything's for him. I don't know why Sister rewards him for being bad."

Tia patted Alice's arm as she held the platter far from Ed. "Tell you what: I'll take you for a treat tomorrow. Just me and you." She bent down to whisper in Alice's ear. "We'll get ice cream."

Alice beamed, her dentures hanging a bit low. Tia needed to take Alice to the ladies' room.

If Tia had felt tired at the JP Senior Advocate Center, here she'd begun dying of sadness. She wondered if God was making her do penance for her life, for giving away Savannah, for sleeping with and then pining for Nathan. For how she'd failed the Grahams. The idea of fighting God terrified her.

"Brain games in fifteen minutes, folks!" Sister Patrice called. She held up a large box printed with bright blue outlines of lively seniors shouting.

"Ooh, look!" Alice Gomez grinned. "Tia, your boyfriend is here," she said in singsong fashion.

Bobby beamed as he bounded down the stairs. They loved him.

"Mrs. Gomez." Bobby gave the frail old woman a squeeze around the shoulders. "You look lovely as always."

"You're early, Bobby," Tia said. "It's only three thirty."

He gave Mrs. Gomez a final pat and turned to Tia. "Good news. Guess what finally happened to yours truly today?"

The entire room hushed, waiting to hear Bobby's news. Even Sister Patrice looked up from the eternal paperwork that, in her words, damned the good sister to hell on earth.

Tia's stomach clutched. She had a bad feeling that she knew exactly what the good news would be.

"I sold it! I did it, Tia!" Bobby did a little victory dance, shaking his shoulders back and forth. He smothered Tia in a bear hug. "Easy street, baby. That's where we're headed," he whispered. "Easy street."

"You won the boss lottery, baby," Bobby said.

He put his hand on the small of her back and led her toward the bridge in the Public Garden. Everything about this oasis of well-tended trees, shrubs, and flowers whispered romance, a Renoir come alive.

"It's not like she gave me the key to the city; she let me out an hour early."

"But still, she's always good to you."

"Aren't I good to her?" Tia asked.

"Why are you biting my head off, baby?"

Oh, that was surely the question. With anyone else, Tia would be nodding her head off as she agreed how wonderful Sister Patrice had been since she took the job. Tia stopped at the foot of the bridge.

"Please don't call me baby, okay?" Tia asked. "I told you it drives me nuts."

Bobby's face went blank, and Tia hated herself.

"Because that's what I remember my father calling my mother. It's painful."

The lie brought life back to Bobby. He stood straighter and gave her a brotherly peck on her cheek. "Sorry, baby. Oops. Last time. Scout's honor." He held three fingers in the air.

She nodded and gave a weak smile. They reached the middle of the bridge and stopped, looking out at the calm lagoon. The Swan Boats, Boston's famed paddleboats, lazed over the water.

"This is exquisite," Tia said. She swept her hand in a circle, taking in the lush greenery, the happy families waiting on line, the flowers everywhere.

"*You're* exquisite."

Bobby loved her too much. She feared that the moment she melted back, he'd harden. That she'd been his unattainable dream. Worship never lasted.

"Look," Tia changed the subject. "The swans."

"You know what their names are?" Bobby answered his own question before Tia could speak. "Romeo and Juliet."

She pressed her lips together. She'd read that the famed Public Garden's swans were, in fact, both female, despite their Shakespearean heritage.

"Things can really move for us now." Bobby tipped up her face and kissed her. "This deal will change everything."

"To you, Bobby." Tia tipped an imaginary hat. "Condo king! And in this market!"

"I know, I know." He beamed. "I can't believe I finally got all the financing."

Tia tried to imagine his Realtor persona; did he keep his "Aw shucks," or was there a shark inside Bobby, one that took giant bites before a client even noticed? Or did his patience make the deals happen?

"This deal has teetered on the brink for ages, but I believed in it . . . honey," he said.

"I know." Tia gripped the iron railing.

"You know what this means, don't you?"

"That you'll be a big shot with a pocket full of money?"

Bobby grinned. He was a good guy. A real guy.

"That too," he said. "But that's not what I meant. It's going to take plenty of dough to fight for custody."

He patted his chest as though a million-dollar check nestled in his pocket; as though the money were already in the bank. "And now we have it."

Tia imagined the condo where they'd live in the new development. Bobby would pick out the best one. They'd wake each morning to the ocean view spread out just for them. In the summer, she and Savannah would only have to cross the street to go swimming.

It was such a beautiful dream. She'd thought about it every time Bobby brought it up, which he did repeatedly, even as she tried to back away. Nuts. It would be purely insane. Still. She'd pictured holding Savannah's warm hand as they shopped for school clothes. The vision of Savannah swinging between her and Bobby, holding both their hands, was the sweetest thing she could imagine. As was taking her girl to meet Bobby's parents. They lived in the same house on K Street where he'd grown up. They'd probably saved all his toys.

She and Bobby could have a sister for Savannah. Two sisters. A dozen. Tia still felt the loneliness of being an only child. If not for Robin, would she have a soul to turn to?

If only she could make it all up, have a do-over. She'd never have given her away.

She still hadn't told Bobby about the day she and Nathan went to see Savannah. He still didn't have a clue that Nathan had come back in her life, however tangentially.

Instead of living clean, she was building a new set of secrets.

"Not that I'm saying we have to go to court right away." He studied her. "But the sooner the better, right? Look: it's about having options—that's the important thing in life. Knowing you can. Whatever you think is right, that's what we'll do. But she's not getting any younger. The sooner it happens, the easier it will be on her."

"I'm not ready to jump in yet," she said. "But the fact that you care . . . that's worth as much as anything I've ever gotten."

Tia looked to her left and saw children climbing on the bronze duck statues honouring the beloved Boston's children's book *Make Way for Ducklings*. Mothers and fathers looked on with adoration.

"Tia?" She looked back. Bobby held out a closed fist. "Can this be worth something to you also?" He opened his hand to reveal a black velvet box, using his thumb to flip it open, as though he'd practiced for this moment. "From this day forward, I want our decisions to be made together."

A large diamond framed with a square of tiny sparkling ones, so bright it caught even the soft light of the cloudy day, shone at Tia. She longed to wear it. Women with diamonds on their finger showed the world they belonged. How much someone loved them.

Bobby took her hand. He slipped the ring on her finger. It fit. Cool metal kissed her flesh. She looked down at her left hand. She spread her fingers, trying to see the dazzling ring and not her bitten fingernails.

"What do you say? Will you marry me?" Bobby asked. "Be my family? Let me be yours? Bring your baby home?"

His head tipped to the side in anticipation, and he bit his lip as he waited for her answer. After a moment, he answered for her. "Don't say a thing. Just wear it for a couple of days—a week." He grinned. "Maybe a month. Try it on. It might feel better than you think."

She felt the weight of the ring, probably worth more than everything she owned all added up together. A haze of sun caught the diamond and refracted it into a rainbow.

Tia moved her hand to the right to catch more of the sun. Her mother would have loved this ring. She'd have loved knowing Tia had Savannah back. And she'd have loved Bobby.

Once Bobby fell asleep, she slipped into the living room. What if she had Savannah here right now? What if she did what Bobby wanted? What about when he wasn't with them? Would she be a prisoner of the house?

How old did they have to be before you could leave them alone for a few minutes? How long before you stopped needing babysitters? She'd probably have to stop working, right? Although she'd need a job to prove her worthiness to the court.

But how about after? Would Bobby expect her to quit? Tia remembered sitting in a dark living room after school watching television. When Robin came into her life, she at least had someone with whom she could share the shows, but it was still lonely in the house. Just the two of them.

Not that they'd be only two, right? She'd have Bobby.

"You're going to marry him? Move back to Southie? Are you nuts?"

"Why can't you just be happy for me, Robin?"

"Oh, okay. Here I am being happy!"

"What are you drinking?" Tia asked. The Skype screen showed Robin holding a glass, toasting Tia via computer.

"White wine."

"In a jelly glass?"

"I don't have a set of wedding china like you're gonna get. Sorry."

"What time is it there?" Tia whispered. It was midnight in Jamaica Plain. Bobby had fallen asleep hours ago, after a celebratory bout of lovemaking that had nearly made Tia cry. Bobby had been so tender, treating her like a crystal figurine.

"Nine. Can't you ever remember the time difference?"

"Not really." Tia finished off her glass of straight whiskey.

"Is this what you want?" Robin asked.

Tia pressed her lips together and concentrated on the image of crossing Day Boulevard with Savannah to get to see the gentle lapping of Dorchester Bay's calm water. She felt Savannah's small hand resting in hers. She imagined Savannah wearing a blue bathing suit dotted with white stars, one that Bobby's sister, now Savannah's Auntie Eileen, would buy her new niece.

"Tia, Tia," Robin called.

Tia closed her eyes.

"Are you crying?"

Tia shook her head.

"Yes you are. I see it."

Tia shrugged.

"Are you alone?"

"No," Tia whispered. "Yes."

CHAPTER 35

Juliette

Juliette clutched the wheel in a death grip as she drove down the snaky Jamaicaway. The four-lane parkway had no business being any wider than one line of traffic in each direction. Even a fractional error seemed likely to result in a headfirst crash into an oncoming car. There were only inches between the traffic lanes, traffic lights came up with brake-screeching frequency, and cyclists veered off their designated path as though the entire concept of bike lanes were only places for the cyclists' brief respites from their mission of torturing drivers.

The last time she'd driven this road, she'd been on her way to spy on Tia. Not a good memory.

At least today, Nathan knew her destination. The relief of not hiding her meeting with Caroline offered at least some small reprieve for her jangled nerves. Each time she tried to form an adequate apology for having burst into Caroline's life, it sounded either insane or insipid.

My mind snapped?

My deepest apologies?

I became unhinged?

Anger had turned to sorrow, and now, calmer, if sadder, Juliette could see what she'd done to Caroline, scheming like a character in a low-rent version of *Fatal Attraction*. Her cheeks became hot at the memory.

Inviting Caroline to a free juliette&gwynne session? Offering treacly sympathy and manipulating her maternal worry? What the hell had Juliette wanted or expected? Jesus. It was a miracle that Caroline had agreed to meet with her today.

"Come on. Give yourself a break," Nathan had said when they spoke on the phone last night. Lately, they'd talked nightly. It reminded her of when they first dated, with her living in Boston and him in Rhinebeck. "Maybe the miracle isn't that she's seeing you but that you're willing to go and say you're sorry. You realize that most people would write an email, right?"

Nathan's genius for reassuring her had become magnified when she no longer had it on tap. She couldn't access equilibrium without him. People spoke of their husbands and wives as being their best friends, but with Nathan, it felt more essential. Without him, her stability was missing. Friends described feeling that way after their parents died, but Juliette never found comfort or constancy with her mother or father. Only with Nathan had she found an emotional home.

Once again she was reading up on marriage, divorce, adultery, and children—the past five years had borne a new crop of these books. At this point, Juliette hated any sentence containing the word *acknowledge* or *repair*. She wanted to throw the tiresome books out the window. Why didn't they offer something useful, like instructions for how to permanently wash another woman's handprints off her husband's body?

In the end, it came down to two simple declarative sentences:

1. *She loved and missed Nathan.*
2. *She didn't know if she had the forgiveness in her to make it work.*

Father's Day had come and gone. She'd promised herself she'd make her decision before then, but she broke that pledge. Instead she made list after list. Gwynne repeated ad nauseam that Juliette should take as long as she needed. Her mother insisted the time was long overdue for her to "stop this nonsense and get your husband home," while her father urged her to be logical about the decision.

Did *logical* mean following her heart or her pro-and-con list? Yesterday she'd done what some book suggested, setting a timer for three minutes and then writing out a pro-and-con list without thinking about or judging anything she put on paper.

Con	Pro
Trust gone?	Love.
No clarity about Savannah.	Kids.
Freedom from feelings.	Family.
Worry about future.	Security.
He lied.	I miss him.
He hid important things.	I still miss him.
What if he leaves me?	No guarantees in life.

Juliette parked the car on a side street lined with Victorian homes, happy for a few moments to calm down before meeting Caroline. She passed the old Boston Children's Museum, now condos, and a former convent, now condos, and then pushed the signal button to cross the busy Jamaicaway.

Jamaica Pond in August looked like a pastoral postcard from 1895—until you noticed white iPod buds in the runners' ears, dogs straining on leashes, baby carriages specially made to accommodate exercising parents, and T-shirts proclaiming everything from Red Sox Nation to Save Nine Inch Nails.

Juliette shaded her eyes as she searched for Caroline in the glary afternoon sun. Squinting, she saw her waving from a large gazebo perched above the water. A weathered boathouse to the left completed the perfect picture.

After breathing deep for bravery, Juliette climbed up the steps to where Caroline stood.

"Thanks for meeting me." Juliette held out her hand, grateful when Caroline held it for more than a brief second.

"Do you want to walk or sit?" Caroline asked. "It's shady here, but I'm happy to get a bit of exercise while we talk."

"Your choice," Juliette said.

"I'd liked to stretch my legs." Caroline gave a small smile. "It's just one and half miles around. I don't think we'll get in much trouble, no matter what you've come to talk about."

Juliette smiled back. "Sounds good. We'll make the—what?—twenty-minute commitment?"

Caroline placed a baseball cap on her head and slipped on the sunglasses that had been tucked in the breast pocket of her white oxford shirt. "Let's go."

Small talk seemed ridiculous at the moment, but Juliette, social discomfort pressing from all angles, made an attempt. "How was the place?"

They'd met here because it was close to a house a Realtor was showing Caroline. Moving from Dover to Jamaica Plain? That was surely a story, but not one Juliette felt any right to delve into except for polite conversation patter.

"Fine." Caroline's face became animated, *fine* seeming to hold far more than the word would imply, but then she pressed her lips together as though clamping down on whatever response had been close to coming out. "I don't want to jinx it."

"I understand." Actually, she didn't, but Juliette didn't want Caroline to feel compelled to lead the conversation. This was her responsibility to carry. She took in her surroundings, buying a moment by studying the park ranger's horse encircled by enchanted children. A small boy extended a tentative hand toward the animal's chestnut brown flank.

"I came to apologize." Juliette spilled the words in a rush. Might as well dive right in. "My . . . my need for information led me to acting unbelievably inappropriately."

Caroline stopped walking. She turned toward Juliette and tipped her head. "That's one way to put it." The corners of Caroline's mouth softened her mocking words. "Inappropriate. That's what my mother would say to describe serving chocolate in the summer sun."

"That doesn't sound so inappropriate," Juliette said. "I love chocolate. Even soft and melted."

Caroline shivered. "Ugh. I'm picturing a Hershey bar coating my fingers."

"And I'm picturing licking it from my fingers. We're different."

"We are." Caroline began walking again. Juliette fell into step, matching Caroline's clipped cadence.

"Really, though." Juliette looked ahead as she spoke. "I'm sorry. I was a lunatic. Just thinking about it makes me want to die."

"I can imagine," Caroline said.

Juliette appreciated the sardonic response. Polite bullshit was the last thing she wanted. "Not that it's an excuse," she said. "But when I learned about Savannah, when I opened the letter from Tia, the world turned upside down, and I felt like my family, my marriage, that everything was about to fall off the face of the earth."

Caroline nodded without comment.

"Look, I'm not asking for forgiveness. At least I hope not. You owe me nothing. I was awful to you. To Savannah. Your husband. Deceiving you like that . . ." Juliette let her words drift off.

"Do you have a background in the CIA or something?" Caroline asked. "You did quite a job on short notice."

"I don't know where it came from."

"Remind me to never cross you," Caroline said. "It was bad enough just being in the cross fire. Your children are pretty lucky, though."

"Why?"

"Well, let's just say I pity the one who goes after them."

They laughed at the same time.

"I'm shocked by how much I like you," Caroline said.

Juliette blinked against the stupid tears that rushed up at hearing Caroline's words. "That's a nice surprise," she said after clearing her throat.

"Really, though. You *were* insane," Caroline said. "If I hadn't been able to calm Peter down, I think he might have called the police."

Juliette shivered, imagining the outcome if that had happened. Detectives questioning her. Nathan bailing her out. Lawyers. Some awful headline in the paper: "Woman Seeks Husband's Secret Child."

"Thank you," Juliette said. "For not calling them. For calming him down. I'm grateful I didn't do more damage than I probably did. Are you okay? Is Savannah okay? I know Nathan and Tia came to see her. Together."

"They did. We weathered it. How about you? Are you okay?"

They rounded the halfway mark of circling the pond. From here, the boathouse and gazebo looked distantly romantic.

"This isn't about me."

"It can be about anything we want. We're beyond niceties, aren't we?"

"I suppose you're right."

Speaking with Caroline was shockingly soothing. There was little to hide from her. While there was no name for their connection—except perhaps for *mishpoche*, the Yiddish word Nathan's parents used to describe anyone even vaguely connected by family ties—Juliette felt as though she were Caroline's cousin; some sort of relative.

"Nathan and I have separated," Juliette admitted.

"I'm sorry. Because of . . . all this?"

"Because he lied. When he told me about the affair, right when he stopped seeing her, probably when Tia got pregnant, I thought I knew everything. If he hid Savannah, then who was he?"

"Did you ever think that perhaps he wasn't hiding it from you but from himself?" Caroline reached for Juliette's arm. "Not everything is about us. And thinking or feeling something doesn't make it true."

"I don't know. Maybe you're right, but I don't want to deny reality."

Caroline pulled Juliette to a bench. "Sit down. If we're going to talk, let's talk."

Juliette sat, shocked, and more than a little overwhelmed by this woman. Apparently, quiet didn't equal shy.

"Look, it wasn't your goal or even on your mind, but you might have saved our family." Caroline pulled her feet up on the bench and circled her knees with her long arms. She looked at the geese waddling down the path as she spoke.

"I was very unsure of myself with Savannah," she continued. "I saw my feelings as everything real in the world. If you hadn't cut into our lives the way you did, setting the events into motion, I don't know where I'd be right now. Certainly not happy."

"Or I could have ruined your lives."

"*Juliette.*" Caroline spoke sharply. "Don't be so melodramatic. You have to see things from other perspectives than your own. The world is three-dimensional. If you want to divorce Nathan, that's your right. But if you think you *should* divorce him, because of Savannah, make sure your decision is well considered."

"Do you think I should take him back?"

"How could I have an opinion on that? I barely know either of you." Caroline placed her feet firmly on the cement and turned toward Juliette. "But I saw Nathan with Savannah. He isn't a monster. Certainly, judging by his actions—toward you and Tia—he's far from perfect. I know he lied, and lied huge, but if you leave, can you base it all on that lie?"

Caroline held up a finger to stop Juliette's response. "I won't get this out if I don't do it right away. I've had some horrendous feelings about being a mother. Maybe if Peter knew them, he wouldn't want to be with me. Don't we all have moments we'd rather forget, and thoughts we wished never came to us? We say things too awful to remember." Caroline pushed her hair off her forehead. "When we're lucky, the people who really matter never know what we've said. What we've thought or done. Nathan wasn't that lucky."

The doorbell rang.

"Lucas. Max. One of you—open the door!" Juliette shouted from the kitchen.

"I got it!" Max screamed. *"I got it!"*

"No one cares!" Lucas screamed back.

Juliette dribbled pancake batter on the skillet. She poured a careful letter *Y* and then watched for the edges to bubble up. The hardest part of making pancakes was having the patience to let the batter set in the pan. Too soon, and you had a mess, with the pancake sticking to the pan until you had to scrape the whole thing out. Too late, and the bottom scorched.

That's what she'd realized after leaving Caroline on Thursday. She'd been looking for the right spot and the right time when she could unwrap from her pain and disappointment with Nathan. She'd needed to not to see his face for a while and to not be reminded of the Nathan who'd screwed up; the man who'd made such decisions that disappointed her so deeply.

However, if she waited too long, her marriage would be beyond repair. She believed that. They'd lose their rhythm. Everything good about them lived in that beam of belonging to each other. Wonderful things danced inside that connection. The boys. Their merged families. Comfort, support, lust—all of it was wrapped up inside that live wire between her and Nathan.

She didn't want to kill that light.

She worried they'd already gone too far.

Caroline seemed so perfect that Juliette didn't believe she could ever compete on the same level of goodness. How was it that she could see life so layered? Was it because Peter hadn't disappointed his wife or because Caroline had done awful things?

Unimaginable. Juliette simply couldn't see Caroline being bad.

Or perhaps Juliette had put Caroline up on the same sort of pedestal on which she'd placed Nathan.

Juliette slid the pancake letter onto the plate next to the stove. She took the pan from the oven warmer and began spelling *Happy* in pancake letters.

Lucas came in as she placed *P* on the platter.

"Dad's here."

"I figured," Juliette said. She leaned over to kiss Lucas, rising on her toes to press her lips to his forehead.

He gestured at the platter with his chin. "Does this mean he's coming home?"

Juliette placed the spatula on the spoon rest. "We haven't spoken about it, really. Not totally. But, yes, that's what we're going to talk about today. That's what you want, right?"

"I guess. If you do." Lucas reached out for a burnt edge she'd cut away. "Shouldn't it be about you? And about Dad?"

Juliette slipped the spatula under *A* and lifted.

"We're bound together whether we live together or not. Once you have children, wherever you are, you're part of the same family." She stopped for a moment to swallow. "I'd like us to be in that same family here. Together."

Juliette was saying more than Lucas imagined. He and Max, they had to know about Savannah. Which meant knowing about Tia. It would be an awful lot to throw on the kids, but ripping apart their family was an awful lot to throw on them in a far worse way. As for lying, well, she'd learned how well that worked.

Today she and Nathan would begin living in truth.

"There," she said. "Bring me the powdered sugar."

"Mom, it looks fine the way it is. You don't have to make a big fuss all the time."

She put down the spatula and turned to her son. "Lucas, this is who I am. Sometimes I'll make a big fuss because of something bad, and you'll hear me crying my eyes out in the bathroom. And other times, just because I'm happy, I'll make an embarrassing fuss. I make commotions. But I'm your mother, I love you, and I'll always take care of you. Now go get the sugar."

He rolled his eyes, which at that particular moment felt nice and normal and not annoying at all.

"Here," he said, handing her the shaker of sugar.

"Thank you. Bring your father and brother in for breakfast."

She straightened the letters until *Happy Family Day* looked perfect, at least for this one moment.

Yes, she was being kind of goony and making a fuss. But what the hell. At least they'd have pancakes to eat that weren't scorched and weren't lying in a gloppy mess. At the worst, she'd covered them in a little too much sugar.

For God's sake, that should be the worst thing that happened to them.

CHAPTER 36

Caroline

Caroline felt uneasy. Going back to the office hadn't made sense after Caroline left the pond, but being alone in her house on a weekday was just plain odd. Nanny Rose had taken Savannah to the park and probably wouldn't be home for an hour. Peter was at work. Silence and stiff perfection surrounded her.

She placed her briefcase on the side table and tried to imagine what it might be like to walk into the Jamaica Plain house. After kicking off her shoes, she unzipped her case and lifted out the folder of information from the real estate agent. When she slid it onto the kitchen table, the bright colors popped against the stark white room. Once she'd spread the pages in a rectangle, she poured a glass of sparkling water and sat to study the brochures before her.

The red house looked bigger in the photos—of course, real estate pictures were always taken to have everything appear ten times larger—but it had more than enough room for the three of them. Downstairs were four rooms and a tiny bathroom. She traveled the rooms with her finger, following with her eyes as she moved from the living room, stopping at the graceful fireplace mantle, and then passing through the tiny dining room—where windows opened to an enormous side yard, highlighted by lilac trees—and then stopped at the cobalt, white, and wood kitchen. Here she could imagine cooking something. Nothing incredible, but something. The outsized and airy family room opened on all sides to light from the yard. Neighbors' houses, far and close, dotted the view.

Caroline glanced out her kitchen window at the copse of blue spruce. Along with flower beds thick with roses, never tended by her or Peter, they provided a backdrop for Savannah's spacious swing set. Even standing on a tall ladder, they'd be hard pressed to see another house. At the Jamaica Plain house, they could practically spit on their next-door neighbor's driveway. And while the tucked-away street meandered in a pretty circle of mostly single-family homes, one block away was one of the largest train stops in the city, located on a street where rundown bars and a twenty-four-hour grated liquor store mixed in with the newly gentrified restaurants and coffee shops.

Her mother-in-law would have a coronary. As for Caroline's own parents, well, it would probably be best to blindfold her mother and father before driving them to the house.

The Jamaica Plain yard cried to be fixed, but unlike here, Caroline itched to get her hands in the earth. She could see herself and Savannah turning over the soil. Getting dirty. Upstairs, none of the four bedrooms, ranging from small to medium, compared with the ones they slept in now—although the largest would make a more than decent home office for Peter. Golden oak floors reflected the light that flooded in from the two walls of windows.

She looked around. Here everything was plumb, perfect, and gleaming with money and taste. Caroline just didn't know whose taste it reflected.

She looked at the brochures on the table and saw a warm, inviting house. A home for deep-cushioned sofas and bookcases.

Their house. Not a spread from *Architectural Digest*.

She'd take Peter to see it on Saturday, but she bet that he'd love it. A real estate guy once told her that you could see it in people's eyes when they'd found their home, and right now she saw the Jamaica Plain house with eyes of love. Perhaps Peter's mother would think they were downsizing, but Caroline preferred to think of it as finally finding the just-right size. If their apartment in Cambridge had been too small, then this McMansion in Dover had always been too big. They were dwarfed by the size and bombarded by the precision. How could a kid bounce around in a place so flawless?

She held up the shiny sheet showing the family room in Jamaica Plain, filled with windows and punctuated by French doors. In her mind, she populated it with a red oriental rug, lamps pooling warm light, and sofas with curled arms that would cradle your head while you read the Sunday papers.

Not too small. Not too big. Just right.

"Peter, you'll love this place," Caroline insisted later that night. "Trust me."

She slid closer to him, feeling the leather couch grab at her jeans as she moved.

He shook his head. "I don't know. Do we want to live that close to Forest Hills Station? Do you know what it's like there? I'm not sure that's where we want Savannah to grow up."

Calm down. Let him find his own way there.

"Just come look at it. That's all I ask."

Peter put his reading glasses back on and reached for the sheets of paper he'd thrown on the sleek coffee table. "When I spoke about saving money, this wasn't what I pictured."

"What did you picture?"

"I suppose something a little more . . . upscale?" He read the specs again. "We could fit this house into our place twice. Do you really want something so small?"

"I'd like to be able to find each other. I don't want to work for a mortgage payment. And I like the idea of neighbors; of Savannah being able to play with other kids. I saw bikes on lawns."

"You'd let her ride her bike there?"

"For goodness sake, plenty of kids grow up in the city." Caroline took his hand and squeezed. "This doesn't have to be *the* place. But

I want you to come and see it. Walk around the street. See how nice everyone is. The couple next door are both doctors, and across the street is a school principal. It's not like we'd be moving into a war zone. It just isn't a lily-white suburb like here."

"Don't make me sound like a snob." Peter leaned forward. "I'd like her to have friends down the street, but I also want a good life for all of us. I want to give Savannah more than I had."

"Is *more* measured in dollars?" Caroline reached for her wineglass. "Love? Fun? You and I had great childhoods, by any standards. I had plenty of money. You never wanted for anything. You had the wild, big family thing. I had my sisters. Our mothers were always there. And we both knew from where we came."

Caroline's eyes welled up. "We can't give Savannah what we had. It isn't possible. We don't have a house full of kids or sisters for her. She never had a mom at home. Whether we like it or not, we're an unconventional family."

"This isn't about the house, is it?" Peter put a hand on her knee.

She wiped her eyes with the bottom of her T-shirt and shivered. Despite the muggy temperature, it was cold and dry in the living room. "No. I like the house, but that's not why I'm upset. We need to figure out what the true right thing to do for our daughter is, and we can't explore it from across a divide. I don't want to be convincing you, or vice versa."

"You think we're on different sides?"

Caroline looked away from him. He couldn't accept that they'd escaped family dissolution by only a thread.

"Do you ever think what it's like for Savannah?" she asked.

"What do you mean?"

"She's adopted, and whether we like it or not, she's always going to have questions. Maybe we're being selfish. We're trying so hard to make everything just right for her, just right like we had, but maybe we're ignoring what she really needs."

"Which is what?" he asked.

Peter looked uneasy, but she pressed on. Fear of truth had already lead Caroline to an imagined burial of her husband and child.

"Savannah knows about Tia and Nathan now, and that she has brothers. We can't pretend they don't exist."

"What does that mean to you, Caro?"

She laced her fingers. "It means putting our dread away. We can't keep them out of her mind or our lives. That's a fantasy for our own psychic safety. Living as though they never met—it's not only impossible, it's wrong."

"I never suggested we should lie. Or paper over the truth." Peter began pacing. "But are we supposed to share her with them? What do you propose? We have them over for a Labor Day barbeque? Maybe they can come to my mother's for Thanksgiving."

"You're her father. I'm her mother. No one's arguing that. Look, I don't have the answers; I only know that we can't be good parents without asking the questions. Our girl shouldn't have to hide herself from us. I don't want her to feel guilty if she wants to meet her brothers someday. And we have to think about what 'someday' means before she comes to us."

Caroline left the couch and went to her husband. She put her arms around his waist and leaned her head on his shoulder.

"Doesn't it frighten you?" Peter asked. "Don't you ever worry about losing her?"

"I don't think you lose someone from loving them the right way." She pressed her hands into his back. "We're a family. We became one the day we took Savannah in our arms. That miracle will never stop. Maybe now we have another bit of magic to be grateful for. Finally, it's all out in the open, and we can be a family without the holding on to the comfort of lies."

Peter touched the brochure. He traced the outline of the red house in Jamaica Plain and then picked it up.

"What the heck," he said. "It can't hurt to look."

CHAPTER 37

Tia

Tia woke up hung over again. Not a deadly bout. No wretched nausea, so, thank God, she hadn't thrown up. Only a throbbing headache reminded her of the previous night. She reached for the coffee that Bobby had left for her. Since their engagement last month, they'd been spending more time at his place. He already had her picking out furniture and carpeting for the condo where they'd move when construction was finished.

Last week he'd stuck catalogs from Pottery Barn Kids in with the ones from Crate & Barrel and Restoration Hardware.

"Those people aren't the only ones who can give your daughter a terrific life," he'd said. "She can have her real mother *and* everything material she needs. You don't need to sacrifice anymore, hon. By the way, did you call the lawyer?"

She looked away when he asked that dreaded question, as he did more often every week, always using that damned pretend-casual voice. Bobby had become obsessed with having Savannah.

It couldn't happen.

Going after Savannah would become the lead story in things she'd done wrong since meeting Nathan, but every time she meant to tell Bobby, she ended up having another drink.

Last night she'd had beer, scotch, and shots of Sambuca. She should have needed a bucket next to the bed this morning, but coffee and a couple of aspirin would take care of her. That was a bad sign. Being able to drink so much without getting sick showed that her body was further acclimating to large amounts of alcohol. Visits to Fianna's were going from weekends to too many weekdays. How soon before it became every night?

Still groggy, Tia stumbled through the sleek grey living room and into the bathroom, seeking the relief of a shower.

Hot water beat on her head and shoulders. She bent over, leaning her hands against the white tile, trying to breathe in courage with the steam.

Taking special care as she chose her clothes, she buttoned up a white silk blouse and tucked it into a black pencil skirt, staring at the photos of Savannah that Bobby had framed.

She sat on the bed to make her sick call. She hated lying to Sister Patrice, but she couldn't begin to formulate how to be honest about the complicated truth she faced.

Marine Gardens Senior Living in South Boston was walking distance from the Sugar Bowl walkway, Tia's hangout as a kid. The large blue building with deeper blue shutters faced the ocean, providing a clear view. Only a roadway and traffic stood between Marine Gardens and the beach.

Mrs. Graham waited in the lobby, her hands clasped in her lap. Tia had called the staff to let them know she was coming.

"Hey, Marjorie." Tia sat next to the old woman and sank into the soft flowered couch. Apple air freshener, disinfectant, and furniture polish covered odors associated with assisted living homes. A wide mahogany table covered by an outsized silk flower display overwhelmed the achingly clean room.

"You're right on time," Mrs. Graham patted her stiff patent leather pocketbook in nervous rhythm as she spoke.

"And you're as prompt as ever. That's such a good quality." Tia reached for Mrs. Graham's hand. "Marjorie, I'm so sorry I haven't come before today."

Mrs. Graham's pale blue eyes widened. "Oh, no, dear. I never expected you to come here. Why would you want to see me after what I did? Goodness, you're not the one needing to apologize. I put you in an awful position."

Tia bit her lip against apologizing for all the ways she'd failed the Grahams. Mrs. Graham didn't need to take care of her by providing absolution, and Tia had no right to seek it from her.

"What you did took courage, Marjorie, and I should have been here long ago."

Mrs. Graham shook her head, even as a glow of hope lit her face. "Oh. That's lovely to say, but nobody would believe it."

"I do."

"Really?" Mrs Graham squeezed Tia's hand. "Most people think I'm a criminal. I'm not exactly popular here. Hardly anyone invites me to play cards, or sit with them during the movies."

"That's just plain mean. And uncalled for." Tia pressed Mrs. Graham's delicate hand back. Gently. She took a deep breath. "I'm jealous of you. I'm jealous of Mr. Graham."

Bright September sun lit the room. Every line etched in Mrs. Graham's face stood out in sharp relief. Uncertainty and disbelief shaded her expression. "Why in the world would you be jealous of either of us?"

"I'm jealous of you for loving someone so much that you'd put your freedom on the line for him. I'm jealous of your husband, for having someone love him that much. Your last years were hard, very hard. You were so good to him."

Tears spilled down Mrs. Graham's cheeks as Tia spoke.

"You did the very best you could," Tia continued. "No one helped you. You took care of Sam, just like he'd always taken care of you. Then you did what you could to make it easier for him to step away from his pain and confusion."

Mrs. Graham opened her purse, drew out a white handkerchief, and dabbed the thin skin under her eyes. "I miss him every day. He wouldn't recognize me, but I'd know him. But I can't see him. That's my punishment."

"It must be awful not seeing him." Tia bent down to get the large tote bag she'd brought. She reached in and took out a large tin decorated with embossed pictures of needle and thread. "Here. I brought this for you. It's small comfort, but it's something I think you'll like."

Mrs. Graham took it. "Thank you, dear. I wish my eyes were better so I could sew like I used to."

Tia shook her head and then put her finger to her lips to indicate that stealth was required. She looked around to see if anyone was watching, and then pried off the lid to reveal an assortment of red and black licorice. "I thought you might have a hard time getting this here."

Mrs. Graham smiled as though Tia had brought down the stars from heaven. "Oh! Thank you, dear. You have no idea how I've missed my licorice."

"I don't want to get you in trouble." Tia leaned in closer and lowered her voice. "That's why I put it in the sewing tin."

"Don't worry about getting me in trouble. I don't think it can get any worse for me, do you?"

Tia laughed. "Probably not."

"You were a good girl to come, Tia."

"I'll come again, I promise. But I might be going away soon, and when I do, I'll write to you. I want to stay in your life. And I'll keep you supplied with licorice. I promise."

"I'm glad you can finally call me Marjorie."

Tia snuck a piece of candy from the tin and popped it in her mouth. "Me too."

Tia changed from pumps to sneakers and then walked from Mrs. Graham's nursing home to the Sugar Bowl. She made the loop twice, peering through the fog to get a look at Thompson Island in the distance, watching the seagulls go after trash, and nodding at familiar-looking people running, walking dogs, and riding bikes.

Tia and her friends drank their first six-packs at the Sugar Bowl. They smoked their first joints, drank repulsively sweet fruit brandy, and played musical couples. Tia lost her virginity here at the Sugar Bowl.

On that particular Friday night, Tia had already drunk four Buds when Kevin tapped out a line of coke. They shared numbed kisses. He took her down to where they could step out on the rocks, seeking a particular flat one that Kevin swore existed. When they found it, Kevin wordlessly covered the cold surface with his jacket. Sixteen-year-old Tia couldn't imagine anything more tender.

Now she needed to find a way to cover that cold surface in a better way. Tia couldn't rely on covering up the rock with some guy's jacket, nor should that be her dream of rescue.

She and Bobby would never last. It was time to pull the plug.

Despite the clouds, she whipped out her sunglasses to cover up her tear-streaked face. She'd been fooling herself; she was good at that, wasn't she?

Jesus, she wanted him as her brother, not her husband; that's how she loved him. Given enough time, he'd bring out all of her worst qualities.

With Nathan, even if his love hadn't been real, hers had been true. She'd felt wide open when she was with him, and she wanted that again. But this time she wanted it with someone who loved her, and whom she loved back.

Not Bobby. In the back of her mind, she'd always known that even as he kept her safe, she'd always stay small in that comfort.

Tia squinted at the crowd around Sullivan's at Castle Island as she approached the restaurant's parking lot. Fried food scented the air. Bobby waved, breaking into a huge smile, and holding out his arms. She'd called him to meet her. It was time to make a choice. She could let him buy her a frankfurter, or she could break his heart and a little piece of her own.

If she stayed with Bobby, eventually she'd call the lawyer about Savannah, no matter how wrong it would be to choose that path. The temptation was too strong, and Tia couldn't resist much longer. Bobby had begun mapping out her life, and hiring the attorney would be part of implementing his plan.

But it was too late. She didn't want anybody choosing her path. Or Savannah's.

Some things you never know, but she was certain of this: her little girl already lived with her mother and father. Too little, too late. That's what going to the lawyer meant. It wasn't only a pipe dream; Tia didn't even think it was really her dream. Not like that.

A court battle could only hurt Savannah. It wouldn't be for her daughter, it would be for herself. If giving up her baby had been selfish, going after her would implement a scorched-earth policy.

Being with Bobby would be like that also. Leaving now would hurt him, but marrying him would end up devastating them both. She could never be the other half of Bobby.

Ice slicked the roads as Bobby drove her to the airport six months later. The stormy March weather forced them to stop twice so Bobby could get out and scrape ice off the windshield. She prayed her plane would take off.

"Thank you for keeping the ring." Bobby glanced away from the expressway traffic for a moment. He pressed her hand tight, driving with one hand. "Put it on once in a while, so you remember me. No pressure. I promise."

He was a good man. Tia hated remembering the day she broke their engagement and his heart, but she would never put that ring on again. Of course, if she did, at least men would leave her alone while she figured out her life, though Robin swore it would be man catnip. "They'll beg you for dates, knowing you're unavailable," she had advised.

Tia didn't want men like that anymore.

Six years before, after she and Nathan broke up, Tia had walked for hours every day. She walked until she was too tired to do anything but work and sleep. She rented movies simply because they starred actors who resembled Nathan. She looked for him everywhere. She saw him everywhere. Eighty-year-old women in wheelchairs looked like Nathan from a distance.

Tia roamed the city praying to see him. What had she been thinking? That if he saw her, he'd once again become the man who she'd imagined would make her life into a fairy tale?

Nathan never knew her, and she'd never known him. She'd made him into a character, filling in every blank with magical qualities she'd attributed to him. His natural caring she redrew as their soulmate attachment. She'd redrawn his sexual craving into once-in-a-lifetime love. And his family? Tia had blurred them into a barely visible pastel, wash until she'd imagined his leaving his wife and sons would produce no more than a short period of disarray, far away from her own awareness. Somehow she'd believed the lies she told herself. As much as Nathan hurt her, she had hurt Juliette.

Now she wondered if Nathan's unavailability had made him desirable. The thought appalled her, but she had to consider it.

More than anything, Tia was ready to discover a world outside her own head. Moving back to Southie would have meant following the same map day after day.

Maybe that wasn't so bad.

But maybe it was.

They arrived at Logan Airport in silence. Bobby took her luggage from the trunk, and then stood and stared at her. She kissed him good-bye, holding on longer than she'd expected. "You know I'll always care about you, don't you?" she asked.

"But not the way I want, right?" He held her out at arm's length. Snowflakes fell around them. She brushed ice crystals from his shoulders. "Can you stay open to the thought of us?" he asked.

"Oh, Bobby. Promise me something."

"Name it," he said.

"Meet the right girl." Tia hoped the moisture on Bobby's face was only rainwater. "You have to do that for me."

"I don't know if I can, because I think I already have."

Tia didn't have the heart to tell him what she knew. She still hadn't met her true love. She wished she could take away Bobby's unhappiness, but sometimes you could only save your own life.

As the plane rose away from Boston, she dug her nails into her thighs until she thought she'd shred her black jeans. She kept glancing at the guy sitting next to her. She had no idea of plane etiquette, but she knew enough to refrain from following her instinct to grab his hand. She'd keep it together until the antihistamine Robin had advised taking kicked in and made her sleepy.

They should pair seatmates with an eye toward reassurance, coupling rookies with experienced parental types, the sort for whom helping conferred a sense of importance.

Unfortunately, the guy to her right hadn't looked up once. She peeked at his ring finger and saw a gold band. He had the *New York Times* folded in the perfect manner used by smart travelers. Tia unwelded her fingers from her legs and reached for the book she'd brought. A sustaining read, a reread, one she prayed would keep her company well enough that she wouldn't start screaming from fear or order a miniature bottle of courage when the flight attendant offered.

Boston spread under her as they flew away from the place she'd never left. They were still close enough that she could recognize landmarks, including South Boston jutting into the ocean.

She'd given up a lot, right? She wasn't running away. Much of what had been offered had made her mouth water. A man who'd care for her. A home on the water. Security. A package her mother would have loved for Tia.

That life would have sunk her. Maybe the world was made up of two kinds of people: those who flourished by staying in native soil, and those who, like Robin, needed to find the place that held the right nutrients for their souls. Tia now thought she might also be that kind of person.

She blinked in and out of pill-induced groggy sleep during the flight to San Francisco, dreaming of her past and future.

She couldn't be certain that California would feel like home, but being with Robin, her only real family in this world, was a good place to start. She touched her time-softened copy of *Anne of Green Gables: Three Volumes in One*, which her mother had given her so long ago. Orphan makes good—it was the story she wanted to reread.

At the luggage carousel, Tia watched for the shabby red suitcases that had been her mother's. Thinking of her mother was less painful for Tia since she'd seen Savannah. For the first time, she could imagine her mother understanding how Tia had come to her decisions, even if she didn't agree with them. She felt as though her mother had finally lifted her curse.

Now that Tia had seen Savannah being held by Caroline and Peter, she could finally unclench after all the years she'd spent paralyzed since letting go of her baby. Now that she and Caroline were in contact, she'd always know that Savannah was safe.

Tia would never turn away from Savannah. She'd never be a mystery. Either road Tia could have taken, giving her daughter away or keeping her, may have turned out to be the wrong choice. Or the right one. But now, at least Tia had finally faced her decision. Her daughter was no longer a hidden shame that required piling bandage upon bandage.

She didn't have to lie anymore.

Perhaps her mother had been right. Maybe giving away Savannah had been like giving away her legs, but the way Tia saw it, she'd only crippled herself. She had given Savannah a chance. Tia hoped her mother would understand. At the very least, she'd be happy for the same things that gave Tia hope and happiness.

Savannah was in good hands.

Tia finally knew her daughter, and she knew that she'd see her again.

Flying hadn't been so bad. Years of stomach-turning fear melted with an antihistamine. Maybe not the bravest way to change, but at least she was here. Perhaps next time she could even pull it off without the Allerest. If not, who cared?

She pulled her luggage through large glass doors that opened automatically and shielded her eyes from the early morning glare as she stepped outside. California's brilliant blue sky appeared wide open.

At that moment, Robin pulled up in the tomato-red Honda she'd described the previous night as she waved a picture of the car at the Skype screen.

"Do you honestly think I can see that?" Tia had laughed. "Don't worry. Trust me, I can find a car."

Still, her friend's protectiveness touched Tia.

"A year, that's all I ask," Robin had said. "Okay, six months, then," she'd immediately compromised when Tia insisted that a year was too long. "Just give California that long a chance."

While planning her trip to California, Tia had emailed Robin's California address to Caroline, who'd written back with her and Peter's new address—in Jamaica Plain, of all places. Attached to Caroline's email were photos of Savannah getting ready for her first day of kindergarten. Caroline had sent autumn photos.

Tia no longer worried about losing touch. Caroline was more than trustworthy. No more waiting for a whole year to see pictures of her daughter. They were already talking about how and when Tia would next see Savannah.

The last time she'd spoken with Nathan had been right before Memorial Day, not long after they saw Savannah. Tia suspected she was the only one to whom he could talk about the situation. It had been obvious he'd had too much to drink. Not that he'd been drunk, just loose enough that he didn't talk to Tia as though she were a spider about to crawl up his back.

"I just don't know if Juliette will take me back," he'd said. "I'm afraid she's lost respect for me. That really hurts. You know what I mean?"

Hearing how much Juliette's respect meant to Nathan broke Tia's final bits of obsession with him. He never valued her opinion with that depth. Wanted her, yes. Maybe even briefly thought he needed her and convinced himself he loved her, but Tia's estimation of Nathan had never mattered like Juliette's. In the hierarchy of Nathan's family and friends, Tia barely had a foothold.

Juliette took him back. Caroline let her know. How odd that Caroline had become her conduit for information. Odder still, Tia found herself happy that Nathan and Juliette had reunited. It meant one less sin for which she had to atone.

Tia slipped into Robin's car. They hugged as sisters.

"Welcome, Tee," Robin stroked her cheek. "You look like hell."

"Good to see you too. It was a long flight."

"The first trip is always the hardest," Robin said. "You'll recover."

Tia slipped on the sunglasses Robin held out to her. "That's exactly what I'm planning."

As they drove from the airport, Tia felt the misery of the past years start lifting. She'd saved herself from the rabbit hole of despair after waiting for so many years for rescue to ride in on a white horse, with Nathan the face of her savior.

For a while, she'd thought Bobby's hand was the one that would lift her out of misery, and in truth, the comfort of Bobby still beckoned like an eiderdown quilt. But scraping away the layers of denial she'd been using—Bobby, drinking, impossible dreams—had set her free.

Tia swore that she'd never muffle her mind again. The right place, the right person, and exactly the path she should walk waited out there—none of which would require her to catalog her life into on-limits and off-limits.

Braiding Savannah's hair or swinging her in a circle might not be in Tia's future, but she didn't have to hide her daughter's existence. She could feel love for Savannah without reaching for a drink. On Savannah's sixth birthday, Caroline would send pictures; Tia would send a doll, maybe a necklace made by Robin, or a teddy bear: for the first time, she'd buy her child a birthday present.

Whether or not Savannah's parents gave it to her was their choice. Sending it would be Tia's.

She'd always be there for her daughter, and Savannah was in the right place. Tia's willingness to endure for her child meant walking away, not fighting for her, and through that choice, she'd gained the possibility for a someday future with Savannah.

They were all connected. And in the oddest way, they had all become a family.

ACKNOWLEDGMENTS

Many people supported me in writing *The Comfort of Lies*, but none more than my husband, Jeff Rand, who gifted me a life without sad songs and made it possible to fearlessly visit the past, and Ginny DeLuca, my best friend and partner in all things in life—including writing. We've held hands through all our choices, smart and stupid, since we were twenty-three, and will continue until we're trading canes.

Family, friends, and colleagues helped me breathe life into these characters I love. Stéphanie Abou has been my wise, warm, and determined partner from the beginning, as has everyone at Foundry Literary + Media. Atria Books is everything you want a publisher to be. Judith Cuff is whip-smart warm, and I thank her for bringing me into the Atria fold. Greer Hendricks is truly a dream-come-true editor, who pushed me perfectly, and I am forever grateful to be working with her. Sarah Cantin makes everything about publishing happier, easier, and better. Within moments of asking for help, Julia Scribner was there. Lisa Sciambra, Cristina Suarez, and Anne Spieth provided a welcome that portends a lasting mountain of thanks from me. Phil Bashe allowed me to appear far smarter than reality. Laywan Kwan, I am still smiling from your extraordinary cover. My journey with Atria has just begun, but I know I have found a home. Nancy Mac-Donald, you are a touchstone of perception, wisdom, comfort, and help; you improve everything you touch. Kathleen Carter Zrelak, from Goldberg McDuffie, how did you become such a terrific publicist *and* a therapist? Rose Daniels, your great design talent actually made building a website fun.

To "team"—beloved Nichole Bemier and Kathy Crowley—thank you for absorbing my tears, celebrating my joy, and holding my secrets. Melisse Shapiro, the quality of my life jumped many levels when I met you. To my circle of trusted writer friends—bless our virtual water fountain: my dearly loved Robin Black, Jenna Blum, Juliette Fay, Beth Hoffman, Marianne Leone, Ellen Meeropol, Elizabeth Moore, Laura Zigman: everyone should have such trust, wisdom and support surrounding them. Chris Abouzeid, Christiane Alsop, Stephanie Ebbert, Leslie Greffenius, Javed Jahangir, Necee Regis, Dell Smith, Becky Tuch, and Julie Wu—you are all way *Beyond the Margins*: wonderful partners, great for depth, and incredible for parties. Amin Ahmad, may we always be such wonderful (honest!) readers for each other.

Special thanks to Linda Percy, you and the rubber duck offered special faith, smiles, and optimism; and to Stacy Meyers Ames, you sure gave this wildly neurotic woman a shot of confidence.

Heartfelt thanks to the Grub Street Writer's Center of Boston, especially Eve Bridburg, Chris Castellani, Whitney Scharer, and Sonya Larson, for bringing us all together and making dreams come true. Real-life hugs to everyone in the fabulous online Fiction Writer's Co-op, with a special shout out to Cathy Buchanan for taking the time to put it together.

My deep love and thanks belong to my family, including the sisters of my heart, Diane Butkus and Susan Knight. I bask in the love of my sisters-in-law, Nicole Todini and Jean Rand, and my brother-in-law, Bruce Rand. A special thanks to my dear mother-in-law, Jeanne Rand, for her constant pride. And Mom, you are always with me.

Those who own my heart, the loves of my life, offer comfort, joy, and understanding: my sister (and best friend), Jill Meyers; my children and my granddaughter: Becca Wolfson, Sara, Jason, and Nora Hoots, and, again, the love of my life, Jeff Rand.